Kissed

"Once upon a time"

IS TIMELESS WITH THESE RETOLD TALES:

Kissed

Includes:
BELLE
SUNLIGHT AND SHADOW
WINTER'S CHILD

CAMERON DOKEY

Simon Pulse

NEW YORK   LONDON   TORONTO   SYDNEY   NEW DELHI

SIMON PULSE

An imprint of Simon & Schuster Children's Publishing Division

1230 Avenue of the Americas, New York, NY 10020

This Simon Pulse paperback edition February 2013

Belle copyright © 2008 by Cameron Dokey

Sunlight and Shadow copyright © 2004 by Cameron Dokey

Winter's Child copyright © 2009 by Cameron Dokey

All rights reserved, including the right of reproduction in whole or in part in any form.

SIMON PULSE and colophon are registered trademarks of Simon & Schuster, Inc.

For information about special discounts for bulk purchases, please contact

Simon & Schuster Special Sales at 1-866-506-1949 or business@simonandschuster.com.

The Simon & Schuster Speakers Bureau can bring authors to your live event.

For more information or to book an event contact the Simon & Schuster Speakers

Bureau at 1-866-248-3049 or visit our website at www.simonspeakers.com.

Designed by Mike Rosamilia

The text of this book was set in Bembo.

Manufactured in the United States of America

2 4 6 8 10 9 7 5 3 1

Library of Congress Control Number 2012936479

ISBN 978-1-4424-7220-4

ISBN 978-1-4424-7221-1 (eBook)

These books were previously published individually by Simon Pulse.

Contents

Kissed

BELLE

To Jim, as they all have been,

once upon a time and always

One

I'VE HEARD IT SAID—AND MY GUESS IS YOU HAVE TOO—
that beauty is in the eye of the beholder. But I've never been
certain it's true.

Think about it for a moment.

It sounds nice. I'll give you that. A way for every face to be
beautiful, if only you wait for the right pair of eyes. If only you
wait long enough. I'll even grant you that beauty isn't universal.
A girl who is considered drop-dead gorgeous in a town by the
sea may find herself completely overlooked in a village the next
county over.

Even so, *beauty is in the eye of the beholder* doesn't quite work,
does it?

Because there's something missing, and I can even tell you what: the belief we all harbor in our secret heart of hearts that beauty stands alone. That, by its very nature, it is obvious. In other words, Beauty with a capital *B*.

Beauty is in the eye of the beholder.

Now that's another statement entirely.

And what it means, as far as I can see, is that those of us whose looks aren't of the capital *B* variety can pretty much stop holding our breaths, stop waiting for the right eyes to show up and gaze upon us. Our Beauty—or, more precisely, our lack thereof—has already been established. It's as plain as the noses on our small *b* faces.

That sounds more like the way things actually work, doesn't it?

I suppose you could say that finding out just what a pair of eyes can do, and what they can't, is what the story I'm about to tell you is really all about. It will come as no surprise that it is, of course, my story. Which means I should probably back up and introduce myself.

Annabelle Evangeline Delaurier. That is my name. After my father's mother and my mother's mother, in that order. But, though it was my father who decided the entirety of what I would be called, it was my mother who sealed my fate and set my tale in motion. For she was the one who decreed I would be known as *Belle*, a name that means Beauty in the land of my birth.

There were problems with this decision, though nobody

realized it at the time. Two problems, to be precise: my older sisters, who displayed such extraordinary Beauty that they were famous for miles around.

My oldest sister was born at straight-up midnight, on a night so clear and cold it snatched the breath. A night that made the stars burn sharp and bright as knives. The baby's hair was as dark as the arc of heaven overhead, her eyes a blue both fierce and sparkling, like the stars.

In celebration of my sister's arrival, Maman, who has a tendency to be extravagant even in life's simple moments, named the infant Celestial Heavens, having earlier extracted a promise from my father that she could name their first child anything she wanted.

As I'm sure I don't need to point out, Celestial Heavens is quite a mouthful.

Fortunately for all concerned, and for my sister most of all, my father's more practical approach to life won out. Celestial Heavens the baby might be, but even before the ink on her birth certificate was dry, my sister was being called Celeste, as she has been from that day forward.

My second sister was born on the first day of the month of April, just as the sun rose over the horizon. Her hair was as golden as the sun's first light, her eyes as green as the meadow that the sun ran through on its way to make the morning. My father, now somewhat prepared for what might come next, took it in quiet stride when my mother named this daughter

April Dawn. By the time the baby had been tucked into her cradle that night, she was being called just April, and she has been ever since.

And then there was the day that I arrived.

At noon, on a day in September that could have been either spring or autumn, judging by the blueness of the sky. Or by the temperature, which was neither too hot nor too cold. A quiet, peaceful kind of day. The kind that, at its end, makes you wonder where the time has gone. A day that doesn't feel like a gift until it's done. For it's only as you're drifting off to sleep that you realize how happy you are, how happy you'd been every moment you were awake.

It was on just such a day as this that I was born.

Even my coming into the world was straightforward, for my mother later related that the time of her labor seemed neither too short, nor too long. Following these exertions, I was placed into my mother's arms. My father sat beside her on the bed, and both of them (or so I am told) gazed lovingly down at me. And if my father felt a small pang that his third child was yet another daughter and not a son, I'm willing to forgive him for it.

It wasn't that he valued daughters any less, but that, after two such extraordinary children, he was ready for one that was, perhaps, a little less remarkable. A child who might be more like him, follow in his footsteps rather than my mother's. And as he could not imagine how a girl's feet might accomplish such a task, in secret, my father had longed for a boy.

"Well, my dear?" my father asked my mother after several moments. He was referring, of course, to what I would be named, for, as always, the choice would be Maman's. She knew what to call my two sisters without hesitation. But here a curious and unexpected event transpired.

Accustomed as my mother was to the spectacular arrivals of Celeste and April, my appearance called forth not a single inspiration. Though her imagination was vivid, my mother simply could not conjure what to call a child who had arrived with so little fanfare, on a day that was so very unremarkable.

My mother opened her mouth, then closed it, without making a single sound. She took a breath, then tried again. And when this attempt also failed to produce a name, she tried a third time. Finally, she closed her mouth and kept it shut, looking at my father with beseeching eyes.

Fortunately, my father is quick on his feet, even when he isn't standing on them.

"My dear," he said to Maman once more. "You have given me a beautiful and healthy daughter, and surely that is gift enough. But I wonder if I might ask for one thing more. I wonder if you would allow *me* to name this child."

Her lips still firmly closed, my mother nodded her head, and my father bestowed a name he had long cherished: Annabelle, after his own mother, who had had the raising of him all on her own. Then, mindful of my mother's feelings, he gave me the name of her mother as well.

In this way, I became Annabelle Evangeline, and no sooner had my father proclaimed his choice than my mother recovered enough to announce that she wished me to be known as *Belle*. If I could not have an arrival quite as remarkable as those of my sisters, I could at least have an everyday name that, like my sisters, would match the Beauty I would surely become.

Allow me to set something straight at this point.

There's nothing actually wrong with the way I look. I have long brown hair that generally does what I ask it to, except on very rainy days when it does whatever it wants. I have eyes of a deep chestnut color that are not set too far from each other so that I appear to look over my own shoulder, nor so close that they appear to be trying to catch each other's glance across the bridge of my nose. And there's nothing wrong with my nose, either, thank you very much.

In fact, I have a face that is much like the day on which I was born. It contains neither too much of one thing, nor too little of another. A perfectly fine face. Just not an extraordinary face. And therein lies the problem. For the Beauty of my sisters can actually take a person's breath away.

I think my favorite example was when April surprised a would-be burglar in the middle of the night. She was no more than nine years old—which would have made me seven and Celeste eleven, just so you know where we are.

The thief, who turned out to be not much older than Celeste, had come to steal the brace of silver candlesticks that always stood on the sideboard in our dining room. April had gotten out of bed for a drink of water. They encountered each other in the downstairs hall.

All it took to subdue the boy was one look at April's golden hair, shining ever so faintly in the darkness, giving off a light of its own. The thief saw all that Beauty, sucked in an astonished breath, then fell to the floor like a sackful of rocks. The noise of this, not to mention April's sudden cry, roused the rest of the house. The would-be robber was still passed out cold, the candlesticks on the floor beside him, when my father summoned the constable.

The story has a happier ending than you might suppose. For April took pity on the lad and convinced my father to do the same.

Shortly after the constable arrived, and with his permission, Papa offered the unsuccessful thief, who had the extremely un-thief-like name of Dominic Boudreaux, a choice: Dominic could go to jail or he could go to sea. Papa is one of the most successful merchants in all our city. His ships sail to every part of the globe, and he had a ship scheduled to set sail with that morning's tide.

Not surprisingly, Dominic Boudreaux chose the second course. As a result, he departed for his new life almost as soon as he'd made up his mind to have one. To the astonishment of all concerned, Dominic took to the sea like a sailor born. He's been sailing for Papa ever since, for about ten years now.

Papa gave him command of the newest ship in the fleet when he turned twenty-one, the youngest man he'd ever raised to captain. When Papa asked Dominic what he thought his ship should be called, Dominic answered without hesitation: the *April Dawn*.

It's a nice story, isn't it? But I've told it to you for a reason other than the obvious one. Because what happened to Dominic and April in the middle of that night tells a second story. A tale about Beauty that I've often murmured to myself, but that I've never heard anyone else so much as whisper aloud. And that tale is this: Beauty does more than stand alone. It also creates a space around itself. Beauty casts its own shadow, because it finds its own way to shine.

There's a catch, of course: For every moment that Beauty shines bright, something—or someone—standing right beside it gets covered up by Beauty's shadow. Goes overlooked, unnoticed.

You can trust me on this one. I know what I'm talking about.

On the twenty-fifth day of September, ten days after my tenth birthday, it happened to me, for on that day I performed an act I never had before. I stepped between my two sisters, and the shadows cast by their two Beauties so overlapped each other that they completely filled the place in which I stood.

As a result, I disappeared entirely.

Two

I DIDN'T *LITERALLY* DISAPPEAR, OF COURSE. I WAS STILL right there, just like always. Or rather, not like always because, incredible as it may seem, I had never actually occupied the space between my sisters.

Maybe it was because Maman sensed the possibility of what did, in fact, occur. Or perhaps it was simply that, in spite of her sometimes impulsive nature, Maman liked everything, including her daughters, to be well-organized. Whatever the reason, until that fateful moment, I had never occupied the space between my sisters for the simple reason that we spent our lives in chronological order.

Celeste. April. Belle.

Everything about my sisters and me was arranged in this fashion, in fact. It was the way our beds were lined up in our bedroom; our places at the dining table, where we all sat in a row along one side. It was the order in which we got dressed each morning and had our hair brushed for one hundred and one strokes each night. The order in which we entered a room or left it, and were introduced to guests. The only exception was when we were allowed to open our presents all together, in a great frenzy of paper and ribbons, on Christmas morning.

This may seem very odd to you, and you may wonder why it didn't to any of us. All that I can say is that order in general, but most especially the order in which one was born, was considered very important in the place where I grew up. The oldest son inherited his father's house and lands. Younger daughters did not marry unless the oldest had first walked down the aisle. So if our household paid strict attention to which sister came first, second, and (at long last) third, the truth is that none of us thought anything about the arrangement at all.

Until the day Monsieur LeGrand came to call.

Monsieur LeGrand was my father's oldest and closest friend, though Papa had seen him only once and that when he was five years old. In his own youth, Monsieur LeGrand had been the boyhood friend of Papa's father, Grand-père Georges. It was Monsieur LeGrand who had brought to Grand-mère Annabelle the sad news that her young husband had been snatched off the deck of his ship by a wave that curled around him like a giant fist, then picked him up and carried him down to the bottom of the ocean.

In some other story, Monsieur LeGrand might have stuck around, consoled the young widow in her grief, then married her after a suitable period of time. But that story is not this one. Instead, soon after reporting his sad news, Monsieur LeGrand returned to the sea, determined to put as much water as he could between himself and his boyhood home.

Eventually, Monsieur LeGrand became a merchant specializing in silk, and settled in a land where silkworms flourished, a place so removed from where he'd started out that if you marked each city with a finger on a globe, you'd need both hands. Yet even from this great distance, Monsieur LeGrand did not forget his childhood friend's young son.

When Papa was old enough, Grand-mère Annabelle took him by the hand and marched him down to the waterfront offices of the LeGrand Shipping Company. For, though he no longer lived in the place where he'd grown up, Monsieur LeGrand maintained a presence in our seaport town. My father then began the process that took him from being the boy who swept the floors and filled the coal scuttles to the man who knew as much about the safe passage of sailors and cargo as anyone.

When that day arrived, Monsieur LeGrand made Papa his partner, and the sign above the waterfront office door was changed to read LEGRAND, DELAURIER AND COMPANY. But nothing

Papa ever did, not marrying Maman nor helping to bring three lovely daughers into the world, could entice Monsieur LeGrand back to where he'd started.

Over the years, he had become something of a legend in our house. The tales my sisters and I spun of his adventures were as good as any bedtime stories our nursemaids ever told. We pestered our father with endless questions to which he had no answers. All that he remembered was that Monsieur LeGrand had been straight and tall. This was not very satisfying, as I'm sure you can imagine, for any grown-up might have looked that way to a five-year-old.

Then one day—on my tenth birthday, to be precise—a letter arrived. A letter that caused my father to return home from the office in the middle of the day, a thing he never does. I was the first to spot Papa, for I had been careful to position myself near the biggest of our living room windows, the better to watch for any presents that might arrive.

At first, the sight of Papa alarmed me. His face was flushed, as if he'd run all the way from the waterfront. He burst through the door, calling for my mother, then dashed into the living room and caught me up in his arms. He twirled me in so great a circle that my legs flew out straight and nearly knocked Maman's favorite vase to the floor.

He'd had a letter, Papa explained when my feet were firmly on the ground. One that was better than any birthday present he could have planned. It came from far away, from the land where the silkworms flourished, and it informed us all that, at long last, Monsieur LeGrand was coming home.

Not surprisingly, this threw our household into an uproar. For it went without saying that ours would be the first house Monsieur LeGrand would come to visit. It also went without saying that everything needed to be perfect for his arrival.

The work began as soon as my birthday celebrations were complete. Maman hired a small army of extra servants, as those who usually cared for our house were not great enough in number. They swept the floors, then polished them until they gleamed like gems. They hauled the carpets out of doors and beat them. Every single picture in the house was taken down from its place on the walls and inspected for even the most minute particle of dust. While all this was going on, the walls themselves were given a new coat of whitewash.

But the house wasn't the only thing that got polished. The inhabitants got a new shine as well. Maman was all for us being reoutfitted from head to foot, but here, Papa put his foot down. We must not be extravagant, he said. It would give the wrong impression to Monsieur LeGrand. Instead, we must provide his mentor and our benefactor with a warm welcome that also showed good sense, by which my father meant a sense of proportion.

So, in the end, it was only Papa and Maman who had new outfits from head to foot. My sisters and I each received one new garment. Celeste, being the oldest, had a new dress. April had a new silk shawl. As for me, I was the proud owner of a new pair of shoes.

It was the shoes that started all the trouble, you could say. Or, to be more precise, the buckles.

They were made of silver, polished as bright as mirrors. They were gorgeous and I loved them. Unfortunately, the buckles caused the shoes to pinch my feet, which in turn made taking anything more than a few steps absolute torture. Maman had tried to warn me in the shoe shop that this would be the case, but I had refused to listen and insisted the shoes be purchased anyhow.

"She should never have let you have your own way in the first place," Celeste pronounced on the morning we expected Monsieur LeGrand.

My sisters and I were in our bedroom, watching and listening for the carriage that would herald Monsieur LeGrand's arrival. Celeste was standing beside her dressing table, unwilling to sit lest she wrinkle her new dress. April was kneeling on a cushion near the window, the silk shawl draped around her shoulders, her own skirts carefully spread out around her. I was the only one actually sitting down. Given the choice between the possibility of wrinkles or the guarantee of sore feet, I had decided to take my chances with the wrinkles.

But though I was seated, I was hardly sitting still. Instead, I turned my favorite birthday present and gift from Papa—a small knife for wood carving that was cunningly crafted so that the blade folded into the handle—over and over between my hands, as if the action might help to calm me.

Maman disapproves of my wood carving. She says it isn't ladylike and is dangerous. I have pointed out that I'm just as likely to stab myself with an embroidery needle as I am to cut myself with a wood knife. My mother remains unconvinced, but Papa is delighted that I inherited his talent for woodwork.

"And put that knife away," Celeste went on. "Do you mean to frighten Monsieur LeGrand?"

"Celeste," April said, without taking her eyes from the street scene below. "Not today. Stop it."

Thinking back on it now, I see that Celeste was feeling just as nervous and excited as I was. But Celeste almost never handles things the way I do, or April either, for that matter. She always goes at things head-on. I think it's because she's always first. It gives her a different view of the world, a different set of boundaries.

"Stop what?" Celeste asked now, opening her eyes innocently wide. "I'm just saying Maman hates Belle's knives, that's all. If she shows up with one today, Maman will have an absolute fit."

"I know better than to take my wood-carving knife into the parlor to meet a guest," I said as I set it down beside me on my dressing table.

"Well, yes, you may *know* better, but you don't always *think*, do you?" Celeste came right back. She swayed a little, making her new skirts whisper to the petticoats beneath as they moved from side to side. Celeste's new dress was a pale blue, almost an exact match for her eyes. She'd wanted it every bit as much as I'd wanted my new shoes.

"For instance, if you'd thought about how your feet might *feel* instead of how they'd *look*, you'd have saved yourself a lot of pain, and us the trouble of listening to you whine."

I opened my mouth to deny it, then changed my mind. Instead, I gave Celeste my very best smile. One that showed as many of my even, white teeth as I could. I have very nice teeth. Even Maman says so.

I gave the bed beside me a pat. "If you're so unconcerned about the way *you* look," I said sweetly, "why don't you come over here and sit down?"

Celeste's cheeks flushed. "Maybe I don't want to," she answered.

"And maybe you're a phony," I replied. "You care just as much about how you look as I do, Celeste. It just doesn't suit you to admit it, that's all."

"If you're calling me a liar—," Celeste began hotly.

"Be quiet!" April interrupted. "I think the carriage is arriving!"

Quick as lightning, Celeste darted to the window, her skirts billowing out behind her. I got to my feet, doing my best to ignore how much they hurt, and followed. Sure enough, in the street below, the grandest carriage I had ever seen was pulling up before our door.

"Oh, I can't see his face!" Celeste cried in frustration as we saw a gentleman alight. A moment later, the peal of the front doorbell echoed throughout the house. April got to her feet, smoothing out her skirts as she did so. In the pit of my stomach, I felt a group of butterflies suddenly take flight.

I really *did* care about the way I looked, if for no other reason than how I looked and behaved would reflect upon Papa and Maman. All of us wanted to make a good impression on Monsieur LeGrand.

"My dress isn't too wrinkled, is it?" I asked anxiously, and felt the butterflies settle down a little when it was Celeste who answered.

"You look just fine."

"The young ladies' presence is requested in the parlor," our housekeeper, Marie Louise, announced from the bedroom door. Marie Louise's back is always as straight as a ruler, and her skirts are impeccably starched. She cast a critical eye over the three of us, then gave a satisfied nod.

"What does Monsieur LeGrand look like, Marie Louise?" I asked. "Did you see him? Tell us!"

Marie Louise gave a sniff to show she disapproved of such questions, though her eyes were not unkind.

"Of course I saw him," she answered, "for who was it who answered the door? But I don't have time to stand around gossiping any more than you have time to stand around and listen. Get along with you, now. Your parents and Monsieur LeGrand are waiting for you in the parlor."

With a rustle of skirts, she left.

My sisters and I looked at one another for a moment, as if catching our collective breath.

"Come on," Celeste said. And, just like that, she was off. April followed hard on her heels.

"Celeste," I begged, my feet screaming in agony as I tried to keep up. "Don't go so fast. Slow down."

But I was talking to the open air, for my sisters were already gone. By the time I made it to the bedroom door, they were at the top of the stairs. And by the time I made it to the top of the stairs, they were at the bottom. Celeste streaked across the entryway, then paused before the parlor door, just long enough to give her curls a brisk shake and clasp her hands in front of her as was proper. Then, without a backward glance, she marched straight into the parlor with April trailing along behind her.

Slowly, I descended the stairs, then came to a miserable stop in the downstairs hall.

Should I go forward, I wondered, *or should I stay right where I am?*

No matter who got taken to task over our entry later—and someone most certainly would be—there could be no denying that I was the one who would look bad at present. I was the one who was late. I'd probably already embarrassed my parents and insulted our honored guest. *Perhaps I should simply slink away, back to my room,* I thought. I could claim I'd suddenly become ill between the top of the stairs and the bottom, that it was in everyone's best interest that I hadn't made an appearance, particularly Monsieur LeGrand's.

And perhaps I could flap my arms and fly to the moon.

That's when I heard the voices drifting out of the parlor.

There was Maman's, high and piping like a flute. Papa's with its quiet ebb and flow that always reminds me of the sea. Celeste and April I could not hear at all, of course. They were children and would not speak unless spoken to first. And then I heard a voice like the great rumble of distant thunder say:

"But where is *la petite Belle*?"

And, just as real thunder will sometimes inspire my feet to carry me from my own room into my parents', so too the sound of what could be no other than Monsieur LeGrand's voice carried me through the parlor door and into the room beyond. As if to make up for how slowly my feet had moved before, I overshot my usual place in line. Instead of ending up at the end of the row, next to April, I came to a halt between my two sisters. April was to my left and Celeste to my right. We were out of order for the first and only time in our lives.

I faltered, appalled. For I was more than simply out of place; I was also directly in front of Monsieur LeGrand.

Three

He really *was* tall. So tall it almost made me dizzy to tilt my neck back to look up at him. Unlike the implications of his name, Monsieur LeGrand wasn't relaxed and round. Instead, he was all sharpness and angles—like one of the tools Papa keeps in his workshop for shaping wood. His skin was tanned, permanently stained by the combination of sun and salt. Even his eyes reminded me of the sea, for they were the blue-black of deep water.

I noticed all this in the time it took his eyes to scan the room, as if I might be hiding in one of the corners.

"Where is *la petite Belle*?" he asked again. "Is she not coming?"

How is it possible he does not see me? I wondered. For I was standing right in front of him, so close that I could have taken no more than two steps and touched his toes with mine.

I pulled in a breath, determined to speak and call his attention to me, but felt the air refuse to leave my lungs. My entire body began to flush with embarrassment, the way it does when you've been caught in an outright lie—for suddenly it seemed that this was precisely what had happened. Monsieur LeGrand's inability to see me had exposed a falsehood. The only problem was that I didn't have the faintest idea what it was.

I've got to get back to my proper place, I thought. *Surely everything will start to make sense again if I can just get back to my place in line.*

Slowly, fearing to call attention to myself now, I took one step back, while my sisters each took a sidling step toward each other. The space between them was now filled. There was no room for me anymore. Safely behind their backs, I took two quick sidesteps to the left. I was on the far side of April now. All I had to do was take two more steps, forward this time, and I would be exactly where I was expected to be.

Releasing the breath I'd been holding, I eased forward into my proper place in line.

"Ah." I heard Maman exhale, as if she'd been holding her breath as well.

"Here she is, Alphonse," Papa said, for that was Monsieur LeGrand's name. "Here is Belle."

I stepped forward again, intending to make a curtsy, though

my legs had begun to tremble so much that I was afraid they might not hold me if I tried. But before I could even make the attempt, Monsieur LeGrand stepped forward as well. To my astonishment, he knelt down—in that way grown-ups have sometimes when meeting a young person for the first time. Not condescendingly, just wanting to view the world from their perspective.

For several moments, Monsieur LeGrand and I gazed at each other, face-to-face and eye-to-eye. I've often wondered whether I'd have seen what happened next if we hadn't been so close.

For, ever so slowly, Monsieur LeGrand's face began to change. The only way I can describe it is to say it became kind. As if he found the way to smooth out all the harsh angles until what lay beneath was revealed: kindness in its purest, most generous form.

I forgot my aching feet and trembling legs then, as a terrible possibility, an explanation for everything that had happened since I'd first entered the room, shot like a bolt of lightning across my ten-year-old mind.

What if my name was wrong? What if Monsieur LeGrand's kindness was not only a simple gift but also a consolation prize, one designed to make up for the fact that I was not a Beauty, not truly *Belle* at all? What if my name was not my true measure, but was the lie I told?

It would explain so much, I thought. Such as why Monsieur

BELLE

LeGrand had not seen me standing between my sisters, as close as the reach of his arm. He had looked for a Beauty to go with theirs, but he had failed to find it. My face did not live up to the promise of my name.

My legs did give way then, and I heard Monsieur LeGrand give a startled exclamation as I suddenly swayed and closed my eyes. If I stared into his one moment longer, I feared I might begin to weep, for now I could see that there was more than kindness in his look. There was pity there as well.

"Why, Belle!" I heard my mother exclaim as, with a swish of silk, she, too, knelt down. I sensed Monsieur LeGrand getting to his feet even as I felt my mother's arms enfold me. I leaned my head against her shoulder, drinking in the scent of lavender that always hovers about her like a soft and fragrant cloud.

"Whatever is the matter? Are you ill?" my mother inquired.

Maman, my heart pounded out in hard, fast strokes. *Oh, Maman. Maman. Why didn't you say something? Why didn't you warn me that this day would come?*

For I had heard more than just the way my mother's dress moved. My legs might have been refusing to function, but my ears still worked just fine. Running through my mother's voice like a strand of errant-colored thread was a tone that was the perfect match for the expression in Monsieur LeGrand's eyes. Maman pitied me too.

It must be true, then, I thought.

I was not a Beauty, and my own mother knew it.

27

How long had she known? Surely she must have believed I was beautiful on the day of my birth, or she would not have insisted on calling me *Belle*.

When had I lost my Beauty? I wondered. Where had it gone?

"Belle?" I suddenly heard my father's quiet voice say. "Are you all right?"

At the sound of it, I felt the rapid beating of my heart begin to slow. For Papa's voice sounded just as it always did. There was nothing in it to show that he had noticed anything different about me, nothing to indicate that anything was wrong.

And suddenly, with that, nothing was. I opened my eyes and stepped out of the circle of my mother's arms.

"I'm fine, Papa," I assured him.

Maman got to her feet and went to stand at Papa's side, a faint frown between her brows. I curtsied then, the buckles on my new shoes squeezing like vise grips. As I straightened, I snuck a quick glance upward at Monsieur LeGrand. If his expression held any hidden meaning now, for the life of me, I could not see it.

"I am pleased to meet you, Monsieur," I went on. "I apologize for causing a fuss. . . . I didn't mean . . . it's just . . ."

"It's just that she's so excited to meet you, Alphonse," my father said, coming to my rescue. "It's all she's talked about since your letter arrived. It came on her birthday. Did I tell you that? She declared it her favorite gift."

"Is that so?" Monsieur LeGrand inquired, and then he smiled. His eyes grew brighter, and all the wrinkles in his face seemed to join together to form a new pattern of lines more complex than that on any sea chart. "That's the nicest bit of news I've had in a good long while."

"Yes, Marie Louise?" my mother's voice slid beneath Monsieur LeGrand's.

"Luncheon is served, Madame," Marie Louise murmured from just inside the parlor door. Three paces in and not a step farther unless she is requested to do so.

"Thank you," my mother said, nodding. I stepped back, so that my sisters and I were standing in a perfect straight line.

We all knew what would happen next. Monsieur LeGrand would offer Maman his arm. He would lead her into the dining room, pull out her chair, then sit down to her right, the position a guest of honor always occupies. Papa would take Celeste in. April and I would follow along behind. All of us would be in our proper place, our proper order. Things would be completely back to normal.

But Monsieur LeGrand surprised us all. For instead of turning to offer his arm to Maman, he closed the distance between us and offered it to me.

"Will you give me the pleasure of taking you in to lunch, *ma Belle*?" he asked as he executed an expert bow. "Think of it as the rest of your birthday present."

I laughed in astonished delight before I could help myself.

For here was a gift I had never even thought to wish for: the chance to be first in line.

I shot a quick glance in Papa's direction and saw his lips lift in an encouraging smile. I didn't quite dare to glance at Celeste, who was now destined to follow along behind. I wondered if she would recognize my back, for it would be unfamiliar to her. I remembered to keep it perfectly straight as I dipped a curtsy in response to Monsieur LeGrand's bow.

"Thank you, Monsieur," I said. "I accept your gift with pleasure."

Both of us straightened up, and I stepped forward to meet him. Slipping my fingers into the crook of his elbow, I let him lead me out of the parlor and into the hall.

It wasn't until at least an hour later, when lunch was nearly over, that I realized I'd walked the entire distance from the parlor to the dining room without feeling the pinch of my new shoes at all.

Four

LATE THAT NIGHT I LAY IN BED, ROLLING THE EVENTS OF the day over in my mind.

The rest of Monsieur LeGrand's visit had passed as smoothly as the silk he had exported for so long. In the excitement of the day and listening to his stories of lands far away, I had allowed the strange and unhappy moments in the parlor to steal away to the farthest corner of my mind.

This was not the same as saying I'd banished them forever, though. They were still there, simply biding their time. Now that the house was quiet and my mind had no other distractions, the memories of what had happened crept forward once more.

Belle. I mouthed the word silently in the darkness. *I am Annabelle Evangeline Delaurier, but everybody calls me Belle.*

Everybody called me Beauty, in other words. But what if what I had feared in the parlor this afternoon was true, and I wasn't so very Beautiful after all?

How do you recognize Beauty when you see it?

What *is* Beauty, anyhow?

I turned my head, the better to see April's where she rested in the bed beside mine. Even in the dim light of the moon coming through the window, April's hair glimmered ever so faintly, like a spill of golden coins. I was pretty sure there wasn't another head in our entire city that could even dream of doing this, of shining in the dark.

If anything is Beautiful, surely that is it, I thought.

But was shining hair enough? Was that all it took to make my sister Beautiful? Or was it not also the way her green eyes sparkled when she laughed? The way her laughter sounded like clear water dancing over stones. Everything about April was like a hand outstretched, inviting you to reach out to join her.

That is truly what makes her Beautiful, I thought.

I lifted myself up onto one elbow now, straining to see beyond April to Celeste's sleeping form. My oldest sister did not give off her own light. If anything, it was just the opposite. The place where she lay seemed plunged in shadow, as if Celeste always carried some part of midnight, the time of her birth, with her.

Whereas April's looks shone out to meet you, Celeste's looks were of a different kind. Something about her always seemed mysterious, hidden from view, even when she was standing in direct sunlight. She made you look once, then look again, as if to make certain you hadn't missed anything the first time around.

That is Beauty too, I decided. Not as comfortable a kind of Beauty as April's, perhaps, but Beauty just the same, for it made you want more. So that made both my sisters Beautiful with a capital *B*.

Where does that leave me? I wondered.

Yes, I know. It sounds as if I was edging right up to self-pity, but I swear to you that wasn't how it seemed at the time. It was simply the logical next question, the next piece of the puzzle I had suddenly discovered I needed to solve.

All of us come to some moment in our childhoods when we realize that the world is bigger than what we have previously known. Larger than we imagined it could be. Wider than the reach of our arms, even when they are stretched out as far as they can go. That is what happened to me on the day of Monsieur LeGrand's visit, I think. As if standing between my two sisters had hidden me from view, but opened up the world all at the same time.

Before Monsieur LeGrand's arrival, I had never really taken the time to consider my relationship with my sisters. Or if I had, it was only to think about our order: Celeste. April. Belle.

But if my name was not the true match to my face, was last

my true place in line? What if there was something different mapped out for me? If I didn't even know myself, how could I begin to find out what that something was?

All of a sudden, I couldn't bear lying in bed one moment longer. My body felt foreign, as if it belonged to someone else. So I tossed back the covers and swung my legs over the side of the bed and sat up, hissing ever so slightly as my bare feet hit the cold floor. Quietly, so as not to awaken my sleeping sisters in all their loveliness, I pulled a robe on over my nightdress, slid my feet into my oldest and most soft-soled pair of shoes, and slipped out the bedroom door.

A house is a strange thing at night, even when that house is your own. For even the most comfortable, well-lived-in of houses has its secrets. If you get up unexpectedly in the night, you can sometimes catch a glimpse of them. Our house seemed to whisper to itself in voices that were quickly hushed as I hurried along its darkened corridors.

Was it talking about me? Discussing my lost Beauty, perhaps? I pursed my lips, pressing them tightly together so I wouldn't be tempted to pose the question. I wasn't all that sure I wanted to know.

I sped along the upstairs hallway on swift and silent feet, then hurried down the stairs at a pace I would dearly have loved earlier that day. I swung right, toward the kitchen at the back of the house. Easing open the door, I poked my head around it, then slid all the way inside.

There, resting on the kitchen windowsill, between a pot of marjoram on one side and oregano on the other, was a single lantern, its flame burning clear and bright. At the sight of this, I felt some of the terrible strangeness that pulled me out of bed begin to ease.

Papa was working late in his workshop.

Do you feel closer to one of your parents than to the other? I do, and I here admit that, much as I love my mother, I have always been closer to Papa. I think it's that the way his mind works makes sense to me, in a way that Maman's never does. I understand the world better when I catch a glimpse of it through Papa's eyes. Even when he shows me a bigger piece of it than what I'm used to, it's still a world I recognize.

And so it was to Papa that I had always gone with any new discovery, any important question, any joy or hurt or sorrow. Most of these conferences had taken place where my father did his own problem-solving: his workshop. Papa had built it with his own two hands, right in our backyard. The lighted lantern was the signal that he was there.

I pulled my robe a little tighter to my chest, for the autumn night was clear and I knew it would be cold. I eased open the kitchen door as quietly as I could, and slipped outside. A path made of broken seashells stretched before me, gleaming pale in the moonlight. Papa had created this, too, so that it would be easy to see the way to and from the house. I loved the faint crunching the shells made underfoot, which also helped to warn Papa of anyone's approach. He used sharp tools inside the workshop. Surprise was not always welcome.

Reaching the door, I used the secret knock I'd developed when I was three, thinking it was the height of cleverness: two knocks, a pause, and then two more. My father's voice sounded even before I had finished knocking.

"Yes. Come in," he called.

I lifted the latch and pushed open the door, blinking a little at the sudden change of light. Papa kept the workshop very bright.

"Hello, Papa," I said.

"Well," my father said, as if clearing his head of whatever thoughts had been there before I arrived and making room for whatever I might have brought with me. "Hello, Belle. Come all the way in and shut the door, will you? You'll let in the moths, otherwise."

I did as I was asked, leaving a small cloud of moths jockeying for position outside the window, trying to reach the lights inside. I always feel sorry for them. They seem so frantic. Not only that, they always come in last, just like I do. Most people prefer butterflies.

"You're up late," my father commented. He set down the project on which he had been working, and I recognized it as a jewelry box. Monsieur LeGrand had given Maman a fine string of pearls just that afternoon. No doubt Papa was making her a special place to store them.

"I was just about to take a break and make some hot chocolate," he said. "Might I interest you in some?"

"Can I have cinnamon in mine?" I asked at once. This was the way I liked it best. It was Papa's favorite too.

"I think that can be arranged," he answered with a smile. I took the spot he'd vacated as he went to the small potbellied stove in the corner of the room, stirred up the coals, and put a pan of milk on to warm.

I watched Papa work, cutting slices of chocolate so thin they curled like wood shavings, before plopping them into the steaming pot with each deft flick of the knife. Papa makes hot chocolate the same way he makes everything else, with smooth, deliberate, and precise movement. I love these qualities about him. He's self-assured, like he's thought things through and knows where he's going. It makes me feel that it's safe to follow him, even into unknown territory.

When the hot chocolate was prepared to his satisfaction, Papa poured two mugs full, slid a stick of cinnamon into each, then brought me mine. Papa sat down beside me and we sipped in thoughtful silence for several moments. I also love this about my father. He doesn't badger me to get going right away. He always lets me take my time.

I was halfway through my mug and Papa had almost finished his before the time was right.

"Papa, may I ask you something?"

"You may ask me anything you like, *ma Belle*," my father

replied. He set his mug down, as if to indicate he was ready for whatever I might ask him. As for myself, I took one more fortifying sip.

"Am I Beautiful?" I blurted out.

It wasn't precisely the question I'd intended to start with, but sometimes, even when you tell yourself you want to ease into things, the question you want to ask the most just pops right out of your mouth.

My father's eyebrows leaped toward his hairline. This was the only sign that my question had taken him by surprise.

"Of course you are beautiful, Belle," he said.

But I could tell that he hadn't really understood what I meant. The way my father said the word, it was just another adjective and nothing more. I stirred my chocolate with my cinnamon stick, trying to figure out how to ask in a way that would tell him what I needed to know.

"But am I *Beautiful*?" I said again, trying to give the word the extra emphasis I thought it deserved. "As Beautiful as Celeste and April?"

My father picked up his mug, a frown between his brows.

"What makes you ask that?"

"Papa," I said, drawing out the second syllable, and trying not to let the fear that he was putting me off get the better of me. "Why does anyone ask a question? Because I want to know the answer."

"Now, Belle," my father began.

"I know," I interrupted. "Pretend we're bolts of silk you're thinking about buying. We're all lined up together, but you can choose only one. Which one of us would you want the most?"

"But surely that question is impossible to answer," my father replied. "For it would depend on why I wanted it. Everything is beautiful in its own way, *ma Belle*, even if you have to look hard to find it."

I felt a hard knot form in the pit of my stomach. "I'm not sure that can be right, Papa. How can it be real Beauty if you have to look hard to see it? Isn't Beauty supposed to be easy to recognize?"

My father narrowed his eyes. "To tell you the truth, I don't think I've ever thought of it in quite that way before," he said, drawing the words out slowly. "I think I'd like a few more minutes to think it over, if that's all right."

This is the downside to the fact that my father never rushes others. You can't rush him, either.

"That's fine, Papa," I said grudgingly.

Giving my father more time was one thing. Sitting still while he pondered my fate was quite another. So, while my father cogitated, I got up from the bench and prowled around the workshop. I knew its nooks and crannies well, and not simply because I often came to talk with my father. I have what Papa calls *quick hands*, the hands of a true wood-carver. If I hold a piece of wood long enough, I can hear the story that it has to tell.

Actually, that's not quite the right way to put it. What really happens is that I *feel* the story the wood is telling. It's as if I become part of the tree the wood once belonged to. It begins with a tingling in my hands, then it flows up my arms and throughout my body. When the story reaches my heart, I can see the image that the wood has cherished deep inside itself. After that, it is simply a matter of gently carving away the extra wood.

We discovered my talent quite by accident when I was about six. Playing outside one day, I picked up a small branch that had come down in a windstorm. Instead of discarding it, I insisted on taking it straight to Papa's workshop. It took a while for him to understand that I was both sincere and determined when I claimed there was a bird inside and I wished to carve it out of the branch. Maman, I think, was genuinely alarmed.

But eventually Papa took me at my word, sitting beside me on the workbench, adding the strength and skill of his hands when my own weren't quite enough. By the end of the day, a small carved bird perched at one end of the branch. All that was needed was a dash of red paint, my father said, to complete the image of a cardinal. I've been a wood-carver ever since.

Now I selected a piece at random—alder, I think—and fetched my carving tools from the workbench Papa had made for me. Then I dragged a packing crate over so that it faced the bench on which my father sat. The piece of alder wasn't large, only a little longer than the palm of my hand, and newly cut, for all its edges felt hard and clean to the touch. I held it in my hands on my lap for a moment, feeling the tingling first in my hands and then my wrists before it shot straight up my arms.

All right, then, I thought. *I see you well enough.* I opened the leather satchel, drew out the knife I wanted, and began to carve.

Five

AFTER WHAT FELT LIKE A GREAT DEAL OF TIME HAD GONE
by, my father finally spoke. "I am not sure what to make of what
you've asked me, Belle."

I concentrated on my carving, not letting my eyes stray to
Papa's face.

"I never thought to compare you and your sisters, one
to the other," my father went on. "Even when you stand all
together, I see you one by one."

I pulled in a breath to protest that this could not be the case,
then expelled it slowly. For I could tell my father was speaking
the truth. Goods he compares on a daily basis because he must.
But I realized I had never heard him compare one person to

another. If anything, he compares you to yourself. Where you are now versus where he thinks you might be able to go. This is the ability that enabled him to give Dominic Boudreaux a second chance. As if Papa could literally see there was more to Dom than met most eyes.

"And as for beauty being something you must see at first glance, I don't think that can be right either," my father went on.

I gouged into the wood and flicked a piece away. "I think you're wrong, Papa."

"I don't see why," my father said, not arguing, but in a tone that told me he didn't think I was making any sense at all. "Don't they say that beauty is in the eye of the beholder?"

The knife jerked, skittering down the side of the alder to bite deep into the pad of my left hand. I didn't even feel the pain. Instead, I watched the blood well up, then run down onto my white nightgown.

In a quiet voice I asked, "But what if people can't see you at all? What if you're as good as invisible, Papa?"

"For heaven's sake, Belle!" my father exclaimed. He got up quickly, crossed to where I sat, and knelt in front of me. Papa carefully eased the wood and knife from my fingers and set them on the floor beside him. He pulled a clean handkerchief from the pocket of his smock and placed it against my cut, curling my right hand over my left to apply pressure to make the bleeding stop.

"I think it's high time you told me what the matter really

is," my father said. "In all these years, I've never known you to cut yourself."

"He didn't see me," I choked, and felt the words burn all the way up my throat. "He didn't see me, but I was standing right in front of him."

My father sat back on his heels. "Who didn't see you?" he demanded. "What are you talking about?"

"This afternoon," I said, answering the questions in reverse order. "Monsieur LeGrand."

My blood was seeping through the handkerchief now, in spite of my best efforts. The cut was deep, perhaps deep enough to leave a scar.

"This afternoon," my father said. "In the parlor, do you mean?"

I nodded. "I didn't mean to be late." My words came out in a great rush. "But my feet hurt and Celeste was going so fast and she wouldn't stop. So when I finally came in, I went too far. I ended up between Celeste and April, right in front of Monsieur LeGrand.

"But he didn't see me, Papa. He *couldn't* see me, and I think . . ." I paused, pulled in a shaky breath. "I think that I know why."

"And what is it that you think you know?" my father asked.

I began to cry then, hot, fat tears that slipped down my cheeks and fell onto the handkerchief, turning my red blood the pink of my mother's favorite rose.

"I think it's because my name is wrong. It doesn't match my face. I shouldn't be called Belle, because I'm not Beautiful. Not really. Not like Celeste and April are. That's why Monsieur LeGrand couldn't see me. He looked for a face to go with theirs, a Beautiful face. Only I don't have one. You can ask Maman if you don't believe me. She knows it's true. I saw it in her eyes."

My father looked as though I'd taken the piece of wood I'd been carving and knocked him over the head with it.

"Why, Belle," he murmured. "Belle."

"But that's just the problem, don't you understand?" I cried out. "I'm not *Beautiful*. My name is nothing but a lie. I don't want to be *Belle* anymore, Papa."

"Then who do you want to be?" my father asked quietly.

"I don't know," I sobbed. For this was the crux of the problem. "I don't know."

At this, my father stood and plucked me from the packing crate. Then he sat down upon it himself, settling me into his lap the way he'd done when I was very small. I tucked my head into the notch of his neck and cried as though I might never stop. My father remained silent throughout.

His arms around me were gentle, and even through my shaking, I could feel the beat of his heart against mine, firm and sure and strong. At last, my tears subsided and I let my head rest against his shoulder, pulling in long, deep breaths. Still, my father held his tongue.

"Couldn't I be Annabelle?" I asked. "I think, maybe . . ."

My voice wobbled and I took a breath to steady it. "Maybe if people weren't expecting to see a Beauty in the first place, it might be easier when it turns out I'm not."

My father was silent for several moments more, just long enough that I had to resist squirming within the circle of his arms.

"Annabelle is a fine name," he said at last. "It was my mother's name and I chose it for you myself. But I'm not so sure that changing what you're called will accomplish what you want it to, my little one.

"We all are more than what others call us, whether we like our names or not. We are also who we choose to be and what we decide to make of ourselves. Changing your name won't change that, nor will it change who you are inside."

"Oh, Papa," I sighed. Just this once, I would have liked it if he'd let me have my way. "Don't you ever answer just *yes* or *no*?"

"Sometimes," my father said. And I heard myself laugh before I quite realized what I'd done.

"There now, that's better," Papa declared, and he dropped a kiss on the top of my head. "I am sorry that what happened today has given you such pain, *ma petite Belle*. But you must remember that you are still young. Perhaps you and your name just need a little more time to find each other."

"Papa," I said, keeping my voice as neutral as I could. "Are you by any chance telling me I need to grow up?"

This time it was my father who laughed. He set me on my feet, then rose and gave a mighty stretch.

"I don't think I would have put it *quite* that way, but I suppose I do mean that." Then he knelt in front of me once again, reaching out to gently take me by the shoulders.

"I'm not quite sure what happened today," my father went on. "First impressions can be tricky things, for they can be both shallow and lasting, all at once. But of one thing I am absolutely certain: Anyone with the right eyes and heart to match will see your beauty, Belle. If not at first, then for the long run. Whether or not your beauty is like your sisters' is another thing entirely. Personally, I think that's beside the point."

"It doesn't feel beside the point," I said.

My father kissed my forehead. "I know it doesn't."

"Don't tell me," I said, sighing. "I'm going to have to wait to grow up for this one too."

"I'm afraid so," Papa said with a smile. "Now, how's the hand?"

"Better." I held it out. Papa eased the bloodstained handkerchief away from my skin. The place where the knife had slipped had left an angry red gash, but the bleeding had stopped.

"That's good," my father said. "We'll wash it when we get back to the kitchen, then bandage it up."

"We're going to have to tell Maman, aren't we?" If it had been a little cut, I might have gotten away without Maman noticing, but a bandage was going to be hard to disguise.

My father nodded sympathetically. "I'm afraid so. But I will make sure she knows that you were being careful. If she asks, I'll say I posed a question that took you by surprise. Not that we need go into the subject matter, of course," he added.

"Thank you, Papa," I said.

"Ça ne fait rien," my father said. "It's nothing, little one." He fell silent, as if trying to decide whether to say more. "Though you know," he finally said, "perhaps if you spoke with your mother—"

"No," I said at once, for I could see where he was going. As far as I was concerned, there was no need to share my feelings regarding the unfortunate combination of my name and face with Maman. I had learned what she believed that afternoon. There was no point in having a discussion.

"If you say so," said my father. "Now, show me what you were carving, and then we will go in."

I bent to retrieve the wood, and held it out. Papa and I regarded it together. He grunted in surprise.

"That's Alphonse," he said. And so it was.

My father took it from me and held it up, the better to see it in the workshop light.

"That is a very clever likeness, Belle," he pronounced. "Not complete—you hardly had time enough for that. But I think that you have captured him, even so." He chuckled and ran his thumb along the wood. "You see how that bump in the wood is precisely like the bump on his nose?"

"I'm glad you like it, Papa," I said.

My father's expression grew thoughtful. "I think you have

a Gift, Belle," he said softly, and here, at last, I heard the capital letter in his voice. "I would like it if you could believe that true beauty springs from the same place."

"And where is that?" I asked.

"Why, from the heart, of course."

Again, I felt tears threaten. "I'd like that too," I said. "I'm just not sure I know how to believe it."

"Of course you don't," my father said simply. "That's what growing up is for."

"Oh, *Papa*," I said, my tone as good as rolling my eyes.

"I wouldn't worry about it too much," my father said, a twinkle in his eye. "In my experience, growing up happens on its own. But now I think I should get you to bed, before your mother comes looking for us and expresses a desire for both our hides."

"I love you, Papa," I said.

He reached down and took my uninjured hand in his. "And I love you, *ma petite Belle*. That sounds like a good starting place for whatever comes next, don't you think?"

"I do," I said.

Hand in hand, we walked in silence back to the house.

Six

WHAT HAPPENED NEXT WAS PRETTY MUCH JUST AS PAPA had predicted: I grew up, with my sisters beside me. But whereas Celeste and April journeyed along the paths I imagine all parents hope for their children—walkways with surfaces just bumpy enough to keep you paying attention and with enough curves so that you learn to think on your feet and develop character—the path I walked turned out to be a good deal more challenging.

I had promised my father I would try to be patient, try to give my name and face time to find each other. I fully intended to keep that promise, if for no other reason than I wanted Papa to be proud of me. There is a problem with unhappy memories, though; I wonder if you have discovered it.

Unhappy memories are persistent. They're specific, and it's the details that refuse to leave us alone. Though a happy memory may stay with you just as long as one that makes you miserable, what you remember softens over time. What you recall is simply that you were happy, not necessarily the individual moments that brought about your joy.

But the memory of something painful does just the opposite. It retains its original shape, all bony fingers and pointy elbows. Every time it returns, you get a quick poke in the eye or jab in the stomach. The memory of being unhappy has the power to hurt us long after the fact. We feel the injury anew each and every time we think of it. And so, despite my efforts to the contrary, this is how it was with me and the memory of my first meeting with Monsieur LeGrand.

It didn't matter that afterward he took notice of me no matter where I stood. That he moved in next door, we saw him every day, and I soon grew to love him and call him Grand-père Alphonse. The memory of our first meeting refused to leave me. Each time it surfaced, it created a new wound, brought me fresh pain. Pain and patience do not make for a comfortable combination.

And then, of course, there was Maman.

I'd like to say what happened that first afternoon with Grand-père Alphonse, the pity I had heard in my mother's voice even as she held me in her arms, came to make no difference in our relationship. But that would be a lie.

The truth is that it did make a difference. And not a little one at that. For every time my mother spoke my name, every time she looked at me, I felt her pity all over again.

For the first time in my life, I was glad to come last in line.

It meant I could lag behind, putting some distance between me and my Beautiful sisters—particularly when we had company or went out in public. Though we might arrive at some social engagement all together, I became adept at hanging back. The more distance I put between my sisters and me, the less painful the comparisons between us seemed to be. Eventually what people remembered most about me was that they didn't really remember me at all.

Celeste and April could always be found at the center of gatherings. Their faces were easy to call to mind. But the youngest Delaurier girl, the one named Belle, her image was much harder to summon, in spite of all her name might promise.

Finally, I just stayed home.

I expected Maman to protest, but she did not. If I'd needed any more proof that my mother thought I was not as Beautiful as her older daughters, she provided it then. For if she'd truly believed I was as Beautiful as my name proclaimed, she would have insisted I take my place in society with my sisters. But she did not. I was simply Annabelle Evangeline, not Celestial Heavens or April Dawn.

And so, while my sisters went to parties and balls, and did all the things girls do as they grow into young women, I did something entirely different: I spent my days in Papa's workshop. There, I carved every available piece of wood. The beauty I found within the wood always seemed much lovelier than my own countenance. In this way, the years went by. And if I was not completely happy, I wasn't exactly miserable either. It seemed a satisfactory compromise.

But even the best of compromises unravels sooner or later, and so it proved with mine. For I'd failed to consider the very thing that growing up means: passage of time. No matter where I spent my days, no matter what my face might look like, I was now a young lady. And young ladies have responsibilities to their families that cannot be shirked or avoided.

Or so my mother informed me at the breakfast table one fine morning in late summer when I was fifteen years old. It was just Maman, Celeste, April, and me. Papa had already departed for his waterfront office, which I considered significant when Maman chose that morning to announce that I would be required to attend the de la Montaignes' upcoming garden party.

The de la Montaignes were my father's bankers and one of the wealthiest families in the city. Their son, Paul, was considered the most eligible bachelor in town. Celeste had been discreetly mooning over him for months, ever since the invitation to the party had arrived. The de la Montaignes' garden party was an annual event, a highlight of the summer.

"I didn't have to go last year," I protested. "How come I have to go now?"

"Because you're almost sixteen," my mother answered, daintily spreading marmalade on a piece of toast. The look of great determination on her face, however, did not bode well for my changing her mind. When Maman spreads marmalade like that, there's pretty much no talking her out of anything.

"Almost old enough to be married," my mother went on. "Your sisters are certainly old enough to be."

So that's it, I thought. She was hoping for a match between Celeste and Paul de la Montaigne.

"He may be good-looking, but he's got no more sense than a pailful of earthworms," I remarked.

My mother paused, her eyes narrowing as she gazed in my direction, the knife with which she'd been applying the marmalade poised in midair. "Who?" she inquired.

"Paul de la Montaigne," I answered. "I heard Papa say so."

"You did not," Celeste said at once.

"I did so," I replied. "Though I wasn't meant to hear it," I relented, as I saw Celeste's face flush. "He was talking to Grand-père Alphonse. We were in the workshop. I was working in the corner and I think they forgot I was there."

"He should not have spoken so," Maman pronounced. She set the knife down on her plate with a sharp *click.* "But it makes no difference, as he did so in private. Paul de la Montaigne is the most suitable young man in our circle. Everybody knows it. And as Celeste is certainly one of the loveliest young women . . ."

Her voice trailed off, as there was little more to be said on the subject. She bit into her toast.

"So what do you want me along for?" I asked, when I was certain my mother's mouth was full. "Contrast?"

"Belle!" April said in a shocked voice.

My mother brought the palm of her free hand down on the tabletop so hard it made the silverware rattle. I watched her jaw work as she struggled to finish her food, the muscles of her throat constricting as she swallowed.

"No, I do not want you along for *contrast*," she said when she could speak, her voice hot enough to scald. As if in answer, I felt a painful blush rise in my face. I knew I'd gone too far.

"I want you along because you are a member of this family. Because you have family obligations, and it's time you began to honor them. You have been selfish long enough, Belle."

"Selfish!" I cried.

My mother placed her half-eaten toast precisely in the center of her plate, then rose to her feet.

"I will not discuss this matter with you any further," she said, her voice now cold as ice. "And you will not take it up with your father. I have spoken to him, and he agrees. It's time you take your place in society. You will wear the dress I select for you and attend the de la Montaignes' garden party in one week's time. Both your father and I expect you to behave in a way that does our family honor in public. It's unfortunate you can't seem to bring yourself to do so at home."

My mother flung her napkin onto her plate, and it landed squarely atop the piece of toast on which she'd so determinedly spread marmalade just moments before.

"You have ruined my appetite with your behavior," she said. "I am going upstairs to lie down. Be so good as to ring for Marie Louise and ask her to bring a cool compress for my forehead."

"I'll do it, Maman," Celeste said.

"Mais non!" my mother replied. "It must be Belle. It is time she acknowledged she is a part of this family. Celeste, you may see me to my room." She extended an arm. Celeste took it. Without a backward glance, my mother and my oldest sister walked out.

Slowly, as if my joints ached, I walked across the room to the bell cord. I gave it a swift tug to summon Marie Louise, and gave her my mother's instructions when she arrived. April sat quietly, her breakfast untouched.

"I suppose you think I'm selfish too," I said, when our housekeeper was gone.

"Not exactly," April answered. Her green eyes regarded me thoughtfully, though not without compassion. It was as if she was weighing how much more to say, how much more I could take.

"But I do think Maman has a point, Belle. The way things are now—it's just not right. I would think you'd feel that more than anyone. Don't you want to find someone who will see you for who you really are?"

"There's not very much chance of that," I said, unable to keep the bitterness from my voice. "Not with you and Celeste around."

April winced, and I instantly wished I could call the words back. It wasn't her fault she was so much more Beautiful than I was.

"I think," she said, calmly and succinctly, without a hint of upset in her voice, "that you are wrong. And I think outsiders are not the only ones who fail to see you clearly."

"What's that supposed to mean?" I said.

April stood up. "Now who's being dumb as a pailful of earthworms?" she asked. She walked to the door. "I saw the dress Maman picked out for you," she added. "It's every bit as lovely as mine or Celeste's."

And with that, she left me alone to my thoughts.

Seven

THE DAY OF THE GARDEN PARTY ARRIVED CLEAR AND bright. *Naturally,* I thought, somewhat sourly, as I stood in the bedroom, gazing at myself in all my new finery, trying to convince my stomach to calm down. It seemed that even the weather wished to impress the de la Montaignes.

I, of course, had prayed for rain all week long.

The episode at the breakfast table had not been mentioned again. Not even Papa brought it up, though I felt sure Maman had told him of it. By tacit agreement, neither my sisters nor I mentioned Paul de la Montaigne. Instead, we pretended it was a week like any other, and not one ending with an event of the utmost importance.

I caught a glimpse of movement in the mirror and realized I was passing my folding knife from hand to hand in an effort to calm myself. Deliberately, I set it on my nightstand and instead picked up the nosegay of flowers I was supposed to carry. Then I gazed back at my reflection.

April had been right, I had to admit. The dress Maman had chosen for me was lovely—every bit as lovely as those she'd chosen for Celeste, for April, and for herself. It was a pale color just edging into pink, like a spring rosebud caught in a late frost. The bodice was stitched with row upon row of tiny seed pearls and the full skirt seemed to go on for miles. I even had matching satin slippers, tied with pink ribbons. There would be no buckles to pinch my feet this time. Thin ropes of seed pearls were threaded through my hair, which fell in great rippling waves to my waist. A circlet of tiny pink rosebuds framed my forehead.

If I hadn't known for certain it was me, I never would have recognized myself.

I stared at the girl in the mirror, her long hair shining like mahogany in the afternoon sun. Eyes as dark as chestnut gazed right back.

Who are you? I wondered. *Are you Belle? Are you Beauty enough to stand beside your sisters without being afraid? To stand beside them proudly, sure of who you are both inside and out?*

I had absolutely no idea, but I knew this much: The time had come to find out.

* * *

The de la Montaignes' house was set upon a hill, its gardens cascading down the hillside in a series of graceful terraces, all of which overlooked the ocean. As much as I did not want to be impressed, even I had to admit I had never seen anything like it. Tables covered in white linens all but groaned under the weight of food and flowers. Women and girls in their finery looked like more beautiful blossoms.

My nerve held through our arrival, as Monsieur and Madame de la Montaigne received their guests, one by one.

"So this is the famous Belle," Henri de la Montaigne said, as he took my hand and bowed low over it.

I had expected the richest man in town to be tall and imposing, sort of like Grand-père Alphonse. But my father's banker was round and pale. He looked like he rarely set foot out of doors. His hands were soft, making me self-conscious of the calluses on mine. I felt my courage teeter, then slowly slide down the hillside toward the sea.

What did he mean, "the famous Belle"?

"You must make sure my son catches a glimpse of you," Monsieur de la Montaigne went on.

"Of course, Monsieur, if that is what you wish," I said, remembering my manners, though I had no intention of doing any such thing. It was Celeste that Paul de la Montaigne ought to look at, not me.

"Excellent, excellent," Henri de la Montaigne proclaimed.

And then, much to my relief, he released my hand and turned his attention to the next guest in line.

My mother kept a sharp eye on me as we began to circulate, but soon she was engaged in conversation. The terrace became filled with so many people, it was easy to render myself invisible and fade into the crowd. You can call me a coward if you want to. I came close to doing so myself.

But the simple truth was that, once I didn't have to worry about the inevitable comparison when standing beside my sisters, I actually began to enjoy myself. The garden was gorgeous: lush green lawns and flowers overflowing carefully tended beds, all set against the jewel of the sea below. Slowly, I made my way from one garden terrace to the next, admiring the views, sampling various delicacies, until, at last, I came to the lowest level, the one by the water.

The garden here was all roses. *How Maman would love this,* I thought. She loved flowers of all sorts, but roses most of all. Her own rose garden was her pride and joy, the only place in our entire house and grounds she cared for all herself. Across the front of the terrace, as if framing images of the sea, stood a series of arbors with roses clambering joyfully up the sides and over the top. Each had a bench on either side. I headed for the one on the far right, certain it would be the most private.

It wasn't until I'd almost reached the bench that I realized it was occupied. Celeste was sitting there, a young man at her side. Though it had been many years since I had seen Paul de la Montaigne, I was certain it could be no other. He had his father's shape. I could not see his face, as his back was toward me, but I was sure that I would find it pale and round.

How on earth can Celeste even contemplate marrying him? I wondered as I stopped short. *Even if he is the most eligible bachelor in town.* I had no wish to disturb them, and I was certain an interruption was the last thing Celeste wanted. Fortunately, they had not seen me. They were too wrapped up in each other.

"I'm so pleased to get you alone," Paul de la Montaigne said, leaning toward Celeste. I eased myself backward, holding my breath. "There's a question I've been dying to ask you ever since you arrived."

I stopped in spite of myself. *He's really going to do it,* I thought. *Paul is going to ask Celeste to marry him.* I was going to have a brother-in-law who was as dumb as a pailful of earthworms.

"Yes, Paul?" Celeste asked expectantly.

"Is it true what they say about your sister?"

I froze in place, my eyes fixed on Celeste's face. Never had she looked more Beautiful, and never had I had more cause to admire her, for she never flinched. Not so much as a flicker of an eyelash revealed that Paul's question was not the one for which she'd hoped.

"I have two sisters. Which one?"

Paul de la Montaigne laughed, and I learned how quickly

it is possible to hate. For the laugh cut like a dagger, sharp on both edges. *You are wrong, Papa,* I thought. *Paul de la Montaigne isn't dumb at all.* He was smart in a way my father would never understand. Smart in the ways of giving pain.

"Why, Belle, of course," he answered. "After all, you must know what they say."

For a fraction of a second, Celeste's gaze shifted so that her eyes looked back straight into mine. "Well, yes, of course I do," she said, her eyes back on Paul de la Montaigne once more. "But I would so love to hear *you* say it."

Paul de la Montaigne smiled. "Why, that she is the living embodiment of her name! That's the reason she never goes out in public, because she's so Beautiful, too Beautiful for all but a few privileged pairs of eyes to gaze upon."

Suddenly, I felt cold all over, not just in my limbs but in my very soul.

"And naturally you're hoping yours will be one of those pairs," my sister said evenly.

"Well, of course," Paul de la Montaigne responded. He reached out and captured Celeste's hand. "So tell me: Is it true?"

My heart began to pound in hard and painful strokes.

Turn around and see for yourself was all Celeste needed to say.

She never so much as glanced in my direction. Instead, she gave a laugh like a chime of bright silver bells. "Surely you don't expect me to answer a question like that," she said playfully. As if chastising a naughty child, she reached out to swat

Paul de la Montaigne on one arm. "You don't give away your family's secrets, do you?"

"Of course not."

"Then why should you expect me to give away mine?"

Celeste got to her feet, carefully gathering her silk skirts before Paul de la Montaigne could reply. As if awakened from a dream, I started, clutched my own skirts in my hand, and darted around the arbor, out of sight.

"And now, if you'll excuse me," I heard Celeste go on, "I really must rejoin my family. Belle is here somewhere, of course. But I wonder if you'll be able to recognize her. Beauty is not always what you expect, you know."

With her head held high, my sister walked out of the rose garden. I waited until a frowning Paul de la Montaigne had departed as well before leaving my hiding place. Any pleasure I'd felt that day had been completely spoiled.

Never before had I been used by another to inflict pain on somebody I loved. More than anything in the world, I wished I had been brave enough to confront Paul de la Montaigne myself. But I was not.

And it would be a very long time, I thought, before I banished the image of Celeste turning her own Beauty into a mask to hide her wounded heart.

Eight

THE EVENTS OF THE DE LA MONTAIGNE GARDEN PARTY
marked a change in our household, though I don't think any of
us realized how great a change at the time. The unhappiness, the
sense of good intentions gone awry, came home with us and
took up permanent residence. It became one of us.

My mother did not make me go out again. Paul de la Montaigne's name was no longer mentioned in our house. When
I tried to express my appreciation to Celeste for what she'd
done, she simply turned and walked away. But whether this was
because she was angry with me, or found the subject too painful to revisit, I could not tell.

Even the weather seemed out of sorts. That summer was

the hottest any of us could remember—fierce, blazing weather, so blistering some days that not so much as a breath of air seemed to be stirring. We could not sit outdoors at all, not even in the shade of the large oak tree in the yard.

Overnight, storm clouds would appear, sliding silently across the sky, though the wind that blew them never seemed to touch the ground. The clouds would hunker down for days, thick and black, as if determined to choke out the sky. On those days, the air would become so thick with moisture that breathing became an effort. But it refused to rain. Instead, we'd wake up one morning to find the storm clouds had gone and the scorching sun was back.

And so that long, strange summer turned into a tense and troubled autumn.

The signs that something serious was going on were small at first. Papa went to his shipping office at the waterfront each morning and returned each evening with a furrowed brow. But slowly, as autumn changed to winter, the frown became a permanent addition to my father's face, and he no longer went to his workshop after the regular day's work was done.

Instead, Papa and Grand-père Alphonse spent their evenings together, poring over sea charts. At night, as my sisters and I lay in bed, we could hear our parents' voices melding together—Papa's calm and steady; Maman's rising sharply, then abruptly falling silent. It didn't take a fortune-teller or a genius to read these signs.

Something was terribly wrong.

Papa's ships weren't returning as expected. It was as if the weather that had so affected us was affecting all the globe. Usually, most of my father's fleet of merchant vessels was safe in port by now. For soon it would be winter, the time to make repairs and plan for the new year. But without ships, without even knowledge of their whereabouts, Papa could make no plans for the future. Even worse, unable to sell the missing ships' cargoes, my father could generate no income.

If it had been only a few ships that did not return, we might have managed. Shipping is a risky business even in the best of times. And my father is a careful man, always cautious not to overextend himself. But this was different—not a portion of that on which our livelihood depended, but all of it. A disaster so large, it was impossible to plan for.

If Papa had been a different sort of man, a greedy man, all might still have gone well for us. But he was not. My father felt keenly his responsibility to the families of the men who sailed for him, families who often struggled to make ends meet despite the decent wages paid to them by LeGrand, Delaurier and Company. Had not my father been a poor man, a poor sailor's son? He would not let the families of his men struggle while his own family lived in luxury. For the truth was, they stood to lose far more than we did: fathers, husbands, sons.

First, Maman began to sell her jewelry. I gladly added the buckles that had so plagued my feet to the pile. The forks, knives, and spoons we'd always saved for company came next, followed shortly thereafter by the everyday silver. We sold the paintings in their gilded frames off our walls, the dresses from out of our wardrobes. None of us went out now. But nothing we relinquished quite equaled our financial responsibilities. It was as if we were pouring our money and possessions into a dark and bottomless hole.

Finally, only the house, our horses, and a few cherished possessions remained. I still remember that evening when Papa called us into the dining room. We still had a dining room table, though the elaborately carved sideboard and its contents of silver serving dishes, crystal, and china were gone. Papa had sold them to Henri de la Montaigne just that morning. Then Papa and I had spent the afternoon distributing the proceeds among the families of the men aboard Dominic Boudreaux's ship, the *April Dawn*.

Beside me at the table, April's eyes were teary. She claimed it was her sorrow at having to part with our belongings, but I think we all knew that it was something more. Dominic had been a frequent visitor to our home before he sailed away on this last voyage, and, though he had paid my parents all the proper respect, the real purpose for his visits was clear enough. The fact that April returned Dominic's affection was equally clear, though Dominic had not spoken to my father before he sailed, and April had kept her feelings to herself. Naturally, this made it all the more difficult to offer her comfort.

"Girls," my father said, "your mother and I have been talking things over. . . ."

I think Papa would have reached out to hold Maman's hand for comfort if he could have, but we were sitting in our usual places: Maman and Papa at either end of the long table, Celeste, April, and I in between them.

Maman's eyes were red. But her face looked determined and calm. The last few months had wrought a change in my mother. After the initial shock, Maman had weathered the sale of nearly all the fine things she'd once so treasured and the snubbing by those she'd once considered friends. Her fortitude was nothing short of inspirational. I think even she had been surprised to discover that, beneath all her fine satins and silks, my mother possessed a backbone of iron.

"It's the house, isn't it?" I asked.

My father nodded. "I'm sorry to say it," he said, "but the house must be sold. I had a letter from Alphonse this morning." He let his fingers rest on an envelope in front of him. Grand-père Alphonse had been gone for at least a week, on an errand whose purpose I was just now beginning to comprehend.

"He writes that he has found us a place in the country," my father went on. "We will move by the end of the month."

"Are the ships all lost then, Papa?" April asked, her voice no more than a thin ribbon of sound. "Have we given up hope?"

"Of course not," my father said at once, though the weariness and sadness were plain in his voice. "It is never a good idea to abandon hope."

"But hope is not the same as a ship safely returned to port, is it?" April continued softly. "Hope does not reunite your sailors with those who love them, with those they love."

"No," my father answered steadily, as he met April's gaze. "It does not. But it does teach us not to despair. It gives us something to hold on to, until word comes of what has happened.

"All may yet be well. I pray for this with all my heart. But I cannot run a business on hopes and prayers, even if my bankers would allow it. I have tried to put this day off for as long as possible, but . . ."

"Where is this new house, Papa?" Celeste inquired.

"A day and a half's journey inland," my father said. "One day through the Wood, and another half day beyond. Alphonse writes that of all the places he saw, this is the one he thinks will suit us best, and I am willing to trust his judgment."

Papa's gaze roamed around our spacious dining room. "It will be smaller than what we're used to, of course," he said, almost as an afterthought. "But Alphonse says that the house itself is well-made and snug. The land has a stream and there is a barn for the horses and for livestock."

"But if there is no money, how will we pay for a new place to live?" Celeste asked.

My father cleared his throat, as if the words were stuck there and he had to force them out.

"Alphonse has sold his own house," Papa replied. "He will see us safely settled in the country, then return to the city and live in the rooms above the office."

"Oh, but—," Celeste began, then stopped abruptly. The question she'd kept herself from asking still hung in the air: If Grand-père Alphonse could stay in town, why couldn't we all stay?

"We cannot afford it," my mother spoke up. "One person can live in the city much less expensively than five."

I saw her look down the length of the table to meet my father's eyes. "Making a clean break is the best thing, for all of us," she continued. "And as your father says, all may yet be well."

But in the present, things were far from well. We spent the rest of that month packing those belongings we felt we could not live without. On the first day of February, we set out for our new home.

Nine

HAVE YOU EVER HAD SOMETHING SO MOMENTOUS AND unexpected happen that it makes you reconsider all the things you used to agonize over?

That's what moving to the country did for me. Whether or not my name was the true match for my face just didn't seem so important anymore.

This is hardly to say I set off for the country with a brave heart, however. How could I? I was leaving behind everything I'd loved, everything familiar.

But no matter what you do to postpone it, the future always shows up at your door. The fact that our door was changing wouldn't make one bit of difference.

We got up early on the morning of our departure. It would be a day and a half of travel overall, according to my father. And we knew the first day's travel would be the longest, for we must be clear of the Wood by nightfall.

I should probably explain about the Wood, shouldn't I?

In fact, considering the importance it came to have for all of us, most especially for me, perhaps I should have mentioned it long before now. But that would have been cheating, putting the middle and end of my story before its start. Introducing you to it now means we enter the Wood together.

The town of my birth looks out toward the sea, curving as if in one slow smile along the coastline. But at its back, snuggled up against it like a cat seeking warmth in winter, lies a great green swath. For as long as anyone can remember, people have simply called it "the Wood." You can traverse it in a day if you go straight through, but it takes three whole days to ride around it.

In spite of this difference, most travelers take the long way around. You can probably guess why. There are tales about what happens beneath the boughs of the Wood—as many as there are trees in the Wood itself. Growing up, my sisters and I heard many of them. Tales of the Wood were our second-favorite bedtime stories, just after the ones we had once made up ourselves about Monsieur LeGrand.

There was the tale of a stand of trees with bark as pale as pearls and leaves of such a color that, when they fell from the branches in autumn, it was like watching a shower of the finest gold. The nursemaid who told us this claimed if you found these trees and stood beneath them as the wind blew, you would come away with your pockets filled with golden coins.

We heard of places in the Wood where the snow fell all year long, sweet as sugar on the tongue, and places where winter never came at all. Places filled with the voices of birds too numerous to count and places where it was so quiet that you could hear the sap run and the trees themselves grow taller.

And finally there were the tales of the Wood's dark places, tales that kept us up at night, tales that could only be told in a whisper, for to speak them any louder might invite the dark into the room with you. It goes without saying that my sisters and I loved these tales the best.

And the one we loved the very most, which kept us from falling asleep the longest, was the tale of a monster dwelling in the most secret heart of the Wood.

It was no ordinary monster, of course. This monster could command the elements. Bend time so as to never grow old. Shape light and dark, becoming visible or invisible at will. The only thing the monster could not do was no doubt the thing it wanted most: It could not leave the Wood.

This last part was all that kept Celeste, April, and me from complete and utter terror. As it was, the first time we heard the tale of the monster in the Wood, we lay awake for three nights running. On the fourth day, Maman dismissed the nursemaid who'd seen fit to tell us the story in the first place. It was Papa who tucked us into bed that night, and as he did so, he soothed away our fears.

It's not so much that what they say is truthful, Papa assured us in his quiet, steady voice, but that certain kinds of stories have the ability to teach us truths about ourselves. There was no real monster living in the heart of the Wood. Rather, the story was a way to think about the monster that might dwell in our own hearts. *That* was the monster we should fear the most, or so my father said.

Papa's explanation made it easier to fall asleep at night, but I wasn't altogether sure I accepted it.

Any child can tell you that monsters are as real as you and I are. So why shouldn't the tales be true? Why shouldn't there be a monster dwelling in the Wood's most secret heart? Such a hidden place seemed as fine as any for a being bound by rules of enchantment, but not those that fettered the rest of us, to call his home.

And now you know as much about the Wood as I did when I first set foot beneath its boughs.

On the first day of our journey, we set off long before the sun was up. It felt a strange, unnatural time to be leaving, as if we were beginning our new life before the old one was truly over. But it had been both of my parents' choice. Neither of them wished to attract a crowd, I think, even of well-wishers, and certainly not those who pitied us or would gloat over our misfortune. It was better to slip away quietly, though not so quickly as to seem like we were running away.

Winding our way through the city streets, the jangle of harnesses and the steady clop of our horses' hooves on the cobblestone were the only sounds. After a time, we reached the stone wall that wraps around the town like outstretched arms. There are gates set into the wall at regular intervals so that no one from the outside can sneak up on the city.

Neither my sisters nor I had ever left the protection of the city walls. We did so now, in single file. Just as my horse stepped through the gate, the sun came up. I pulled back on the reins in surprise.

For instead of the blue of the ocean to which I was accustomed, I found myself looking out into a waving sea of green, flecked with rose and gold. And so it was that I saw the Wood for the very first time, while it looked to hold the greatest promise: at dawn.

Unexpectedly, I felt my heart lift. *Perhaps Papa is right,* I thought. *Perhaps all may yet be well after all.*

Then I put my heels to my horse and followed my family toward whatever lay in store.

"Where is the heart of the Wood, Grand-père Alphonse?" I asked several hours later. "Do you know?"

Out of the corner of my eye, I thought I saw him smile.

The two of us were now riding at the head of the party,

instead of bringing up the rear in single file as we had been before. Beyond the city gate, the narrow streets of the city opened out into a great causeway that ran the length of the wall, making it easier for the large wagons of trade caravans to navigate. Something about all that space just plain went to my head, as far as I can tell.

Having spurred my horse on once, I had done so again, moving forward to the front of the line. Hardly my usual position, but why shouldn't I go first? We were beginning a new life. Surely, the old order of things need not apply.

It was exciting to feel the wind in my face and to know my eyes were the first to gaze upon whatever was to come. After a few moments, Grand-père Alphonse joined me, for even once we entered the Wood, the path stayed broad enough for two to travel side by side. Besides that, it made good sense for Grand-père Alphonse to take the lead. He was the only one who actually knew where we were going.

Not that any of us could have gotten lost. The path ran as straight as that of an arrow. The trees grew so close along the roadway that I could have reached out and brushed them with my fingertips. I inhaled deeply, tasting the sharp scent of pine at the back of my throat.

"You are thinking of the story," Grand-père Alphonse said.

"I suppose I am," I answered with a smile. "Perhaps I'm simply being childish. We've heard dozens of stories over the years, but I never thought I'd actually set foot inside the Wood itself. That makes the tales feel . . . different, somehow."

"I know just what you mean," Grand-père Alphonse said with a nod. "I felt the same way myself, the first time I came here, as if all the tales were going to come to life around me."

"Well, if they're going to do that," Celeste piped up behind us, "why not look for the grove that rains down golden coins? If we gathered some of those, we could go back home where we belong."

"I didn't say I wanted to find the heart of the Wood," I said into the charged silence that followed my sister's words. There was no home to go back to, even if we could. After all that had happened, who was to say where we belonged?

"I only asked Grand-père Alphonse if he knew where it was."

"I do not," Grand-père Alphonse said simply. He twisted in his saddle to look back at Celeste. "And I think that we are safe enough, Celeste. No road leads to the heart of the Wood, as far as I know. It is a place that gives up its secrets only when it chooses. That's what I've heard said, anyhow."

"Well, I, for one, hope it keeps them to itself," remarked my mother as Grand-père Alphonse faced forward again. "Things are bad enough without monsters popping out to frighten us."

As if the Wood understood her words, a sudden wind swept through the trees, followed by an absolute stillness, which even momentarily muffled the sounds of our horses' hooves.

"I think," my father said carefully, "that we have had quite enough talk of monsters."

We rode in silence for a while. I kept my eyes trained on the path, each one of my senses heightened.

"There is another tale of the Wood that I could tell you, if you like," Grand-père Alphonse offered, breaking the uncomfortable silence that had fallen upon us all. "One that I think will appeal to you especially, Belle."

Celeste gave an unladylike snort. "In that case, it must be about a piece of wood."

I swiveled in my saddle to stick out my tongue.

"As a matter of fact, you're right," Grand-père Alphonse answered with a chuckle. "But there's something in it for you, too, Celeste, for it's also a tale of love."

"That would make it a tale for April, then," Celeste contradicted.

"That will do, Celeste," my mother interjected. "What is this tale that you would tell us, Alphonse?"

"It is the story of the Heartwood Tree. Do you not know it?"

"I do not," replied Maman.

"Well, I will tell it to you," Grand-père Alphonse said. And this is the tale that he told us as we rode.

Ten

"ONCE UPON A TIME THERE LIVED A YOUNG HUSBAND AND wife. Though they had been married less than a year's time, it seemed they had known each other forever, for they had been childhood sweethearts and loved each other almost all of their lives.

"The couple often took walks beside a glistening lake, and when they paused to look at their reflections in the water, even as their eyes beheld two individual people, they felt they were seeing just one being, so closely were their two hearts joined."

"So this *is* a tale of true love, then," April spoke for the first time.

"It is," Grand-père Alphonse agreed, his eyes fixed on the

road ahead. "And so I would like to tell you this couple lived happily ever after. That they lived long and prosperous lives together. But they did not.

"Not long after their wedding, the wife became sick with an illness that had no cure. She grew very frail and died in her husband's arms. His grief was so intense that it caused others pain to behold it, for there is something truly terrible about a love that is snatched away too soon."

Grand-père Alphonse paused to take a breath, and in the silence I could almost hear Dominic Boudreaux's name whispered through the treetops. Had he met a watery grave? I yanked myself back to the present at the sound of Grand-père Alphonse's voice.

"The young widower chose his wife's gravesite with great care," Grand-père Alphonse continued. "He buried her beside the lake where they had so loved to walk. And over her heart, he planted her favorite tree: a pink-blossomed dogwood.

"When this was done, the young man sat down upon the grave that now contained all he held dear, and wept for eight full days and seven full nights until his heart was empty and his eyes were dry.

"And then the young man put his head down on the earth, just as he had once set it on the pillow beside his wife's, and went to sleep, no longer caring if he awoke the next morning."

"What a strange, sad story this is, Alphonse," commented my mother.

"It is," Grand-père Alphonse said with a nod. "But it is also full of wonder. For on the eighth night, as the young man slept, a strange event transpired. The dogwood tree took root, then grew into something else entirely.

"For it was a tree unlike any other: nurtured by the bones of true love below it, and watered by the tears of heartfelt grief above it. And so, when the new day dawned, and the widower opened his eyes, he found himself lying beneath the boughs of a ten-foot tree.

"As he gazed upon it, the tree burst into bloom, and its branches bore flowers such as no one had ever seen before. Some carried blooms of a white more pure than winter's first snowfall, while others bore those as red as freshly spilled blood.

"Though startled, the young man understood at once: The white blossoms were the symbol of his grief, sprung from the bones of his beloved. And the red were the symbol of his love, borne from his own heart.

"No sooner did he comprehend this than a wind came up, streaming through the branches over his head, raining petals down upon him. As they mingled together, the petals formed a third color: a pink precisely the same shade as the first blush of dawn.

"The widower rose to his feet, gathered as many of the soft, delicate petals as he could, and set off for home. There, he placed them in a clear glass jar and set the jar on the windowsill beside his bed, so the petals would be the first thing he would see when he awoke each morning.

"One new day dawned, and then another, and so, first days, then weeks, then months, and, finally, years went by. But no matter how much time passed, the petals always remained true and never faded.

"And in this way, the husband was comforted. For it seemed to him that, though he could no longer hear her laughter, no longer reach out and take her by the hand as he had once so loved to do, his wife had not completely left him. Her love still kept pace with his. It still walked the earth beside him though she could not.

"Her love was in the sound of the wind as it danced through the treetops, the sound the brook made, running swift and high. It was in the busy talk of chickadees on a cold morning and the call of a single raven just at nightfall. But most of all, it was in the petals in the jar on the windowsill—petals that retained the same color as the day he had first gathered them.

"And so he called the tree that had started as one thing but blossomed into another, the Heartwood Tree. And he decreed that no one must cut its boughs. For, like love, the gifts the Heartwood has to offer cannot be forced. They must be given freely, or not at all. For anything less is no true gift.

"The man never married again, but spent his days living quietly by the lakeside. When he died peacefully in his sleep, he was buried beneath the Heartwood Tree, alongside his wife. Never once, in all those years, did the tree shed more than its petals. All heeded the young widower's words, none daring to cut the Heartwood's limbs.

"For it is whispered that when the Heartwood Tree gives itself at last, letting loose a branch of its own accord, it will be to one with the heart to see what lies within the wood. To see what the husband and wife grew together out of their joy and sorrow combined: the face of true love."

We rode for some distance, none of us speaking. But the Wood around us was far from silent. It seemed to whisper secrets to itself.

"I told you it was going to be a story about wood," Celeste said at last, breaking the long silence.

"Oh, Celeste," April protested, but I could hear the laughter in her voice.

I laughed too, though my heart was beating as if I'd run all the way from town. I knew why Grand-père Alphonse had told the story. What better hands for a piece of the Heartwood Tree to fall into than my own?

If only such a tale were true, I thought. *If I could hold a piece of Heartwood in my hand, then I might see the face inside it. The face of the one person who would see me as I am, Beautiful or not, and cherish me for it.*

My true love.

"Oh, Celeste's just afraid the tree wouldn't share its secrets with her," I teased. "Or if it did, it would be by a branch falling on her head."

"Well, maybe that's how it works," April said. "The branch conks you on the head, and then you see visions."

"You two are absolutely impossible," Celeste cried. She kicked her heels against her horse's flanks, urging him forward, through the narrow gap between Grand-père Alphonse and me.

"Oh, no you don't!" I called. "I like being first, and I intend to stay there."

"You'll have to catch me, too, then!" April suddenly exclaimed as she followed Celeste's example.

I thumped my heels against my horse's sides again. And so, inspired by a story of loss and redemption, my sisters and I raced toward whatever the future might bring.

We left the Wood just at nightfall.

Eleven

THE SECOND PART OF OUR JOURNEY WAS SWIFT, FOR THE road continued fine and even and soon brought us into the countryside. The landscape was one of tiny valleys nestled between gently rolling hills. The hills would be a soft golden color in the summer, Grand-père Alphonse told us. At the moment they were covered with light green fuzz, which would turn into a green so bright it would bring tears to our eyes. Or so Grand-père Alphonse promised, anyway.

Half a day's travel along the winding country road brought us, at last, to our new home.

Papa had said there was a stream on our new land, and we heard it long before we ever saw it. At first, it was no more than a teasing whisper of water, always just out of sight, as if it were playing hide-and-seek with us. But soon we caught glimpses of it snaking through the hills. Gradually, it grew closer, and the whisper became a murmur and, finally, a pure, clear song of liquid flowing over stones.

The stream greeted us as we rounded the bend and the view opened up. The house that was to be our new home was some distance from the main road, though plainly visible from it, nestled against the base of a small hill. The stream flowed toward the house, then made a quick, darting curve behind it, as if hurrying to get wherever it was going. The barn sat to one side of the house.

The house itself was faced in weathered gray shingles and had a roof of sod. I had never seen such a thing before. The front windows sparkled in the midday sunlight and between them, in an unexpected burst of color, was a bright blue door.

For several moments, no one spoke.

"It doesn't have a dirt floor, does it?" Celeste inquired.

"Oh, for heaven's sake, Celeste," my mother exclaimed.

"It's not that far-fetched," my sister protested. "There's grass on the roof."

"That is an old trick," said Grand-père Alphonse. "It helps keep the house warm in the winter and cool in the summer. There's hay in the walls for the same reason."

"It looks a snug and cheerful place," my father said.

"I hope that you will find it so," Grand-père Alphonse

replied. "But to answer your question, Celeste, the floors are made of wood."

"Thank goodness for that," my sister said. "At least there will be something that I recognize."

"Oh, hush, Celeste," I said, as I swung down from my horse. "You're not being clever, just unhelpful."

Grand-père Alphonse dismounted, then turned and held one hand up to my oldest sister.

"She is nervous," he said calmly. "Which is perfectly reasonable. Come inside, all of you, and see your new home."

Grand-père Alphonse stayed several weeks, helping us unpack and arrange our belongings—the few treasures we could not bear to leave behind—and grow accustomed to our new surroundings.

Maman still had her favorite chair, the one in which she sat to work her fancy embroidery. This was placed in the room to the left of the short set of central stairs, for Maman had decreed that this would be the living room. Though, when you got right down to it, the room on the right would have done just as well, for the two rooms were precisely the same size. We had discovered almost at once that our new home had been built along strict symmetrical lines.

Maman's chair went nearest the fireplace, with the great, round freestanding hoop for holding her linen to the right of the chair, and the basket that held her needles and skeins of silk on the left. Papa had made them both as a gift for their first anniversary, many years ago.

April brought with her an elaborately carved chest of sandalwood that had been a gift from Dominic following his first voyage as captain of the *April Dawn*. I had no idea if it was empty, or if she had placed other treasures inside. Celeste had her dressing table with its stool of padded silk, and the ivory-backed brushes with which she gave her hair its one hundred and one strokes both morning and night.

As for me, I had a chest, as well, fashioned of hemlock wood. I had made it myself. After it was finished, I had rubbed it gently with linseed oil to make it shine. Hemlock is a soft wood, so the chest had to be treated carefully, but I loved its golden color.

Inside the chest, I had carefully placed the canvas bundle that contained my carving tools, some treasured pieces of uncarved wood, and as many of my father's woodworking tools as the chest would hold. Grand-père Alphonse and I had schemed together on this, for Papa had decided that, now that he would be without his workshop, he would leave behind all but his most basic carpentry tools.

But I knew how important it was to Papa to work with his hands. I simply could not imagine him without a project of some kind. And I was afraid that, without a task to occupy his hands and mind, my father would worry himself into an illness, for I had only to look at him to see how the last few months had taken their toll.

At the back of the first floor, behind the central stair, were two more rooms, a kitchen and a pantry. The upstairs was divided into two long, narrow rooms that ran from the front of the house to the back, as opposed to the downstairs rooms, which were side to side.

One of these would serve as a bedroom for my parents, the other, for my sisters and me. Maman had actually given us permission to place our beds in whatever position we liked, though we had selected our places in order of birth. Old habits are hard to shake.

Celeste placed her bed in the center of the long wall that divided the two rooms, with her dressing table alongside. April tucked hers under the eaves. That left me to place mine precisely where I would have chosen, had I been allowed to go first: beneath the center window along the outside wall. During the day, I could look out and see the hills rolling away toward the Wood. At night, I could look out and see the stars.

Those first weeks, we kept busy, putting all thoughts of the city resolutely from our minds as we moved furniture and supplies, arranging and rearranging them as we learned how to make this strange new house our own.

It was Papa and Grand-père Alphonse, both of whom had grown up without servants, who showed the rest of us how to build a fire in the wood stove in the kitchen, how to bank it at night so that it would not go out, and then how to stoke it up once more the following morning.

I learned to tell—by how fast water dried on my hand—whether the oven was a fast oven, hot enough to bake a pie, or had cooled down enough to be called medium, just right for bread or rolls. Last was the slow oven to be used for things like custard, which would curdle if it got too hot too fast, but which could stay in a cooler oven for a long time.

Celeste caught on to this the quickest and soon assumed most of the cooking duties, much to all of our surprise, including, I think, her own. She had always been clever. This much, we knew, for all too often we had felt her cleverness through her sharp tongue.

But I don't think it had once occurred to any of us that part of Celeste's sharpness might have been because she was bored by what our old life had to offer. To me it had seemed as if my oldest sister had always had the life she wanted, though all it asked of her was that she be Beautiful. And this she could do as easily as breathing; it took no thought or effort at all. Now it was as if working in the kitchen gave Celeste a purpose, a reason to be clever, where she'd had none before.

While Celeste took on the cooking, April and I struggled to master the rest of the tasks needed to keep a household running, for we were determined to spare Maman as much of the heavy work as possible. She protested at this until Papa remarked how much lovelier the downstairs rooms would look with new curtains at the windows, and, personally, he'd always been very fond of embroidered ones.

That was all it took to get Maman to settle right to work making some. This left April and me free to take on the remainder of the chores, all of which seemed to involve mopping, dusting, or scrubbing. By the end of the very first week, I had a whole new appreciation for Marie Louise, the housekeeper we'd had to leave behind in the city, as well as all the maids we'd employed.

Now it was April's turn to surprise us, for no task seemed too difficult or dirty for her. The more challenging the task, the more she seemed to like it, in fact. It was almost as if she wanted to wear herself out, so that she wouldn't have the energy to worry about Dominic—though this was pure supposition on my part, as she still refused to speak of him at all.

With Celeste mastering the kitchen and April the cleaning, I worked outdoors with Papa and Grand-père Alphonse. Together, we laid out a plot for a kitchen garden. It was still too early, the ground too cold, to plant the seeds that we had brought. But at least I could get a head start on deciding where they'd go.

After Papa, Grand-père Alphonse, and I had laid out the garden, we went to work refurbishing the barn. It was as well-made as the house, so this was mostly a matter of getting the horses settled into their new homes.

But at the very back, in a space that had once been a tack room, I did my best to create a new workshop for Papa. This was a tricky task, as I had to do it on the sly. The rest of the family was in on the secret, of course. Everyone helped to keep Papa distracted and out of the way. Grand-père Alphonse turned out to be the greatest help.

You could live in the city without knowing who your neighbors were, he said. But in the country, it was a good idea to at least know *where* they were, in case you needed to ride for help. So, while Celeste mastered the kitchen, Maman the curtains, and April the rest of the house in general, Grand-père Alphonse took Papa farther into the countryside.

It felt strange and lonely to be in a new place without him, but it *did* give me time to complete my surprise, and the new workshop was ready the day they returned. Grand-père Alphonse would begin the trip back to the city the following morning.

"Papa," I said, as I came into the kitchen. It was early evening, not quite time for dinner, and Papa was sitting at one end of the table drinking a mug of tea. At the other end of the table, Celeste was busy peeling potatoes.

"I'm sorry to bother you," I went on. "But there's something I need your help with in the barn."

Celeste met my eyes swiftly, a look of question in them. I nodded my head ever so slightly. Celeste turned her attention back to the potatoes.

"You can see that Papa is having his tea, Belle," she remarked. "Couldn't your problem at least wait until he's done?"

She sounded so precisely like her old cross self that I bit the inside of my cheek to keep from smiling.

"I didn't say there was a problem," I replied. "I only said I needed him to come and look at something."

Papa pushed back from the table. "I can do that easily enough," he said. "The tea will still be here when I get back."

Celeste dropped a potato into a pot of cold water with a *plop* and said nothing more.

"I *am* sorry to make you get up," I said to my father, as we walked toward the barn, side by side. "I know you must be tired."

"I am, a little," my father replied. He gave the seat of his pants a rub, a rueful expression on his face. "I'm afraid I'm not cut out to be much of a rider. I'm happy to stretch my legs a bit, to tell you the truth.

"Now," my father continued briskly, as he pushed open the barn's great sliding door. "What is so important that you must interrupt my tea for help?"

"It's back here," I said, as I led the way. "I've wanted to ask about this ever since you left. I'm just not sure I've set up this room quite right."

I reached the room I'd worked so hard to keep secret, lifted the latch, and pushed open the door, gesturing for Papa to go in first. I'd left a lantern burning, placing it carefully so that it was safe, and so that it would illuminate as much of the room as possible.

"What do you think?" I asked. "Did I do a good job?"

My father took several steps forward, then stopped abruptly.

He pivoted in a complete circle on one heel, without making a single sound. But I saw the way his eyes moved around the room, taking in all the details. It was as close to his workshop in town as I could make it.

"You did this?" he said finally.

I nodded. "With Grand-père Alphonse's help. With everyone's help, actually, for they all kept you busy."

My father let out a long, slow breath. Until that moment, I hadn't realized I'd been holding mine.

"Thank you, Belle," he said. "I have tried not to be selfish, but I admit it gave me a pang to leave my workshop behind."

"You are the least selfish person I know," I said. "A selfish man would not have given up his fine city house to care for the wives and children of sailors."

"Ah, but you forget," my father answered quietly. "I am a sailor's child. Without Alphonse, I'd have had no fine things to give away." He moved to me, and put an arm around my shoulders. "Like him, you have given me something that costs you very little, but counts for much."

I leaned against him, putting my head on his shoulder. "And what is that?" I asked.

"Kindness," said my father. He dropped a kiss on the top of my head. "Now, let's go back inside. I think Celeste is making something special for Alphonse's last night with us."

With his arm still around my shoulders, my father and I walked back to the house.

Twelve

GRAND-PÈRE ALPHONSE DEPARTED THE NEXT DAY, RIDING out shortly after noon, beneath a cloudy sky. He promised to let us know the moment there was reliable word on any of Papa's ships. Our tiny new house felt large and empty after he was gone. And, though we had been working hard at many different things, Grand-père Alphonse's return to the city marked the true beginning of our new lives.

Our days soon fell into a rhythm, each day with its own chore. On Monday, Celeste rose early to bake pies and bread. Tuesday, she sat and sewed with Maman while April and I heated endless kettles of water to do the washing. I quickly grew to dislike washing day. It was exhausting work and my arms and back ached by the time we were done.

Wednesday, Celeste baked again, while April did the ironing and I worked outdoors.

In addition to the patch for vegetables, Papa and I were digging flower beds, particularly outside the window of the room where Maman sat and sewed. The gardens in our yard in the city had been her pride and joy. She'd brought blossoms indoors every day when the weather was fine.

While I'd been busy preparing a surprise for Papa, April had been saving one for Maman: The trunk April had brought with her was filled with rose cuttings, one from every bush Maman had had to leave behind. At the rate things were warming up, I'd be able to plant them soon. For, though our days were often damp and chilly, we were well on our way to spring.

And we'd discovered the reason the hills around us turned a green so intense it brought tears to the eyes. It was because, during early springtime, the weather drizzled almost nonstop.

"I think I'm beginning to grow mold," I remarked late one afternoon as I came into the kitchen. For once, it wasn't raining, but was still wet and muddy outdoors. "Maybe that's why the hills get so green. They're moldy too."

Celeste opened the oven door and peered inside. It was the first day of April, our own April's birthday. Celeste was baking a cake, her first, as a surprise.

"You take those muddy shoes off before you set one foot in this kitchen, Belle Delaurier," she said without turning around.

"Thank you for the reminder," I said tartly. Celeste may have gotten easier to live with, but she was still bossy. I sat down on the chair that was kept just inside the door for precisely the purpose of removing muddy shoes, though I made no move to take mine off.

"This may come as a surprise to you, old and wise as you have become, but I do know better than to track mud all over the floor."

"Who's old and wise?" April asked as she came into the room. She had a big apron tied over her dress. It was her afternoon to do the dusting, a task she'd refused to relinquish, birthday or not.

"Celeste," I replied.

April's eyebrows shot up. "When did all this happen?" she inquired.

"I'd be careful, if I were you," Celeste remarked. She set the pan with the cake at the back of the stove with a *clank*. Apparently, it was done. "Remember who cooks the meals around here."

"But never does the washing up," I replied. That task usually fell to me these days. My one consolation was that it helped keep my hands clean. No matter how careful I was to wear gloves, I always seemed to end up with dirt under my nails from working in the garden.

"Well, of course not," Celeste said, in a tone that told me this should have been obvious.

April shot me a quick wink.

"Of course not," she echoed.

Without warning, Celeste whirled around, the towel she'd used to protect her fingers from the hot cake pan still in her hands. She wadded it up into a ball and tossed it straight at April. April dodged aside. The towel hit the wall behind her, then slid to the floor.

"Thank you very much," April said. "That's one more thing for me to wash."

"It's not my fault," Celeste said quickly. "I was minding my own business until a few minutes ago." She actually went so far as to point a finger at me. "Blame Belle."

I made a strangled sound of amusement and outrage, both. "What do you mean 'blame Belle'? I didn't do a thing."

"You don't have to *do* anything," Celeste explained, as if I were an idiot. "You're the youngest. You get blamed by default."

"You want something to blame me for?" I inquired.

I stood up. Then I lifted one foot, still in its muddy shoe, and held it beyond the edge of the kitchen mat.

Celeste's eyes narrowed. "You wouldn't *dare*," she said.

"Get mud on my clean kitchen floor and you're mopping it up yourself," April warned.

I brought my foot down, then lifted it straight back up, creating one perfect, muddy footprint.

"That's it," April said. "Now you've done it."

"What do you say we give her *your* birthday spanking right here and now?" Celeste proposed.

"You'll have to catch me first!" I cried out.

I whirled, yanked open the door to the yard, and dashed down the kitchen steps. The clatter of footsteps behind me told me my sisters weren't wasting any time in pursuit. I turned to face them, once again lifting my foot. I held it poised over a very large mud puddle.

"Think carefully before you come any closer," I threatened.

"Go ahead, April. She doesn't really mean it," Celeste said. But we all noticed she'd stopped right where she was.

"Oh, yes, I do," I taunted.

April skidded to a stop beside Celeste. "She says she does."

"Guess there's only one way to find out, isn't there?" Celeste said.

"Guess so."

"No. Wait. Stop!" I cried. But by then it was too late. My sisters had called my bluff. Hands linked, Celeste and April dashed forward, leaped up, and landed full force in the mud puddle.

Water and mud flew in every direction, but mostly, of course, up and out. Within seconds, our skirts were filthy and soaked. I bent down and scooped up two brimming handfuls of mud.

"You're about to be very sorry you did that," I said.

"Look out!" Celeste cried.

I let the mud fly. After that, it was pretty much a free-for-all. I have no idea how long my sisters and I stood in the puddle, shrieking and flinging mud and dirty water at one another. I do know it began to rain at some point. As if this were some previously determined signal, my sisters and I stopped all at once and lifted our filthy faces to the sky.

"If we stand out here long enough, do you think we'll get clean?" April asked after a few moments. She was breathing heavily, as we all were.

I wiped a hand across the front of my dress, leaving behind a trail of mud. "I guess it's not been long enough yet," I remarked.

Celeste laughed first, and before we knew it the three of us were roaring with helpless laughter.

"Well, I guess we all needed that," April remarked. A moment of silence fell. We stood together, our arms around one another.

"I guess we did," Celeste acknowledged. She gazed down at her muddy skirts. "How come we never did things like this before?"

"You've got to be joking," I said. "Can you just see us doing this in town? We'd never have been invited anywhere again."

"You wouldn't have cared about that," Celeste answered. "You never went anywhere anyhow."

I heard April suck in a sudden breath. "No, wait," Celeste said quickly, before anyone else could speak. "I didn't mean it like that. Not sharp, the way it sounded."

"It would be all right even if you did," I answered somberly. "It's true enough." I looked down at my soaked and mud-spattered dress. "I'm not so invisible now, am I?"

"And we're not so very fine and fashionable," April said quietly. "We've only been here a couple of months. How can being in the country have changed us all so much in so little time?"

"Maybe it hasn't," Celeste said. "Maybe this is who we were all along, and we just couldn't see it before. But there aren't so many other eyes to look at us now, are there? Only our own."

"So now the question is," I said, "do we like what we see, or not?"

"What's that?" April interrupted, her head cocked as if she was straining to hear some new sound.

That was the moment I realized I'd been hearing it too, without quite registering what *it* was.

"That's a horse," I said. "Someone's coming."

There was a moment of electric silence. Then, hands still clasped, my sisters and I dashed around to the front of the house. We were just in time to see a single horse leave the main road and start down the one that led to our front door. Its rider swayed in the saddle, clinging to it with both hands, as if this and sheer willpower were the only things keeping him from falling off the horse and into the mud.

"That's not Grand-père Alphonse," Celeste said.

"No," I answered. "It's not. I think maybe it's—"

But by then, April was in motion. Picking up her skirts with both hands, she ran flat out, like a small boy. She reached the horse just as its exhausted rider finally reached our yard. The horse stopped.

"I'm sorry," I heard the horseman say. "I hate to repeat myself. But I'm afraid I'm going to pass out. Again."

Then he pitched sideways in the saddle and slid to the ground just as he had once before, many years ago. April sat down in the mud and cradled his head in her lap.

"Go get Papa," she said. "Go get help."

And then she began to weep the kind of tears no one minds shedding. Tears of joy.

Dominic Boudreaux was home.

Thirteen

"It was the worst possible combination of circumstances," Dominic told us later that night.

We were sitting in the living room, a cheery fire in the grate. All of us had changed out of our filthy, wet clothes. Though in Dominic's case, his only option was to borrow some of Papa's. At my mother's insistence, Dominic was now seated in her chair, the most comfortable in the room. April sat on a low stool beside him. In her hands, she held a mug of steaming broth, from which she urged him to drink from time to time.

Any doubt as to their feelings for each other had been dispelled by the time Dominic and my father staggered through the front door. April had left Dom only long enough for them both to get out of their wet and muddy garments. After that, she'd refused to leave his side.

"What happened?" she asked now.

"It's more a matter of what didn't," Dominic answered, with a tired smile.

First, the *April Dawn* had been blown off course. Then, she'd been becalmed. Seemingly endless days had passed without a stir of air. Food and fresh water had begun to run low. The men had started to fear they would never get home.

"If I'd been sailing for any man but you, Monsieur Delaurier," Dominic said quietly, "been captain of any ship but one of yours, sooner or later I'd have come to a day when I feared for my life. For hungry men become desperate ones in the time it takes to blink, and desperate men commit desperate acts, things they would never consider otherwise."

He paused. April reached up and pressed the mug into his hands. Dominic took a long, slow sip, as if savoring every drop. Papa was a smaller man than Dominic, but Dominic looked thin and frail in Papa's borrowed clothes.

"But the men love you, sir," Dominic went on. "I don't know how to say it any way but that. They know you're a man who honors his word, and sooner than dishonor you, I think they'd have starved. Not one word of mutiny did I hear, and, finally, the wind came back and we made sail for home."

Dominic paused to take another sip of broth, then handed the mug back to April.

"When we finally made port, when we got back and the men learned what you'd done—how you'd sold your own things to care for their families—it was everything I could do to keep them all from coming here with me. There's not one man who won't be willing to set sail again, to look for those lost ships, that is—just as soon as we make repairs to the *April Dawn*."

"Oh, but surely—," April began, then stopped. I could almost see her bite down on her tongue.

"Let's have no more talk of setting sail tonight," my father said into the quick silence that followed April's outburst. "There'll be time enough for that. The men are all well, you say?"

"As well as can be expected, given what they've been though," Dominic replied. "Some will heal faster than others."

"And I imagine good food will soon set most things to rights," my father said.

"True enough, sir," Dominic concurred. "That's true enough."

My father seemed to hesitate, almost as if he wanted to postpone the question we all knew must come next.

"And the cargo?" he finally inquired.

"Safe and sound, every last bit of it," Dominic answered, and I could hear the fierce pride in his voice. "I brought it all home to you, sir. Every last man, every single chest of cargo. It just took a little longer than planned."

All of a sudden, a smile lit Dominic's drawn and tired face.

"Not too bad for the lad who began life as a thief, wouldn't you say?"

"I would," my father replied. He reached out to grip Dom by the arm. "I would indeed say so, and more. You've given back more than you ever tried to take."

"I learned that from you, sir," said Dominic Boudreaux.

My father gave Dominic's arm a final squeeze and then released it, making no attempt to hide the tears that filled his eyes.

"Monsieur LeGrand asked me to tell you you should come without delay, sir, if it can be managed," Dominic went on. "He'd have come himself, but there is much to do."

"That there is," my father said with a smile. "But you have done enough for now. Stay here and rest, Dom. I'll go tomorrow morning. That will put me in the city within two days' time."

Papa left shortly after breakfast the following morning, earlier than he might have when the roads were dry, but the rain continued and, even for a single man on horseback, the going would be muddy and slow. Celeste packed food and water in Papa's saddlebags.

"I cannot promise," my father said, as we all stood together in the kitchen, "but if there is money left over after paying off debts, I may be able to bring you something from town. Tell me what you'd like, girls, and I'll do my best to manage it."

"I don't need anything, Papa," April said at once. "Unless there is something that would help Dominic."

As she spoke, the color rose in her cheeks, but she kept her eyes steady on my father's.

"I think food and rest will be enough for him," Papa answered. He reached out and brushed a thumb over one of April's blazing cheeks. "And, of course, your company. I'll expect the two of you to have settled things by the time I return."

He gave April's cheek a sudden pinch, then shifted his attention. "What about you, Celeste?"

"Could you bring some lavender plants, Papa?" my oldest sister asked. "Belle says the cuttings from the rose bushes are almost ready to plant. But if we could have lavender as well . . ."

"You're thinking of your mother," my father said. For though roses were her favorite flower, lavender had always been the fragrance she loved best.

Celeste nodded. "But what would you like for yourself?" my father asked.

Celeste cast her eyes around the kitchen, as if searching for inspiration. "Well, it would be nice to have one more cast-iron skillet," she said. "A really big one."

"A cast-iron skillet," my father echoed.

"I know it would be heavy," Celeste said quickly, as if she'd heard some objection in my father's voice, "but there's Dominic to feed as well now, for as long as he stays, and a bigger pan would be useful, Papa."

"You could always bring sugar, if a new pan is too difficult to carry," I suggested.

Celeste nodded. "Or that, yes. That's a good thought, Belle."

My father put his hands on his hips. "Now, let me see if I have this straight," he said. "My daughters, who not three months past were as fine a collection of fashionable young ladies as anyone could hope to meet, are asking for a pan it takes both arms to lift, and a tonic for a sweetheart? Not one piece of finery among you? Not one ribbon or bow?"

"Well, certainly no buckles," I said, and earned a laugh from everyone present.

"I have no use for fancy ribbons in the kitchen," Celeste said simply. "I'd always be worrying about the ends dragging in the batter or, even worse, catching fire as I work at the stove."

"And they're no good to me when I'm dusting or scrubbing a floor," April chimed in.

"I'll take theirs, Papa," I offered. "I can use it to mark straight rows in the vegetable garden."

"Well," my father said. "Well, then." He stood facing us as we made a little half circle before him. For the second time in as many days, my father had tears in his eyes.

For my sisters and I were sending a message, and my father had heard it, clear as a bell. We would not ask for what we'd valued in our old lives. It would take more than one shipload of cargo to buy those lives back, and I, for one, was far from certain that I wanted mine.

In my old life, I had become invisible. In my new one I was . . . I wasn't quite sure what. But I knew this much: I wanted to find out, for I liked who I was in this new life better than who I'd been before.

But most remarkable was the fact that my sisters and I had each spoken spontaneously. We weren't putting on a brave face we'd discussed ahead of time. We had each spoken truly, from our hearts. We did not want the past. We wanted the future, whatever it might hold.

I don't think I'd ever loved my sisters more than I did in that moment.

"If you're sure," my father said.

"We're sure, Papa," I replied. "Though if you chance to come upon the Heartwood Tree and one of the branches just happens to break off and fall on your head . . ."

My father tossed the saddlebags over one shoulder with a laugh. "I think it's time that I was going. I'll come back as soon as I can. Don't let your mother worry."

"We won't, Papa," April promised.

Together, our arms around one another, my sisters and I crowded into the kitchen doorway, watching until the rain hid my father from view.

And then we began to wait once more.

Fourteen

WE WAITED FOUR LONG WEEKS, UNTIL THE DAYS SLID FROM April into May. At last, the weather turned fine: Glorious spring days filled our hearts with hope for the future.

And so, at last, my father came home.

He arrived at noon, just as Celeste was preparing to set our midday meal on the table. We'd had a brief and unexpected burst of rain that morning, but it had quickly passed, leaving the day sparkling and warm.

Celeste was just taking a fresh-baked pie from the oven when she heard footsteps at the kitchen door. Her cry brought us hurrying in from all parts of the house. Within moments, Papa was seated at the kitchen table, a mug of the tea he so loved close at hand, while Maman, Dominic, and we girls ranged around him.

"It's all right, *mes enfants,*" he kept saying over and over. "*I'm all right.*"

But it was clear that he was not.

The man who had ridden out to the city four weeks ago had been in high spirits. He'd had a glimmer in his eyes. The man sitting now at the kitchen table was bowed down, as if by some hidden weight almost too great to bear. I'd never seen my father look like this, not even in the days before we'd moved to the country, when each morning brought word of some new loss.

My mother sat beside Papa, an arm around his waist as if to shore him up.

"Drink your tea, Roger," she urged in a soft, firm voice. "You got caught in that rain squall this morning, didn't you? The tea will warm you up."

My father took a sip, obediently, like a child.

"I'm sorry to be such trouble," he said.

"Papa," I said, shocked. "How can you talk so? We love you. How can anything we do for you trouble us?"

The mug of tea slipped from my father's fingers, then bounced off the tabletop and smashed on the floor. Hot liquid and broken crockery shot every which way. None of us moved or made a sound.

Our attention was riveted on my father's face, on the tortured expression in his eyes as they stared into mine.

"Belle," my father said hoarsely, and I felt the hairs on the back of my neck rise at his tone. "*Ma petite Belle.* I wonder if you will say that when you know what I have done."

"I stayed in the city too long. It's as plain as that," my father said some time later. At Maman's urging, we had deferred any explanation of Papa's strange and dire remark until we'd all eaten lunch. If we were about to face some new crisis, she declared, we would need our strength, and no one could be strong on an empty stomach.

Much to my surprise, the food helped—as did the simple act of sitting down and eating together, a family once more. Gradually, the lines in my father's face seemed to ease a little, and his shoulders straightened, though his eyes were still full of worry when he gazed at me from time to time. At last, the meal over, April brewed a fresh pot of tea while Celeste brought out the pie. Then, once more at Maman's urging, Papa began to tell his tale.

"Let me share the good news first," he said, "for there is much that is good to tell. The *April Dawn's* safe arrival was just the first, Dominic. By the time I reached the city, two more of our ships had arrived at port. This went a fair way toward settling our remaining debts, enough so that my credit is good in the city again and we can begin repairs. Although," my father went on with the ghost of a smile, "I have decided that we will no longer bank with Henri de la Montaigne."

"Good for you, Papa," Celeste said.

Papa drew a deep breath, then let it out. "I stayed in the city longer than I should have," he said again. "But there was so much to accomplish, so much I wanted to see and do. I wanted to visit as many of the men as I could. And then there were the ships to inspect, trying to decide what repairs must be made, when the ships could be ready to sail once more.

"Perhaps I have grown too cautious in my old age," my father went on. "Perhaps I was too anxious to make sure everything would turn out well, that no harm would come to my sailors, or dishonor to us, again."

"But surely no man can truly do that," said my mother.

"You're absolutely right, my dear," my father replied. "At any rate, I realized I'd been gone for nearly four weeks, and, even worse, I'd sent you no word of what was going on. By that time, even Alphonse was urging me to return. I'd been away from all of you quite long enough, he said, and he could manage what still remained to be done."

My father paused to take a sip of tea, as if to fortify himself before continuing.

"So first I stayed too long in the city, and then I left later in the day than I should have. I knew it at the time. But, once I had decided to leave, I felt so eager to be home that even another night away from you seemed too much. And the journey itself was so simple and straightforward. All I had to do was keep to the road. I had been through the Wood twice now. I did not think it held any danger for me.

"But I did not count on the storm."

"What storm, sir?" Dominic asked in the startled silence that followed my father's words. "With the exception of that bit of rain we had this morning, the weather has been fine here the whole time you've been gone."

"You set my mind at ease," my father answered, "strange as that may sound. For the storm I encountered on that night was like none I have ever experienced. It was almost as if it had a will, a mind of its own. As if it sought me out.

"I'd not been in the Wood more than half an hour when it struck. After that, I could not keep track of the time."

"But surely nothing dangerous could happen," Maman said. "As long as you did what you said and stayed on the road."

"That's precisely what I did," my father replied. "But on that day, in that storm, the road led to a place it had not before. I think, perhaps, that this destination was always there, waiting for the right set of circumstances and the right person to come along."

Silence filled the kitchen, but in it was the question that resonated in every mind.

"Where did the road take you, Papa?" I finally asked.

"To the heart of the Wood," my father replied.

Fifteen

"I THINK IT WAS THE WIND THAT DID IT," MY FATHER CONtinued. "The wind made it so hard to see where I was going. For it drove the rain straight into my face, forcing me to bow my head down. And the sound . . ."

He broke off and shook his head, as if to dispel the memory.

"Not filled with rage, as high winds so often are. But if true loneliness ever had a voice, it would cry out with the sound of that wind. Even as it pushed against me, it seemed to pull me forward.

"I have no idea how long I traveled," my father said. "I rode until I was soaked clear through to the skin, and my horse began to stumble. Finally, I got down and led him, fearful that

I'd take a fall and injure myself. But also so that I could feel the road beneath my feet and know that I still traveled on it."

"But you said you never left the road," Celeste countered.

"Nor did I," replied my father. "Remember how we marveled at how smooth and even the surface of the roadway was? The longer I went on, the more it seemed the road began to change beneath my feet, even as I walked along it. It became rough and uneven as if, instead of being well kept up, it had been abandoned, forgotten. It was all I could do to keep my balance.

"In the end, I didn't. My foot turned on a loose stone and I pitched forward, letting go of the horse's reins so that I wouldn't pull him down on top of me. I expected to land flat on my face. Instead, when I reached out to brace myself, my hands found cold, wet metal, and I held on tight.

"I had come to a pair of iron gates."

"You should have turned right around and gone back the other way," my mother announced.

"Maybe," said my father. "But the solution to my situation did not seem so simple at the time. I was wet and I was tired. And, though I don't like to admit it, I was as afraid as I've been in a good long while. Beyond the gates might lie rescue or shelter. Outside them, I knew that there was none.

"So I pushed on the gates. They did not budge. Three times I pushed with all my might, and on the third try, they opened."

"Three," I murmured. "Just like in one of Grand-père Alphonse's stories."

"Even so," my father said with a nod, "for as hard as they'd been to open, those gates swung back without a sound. I gathered the horse's reins and my courage, then walked forward. As we passed through the gates, the storm died down. For the first time in what seemed like hours, I did not have the sound of that terrible wind in my ears.

"I turned back. Through the open gates and beyond them, I could see that the storm still raged. But where I stood, all was still and calm. The path was solid again beneath my feet, and I could see that it was made of stones so smooth and white they looked like polished ivory.

"As I stood hesitating, suddenly unable to decide what I feared more—going forward or turning back—the gates swung closed behind me as silently as they'd opened.

"'That settles that,' I thought. Forward I went, and I did not look back again. I was half convinced the world was unraveling behind me."

"I think you were very brave, Papa," I said.

"Thank you, Belle," my father answered with a tired smile. But when he looked at me, I noticed the sadness still remained in his eyes. There was something he hadn't told yet, the part of the tale that gave him pain.

"Since going forward was my only real choice, I continued to do that," my father went on. "It seemed to me I must have been on the grounds of some great estate. On one side of the road was an orchard of fruit trees, on the other, a garden filled with roses. I could not see their colors in the fading light, but their scent was all around me.

"I'm not sure how long I walked, for I had reached that strange stage of weariness where time seems to fold back upon itself.

"At long last, I came to a short rise, and saw before me a great house made of stone. It seemed to fling itself across the hilltop, as if longing to break free of the constraints of its own construction. To its left sat a row of buildings I thought must be stables. I approached, and found that this was so.

"I stabled my horse, caring for him well and tenderly, for he had been brave that day. Though there were no other horses in the stables, there was food for him in abundance. This reminded me that I was hungry as well. I then approached the house with some trepidation, for I had no idea what I would find inside."

"Oh, but surely you had to know," Celeste interrupted. "The heart of the Wood. That's what you said. So you must have seen the very house of the monster."

"Celeste!" April cried.

"What?" Celeste snapped back, and suddenly the tension in the room ratcheted up sharply. "We're all thinking it. We have been ever since Papa told us that he thought he traveled to the heart of the Wood. Don't get mad at me just because I had the guts to say it out loud."

"Since when do monsters live in houses?" I asked, trying to defuse the situation.

"It's a *monster*," Celeste replied. "Surely that means it can live wherever it wants. Who's going to tell it no? You?"

"Girls," my mother said. "That's enough."

"What *was* inside the house, Papa?" April asked.

"No one," my father replied. "That is to say, no living soul that I encountered. But the front doors parted at my touch as easily as the gates had, and closed behind me just as silently once I had crossed the threshold. Inside, I found myself in a great entry hall. The floor was a mosaic of images beneath my feet, but I did not take time to study the story they might tell.

"I called out, for I did not wish to give offense. There was no reply. Then, as if by way of answer, a door at the hall's far end swung open, and through it, I could see a glow. I called again, and still there was no answer. So, hearing no sound but my own loud breathing and footsteps, I walked the length of the hall until I stood in the open door.

"Before me was what I took to be a small study, for bookcases lined the walls. Directly across from me burned a cheerful fire. This was the glow I had seen from the hall. In front of the fire was a low table set with meat, bread, cheese, and a flagon of wine. A chair was alongside the table, positioned so that its occupant might eat and be warm at the same time.

"I stood in that doorway for I can't tell you how long, till I'd dripped a great puddle of water on the floor and heard my stomach growl. At that, I finally went in, took a seat in the chair, and ate as hearty and delicious a meal as I'd had in my life. Afterward, I slowly drank a glass of wine, the best I'd ever tasted. Before I knew it, the food and wine, combined with my weariness, got the better of me, and I fell asleep before the fire."

"I'd never have been able to do that," April said. "I'd have felt too afraid."

"Did you not feel afraid, sir?" Dominic inquired.

My father was quiet for a few moments. "No, I did not," he answered finally. "It's difficult to explain, but it's almost as if the house felt welcoming. As if it was made peaceful, even joyful, by my presence, and wished to do me good rather than harm."

Papa gazed at us as we sat around the table, holding each of our eyes in turn. "You all know that I am not a fanciful man," my father said. "I have never really believed the old tales of the Wood. To me, they seemed best suited to what they have become: bedtime stories. But I swear to you that I felt something in that house, as if the very stones of which it was made were, themselves, alive. And I felt it welcome me as surely as I felt you welcome me here today.

"But, beneath the welcome, there was something else."

"What was it, Papa?" I asked.

"Loneliness," my father answered. "The silence of that house spoke with the same voice that the windstorm had, with one fierce and endless cry against being alone.

"So, no," my father said once more, turning his gaze again

to Dominic. "I did not feel afraid. If anything, I felt my own good fortune.

"I had been rescued. I was being offered shelter. But in the morning, I would ride away. I could return to my home and those I loved. But the spirit that haunted that place would have no such reprieve. It had to stay behind. I'm not certain how I knew this, but I did. I seemed to feel it in my bones.

"I slept through the night," my father continued. "And awoke refreshed the next morning. My clothes were dry. They bore no trace of having come through a storm, no trace of having been slept in. Nor, for that matter, did I. I wasn't stiff or sore from sleeping in a chair all night. The table beside me had been reset for breakfast. There was fruit and cheese, and a steaming pot of coffee. I breakfasted as well and heartily as I had dined the night before.

"I had half a mind to explore the house, then changed my mind. For the loneliness seemed heavier this morning, as if anticipating my departure, and at that I felt a sharp and sudden longing to be safe in my own home.

"I went to the stable and saddled my horse, who had breakfasted just as well as I. I still had no idea who had provided the food and fresh water, for I neither saw nor heard a single soul.

"'Thank you,' I said to the air in general. I felt slightly foolish, but to go without expressing some thanks did not seem right. 'I don't know who you are, but you have shown me great kindness. I will always honor you for it.' I gathered up the horse's reins and prepared to go.

"As I led the horse from the stable, I caught sight of a smaller path, one I had not noticed in the gloaming the night before. And down the path, I saw a small but beautiful lake with a white pergola near the shore.

"Not far from the pergola, there was a tree in bloom, the loveliest I'd ever seen, or so it seemed, but I could not tell what kind of tree it was. And here, at last, I finally gave in to my curiosity.

" 'What harm can come from going to look at a tree?' I thought. So I left my horse where he stood and went down the hill on foot.

"You will remember I said the house sat at the top of a rise."

"We remember, Papa," I said, nodding.

"The distance was greater than I had thought. Or perhaps it was simply that the closer I came to the tree, the more slowly I walked.

"For as I approached, I began to understand why the tree had caught my eye. The boughs bore blooms of two different colors. Some were a white so pure it was like looking at sunlight on new-fallen snow. Others bore blossoms of a red more rich than any rose. A faint scent filled the air, sweet and promising, like hope.

"Then, as I watched, a faint breeze moved through the branches and a handful of petals released their hold. They

CAMERON DOKEY

tumbled toward the earth, mingling together, and finally came to rest upon the ground below. And there they formed a third color, the soft pink of a new dawn."

I felt a wave of emotion roll through me, so many different things at once I couldn't even begin to identify them all.

"The Heartwood Tree," I said, barely recognizing the sound of my own voice.

"The Heartwood Tree," my father echoed. "As if in a dream, I walked forward until I stood beneath its boughs. I looked up and beheld a fluttering mass of red and white and every variation in between that you can think of. For the petals were in constant motion, like a flock of birds in flight. Where the petals overlapped, new colors formed.

"I have never seen anything so beautiful in my entire life," my father said. "Nor anything so alive. I did not feel the loneliness that had been my constant companion in the house quite so keenly while I was beneath the Heartwood's boughs. Instead I let the sweetness of the air fill up my lungs."

"Papa, please tell me that you didn't," I burst out, unable to contain myself a moment longer. For surely, having come to the Heartwood Tree, we had also come to the heart of my father's story.

"No," my father answered. "I did not. I might have doubted the truth of Alphonse's tales, but I could hardly doubt the evidence of my own eyes. I was standing beneath the Heartwood Tree, and it would have been sacrilege to take one of its boughs.

124

I would not have done this, Belle, not even for you."

"Then what happened, Roger?" my mother asked quietly.

"I stepped up close to the tree," my father said, "and placed my palm against the trunk. I'm not quite certain why. To verify by touch that which my eyes were seeing. Or perhaps simply to feel a part of something I had been so certain could not exist. Something so extraordinary."

He looked at my sisters and me, each in turn. "I have seen each of you being born," my father told us. "Held you in my hands within moments of your first breaths, yet still I had never touched anything as alive as the Heartwood Tree felt in that moment.

"I could feel its roots, curling deep into the earth. Feel its sap rising. I could feel new leaves unfurl, petals quiver. And, at the core of it all, it seemed to me that I could feel the very heart of the tree itself, that sweet and bitter combination of love and grief, entwined. Inseparable for as long as the tree should live."

My father paused. "And when I finally dropped my hand," he said, "I felt I saw the world around me with new eyes. For how could one stand in the presence of such strength forged from pain and joy, and not be transformed?"

He gazed into space, as if he could still see the Heartwood Tree in his mind's eye.

"Did you say you had brought in my saddlebags, Dominic?" he asked quietly.

"I did, sir," Dominic answered, his tone slightly mystified. "They are by the door. Shall I bring them to you?"

"If you please," my father replied.

Dominic brought my father's saddlebags to him, placing them on the table, spread out so that the leather strap that passed across the horse's back was in front of Papa and the bags stretched across the width of the table. Then Dominic stepped back, but I noticed he did not return to sit beside April, but stayed close, just behind my father.

Papa rested his hands atop the saddlebags for a moment as if mustering the courage to reveal what was inside. Then he undid the lacing on one bag and flipped back the flap.

A sweet fragrance wafted out, one that made me think of the whir of bees, of spring birdcalls. My father reached inside the bag and removed a small branch about the same length and width as my forearm. Its bark was dark and ridged, like that of an almond tree. Bursting from the main limb were many fine, short branches, each covered in either red or white blossoms.

My father held the branch in his hands a moment, as if weighing its cost, then reached out and placed it in front of me on the table.

"I did not break a branch from the Heartwood Tree, yet still I have one. But I do not think that it was meant to come to me. I think that it was meant for you, Belle."

Sixteen

"But how, Papa? *How?*" I cried.

I could not quite bring myself to touch the Heartwood branch, for fear it should melt like snow beneath my fingers.

"In just the way Alphonse's tale said it would," my father answered simply. "The tree gave up a branch of its own accord.

"As I stepped away from the trunk, I heard a sharp *crack* overhead and a single limb"—he gestured to the one that now rested on the table in front of me—"*this* limb, came plummeting down. It landed at my feet, directly in front of my boots, in fact. As if anxious to make sure I didn't miss it. I bent down and picked it up."

My father sighed, and I had never seen him look so old.

"There have been moments since," he said, his voice very quiet, "when I have wondered if I might have escaped if I hadn't done this, if I had stepped over the branch of the Heartwood Tree and let it lie where it fell."

"Escape from what?" Dominic asked softly.

My father started, as if he'd forgotten Dominic was standing behind him. "From the Beast," he said. "For that is all I can think to call it."

"The monster," I whispered. "So there *is* a monster in the heart of the Wood."

"There is, indeed," my father said grimly. "And though I still don't understand, its fate is tied to that of the Heartwood. By its own desire, if nothing else."

"What can a Beast desire?" April asked with a shudder.

"Many things, I would imagine," my father said. "But in this case, in the case of the Heartwood Tree, the same as you or I."

"To see the face of true love," I said.

Papa nodded. "No sooner did I pick up the branch of the Heartwood Tree than the Beast was there. It—he—seemed to come from everywhere, and nowhere, all at once. One moment I was bending over to pick up a treasure, the next I was felled by a cry more terrible than anything I have ever heard on this earth. I tumbled to my knees, shielding my face with my hands, no thought of bravery in my mind. That awful cry left no room for it. I was sure I would die."

"'So this is how you repay my kindness!' the creature roared.

'I feed and shelter you, and then you attempt to steal my heart's best hope? Give me one good reason why I shouldn't tear you to pieces right here and now.'

"The cry had been that of a wild animal," my father said. "But the thing before me spoke with a man's voice. At this, my courage broke altogether, for that seemed the most terrible thing of all.

" 'Speak,' the thing before me said. 'Or you will lose the chance to do so.'

" 'I am not a thief,' I said, though I was talking to its feet as I could not bring myself to raise my eyes. 'All my life, I have tried to be a just and honorable man. That has not changed overnight.'

"I felt my heart grow bolder as I spoke, for I knew I spoke the truth. I wasn't about to let some creature of enchantment suggest otherwise, no matter how terrifying it was."

"Good for you, Papa," I murmured.

"I sincerely hope you continue to think so, Belle," my father replied. "I explained how the branch had fallen at my feet and that all I'd done was to pick it up off of the ground.

" 'I have heard the tales about this tree,' I told the Beast. 'Though I never put much stock in them, until now. But if this is truly the Heartwood Tree, then I know it must give of itself freely, or not at all.'

"When I had finished speaking, the Beast was silent for what seemed like a very long time. He made a slow circle around me, his leather boots making no sound as he moved across the grass. Oh, yes. He was clad as a man is," Papa said, to Maman's startled exclamation. "And a rich man, at that, in velvet, leather, and linen. His clothing was more fine than mine. Finally, he came to a halt directly in front of me, precisely where he'd started.

"'Why should the Heartwood choose you?' he demanded. 'It has grown on these lands, my lands, for time out of mind. Why should the tree give you what it has given no one else? You have said that you are honest. Prove it. Speak truth to me now, and do so carefully, for I will know if you lie.'"

My father put a weathered hand over his eyes.

"You told him about me," I said.

"God forgive me," my father answered. "But I did, Belle. I told him of the way you see things in the wood, things that no other eyes nor heart can find."

"Oh, Roger," my mother cried softly.

"No, Maman," I said swiftly, as I laid a hand on hers. "Don't. Papa was right to tell the truth."

"I had thought my words might calm the Beast," my father said. "But if anything, they made him more agitated than before. He paced in front of me, his long legs tramping down the grass. Time and again, I tried to raise my eyes. It seemed pitiful that I should kneel on the ground, too terrified to even lift my face when I had done no wrong.

"But try as I might, I could not do it. At last, the Beast stopped pacing and spoke.

"'I will make you a bargain, merchant,' he said. 'For I believe that you have answered my questions honestly and bravely, and that deserves a chance I might not bestow on one who is not as moral as yourself.

"'If you can do what no other living thing has done, if you can look into my face and hold my eyes for the time it takes to count to five, you may take the branch of the Heartwood, leave this place, and never return.'

"'And if I cannot?' I inquired.

"'Then you may go from this place today, but either you or your daughter must return in one week's time. For now that the Heartwood Tree has at last let go of a bough, I must know what it holds inside. Do not think to escape me once you leave the Wood. You have partaken of the magic of this place, and I will know where you go.

"'What say you?' the Beast demanded. 'Will you try?'

"'I will,' I said. For I could see no other way out but to look the creature in the eyes. Here was a chance to free the both of us, Belle."

My father dropped his face into his hands. "I could not do it," he whispered, his voice an agony. "I could not do it, no matter how hard I tried. For every time I lifted my eyes toward his face, a thousand images, each more horrible than the last, seemed to crowd into my mind.

"I told myself that I was being foolish. That I was a man and a man is not afraid to look into an animal's eyes. Outside the

Wood, if a man and beast's eyes meet, it is always the beast who is the first to look away.

"But nothing I told myself made any difference. I could not pass this test, and so I was left to uphold the rest of the bargain.

"'So, merchant,' the Beast said. 'Though you are true and just, I see you are no more brave than other men. Take the Heartwood branch and leave this place, but either you or your daughter must return in one week. I will send for you, so that you do not mistake the time.'

"He began to move away, and so, at last, I stumbled to my feet, only to fall to my knees again and plead for mercy. He must have heard me behind him, for he stopped.

"'I would send your daughter if I were you,' the Beast said. 'Perhaps she will be able to pass the test that you have failed, since she is able to see what no one else does.'

"I did not see him walk any farther," my father said. "With these last words, he was simply gone. I found my way back to my horse and rode for home. The journey seemed to take no time at all, for the road passed quickly out of the Wood and soon I was at my own door."

"And this is where you will remain," my mother said firmly. "Both you and Belle. Or we can set off today, back to the city. We need not go through the Wood. We can go around. Think of it as a bad dream, Roger. But now you are awake; you are back with us."

"I gave my word," my father said.

"In fear of your life, sir," Dominic put in quietly. "Surely you need not honor a bargain made under such terms."

"Perhaps not," said my father. "But—"

"Papa isn't going to go at all," I heard myself say. "I'm the one this Beast really wants. He's made that clear enough. I'm the one who can carve the wood. If not for me, Papa never would have picked up the branch in the first place. I'm the one who should keep the promise."

"How can I allow that?" my father asked, the anguish in his voice ringing as clear as a bell. "What kind of father sends his daughter into danger while he himself stays safe at home?"

"The kind of father who trusts his daughter," I answered. "And who is wise enough to recognize that he has no choice. Surely this Beast only wants what we all do: to see the face of true love. If I can show him that—"

"True love!" my mother suddenly exclaimed. "What can a Beast know of love?"

"Perhaps that is what he wishes to discover," I said.

"Perhaps," cried Maman. "All I hear you say is if and perhaps. Those are fragile words to pin your hopes on, let alone your life, ma Belle."

I leaned forward then, and did what I'd feared to do, until now. I took the branch of the Heartwood Tree between my hands. The rough bark bit into my palms.

"I have felt . . . different for as long as I can remember," I said quietly. "Even before the space between my name and face became so great that I found a way to disappear inside it."

I lifted up the wood, as if to test its weight, and felt the fine tingling in my hands that always heralded my ability to picture what the wood was holding in its secret heart of hearts.

"I do not know if what I will find inside this wood will be what the Beast wants. But we all know that I'm the only one of us who will find anything at all. I *may* not, but we all know Papa *cannot*. In which case *perhaps* and *if* may be stronger than they sound."

"I do not understand you," my mother said. "It is almost as if you wish to go into danger."

"Of course I don't," I replied. "But I won't send Papa back, not if I can help it."

My father pulled in a breath to speak. I stood up before he could, still cradling the Heartwood bough.

"You are tired, Papa," I said. "All of us are confused and frightened, but none of us need go anywhere right this moment. Let us speak no more of this for now."

I gave Maman a tired smile. "*Perhaps* tomorrow will bring a way out that we cannot see today."

"Perhaps," said my mother. She stood up. "Come upstairs, Roger," she said. "You are tired. A proper rest in your own bed will do you good. Belle is right. Whatever must be decided can wait until at least tomorrow."

Papa and Maman climbed the stairs, their arms around each other. April and Dominic went outside, speaking in quiet voices.

"I'll do the dishes, just this once, mind you," Celeste said. She paused for a moment, gazing at the branch of the Heartwood Tree. "It really is beautiful, isn't it?" she said. "Do you suppose it wants some water?"

"I've been thinking the same thing myself," I said.

And so, while Celeste cleared the dishes, I took the heaviest of our pitchers and filled it with water. I placed the Heartwood branch in the pitcher and carried them both up to my room. I set the pitcher on the windowsill beside my bed. Then I curled up on the bed, gazing at the blossoms of the Heartwood tree, listening to the sound of my parents' voices as they spoke quietly in the next room.

I closed my eyes and felt the small house, which had become our home, safe and snug and comforting, around me. But even with my eyes closed, I saw the petals of the Heartwood Tree, as if their image had been etched onto my eyelids. White as freshly fallen snow; red as heart's blood.

What did the Heartwood hold for the heart of a Beast? I wondered. I fell asleep and dreamed of what my eyes alone might discover.

Seventeen

THE HEARTWOOD BRANCH SAT IN ITS PITCHER ON MY windowsill all week, its petals never fading, its fragrance filling the house. I cannot say my family ever grew comfortable with our strange new situation, but they did become . . . resigned.

There were no more emotional scenes or arguments, though every time I looked at my mother, I saw the fear and sorrow in her eyes. Much as it grieved me to see it, it only strengthened my resolve.

I would not send my father back into the Wood. I must be the one to leave home.

On the morning that Papa or I needed to honor the agreement, I awoke early, even before Celeste, who is always the first one up, to stir up the stove. I washed my hands and face, then stood a moment considering. *What does one wear when going to pay a visit to a Beast?* I wondered. *What else should I bring along?* For I had no idea how long I'd have to stay.

This last thought was all it took to send me hurrying into motion.

Moving quietly, so as not to awaken my sisters, I put on my plainest everyday dress, the one of gray homespun, and laced up my sturdiest pair of shoes. Then I spread my favorite shawl out on the bed and set my bundle of carving tools in the very center, adding an apron and several pairs of stockings to the pile. I folded the ends of the shawl into the middle, and tied it into a bundle I could carry by slipping my arm through the knots.

It wasn't much. But then that was precisely my intention. *That ought to send a message,* I thought. I wasn't coming to impress, and I would stay no longer than I must.

Finally, I lifted the pitcher containing the branch of the Heartwood from off my bedroom windowsill. A scatter of blossoms sifted down. I reached to sweep them up, then decided to let them be. *Let them stay, to welcome me home,* I thought.

I slipped the bundle over my arm and tiptoed from the room. Downstairs in the kitchen, I placed the Heartwood and my belongings on the stool by the back door, went to the stove, stirred up the fire, and put on the kettle. While it was heating up, I opened the back door and looked out. It was as fine a spring morning as anyone could have asked for.

I could see the neat rows of the vegetable garden from where I stood. I had planted carrots, lettuce, beets, peas, pole beans, and tomatoes earlier in the week, trying hard not to wonder whether or not I'd have the opportunity to taste any of the vegetables whose seeds I was so carefully placing in the ground. A faint layer of dew lay on the freshly turned earth. It steamed slightly, where the sun touched it, wisps of ghosts rising up from the ground.

I heard the rattle of the kettle, the signal that the water had begun to boil. I turned toward the stove, but Celeste was already there. She'd come downstairs so quietly I hadn't heard her arrive.

"Thank you for getting things started for me, Belle," Celeste said as she lifted the kettle from the stove and poured the steaming water over the leaves in the teapot.

"I left the real work for you," I said. I stepped back into the kitchen, but left the door open. It was nice to smell the morning air. "All I did was boil water."

"And a fine job you did of it too," Celeste said. "What would you say to pancakes this morning?"

"When have I ever said no to pancakes?" I asked, though, to be honest, I didn't think I could eat a thing. My stomach was full of knots.

Celeste fetched her favorite blue mixing bowl down from the shelf and carried it to the table as if she were preparing to make breakfast as she did on every other morning. But when she went to set down the bowl, it slipped from her hands, gouging the smooth tabletop.

Celeste gave a horrified cry. She rested her hands flat on the table and leaned over them, as if to catch her breath. "I can't do this," she gasped. "I can't act like everything's normal. I just can't. You're really going, aren't you?"

"Yes, I'm really going," I said. I moved to stand beside my sister and laid a consoling hand on her arm. "I have to go. You must see that, Celeste. One of us has to, and I can't let Papa . . ."

My voice faltered, and broke. It was impossible to speak past the enormous weight in my chest, the lump in my throat. All week long, I'd told myself I would be brave. I didn't feel so brave right at that moment.

"Don't," Celeste said. She put her arms around me and held on tight. "Don't you dare cry, Belle. If you start, then I'll start, and we'll wake the whole house. I understand. I think we all do. I just wish there were some other choice."

"I wish that too," I said. "With all my heart. But there isn't one. Unless this Beast, whoever or whatever he is, changes his mind."

"Maybe he will," Celeste said, her tone determined and hopeful. "Or maybe he'll just forget. He said he'd send for you, didn't he? What if—"

She stopped, abruptly, and I felt her arms tighten around my waist. But I was already stepping from the shelter of her arms. For I had heard the same thing she had: the sound of hooves outside.

"Don't look, Belle," Celeste pleaded. "If you don't look, maybe it will go away. We can pretend it isn't there."

"But it *is* there," I said. "And we both know it." I moved to the open door and looked out.

There was a horse standing in the yard beside the vegetable garden. He was the most astonishing color I'd ever seen, a black so deep it was as if the night had changed its form. His mane shimmered blue, like a raven's wing does in bright sunlight.

"I thought princes in fairy tales were supposed to have white horses," Celeste said.

"Ah, but this horse belongs to a Beast and not a prince," I said. "And this is not a fairy tale. It's real life."

"Look," Celeste said. She pointed at the horse's saddle, bit, and bridle. "Silver buckles."

As if he had heard her, the horse tossed his head.

"Silver buckles," I echoed softly. "It seems he doesn't like them any more than I do."

Without warning, Celeste snatched up the Heartwood branch and the shawl with my belongings, and thrust them into my arms.

"Go, Belle," she said. "If you're really determined to do this, then go now, before anyone else comes downstairs. It will only be harder to leave once they do."

I caught my breath. "You're right," I said. "You're absolutely right."

Together, we flew down the back steps and stopped next to

the horse. He took a few prancing steps away, then steadied. I set
my belongings on the ground and turned to Celeste.

"Help me up."

Celeste bent and made a cradle with her hands. I put one
foot onto them, and she boosted me up. I tossed my leg across
the horse's back, riding like a boy. I tucked my skirts in as best
I could.

"Say good-bye to them for me," I panted, as Celeste handed
up my shawl. I set it on the saddle before me, tucking the branch
of the Heartwood through the knot. "Tell April not to wait to
marry Dominic. And . . . I want to say thank you," I said. "I
should have said it long before now."

"Thank you?" my sister asked. "To me? What for?"

"For not telling Paul de la Montaigne I was standing right
behind him at that stupid garden party," I said. "For putting my
pain before your own. I don't know how I'll ever make it up to
you, but I promise you, if I come back, I'll try."

"Don't be ridiculous; of course you'll come back," Celeste
replied. "And for the record, Papa was right. Paul de la Montaigne is as dumb as a pailful of earthworms. Forget about him.
I certainly have. He was never worth your pain, or mine. Now
you'd better get going."

"Tell Papa and Maman I love them," I said.

"I will," Celeste promised, her own voice as breathless as
mine. "But I think I've changed my mind. There is something
you can do to make up for Paul de la Montaigne."

"What's that?" I asked, even as I felt the horse's muscles bunch beneath my legs.

"Come home."

"I will," I vowed. "I swear to you I will. I'll find whatever it is this Beast wants, then come straight home."

"I'll hold you to *that* promise," my sister said.

She stepped back just as the horse reared up, forelegs pawing the air, and uttered one great cry. Then, with a force so hard it made my teeth jar together, his hooves came back down to earth and we galloped from the yard.

"You could consider slowing down," I panted some time later, though it was a miracle I could speak at all. The horse had kept a steady pace, as if afraid to go any slower lest I slip off his back and try to run off on my own.

At the sound of my voice, I saw his ears twitch.

"Our destination isn't going anywhere, is it?" I went on. "I don't expect to make a good impression. I'm already far too windblown for that. And I don't actually imagine your master cares all that much about what I look like anyhow. But it might be nice if I could arrive in one piece. You keep this up, you're going to shake my bones apart."

The horse tossed his head, as if he disapproved of my remarks. But he did slacken his pace, first to a canter and then to a trot. Whether this had to do with my request or the fact that the Wood was up ahead, I could not tell. I brushed my hair back from my face and settled the bundle more firmly in front of me in the saddle.

As we passed beneath the first of the trees, the horse settled into a brisk but easy walk.

"Thank you," I said. "I appreciate your kindness."

He turned his head and lipped the edge of my skirt.

"Oh, so now you want to be friends, do you?" I said with a smile. "After you've gotten your way the whole time."

The horse whickered, a sound like laughter.

"I wonder what you're called," I mused aloud as we continued on. "I hope it's something more imaginative than Midnight. And I wish you could tell me how much farther we have to go."

But here, the horse could provide no answer—none that I could interpret, anyhow. I sat upon his back, my hands resting lightly on the branch of the Heartwood. The trees of the Wood seemed to acknowledge our approach, bending forward as if in stately bows, in a wind they felt but I could not. Dappled sunlight danced across the forest floor.

The horse changed pace again, abandoning his walk for a quick and eager trot. At this, it seemed to me I felt the wind, and more, I heard the sound it made as it brought the treetops together, then pushed them apart, as if they were passing on a message.

Belle is coming. Belle is coming. Belle. Belle. Belle.

Once more the horse shifted pace, into a canter this time. And now I made no request that he hold back, for I thought I understood. He was eager to be home.

"All right," I said. "Go on, boy."

At this, he sprang forward so swiftly that I closed my eyes and held on tight. And so I missed the moment when we passed from the Wood where anyone could travel into the one of enchantment. Whether I would have known the boundary when we crossed it, to this day, I cannot tell.

Finally, with an abruptness that almost tossed me straight over his head, the horse stopped. We'd come to our precipitous halt in front of a pair of elaborately carved wrought-iron gates. In the center of the gate on the right was the silhouette of a man, with one hand outstretched. Opposite him, in the center of the left gate, was a woman, reaching back toward the man.

When the gates were closed, their hands would meet. When the gates were open, they would be apart, yet still reaching for each other. A pair of horses rearing up on their hind legs created a curving arch atop the gates.

"One of those is you, I suppose," I said. The horse gave his head a toss. As if at the sound of my voice, the gates swung open. Just as my father had said, they did not make a sound.

I gasped. Perhaps it was just the shadow of a nearby tree, but as the gate opened, the figure of the man altered, if only for a moment. Instead of the smooth lines that suggested a nobleman in fine clothes, it seemed the silhouette grew jagged; desperation etched in every line. It looked like a soul in torment.

But with the gate swung wide, the shadow passed, and I was gazing once again at a young man reaching toward his sweetheart.

"I guess this means we can go in," I said. The horse tossed

his head and stamped, setting the silver buckles on his harness jangling. But he stayed right where he was. And all of a sudden, I understood.

This Beast doesn't miss a trick, does he? I thought.

"May I please come in?" I called out, my voice clear and strong. I'd been a little concerned about that, if the truth must be told. Talking to the horse was one thing, to his master, quite another. At any rate, there could be no harm in being polite. Less chance of being eaten on the spot, or so I sincerely hoped.

"My name is Annabelle Evangeline Delaurier," I went on. "I have come to honor my father's debt, to return the branch of the Heartwood Tree. I have come of my own accord. I would like to enter, if you'll let me."

The horse whickered its approval. There was a beat of silence. Then, as if he'd heard an answer that I couldn't, the horse walked through the gates.

Don't look back, Belle, I thought. *Don't watch those gates shut fast behind you.*

But of course I did it anyhow. I turned and watched the gates that marked the place between the world I thought I understood and one I was quite certain I did not, close silently behind me. The man's and the woman's outstretched hands were truly clasped together now. The young couple was reunited.

I turned my face away. Toward the heart of the Wood. The home of the Beast, the monster.

Eighteen

THE REMAINDER OF MY JOURNEY WAS JUST AS MY FATHER
had described. The path the horse and I trod was narrow,
and made of ivory-colored stones so cunningly made there
was not a chink for a single blade of grass to grow. On one
side, an orchard of fruit trees stretched into the distance.
On the other, roses grew in great profusion, tumbling over
one another in what must have once been a series of formal
flower beds, long gone wild. The scent of the flowers was
so strong I could almost see it in the air. And, woven in so
tightly it could not be separated out, was also the bitter tang
of loneliness.

The path wound for about half a mile, then broadened out.

The horse rounded a gentle curve, and suddenly, I could see the rise with the great stone house and its courtyard and stable sprawling across the top. The horse moved steadily up the hill until he reached the courtyard, then stopped. The house was to my left now, and the stables to the right. I looked around, but could see nowhere I could easily dismount. So I sat on the horse's back, my palms against the bark of the Heartwood Tree, as if for good luck, and waited.

It's your move, Beast, I thought.

I'd like to be able to say that my first sight of him was magical and supernatural, that he appeared from out of nowhere with a crash of thunder and a puff of smoke. Papa had said the Beast had seemed to come from out of thin air, from everywhere and nowhere, all at once. So expecting the extraordinary hardly seemed far-fetched.

In my case, he came from the stables, as if he were a stable boy preparing the stall for the horse. It was so prosaic, I might have laughed, but even I am not that brave. It's hard to laugh when your heart is in your throat.

Though I suppose it could be said that he did appear magically. For, one moment, the horse and I were alone in the courtyard. And, in the next, there was a figure, a shadow within a shadow, standing in the open stable door.

I gave a jolt, and the horse beneath me shifted a step, steadied, then pawed the ground with one dark hoof, as if annoyed at my response.

"I'm sorry," I whispered. "But this isn't exactly easy for me, you know."

The horse blew out a breath, and the figure in the doorway stepped forward into the light. I shivered, even as the air in the courtyard seemed to ripple with heat. My heart began to beat in hard, fast strokes, so loudly it would have been a miracle if he didn't hear it all the way across the courtyard.

He was tall.

That was my first thought. Even from a distance, and from my vantage point on the back of a high horse, he was tall. Lean and rangy like a wolf, was my second, not particularly comforting, thought. I felt my courage start to waver.

You can do this. You have to do this, Belle, I thought.

Half a dozen steps the Beast strode toward me, the soles of his boots making not a single sound. Then he stopped. I had no idea why. The horse stretched his neck, as if testing the bit between his teeth.

"I suppose," I heard a deep voice say. "That you are quite real."

I gasped, for I felt his voice pass through my skin, through muscle and flesh, until it came to rest in the marrow of my bones. Papa had said the Beast had the voice of a man, but this was not quite accurate, I thought.

For no human being I had ever met spoke in a voice like that, sounding heart and mind together, at once, as one. A Beast may have the ability to camouflage its skin. Men are better at hiding their hearts.

"I don't understand you," I somehow found a way to reply. "I am Belle Delaurier," I said, as I had at the gate. "I am here by your order. You gave my father shelter, and he took away a gift you did not wish to bestow. I have come to bring it back and to fulfill his promise."

The Beast took three more steps. Two more, and he would be close enough to touch.

"So you *are* real," he murmured, almost as if speaking to himself. "I have not imagined you. You are real. You have come. I see a dark gray dress on my horse's back, strong hands on the reins, and your hair . . ."

He paused, and I had the sense he was studying me intently. "Your hair curls and it is brown. But your face . . ." His voice faltered and broke off. "Your face eludes me," he continued after a moment. "Your features slip in and out of focus, like a star at the end of a telescope."

"I am not a star," I said, a sudden ache in my throat. "I'm just a girl named Annabelle."

"Annabelle," he echoed, and I seemed to feel the strange power of his voice in every part of me. As if it were seeking the way to make me visible. "But I thought that you said . . . Belle?"

"Belle is my nickname," I answered. "It's what I've always been called. I think that may be your problem—with my face, I mean. It makes you think you're supposed to look for Beauty."

"And I can't find what isn't there?" the Beast said. "Is that your point?"

"It is," I replied.

He took one more step, and then another until he was standing right beside me.

"Real and honest," he said. "A powerful combination. You do not spare feelings, not even your own. So I will tell you a truth of my own in exchange for yours: What I can and cannot see is not determined by your face, alone, Belle Delaurier. It is . . . part of the reason I reside in this place, so that I might learn to use my eyes."

"I don't understand," I said once more.

"You will," he answered. "Or so I hope, in time."

He placed a hand against the horse's flank then, not an inch from my knee. I stared down. Like the rest of him, his hand was long and lean, though broad across the knuckles.

A strong and capable hand, I thought. One that could both cradle and crush. It was covered in a fine layer of fur, copper-colored, like the coat of a fox. The tapering fingers ended in short nails, pointed at the tips. They looked sharp.

The horse turned his head and rubbed it along the Beast's arm. The Beast lifted that hand and stroked it along the horse's nose.

"What is your horse called?" I blurted out.

The hand stilled for an instant, then continued its motion. "Corbeau."

"Raven," I said. The horse tossed its head, as if acknowledging its name. "It suits him, and it's a much better name than Midnight."

The Beast made a sudden sound, like a strange, harsh bark. I started, and the horse shied. The Beast stepped back.

"I'm sorry," I said, when Corbeau was calm once more. I stroked a hand along the horse's neck, on the opposite side from where the Beast stood. He made no move to step in close again, I noticed. "I'm sorry. I didn't mean to do that."

"I know you didn't," the Beast said. "I think that's the problem. For the record, I don't intend to eat you. I don't intend you any harm."

"What do you want, then?" I asked.

"Company, for one thing," the Beast replied. He made a gesture in my direction, and I managed to keep myself still this time. "And to see what the Heartwood holds. Your father said you might be able to show me this."

"I hope so."

"Will it take long?"

I hope not, I thought. *For both our sakes.*

"That is up to the wood itself, not to me," I answered honestly. "Every piece of wood I've ever touched has shown me its secret eventually. Some take longer to reveal what they hold on the inside than others. The Heartwood has held on to its secrets for a very long time."

"That is so," the Beast concurred. There was a quick pause. "Thank you, Annabelle."

"What for?" I asked. "I haven't done anything yet."

"Oh, but you have," he countered. "You came, and you have

spoken the truth twice now, even though it frightens you to do so. Another person might have given me an easier answer, one they imagined I might like to hear. You did not."

He stepped to stand beside the horse once more. "I'm sure you'd rather be a million miles away, but I am glad that you have come, Annabelle."

"If you will call me that," I answered, "then I will try to be glad I'm here as well." For, in only a few minutes with this stranger, this Beast had done what I had been unable to convince my family to do in nearly ten years: He had called me Annabelle.

"And I will do my best to see, and to reveal, what the Heartwood holds," I went on. "Though, since we're busy appreciating the honesty, I should probably mention that I can't promise that what I find will be what you want. My ability is to see truly, not on command."

"If you see truly, then what you reveal will *be* what I want," the Beast replied. "And now, I don't suppose I could persuade you to come down off Corbeau. I'm sure he's ready for his stall."

"Of course," I said, though my lips felt stiff. It was clear he meant to help me down himself.

I handed down the bundle of my shawl, being careful not to touch him. He took it from me just as carefully, then set it beside him on the cobblestones. I settled the branch of the Heartwood in the nook of one elbow, as if it were an infant.

"Hand it to me," the Beast said simply. "I'll give it back when you're on the ground."

For the space of time it took for me to draw a breath, I was certain that I was going to say no. But, at the last instant, I changed my mind. Cradling the branch between my palms, one on either end, I leaned down. The Beast reached out and grasped the Heartwood in the middle. A tingle, so sharp it was almost pain, shot into my hands and up my arms. I think I made a sound.

The Beast froze, his great hands gripping the Heartwood so tightly that I saw his knuckles beneath the copper-colored fur, for they had turned stark white.

"Look at me, Annabelle," he demanded in that fierce, compelling voice. "Look into my face, into my eyes for the span of time it takes to count to five. Look at me and let me see you. Look at me and free us both."

The tingling in my arms was truly pain now. Spreading across my shoulders, burrowing into my chest, aiming straight for my heart. When it reached it, I would be transformed. Whether it would be as simple as dying, I could not tell. But of one thing I was certain: I would no longer be the Belle Delaurier I knew.

And it was because of him, this strange combination of man and beast that stood before me.

"No," I said. "I can't. I'm sorry."

He made a dark sound, deep within his chest, and I understood that my own pain was nothing.

"Then let go of the Heartwood," he commanded.

I set my teeth. "I'm trying."

It was Corbeau who broke the deadlock, turning his head without warning to sink his teeth deep into the Beast's shoulder. The Beast gave a startled exclamation, released the Heartwood, and stepped back. The second we were no longer touching the wood together, my fingers loosened of their own accord. I released the branch and it fell, landing on the bundle of my belongings.

I cradled my hands in my lap, one curved inside the other. My fingers were stiff and painful. I flexed them, rubbing them as if to bring back the circulation after too long out in the cold. Without a word, the Beast bent to retrieve my bundle and the branch of the Heartwood.

"I can get down myself," I hurried into speech, throwing one leg over Corbeau's neck as I did so. I slid along his flank to the ground, the impact of the cobblestones jarring every bone in my body. I leaned against the horse for a moment, waiting for my legs to steady. "And I can stable Corbeau as well, if you'll let me. I'd like to."

"As you wish," the Beast said, turning away. I turned to the horse.

"All right," I whispered against his neck. "It's going to be all right. Come along now, Corbeau."

The horse followed me obediently, as if I were the one who cared for him every night. Just as we reached the door of the stable, the Beast spoke once more.

"Why did you think the horse would be called Midnight?" he asked. "And why were you pleased when he was not?"

I paused, one hand on Corbeau's neck, though I did not turn back. "Because of his color," I answered. "And because it seemed too obvious a choice."

Again, he made that sound in his throat that had so startled me before. *He's laughing,* I realized.

"I think you'll find not much around here makes the obvious choice. Thank you for caring for my horse, Annabelle."

"You're welcome," I said.

"I'll wait for you inside."

If you're trying to make me hurry, that's not the way to do it, I thought.

I did turn back then, to ask how in the world I would find him inside that great stone house, and discovered he'd pulled the trick I'd expected earlier.

He'd vanished into thin air, for he was nowhere in sight.

Nineteen

I STABLED CORBEAU, TAKING OFF THE SADDLE AND HAR-
ness, finding the place to stow them where they belonged, then
caring for him as carefully as if he were my own horse. I brushed
him so long and well I could almost see myself reflected in his
glossy dark coat, and he, himself, was stamping in impatience,
eager for the meal that was still to come.

At long last, more reluctantly than I liked to admit, I put
the brush and currycomb away and fed Corbeau. I stayed beside
him, leaning my head against his smooth, warm flank, listening
to his strong teeth make fast work of his evening meal of oats.

"You like him, don't you?" I murmured. "And he likes
you." The stable was as immaculate as Corbeau himself.

"That's good news, isn't it? That he's capable of affection?"

Because you're hoping what, precisely, Belle? I thought. *That he'll like you, too? Be satisfied with not being eaten and be done with it.*

Corbeau blew out a great snuffling breath, as clear a request to be left in peace as if he'd spoken. Which, come to think of it, I suppose he had.

"All right," I said. "I'm stalling. I admit it. There's no need to get all huffy."

Corbeau turned his head then, regarding me with one dark eye. "I'm going to go inside the house now," I said. "I am, honestly. Just as soon as I remember how to breathe."

For, abruptly, I felt dizzy and light-headed. My heart pounded, as if I'd been running.

I stamped my foot in frustration, and Corbeau showed his teeth. "This is ridiculous," I said. "And it's going to stop right now. What was the use of coming this far if I won't go any farther? I'm going inside that house. I'm going right now."

On impulse, I leaned over and gave Corbeau's neck a kiss. Then I turned and walked from the stable, wishing I didn't feel like I was leaving behind my one and only friend.

The doors to the great stone house were shut, and though I did not give myself permission to take this as a sign to turn around and run in the opposite direction, I did put off going inside for one moment more. For the doors gave me a surprise. They were made of wood and elaborately carved. And, like the gates I'd passed through to enter the Beast's domain, they showed a man and woman, reaching toward each other.

It was easy to see that the couple was nobly born. For the carving was so intricate and detailed I could see the lace the man wore at collar and cuffs, and the long string of pearls the woman wore at her throat.

Who are you? I wondered.

Once again, with the doors shut fast, the couple's hands were joined. I hesitated a moment longer, reluctant to break that clasp, for it seemed to me that these were two who should never be parted for long.

Nor will they be, I chastised myself. *Only for the amount of time it takes the doors to open and close. Stop putting off going inside, Belle. You can't stand on the front step forever.*

I sighed. Then I walked up the last two steps, setting my hands against the place where the couple's hands met. That was all it took to get the doors to open. As the gates had, the great wooden doors of the house swept back silently. The arms of the figures on the doors swung wide, in a gesture that looked like a grand welcome.

I stepped across the threshold.

The entry hall was a dazzle of colors as the light streamed in from stained glass windows high above. It both obscured and illuminated the images on the tiles beneath my feet. For, just as

Papa had described, the entry hall of the house was covered in a mosaic, many parts working together to form a whole.

Everything here tells a story, I realized. Whether it was the same one, over and over again, or some fresh tale each and every time, I couldn't yet tell. *Perhaps with enough time,* I thought, then caught myself short.

I was here to discover what lay hidden within the Heartwood branch. That, and nothing more. The sooner I did so, the sooner I could keep my promise to Celeste, and to myself: the sooner I could return home. I had no business getting sidetracked by whatever stories might lie hidden in this place, no matter how artfully told.

"There you are," I heard the Beast say, interrupting my thoughts. He materialized at the back of the entry hall, perhaps from the study where my father had sheltered. He strode forward into the light until we were both illuminated by the colors streaming down from the windows above. I, in a pool of yellow; he, in a patch just a shade lighter than indigo. I looked up and saw that the color came from the sunlight passing through the image of a woman dressed in a dark blue gown.

Look how he manages to find the shadows even when the sun is shining on him, I thought.

"I wondered if perhaps you meant to stay in the stables with Corbeau," the Beast went on.

So there was to be no reference to the strange and uncomfortable moment in the courtyard, when he had all but begged me to look into his face, to gaze into his eyes. That was perfectly fine with me.

"I considered it," I answered lightly. I did my best to seem as if I was really looking at him, casting a quick glance upward in the general vicinity of his face, before letting my gaze settle on a place slightly over his left shoulder, at about the height of his earlobe—if I'd actually been able to find his earlobe beneath all that hair. For now, as I did my best *not* to look at him, I seemed to see a hundred things that I had not before.

He had a man's hair upon his head, just a shade darker than the copper fur that covered the backs of his hands. It curled in wild profusion, long enough to brush down to his impossibly broad shoulders. It was almost as if the very form of him could not quite make up its mind. Was he a man, or was he a beast? I wondered, abruptly and uncomfortably, whether this might be the true definition of a monster: a being that was neither one thing nor another.

"Let me show you to your room," the Beast—for by now I was incapable of thinking of him by any other name—said, precisely as if he were an innkeeper and I, a guest to be welcomed and made comfortable. "Perhaps that will make you feel better about coming indoors."

And perhaps I'll learn to sing like a nightingale, I thought, though I chose not to mention that possibility aloud.

I nodded to show that I would follow his lead. We proceeded up a broad set of central stairs, side by side. They were made of the same gray stone as the rest of the house, but running down the center was a wide runner of bright blue.

"I feel as if I'm walking up a waterfall," I said.

He made what I sincerely hoped was an appreciative grunt. *And walking next to you is like hiking up one mountain with another at your side,* I thought.

I had seen that he was tall. It was the first thing that I'd noticed. But it was one thing to *see* it, looking down from the back of a large horse, and another thing to *feel* it, walking with him. My head reached no higher than the center of his chest.

Just high enough to peer into his heart, I thought. Then wished I hadn't, for I wasn't all that sure I wanted to discover what a Beast's heart might hold.

The stairs ended in a broad landing with three halls heading off in different directions. One straight ahead, and one each to the left and right.

"I have put you this direction," the Beast said, indicating that we would proceed along the passage to the right. "On this side of the house, the windows overlook the lake."

And the Heartwood Tree, I thought.

"Where are your rooms?" I asked, then did my best not to wince, for it sounded as if I was trying to find out how far apart our rooms were without asking the question directly.

"All around you," the Beast answered shortly. "For everything here is mine. But if you're asking where I sleep, I have no fixed place. Sometimes I stay indoors at night. More often I do not."

So you are nocturnal, like an animal, I thought.

"Don't you have a favorite room?" I asked, determined to find a safe topic.

"I do," the Beast replied, after a brief pause. "The study. Where your father spent the night."

"You are fond of books, then," I persevered.

"I am," he said. "Though I am also rather hard on them." The Beast made a strange gesture, clicking his long, sharp nails together. "This is your room."

The Beast stopped before a closed door, turned the knob, and pushed the door open wide. Before me stretched an end-less carpet of fresh spring green, precisely the same color as a new lawn. To the left, a great canopy bed swathed in pale peach silk rested on a dais of white marble. On the right was a great wooden wardrobe. But it was what I saw straight ahead that captured my attention and held it.

For the back wall of the room was not a wall at all. Instead, it was a series of windows so clear I would not have known they were there save for the frames that held the panes in place. Through them I could see the sparkle of the lake, the move-ment of the clouds as they scudded across the clear blue sky. I was across the threshold and moving toward the windows almost before I realized what I'd done.

"You like it, then," the Beast said.

"Of course I like it," I responded. I could see that there was a wide balcony bordered by a stone balustrade outside the windows. In the center was a little table with just one chair pulled up before it. Hidden by the bulk of the wardrobe was the door that would take me to the outside. It was made of mahogany, polished until it gleamed ruby red. In its center was a crystal doorknob.

"It's beautiful," I said. "Everything about it is beautiful. Do the windows open?"

"Place your hand upon whichever pane of glass you choose and it will yield before your touch," the Beast said. "When you wish it to return, call it back."

I stopped short, astonished, then continued the rest of the distance to the windows more slowly. I lifted one hand, then pressed my palm against the closest pane of glass. I felt a sharp cold, as if I'd plunged my fingers into ice, and then, with a sound I thought might be laughter, the glass seemed to whisk away and my hand moved through into the open air.

I snatched my hand back, considered it a moment, then extended it again. This time my hand passed straight through. The glass was simply . . . not there. I wiggled my fingers experimentally, then brought them indoors once more.

"Thank you very much for the demonstration. Now come back, please," I said.

I heard a sigh, as if someone had exhaled a breath into the room, and saw that the pane of glass was back in place.

"Stay put now, if you please," I said, and set my fingertips against it. The glass did as I instructed. It was precisely as the

Beast had said. If I willed the pane of glass to open, it would do so. Otherwise, it was simply a pane of glass.

"I thought you might be joking," I said as I turned back toward the Beast.

"Why would I do that?" he asked. "How much humor do you think a beast has?"

"I imagine that depends on the beast," I said. I frowned, for I realized suddenly that he was still standing in the hall. "Why are you out there?"

He shifted his weight, as if uncomfortable.

"This is *your* room," he said. "No one may enter except by your permission."

"Not even you?"

"Not even me."

Slowly, I moved back across the floor until we faced each other across the threshold, just a little too close for comfort.

"You deny yourself a place in your own home? Why would you do that?"

"Because I wanted you to have a place here you could call your own, a place you could feel safe."

"Am I in some danger, then?"

"From me, no," the Beast said. "But from your own fears of me and your surroundings, I think the answer may be yes."

He shifted his weight again. "I would like—" He stopped, then tried again. "Please do not misunderstand me," he said. "You have done an impressive job this morning, Annabelle.

You've been polite, but you've shown also that you have backbone. Both of which are very nice, but they do not alter the heart of the matter.

"You did not come here of your own free will."

"There's an easy way out of that," I answered. "Let me go."

"No," he said without hesitation. "Not yet. Not until you can show me what the Heartwood holds."

"So until then, no matter how lovely and magical it is, this place is still a prison."

Now it was the Beast who took a step forward, until the tips of his boots nudged right up against the doorway. "It has always been a prison," he said. "A very beautiful one, that much is true, but a prison nevertheless. I find it helps if you don't try quite so hard *not* to see the bars."

He took a single step back. "Within the boundaries of this place you may go anywhere you like," he went on. "But you may not go beyond them. The same applies to me, if it makes you feel any better."

"Thank you for telling me," I said. "But it doesn't."

"I didn't think it would," he replied.

He picked up my shawl and the branch of the Heartwood, both of which had been sitting beside the door in the hall. "Here are your belongings. Your time is yours to spend as you wish, though I'd like to make a request."

It's your house, I thought. *You can do whatever you like.*

"I'm listening," I said. Not the most gracious response, but standing there I realized suddenly how very tired I was. Just getting here had taken all my strength, and now he wanted one thing more.

"Please," I said, when he still remained silent. "Go on."

"I'm hoping you will consent to join me each day, just at twilight," the Beast replied. "I have become reconciled to many things, but not to being utterly alone as day gives way to night. If you will give me your company, I think it would make the moment easier to bear."

"How will I know where to find you?" I asked.

"I'll find you," the Beast said. "If you consent."

"I consent, just don't . . ." I sighed. There was no way forward but to sound ridiculous or to give offense, or both. "I would appreciate it if you wouldn't sneak up on me," I said. "Your sudden appearances and disappearances can be a little alarming."

"That is fair enough," the Beast said. "I will do my best not to alarm you. Until tonight then, Annabelle."

Without another word, he turned and strode away. I closed the door quietly behind him. Then, carrying the Heartwood branch, I walked back across the room, opened the door to the balcony, and stepped out. The air was clean and brisk, and I inhaled deeply. I sat down at the table, and though the view beyond my balcony was compelling, all my attention was cradled within my palms.

I closed my eyes, waiting for the tingle that would be the

BELLE

signal that soon I'd know what the wood held within it, the image it carried in its heart of hearts. But, though I sat all that afternoon, sat until the air grew chill and the sun began to sink in the sky, I felt no stirring of my Gift.

I felt nothing, nothing at all.

And finally, for the first time, I felt truly afraid. Afraid for my own life. Not that the Beast would harm me, but that my existence might come to be as his was. That the loneliness of this place, no matter how beautiful it was, would soon become his and mine combined.

I gripped the Heartwood tightly in my hands, the deeply grooved bark biting into my palms.

Help me, I thought. *Help me to see truly. Help me find the secret of your heart.*

Help me to find the way to free the Beast, and myself.

Twenty

OUR DAYS SOON FELL INTO A SOMEWHAT COMFORTABLE routine. The Beast and I kept out of each other's way as much as possible during the day, but, no matter where in the house or on the grounds I was, he always found me, just at twilight. Sometimes we would sit in the study, while he pointed out his favorite books. But more often, as the weather was warm, we stayed outdoors. Soon, I had been all over the grounds that were within easy walking distance of the great stone house.

I was beginning to learn my way around in other ways, as well. In addition to the panes of glass in my windows, there were doors that would open merely with a wish, set side by side with ones I could not open at all. I had only to think of a food I wanted to eat and it would appear, sometimes literally, before me. The first time this happened I was caught completely unawares and put my foot down squarely in a fresh strawberry pie. I soon learned to be stationary (and preferably seated) when I thought of food.

I tried very hard not to think too much of home. For when I did this, the house felt most like a prison, albeit a lovely and magical one.

But I did not let my explorations distract me from my purpose. Every day, I took the Heartwood into my hands, trying to listen as it whispered its secrets, straining to see into its heart of hearts. I stood beneath the tree itself for hours on end, gazing up into its boughs. I laid my hands against the trunk, as Papa had. I even kicked off my shoes and climbed into the branches, the bark snagging holes in my stockings.

But no matter what I did, the Heartwood remained silent. The secrets it carried, it kept to itself. And every evening, just at nightfall, the Beast repeated the request he'd made the day I first arrived. That I look into his face and gaze into his eyes for the time it took to count to five. Each and every night I gave the same reply.

"No. I can't. I'm sorry."

Until, at last, I began to grow tired of the struggle. Of all the things I couldn't do. And I wondered how much longer we could go on as we were.

"Why five?" I asked one night. The Beast and I were sitting

together in the pergola, by the shores of the lake. He had not
made his daily request yet, but I could tell it was coming. The
sun had just begun to sink, plunging into the waters of the lake
like a gold coin tossed to make a wish.

"What?" the Beast asked, as if his mind had been far away,
drifting on the waters of the lake, perhaps, as his body sat, huge
and solid, at my side.

"You always ask the same thing," I said. "You always ask me to
look at you for the time it takes to count to five. Why that number?
Does it mean something, or did you just choose it at random?"

"I didn't choose it at all," the Beast replied. If he was surprised that I'd brought up the matter of his request myself, he
did not show it. But then, I didn't have any of the usual land-
marks to go by. It's hard to learn to know someone when you
can't see their face or look into their eyes.

What a curious couple we are, I thought, then sat up a little
straighter, as if poked by a pin. *You're not a couple at all, Belle,* I
reminded myself.

"Then why?" I inquired. "If you didn't choose the number,
who did?"

He turned his head then, as if he wished he could read my
expression.

"Why do you want to know?"

I felt a burst of emotion, frustration and impatience combined. At least I was making an effort to understand. All he did
was ask the same question every single night.

I stood up. "You know what? Just forget it. I should have known you wouldn't tell me anyhow. You never really explain anything, do you? You just give orders."

I set off, not caring where I was going.

"Belle, wait," the Beast called. I kept on going. If he really wanted to catch up with me, he'd be able to do it in about thirty seconds, I had no doubt. Sure enough, before I'd gone half a dozen steps, he was beside me again, his long stride easily matching mine.

"Please wait," he said. "I wasn't trying to evade your question, I was asking for the simple truth. Why do you want to know?"

I sighed. "I just don't understand why you always ask the same thing," I said.

The energy from my outburst had carried me down to the shores of the lake. The coin of the setting sun had melted now, turning the water a shimmering liquid gold.

"I don't like knowing that you'll ask it, even though we both know what my answer will be, night after night." I paused. "And I suppose it's starting to make me . . . unhappy that I always say no."

"I will never harm you because of your answer," the Beast said quickly.

I considered this for a moment, replaying his words in my mind. I poked my toe at the damp, sandy earth by the shore of the lake.

"I know that," I said at last.

"Do you?"

"I think I do," I replied. "I think that I have come to understand, to believe," I went on, choosing my words very carefully, "that it was never your intention to do me harm. Which is not quite the same thing as saying you're always happy with me, or that I'm always comfortable here."

"No, it isn't," the Beast replied. There was a pause. At any moment, I expected his nightly question. But it did not come.

"What's on the other side of the lake?" I asked at last. "And don't you dare say 'the opposite shore.'"

He made the sound I knew to be laughter. "Beyond the lake is one of the boundaries of this place," he said. "It lies . . . not far beyond the opposite shore."

"Do you ever go out onto the lake?"

He shook his head. "Not often, no."

"But you must sometimes," I persisted. "There's a boat." I could see it from where we stood, moored to a short pier not far from the pergola.

"There is a boat," he agreed. There was a silence. "I take it you're proposing we go now. It's getting dark, Annabelle."

"But there will be a moon soon enough," I countered. "It was almost full last night." I turned toward him then, inching my eyes upward as far as I dared. "Please," I said. "Might we not at least try? Is there something I should be afraid of in the dark? Something that intends me harm?"

Though we were often together as the sun went down, I had always stayed alone in my own room after dark. This had been my own decision, and it had seemed a prudent choice. Even in the world I knew, it was not always safe to be out after dark. And there was so very much about this place I did not know.

"There is nothing in the dark that will deliberately seek you out to harm you, nothing present in the dark that does not dwell in the light, as well," the Beast replied. "But the dark provides a kind of freedom. It is a time when some things here become more of what they truly are."

"And what is that?" I asked.

"Wild."

I let this sink in, weighing the options, for I had the very strong feeling he was including himself.

"Thank you for the warning," I said. "But I believe I would still like to go. I can go on my own, if you don't wish to take me. I know how to row a boat."

But the Beast was already shaking his head. "No. If going out on the lake is what you wish, then it will be my pleasure to take you."

"That is what I wish."

"Then let us go."

Much to my astonishment, he offered an arm, precisely as if we were a young lady and gentleman out for an evening's stroll. I hesitated. Aside from that first day, when he'd tried to lift me

173

from the horse, we had been very careful not to touch each other. And he had not gone near the Heartwood branch again. It was always safe in my room, or on the balcony outside.

I steadied my hand, then tucked my fingers lightly into the crook of his arm. A shudder passed through him, of pain or pleasure I could not tell.

The Beast wore velvet. He almost always did, and the fabric was rich and smooth beneath my fingertips. And for once I was dressed as finely as he, for I had at long last given up the simple dress I'd brought with me in favor of one from the wardrobe. I'd put off doing this for as long as possible. Wearing the clothes the Beast provided felt too much like settling in. But I had brought only one dress, and I couldn't wear it every day forever.

The one I'd finally decided on was a deep blue with a full skirt, and a lace undershift that showed at the bodice and cuffs. It wasn't until I was halfway down the stairs that I realized why I'd chosen it over all the others: The dress was the same shade as the gown worn by the woman in the stained glass window, the window that had hid the Beast in shadow that first afternoon. Like the Beast's own clothing, it was velvet. I felt its luxurious weight with every step I took, a far cry from my usual home-spun.

"Who is the young couple?" I asked. "The one on the gate, and on the front door?"

"You are full of questions tonight," the Beast observed. Not quite the response I was hoping for. We reached the pier and proceeded down it toward the boat, our shoes making hollow sounds against the wood.

"I'm always full of questions," I admitted with a sigh. "It used to drive my mother crazy when I was a child. I'd try my best not to ask them, but it would always make things worse. I'd store them up only to let them loose in a great flood, just like tonight. I therefore solemnly promise not to ask any more questions this evening."

"You will have a hard time keeping that promise, I think," he remarked.

I laughed before I could catch myself. "And I think that sounds just like a clever challenge."

We reached the end of the pier. I released his arm, and watched as the Beast stepped down into the rowboat. It rocked beneath his weight then steadied.

"How about this?" I said, on impulse. "Let's see which one of us can go the longest without asking a question." I heard him pull in a breath. "And the one I asked just now doesn't count," I hurried on. "Whoever gives in and asks first must receive a truthful answer, but then the other gets to ask two questions, and receive two truthful answers in return."

He gave a grunt. "You have brothers and sisters, don't you?"

"Two sisters," I said. "Stop trying to weasel out. Is it settled?"

"I don't suppose that counts either," the Beast said.

"Of course not. We're still establishing the rules. And don't think I didn't notice the way you snuck in a question. Rhetorical questions are considered cheating, by the way."

"You drive a hard bargain," he observed.

So do you, I thought. But I was determined not to stray into potentially unpleasant territory.

"Very well. I will play this questions game," the Beast said. "Now hold still."

I opened my mouth to ask the obvious question, then closed it again. "Very sneaky," I replied. "I am standing still. I eagerly await your explanation as to why."

"So I can lift you down into the boat, of course," he said. Perhaps I was becoming accustomed to the timbre and cadence of his voice, but I could *hear* the smile within it. He was enjoying himself.

"I can get down myself," I protested.

"No," he countered at once. "It's too far for you to step, as I did, and it's not safe for you to jump. If you want to go out on the lake, you have to let me help you down. That's *my* bargain, Belle."

Don't call me that, I almost snapped. Instead I bit down, hard, on the tip of my tongue.

"I'm standing still," I said.

He reached out, grasped me tightly around the waist, and lifted me up. His hands were so large they almost spanned my waist. My stomach made a strange little lurch. I put my hands on his shoulders to steady myself.

He is so strong, I thought. Strong enough to snap me in two without breaking a sweat. Strong enough to shelter me from whatever harm might come. I felt my arms begin to tremble, suddenly, as if it were I who carried some extra weight. The wind whisked by to snatch at my skirts, billowing them into a great cloud of dark blue fabric. I felt like I was flying.

The Beast lifted me up, high above his head. I threw my own head back and laughed at the unexpected glory of it. The stars were just beginning to spangle in the sky overhead. From the unseen far shore of the lake, I heard a night bird call.

The Beast made a half turn, the boat rocking a little under his feet. I put my arms around his neck and held on tighter.

He stopped, the boat steadied, and he set me down, sliding me along the length of his body. Just for a moment, my face brushed against his. I heard him pull in a sudden breath even as I made a sound of wonder. For there was something unexpected here, a thing my senses were trying to tell me but my mind refused to grasp. Then my feet were in the boat. He took a half step back, grasping my forearms to keep me steady as the boat rocked once again. As soon as the motion stopped, he let me go.

Heart roaring in my ears, I sank down onto the wooden seat in the bow. Without a word, the Beast took his place in the stern and unshipped the oars. Then he cast off, using the end of one oar to push us away from the pier. He rowed steadily and quietly for several minutes. I sat, and waited for my heart to steady, watching the stars come out.

"It's very beautiful," I said finally.

"Indeed, it is. It will be even more lovely when the moon is up." He continued to row, the motion smooth and steady. "You asked me a question earlier."

"I asked several questions earlier."

"True enough. This one was of a . . . numeric nature. You wanted to know why I ask you to look into my eyes for the space of time it takes to count to five."

"Only if you feel like telling me," I said quickly.

"It's not so very complicated," the Beast replied. "Five for five heartbeats, the length of time it takes to breathe in or out. For that is how quickly a life may change, for better or for ill. The time it takes to make up, or change, your mind."

"That's it?" I cried. "No story of enchantment, of brother against brother or son against father?"

Then I dropped my head down into my hands when I realized what I'd done.

"There is some of that, as well," the Beast said mildly. "But that tale has not been spoken in many years, and then only in daylight. It is . . . not a tale for the dark." There was a pause, during which he began to row once more. "I believe you owe me several answers, Annabelle."

"Yes, yes," I said. "All right. I know." I lifted my head, straightened my shoulders, and lifted my chin. "I'm ready."

"You might," he observed in a mild voice, "try to sound a little less as if you were about to face a firing squad. You said you came here of your own free will. Did you mean it?"

"Within reason," I replied. "One of us had to come, either Papa or I. I couldn't let it be Papa. Losing him would devastate my mother, I think, but more than that . . ."

I broke off.

"More than that?" the Beast prompted.

"You want to know what lies within the Heartwood," I said. "To see the face of true love. Papa cannot show you that. Only I can."

"Then why haven't you?" he asked, his voice very, very quiet.

"I honestly don't know. It's never been this difficult before. Usually, all I have to do is hold a piece of wood in my hands to see what it holds inside it.

"But with the Heartwood, it's almost as if I'm not looking in the right place, as if there's some extra angle I'm supposed to consider, some additional question I'm supposed to ask.

"I'd like to find the answer just as much as you want me to," I said. "It's the only way I can go home."

The wood of the oars scraped softly against their metal locks as the Beast slid the oars forward, then pulled back, slowly.

"You find it so unpleasant here, then?" he asked.

I shook my head. "No. It isn't that. It's very beautiful here, and I think that you . . ." I paused for a moment, to be certain of what I wanted to say. "You are doing your best to take my mind off the fact that I can't go home. You have been very kind. But this isn't my home. You must see that."

"I see it very well."

"What do you see when you look at me?" I suddenly asked.

The Beast lifted his head. I could feel his eyes on me in the gathering dark. *Just do it, Belle,* I thought. *Look up. How hard can it be to look into his eyes?*

But in spite of my mind's questioning, my eyes would not obey. It was like the Heartwood, only worse. For I wasn't altogether certain I wanted to discover the secrets of the Beast's face.

"Bits and pieces," the Beast said at last. "Tonight, for instance, I can see that you have on a blue velvet dress. I already know that your hair is brown and that it curls, and that the top of your head reaches no higher than the center of my chest.

"But your face defeats me utterly. I cannot see your features, the shape of your lips, the color of your eyes. Although I think ..." He broke off and leaned forward as if to examine something. "That you have a dimple in your chin."

"I do," I acknowledged, not quite sure how I felt that he'd discovered this. He'd seen me more clearly than anyone had in years. "My eyes are—," I began.

"No!" he interrupted swiftly. "Don't tell me. It's important I discover this for myself, with my own eyes."

There was a charged silence. *Here it comes,* I thought.

"Please don't ask me," I said. "Just this once. Just for tonight."

He leaned back then, and I could almost hear the effort that it cost him to do as I asked.

"Look into the water, Annabelle," he said at last. "You can see the stars."

So grateful I thought I might weep, I turned, rested my hands on the gunwale, and gazed down. For several moments, all I saw was the sheen of the water, gleaming like a black pearl. Then, quite suddenly, I could see the stars, as if the universe had flipped upside down, and the heavens blazed up from below the surface of the lake, rather than shining down from above.

Between one breath and the next, I thought. *That's how little time it takes to change perspective. The time it takes to count to five.*

"The waters of this lake can show many things," the Beast said quietly. "If you gaze into the water and wish hard enough, you may be offered a glimpse of what you wish for most."

"Can it show me my family?" I asked, gripping the gunwale tightly. *If I could just see them,* I thought. *Perhaps I would be less homesick. Perhaps I would find it easier to see what the Heartwood held inside.* "Can it show me my sisters, Papa, and Maman?"

"If that is what you truly wish for," the Beast replied.

I leaned out over the water, wishing with all my heart. As if in answer, the surface rippled. The stars seemed to blend together until the lake became filled with a hot, white light.

But I did not see my family. Instead, as if in a mirror, I saw two figures, a young man and a young woman, seated in a row-boat.

She was wearing a dark blue dress. He was clad in russet-colored velvet. As I watched, he leaned forward and held out a hand. She reached back. Their fingers touched. He carried her hand to his lips and pressed a kiss inside her palm.

No! I thought.

For I knew this couple. I had seen them on the gate, on the front door of the great stone house. Their images, their spirits, seemed to be everywhere on the Beast's lands. Until this moment, I had always assumed they were a couple from the past. A rendition of the young husband and wife buried beneath the Heartwood Tree.

But now, gazing down into the lake, I saw the truth in one great, blinding flash. This couple was the future of this place. Its salvation, not its past. What I had seen was still to come. All of a sudden, I was on my feet, heedless to the boat's rocking.

"Belle!" the Beast said sharply. "Sit down."

"Why did it show me that?" I gasped out. "That wasn't what I asked for."

"It must have been, at least in part. For the water shows only what the heart wishes, and when it does this, it cannot lie. That is the heart's true strength, the way it keeps us alive."

"But I don't want those images to be there. That isn't what I want!" I cried.

I tried to back away from him.

"Belle," he said again, urgently. "You must stop moving. You will overturn us both."

He reached up to steady me, but I jerked away from his outstretched hand and tumbled over the side.

The water closed over my head—cold, so very cold. I kicked my legs, desperately trying to get back to the surface, but my long skirts pulled me down and down. I opened my mouth, as if to scream in anguish and fear, and felt the cold kiss of the water against my tongue.

I am going to die, I thought.

But, suddenly, the Beast was there, his strong fingers closing over the hand I'd snatched away from him just moments before. He gave a great yank and my body shot upward. I was flying through the water now. The lights of the stars seemed to shimmer all around me. Then the world went black and I saw nothing more.

When I knew myself again I was lying sideways, cradled in a pair of impossibly strong arms. From a great distance, a voice was speaking—calling my name, begging me to answer, and cursing me, all at once. I pulled one aching breath into my lungs, gave way to a great bout of coughing, then tried again.

"Stop shouting," I managed to croak. "You're hurting my eardrums."

He made a sound then, the most human I'd ever heard him utter save for speech itself, something caught between laughter and a sob.

"For the love of God, what were you thinking, Annabelle?"

"It's no use scolding me," I said.

My stomach was full of jitters and my head felt light. I

wanted to lean my head against his shoulder and leave it there forever; I wanted to claw my way out of his arms.

"I'm sorry about the dress," I said.

He stopped walking. "I don't care about the dress and you know it." He gave me a shake, as if to rattle some sense into me. "Look at me. *Look at me, Annabelle.*"

"I can't!" I cried. "I don't know how. Stop acting like a Beast. Stop asking me to try."

He set me down, releasing me so abruptly the soles of my feet sang with pain as they hit the cobblestones. We were back at the house, in the courtyard. I had no idea we'd come so far, that he'd held me so long in his arms.

"Find what the Heartwood holds soon," he said.

Then he was gone.

Twenty-One

I SLEPT BADLY, MY DREAMS FULL OF WATER, AND AWOKE TO a sky filled with dark and glowering clouds. The air was as thick as damp cotton. I threw back the covers and got out of bed, leaving the bedclothes in a snarl. The change in the weather made me angry somehow, as if it, too, conveyed the Beast's displeasure, and kept me confined indoors.

We'll just see about that, I thought. Ignoring the wardrobe with its selection of fine dresses, I put on my plain homespun once more. Then I set out for the stables in search of Corbeau. I might not be able to do anything about the weather, but I definitely wasn't going to let it, or anything else, boss me around.

Fortunately for the success of my rebellion, Corbeau was in

his stall. This wasn't always the case. Sometimes the horse simply roamed free, other times the Beast rode him himself. Corbeau swiveled his head around as I came into the stall.

"Good morning," I crooned, running my fingers through his mane. "You'd like to go for a run, wouldn't you? You don't want to stay indoors any more than I do, do you, Corbeau?"

The horse whooshed out a breath, whether in agreement or disparagement of my proposed plan of action, I couldn't tell. But he made no objection as I saddled him and led him into the courtyard. I walked over to a stone planter flanking the steps to the house, clambered up it, and mounted Corbeau. As I settled into the saddle, he pranced a little, reaching out with his neck to feel the bit between his teeth.

"Take me somewhere, Corbeau," I commanded. "I don't care where, so long as it's away from here. Now run. *Run!*"

He shot from the courtyard like a bullet, heading for the orchard. Up and down the rolling land between the hills we went, as if running an obstacle course, then through a great meadow that lay beyond. The horse's coat grew shiny with sweat. My hair tumbled loose around my shoulders, curling in every direction as if each strand had a mind of its own. But no matter how far Corbeau and I ran together, I could not outrun the fact that I was trapped. I could no longer see the loveliness of the land all around me. All I saw were prison bars.

At last even Corbeau's strong legs grew tired, and his pace slowed. We settled into a walk, traveling aimlessly. Movement was all that was important. For once I stopped, I would be admitting the truth, admitting defeat: There was nowhere for me to go.

When I saw a pair of iron gates up ahead, I realized we had come to a place I recognized. It was the entrance to the Beast's lands, the same gate I'd passed through I had no idea how many days ago now.

I brought Corbeau to a halt, tossed my leg over his head and slid down. I caressed the black velvet of his nose. Ten steps took me to the gate. It was shut fast, the couple's hands clasped together tightly.

I moved forward until I stood before the image of the woman. *Let go,* I thought. *Let go of his hand and let me out.*

I felt a sob rise up, straight from my heart.

"Let me go," I said. I slammed my fist against the gate, felt the iron bite into my skin. "Let me go. Let me out."

Over and over I cried out my request, beating against the gate until my hands were bloody and raw. And still, the woman and her love clasped hands, pledging their devotion and my imprisonment both. Until at last, I sank to my knees, cradling my torn hands in my lap. Corbeau walked over to nuzzle the top of my head.

"Ah, Belle," I heard the Beast say behind me, so gently that it made me want to weep. "What have you done?"

"Go away," I said, without turning around. "I don't want to talk to you. I don't want to try, and fail, to gaze into your eyes. I don't need to be reminded that I can't see what's hidden in the

Heartwood, that I'm failing at the only thing I ever did well.

"I don't want to be here. I never wanted to be here. I want to go home."

A great stillness filled the air, as if the very land around me held its breath.

"Is that truly what you wish?" the Beast asked.

I did begin to weep then, great scalding tears, as the sob that rose from my heart threatened to split it open wide.

"Yes," I choked out. "I can't do what you need me to. I can't do anything right. I don't know why you even want to keep me here."

"Do you not?" the Beast asked quietly.

But by now I was weeping too hard to speak.

"Very well, then, Annabelle Evangeline Delaurier," he said. "I will not hold you here against your will. I will let you go."

I staggered to my feet. "Wait," I said, frantically wiping tears from my face with the backs of my hands. "Don't go like that, I . . . I don't understand why you're doing this. I haven't done anything you wanted."

"You came in the first place," he said. "Apparently, that must be enough. You should take Corbeau. He will speed your journey. If you hurry, you can be home by lunchtime."

"But you—what will happen to you?" I asked.

The Beast spun around so suddenly I faltered back a step, crashing against the gates. With a scream like an animal caught in a trap, they began to swing apart.

BELLE

"I am finished answering your questions," he snarled. Never had he seemed more like a Beast than he did at this moment. "You asked to go; I have given you leave. I suggest you depart, before I change my mind."

He gave Corbeau a slap on the rump. The horse gave a cry, echoing that of the gate, and bolted forward. I stumbled after him. As I passed through the gate, I saw it had changed. It was broken, rusted. The couple's hands, once so tightly bound together, were shattered at the wrists. No longer would they be able to cling together. They were torn apart forever.

And it was only then that I realized I had left behind the branch of the Heartwood.

Twenty-Two

JUST AS THE BEAST PROMISED, I WAS HOME BY LUNCHTIME. Corbeau had halted not far from the gate. I hauled myself up onto his back, which took some doing as there was nothing to help me mount and my hands were raw. There was no chit-chat between me and the horse as we traveled this time. Before, Corbeau's gait had seemed even and smooth. Now it seemed likely to shake me apart, finding every loose stone or rut.

"I'm sorry," I finally said. "I'm sorry. I didn't mean to hurt him. I didn't know I could. I just wanted to see my family. Why is that so much to ask?"

Corbeau shook his head, as if to drive the sound of my voice from his ears, and kept walking. It didn't take long to leave the Wood behind. We reached the turnoff to the house, my house, just as the sun reached the top of the sky. I reined Corbeau to a halt for a moment, gazing at the place I'd come to think of as home.

The roses I had planted before I'd left had new green leaves. At the side of the house, I could see that April had hung a load of washing out to dry. As I watched, a figure appeared in the kitchen doorway, then came down the steps.

Papa! I thought.

I urged the horse forward then, banging my heels against his sides until at last he gave in and took me where I wanted to go. I saw my father lift a hand to shade his eyes, heard him give a great shout. And then I was in the yard with my family all around me.

I had done it. I was home.

"I still can't believe that Beast let you leave," Maman said several days later, for what felt like at least the millionth time.

I was putting away the clean dinner dishes. April and Dominic had gone for a walk. Celeste was visiting Corbeau in the stables to see if she could interest him in a carrot. The two had taken an unmistakable shine to each other. Papa was working on a project in his workshop. He'd spent more time in the workshop than he had in the house since I went away, according to Maman.

The days following my return had brought the color back

into my father's face, the straightness to his shoulders, though it had not quite erased the worry in his eyes. As for my mother, she had stayed by my side almost constantly, as if I might disappear or set off again if she didn't keep me in sight at all times.

By mutual, and silent, consent, once the general exclamation over my unexpected reappearance had died down, no one questioned me much about what my life had been like during the time that I was gone. It was as if we all wished to simply savor being together again. The explanations could wait, and they would come. Not that I had very satisfactory ones to give. For now, it was enough just to be at home.

"And I can't understand *why* he did it," my mother went on. "Why force you to come, then let you go before you'd accomplished what he wanted?"

I'm not so sure I understand, myself, I thought. Aloud, I gave the only explanation I had.

"He let me go because I asked him to, Maman."

My mother exhaled a quick breath through her nose. "Then you should have asked him to do it earlier," she said. "You would have saved us all a lot of worry, especially your Papa."

"I did," I said, suddenly remembering this. "It was almost the first thing I did ask for, in fact. He said no."

"Then why did he say yes the second time you asked?" my mother said.

"I don't know, Maman," I answered.

I don't know.

*   *   *

Grand-père Alphonse came to find me not long after. He had ridden from town just that morning to bring the news that the last of my father's ships had come safely to port. We were rich again. We could return to our old lives at any time we chose, if that was what we wanted.

Surprising as this news was, there was more to follow, for neither my mother nor my sisters, once so fashionable, seemed at all eager to get back to town. April and Dominic were planning to be married before he went back to sea in a ceremony that would take place beside the vegetable garden. They didn't seem the least bit interested in trading a simple country wedding for a fancier one in town.

We learned to be happy here, to be a true family, I thought. And happiness, once found, is hard to give up.

"Come take a walk with me, Belle," Grand-père Alphonse suggested as I finished the last of the washing-up chores. "We have a few moments of real daylight left before the sun goes down."

Twilight, I thought. I turned to my mother. "Would you like to come with us, Maman?"

"No, no, you go ahead," my mother said with a wave of her hand. "I have some sewing I want to do." My mother was embroidering the bodice of April's wedding dress.

Grand-père Alphonse and I went outdoors together, turning our footsteps toward the stream that ran behind the house.

"I have been watching you all day, Belle," Grand-père Alphonse observed after several minutes had gone by. "You are very quiet, and it seems to me that you are not quite yourself. Are you unhappy?"

"I shouldn't be," I said at once, as much to myself as to him, I think. "I got everything I wanted, didn't I?"

"I don't know. Did you?" asked Grand-père Alphonse.

"Of course I did," I replied. "I got to come home. The Beast let me go before he had to. I'm still not sure I understand why."

"Is that so?"

"Stop playing twenty questions with me, Grand-père Alphonse," I snapped. I stopped walking and gave a strangled laugh. "Oh, for heaven's sake. Now I sound just like him."

In the time I had been gone, Papa had built a bench to sit beside the stream. Grand-père Alphonse led me to it and we sat down.

"Tell me what distresses you so, *ma Belle*."

"I couldn't read the Heartwood, Grand-père Alphonse," I said. "I couldn't see its face, no matter how hard I tried. I failed him, and I'm so afraid . . ."

I broke off, battling a sudden impulse to weep.

"I'm so afraid I've failed us both somehow." I dashed a hand across one cheek, as the tears won the day and began to fall anyhow. I really *was* upset, much more than I had realized. "I hate to cry."

"I know you do," Grand-père Alphonse observed with a

gentle smile. He dug in his pants pocket and produced a hand-kerchief. "You always did, even as a child. Tell me more. What about him?"

"He's a Beast," I said, and blew my nose loudly. "What else is there to know?"

"There must be something, I think," Grand-père Alphonse said. "Or you would not be twisting my second-best handker-chief up into knots."

"He confuses me," I burst out. "He makes me confuse myself. One minute, he's asking for the impossible and all I want to do is run away. The next, all I want to do is give him what he wants."

"But surely you should only do that if it's what you want as well."

"I don't know what I want!" I wailed. "Can't you see that's the problem?"

Grand-père Alphonse opened his arms and enfolded me inside them. I wept as though the end of the world had come. He held me quietly until the storm had passed.

"I've ruined your shirt," I said after many moments.

"I doubt that," Grand-père Alphonse said mildly. "And even if you have, I have others." He ran a hand over my head, the way he did when I was a child. "May I tell you what I think, Belle?"

"I wish you would," I said.

"I think you do know what you want. The problem is you don't want to admit it."

CAMERON DOKEY

I gave another sob, but I sat up. "I can't admit it," I said. "It's admitting the impossible. I'm not sure how long the Beast—I don't have anything else to call him but that—and I have actually known each other. I'm not even sure I like him. So how can it be that now that I'm away from him I find . . ."

I paused and pulled in one shaking breath. "How can it be that I love him? I don't even know when it happened. I wasn't even sure it had."

"It doesn't take very long," Grand-père Alphonse said. "As little as between one heartbeat and the next. Love is many things, *ma Belle*. And the face it wears is not always what we expect. That's one of the things that makes it wonderful."

"I've never seen his face," I said. "He's never seen mine. That's part of the problem."

"You think so?" Grand-père Alphonse asked. "I grant you seeing his face may be necessary to free him. Both you and your father have told us so. But it seems to me that a face is not required for the rest. For what love truly is, where it truly resides, is in a place that none of us can see."

"The heart," I whispered.

"Just so," said Grand-père Alphonse.

So I had seen a true vision in the lake that night, I thought. For I had wished to see what I loved most. And the lake had shown me the Beast and me together. But my eyes had not understood the image my heart rendered at my own request, for I had not yet learned to look with the eyes of love, the eyes of the heart.

196

I lifted my right hand and turned it over to gaze down into the palm, at the place where the young man in the vision had pressed his lips. I felt a fine tingling begin there, spreading out toward my fingertips, up my arm. It was the same sensation I experienced when a piece of wood began to share its secrets. The sensation the Heartwood had denied me for what felt like days without end, save for one moment only. The one in which the Beast and I had held it together.

"Oh, of course," I said aloud.

"Belle?" Grand-père Alphonse said.

"The Heartwood," I replied. "I tried so hard to see what it held within it, to find the face of true love. And all the time, I was going about it the wrong way. Looking for the wrong thing.

"It took two," I said. "Two different people to make the Heartwood what it is. Two different experiences, grief and joy, combined. True love never has just one face, does it? It must always have two, or it isn't true love at all.

"That's why I couldn't see anything, no matter how hard I looked. I was only looking for one thing, one face. I forgot that, to find true love, you must look with love's eyes."

"I think," Grand-père Alphonse said, "that you have grown very wise all of a sudden, *ma petite Belle*. What will you do with such wisdom, I wonder?"

"Go back," I answered at once. "He let me go because he loved me. I see that now. He gave me what I wanted most. He let me leave him. Now I have to go back and finish what I started. But first I must talk to Papa."

I stood up and started for the barn.

"You are sure, Belle?" my father asked a short time later. Following my startling pronouncement in his workshop, Papa had insisted we all go back to the house. Despite my sense of urgency, I had agreed. I had left my family once without saying good-bye. I would not do so a second time.

"As sure as I can be, Papa," I replied. "I think I understand"— I cast a quick look in Grand-père Alphonse's direction—"that I *see* the truth now. I understand why I could not read the Heartwood before."

"But you think you can now," my father said.

"Yes," I answered, just as I had in his workshop. "I do think so." I looked around, at my family's shocked and sober faces. "I can't leave this unfinished. It isn't right. But even more, going back is what is in my own heart."

"Well, then," my father said into the startled silence that greeted these words. "I think that you must follow your heart and go."

"Roger, how can you say such a thing?" my mother exclaimed. "How can you let her go into danger a second time?"

"I'm not so sure she's going into danger," my father said, his eyes on mine. There was not a trace of worry in them now. As if learning what I held in my heart had freed the pain he'd carried in his the whole time I'd been gone. "Perhaps she never was."

My father shifted his gaze to April, sitting at Dominic's side.

"I remember how April looked," he went on quietly, "when we did not know whether or not Dominic was coming home. Perhaps the greater danger lies in not finishing what is started, in carrying unanswerable questions all the days of our lives. And I think, finally, that I will put my trust in my daughter ahead of my own fear. I will put my trust in her strong heart."

"But he is a *Beast*," Maman protested, though I think even she knew that she had lost the argument.

"And Dominic was once a thief," April spoke up. "Not everyone ends the same as they begin, Maman. Papa is right. Belle's heart is strong. Give it the chance to find its own way. Let her go."

"Oh, very well, since I see I am outnumbered," my mother said waspishly, but I saw the sheen of tears in her eyes.

"Thank you," I said as I went to kiss her. I turned to face the rest of my family. "Thank you all."

And so I set out to find the heart of the Wood through no other enchantment than the strength of my will, with a power no greater than that which I carried in my heart.

I never would have made it, but for Corbeau. For it seemed to me that the Wood did not welcome me back. I had injured one it claimed as its own. The path turned and twisted where once it had run straight. Unexpected branches kept sweeping

CAMERON DOKEY

across it, as if to knock me from the back of the horse. A cold, sharp wind blew straight into my face, although it was early summer.

But Corbeau never faltered. I laced my fingers through his mane, closed my eyes, and held on tight. And so, throughout that long, cold night, I searched for the home of my beloved not with the eyes of the mind, but of the heart.

We came to the iron gates just at dawn.

The young woman still stood, one broken hand outstretched, but the right-hand side, the one with the image of the young man, had completely tumbled down. It lay in pieces on the ground. At the sight of it, a terrible fear seized my heart.

"Fly," I urged the horse. "Fly, Corbeau. Take me to him. Don't let me be too late."

Through the ruined gates and along the avenue, we flew, clattering up the hill and into the courtyard.

"I'm here. I've come back. Where are you?" I shouted. And it seemed my heart would break that I had never asked him for his name. I, who had been so very concerned about my own. But I would not call out for him, naming him a Beast.

I found him in the study.

He was sitting in a wingback chair, drawn up before the fireplace, the same one in which my father had fallen asleep, once upon a time. His long legs were stretched out before him. His head was thrown back. His eyes were closed. For one horrible, endless second, it seemed he did not breathe. Then I saw that he had the branch of the Heartwood clasped to his chest. In horror, I saw that the petals had begun to turn a color not a single one had ever been before: brown.

Oh, my love, I thought. *I came so close, so very close to losing you. To not seeing us both in time.*

I knelt down beside him, placed my hand on top of his hand where it clasped the Heartwood. The other I placed against his face, the one I'd tried so hard not to see for so very long.

"I want you to look at me," I said, willing it with all my might, with all my heart. "Open your eyes, and look into mine. I know you can hear me. I know you can do this.

"Please," I said. "Don't leave me, now that I've found you at last. Don't leave me to love alone."

I saw his eyelids flutter then. The power of the Heartwood sang up my arm. I felt his chest rise, as he pulled a single breath.

He opened his eyes, and looked straight into mine.

"One," I said, and watched his eyes widen.

"Two." His other hand came up, and covered mine.

"Three." The petals of the Heartwood flushed, as if they were a young girl blushing.

"Four." And now I could hardly see, for the tears that filled my eyes.

"Five."

There was a sound like a clap of thunder, the wings of wild birds, a single voice singing its favorite song on a clear, bright morning. The great stone house seemed to shake on its foundation. My gaze never faltered. I kept it steady on his, and realized that, at long last, I was seeing myself truly, reflected back through the eyes of true love.

I looked at him and saw a handsome young man with eyes of green and hair the color of copper.

"Tell me your name, if you please," I said. And, for the very first time, I saw him smile.

"Gaspard."

He sat up, then drew me into his lap, and pressed his lips to mine. I felt my heart beat, five deep strokes, and I knew that it was given to him for all time. Then Gaspard drew back and gazed into my face once more.

"I can see your eyes," he said, and his voice sounded just the same as it always had, heart and mind combined. And in it I heard more joy than I had ever believed possible.

"Your eyes are brown, Annabelle."

"Indeed they are," I said, as my heart began the melody it would sing until the day it ceased to beat.

"And my name is Belle."

Twenty-Three

OUR STORY HAS A HAPPY ENDING, BUT THEN YOU'VE probably known that all along.

I gave Gaspard the Heartwood as a wedding present, for it finally revealed the secret it had guarded for so long. The face of true love, which is, of course, not one face at all but two, for true love cannot happen on its own. This was what I'd been missing, the piece of the puzzle you'd think would jump right out, but is, instead, the last one you find.

True love always takes two, for it is about another more than you yourself.

The two of us were married not long after April and Dominic. Like them, we clasped hands and said our vows standing beside the vegetable garden. There wasn't time to make me a dress as fine as April's. But Maman gave me her favorite silk shawl. April wove a wreath of roses for my hair. Celeste baked a cake so tall it almost failed to come out of the oven door. I walked toward my true love with my father on one side of me and Grand-père Alphonse on the other. And so, surrounded by all I loved, we spoke our vows.

Afterward, Gaspard and Dominic carried the kitchen trestle table out of doors, and, beside the stream that ran behind the house, we ate the wedding feast Celeste had prepared. And it was here that Gaspard presented to me the only wedding gift that I had asked for: his story.

"I'd like to be able to tell you that I was once someone important," he began. "A king or a prince, perhaps. But I was not, though my family was a noble one. We lived in the town by the sea, the same town you came from, sir," he said, turning to my father.

When I had first brought Gaspard home, he had immediately gone down on one knee before my father. There he'd asked both his forgiveness for the way he'd behaved in the Wood, and Papa's permission to marry his daughter. My father had given both.

"All my life, I had heard tales of the Wood," Gaspard went on. "Tales of its enchantment, tales of its power, which was said to be that of life itself. It was for these reasons that we did no hunting there, in spite of the game that was abundant. It was said that your eyes could deceive you within the boundaries of the Wood, for only those whose own hearts were true could see what lived there in their own true forms.

"And if you did not see truly yet took what the Wood did not wish to give, then its power would exact a terrible price."

"No one hunts there even today," my father said. "Though the reason you give has been lost over the years."

"How long were you in the Wood?" Dominic asked quietly.

"I'm not certain," Gaspard replied. "A very long time, I think. So long a time I knew no way to count it."

"But why?" I asked.

He gave my hand a squeeze. "As punishment. For, in the arrogance of youth, I decided that the rules need not apply to me. This, in spite of the fact that my heart was far from true, for obviously it was filled with my own desires alone. One day, I shot and killed a doe. I did not know—I did not see—that she had a fawn. The grief of the child for its mother was piteous to see. Even I came to regret what I had done.

"This was the only thing that saved me, in the end, I think. The reason the power of the Wood let me live instead of simply claiming my life as payment for the doe's. She rose up before me, and as she did, her form changed, and she became the loveliest young woman I had ever beheld. She gathered the fawn up into her arms.

"'See the grief your thoughtless act has caused?' she asked, the tears hot upon her cheeks. 'Since you behave no better than a beast, you may wear the form of one. Since you refuse to use your heart to see, your eyesight will be clouded. That which pains you will be easy to see. That which you desire most will be hidden from you.

"'And this is how you will remain until the day that one true heart, with eyes to match, finds the way to free you from this curse you now bring upon yourself.'"

"That's why you wanted to know what the Heartwood held," I said. "For no eyes see more truly than those of true love."

"As you have demonstrated," he said with a smile.

"As we *both* have demonstrated," I replied.

"Oh, for heaven's sake," Celeste exclaimed. "Between the two of you and April and Dominic, all this lovey-dovey carrying on is enough to turn my stomach."

By which you can see that not everything about us had changed. Celeste still had her sharp mind and equally sharp tongue. Today, however, she also had a twinkle in her eyes.

I laughed. "You only say that because you're the oldest," I replied. "You were supposed to get married first."

Celeste shook her head with a smile. "I am finished with the way things are supposed to be," she said. "And so, I think, we all are. No matter what the rest of you decide to do, I'm staying here. I like the country."

"But you can't stay on your own," I protested. Papa and Maman had already announced their intention to return to the city, at least for a while.

"She won't be alone," April said. "I'll stay with her, at least until Dominic comes back from sea."

"I was hoping you'd say that," Celeste said. "Without you, I'd have to do the dishes myself."

"But what about when he comes back?" I asked.

Celeste reached across the table to take my hand. "Do not worry about me, *ma petite Belle*. You and April found your way, and I am happy for you both. Now you must let me find mine. But you and Gaspard—what will you do?"

"We will go back to the great stone house in the Wood," I replied. "There is a story there—more than one, I think— which I would like to understand before we settle anywhere else. And there is the Heartwood, too."

"Come to us at Christmas, all of you," Gaspard proposed. "And we will make the house that was so long a place of loneliness one of joy."

And so, after many days together and of making preparations, those of us who would make the journey through the Wood were ready to go. April stayed behind with Celeste. Papa, Maman, along with Grand-père Alphonse, Gaspard, and I set out. The path through the Wood ran as straight as ever, save for the narrow, winding path that curved into its very heart. There was no way to miss it now.

Gaspard and I parted from my family, and rode to the great stone house in silence, with me seated before him on Corbeau. The iron gates stood open, as if welcoming us home. Every tree in the orchard was in bloom, though the days were shortening now. We left Corbeau in his stable. Then, hand in hand, we walked to where the Heartwood stood by the shore of the lake.

"Look," I said when I saw it. "Oh, look, Gaspard."

The blossoms of the Heartwood tree lay scattered on the ground. But in their place, its boughs were filled with fruit as ripe and golden as the sun. Slowly, almost reverently, I moved to lay a hand against the bark.

"Someday," I said softly, "this tree will die. But what it carried in its heart will never be extinguished. Its roots go too deep, the fruit it bears is too nourishing, and the promise carried on the scent of its blossoms travels too far.

"True love may not always be easy to see, but once it has been discovered it can never be lost."

"You are as honest at the end as you were at the beginning," my true love said.

And I put my arms around him and kissed him beneath the branches of the Heartwood Tree, feeling my heart ache at the pure joy.

SUNLIGHT AND SHADOW

For Amanda, who was there for the finish
For Lisa, who was there at the start
For Jodi, who was there
for everything in between and then some
And for Hilary, who gave me my first glimpse
of the Queen of the Night

A House Divided

COME CLOSE, AND I WILL TELL YOU A STORY.

Or, at the very least, I'll start one.

The story isn't mine alone, so I shouldn't be the only one to tell it. But, as I think it's only fair to say the whole thing started with my parents, it seems equally fair that I should be the one to get the storytelling ball rolling.

This is how the whole thing began, to the best of my knowledge.

In a time when the world was young, and the hows and whys of things you and I now take for granted were still being sorted out, Sarastro, Mage of the Day, wed Pamina, the Queen of the Night. And, in this way, the world was made complete, for light was joined to dark. For all time would they be bound together. Only the breaking of the world could tear them apart.

In other words, in the time in which my parents wed, there was no such thing as divorce.

I don't know how long they were married before I came along. How many days and nights went by. Of all the questions I asked as I grew, and I asked plenty, until I learned that questions didn't always equal answers, that particular question was one I never voiced. I think this is because I wasn't all that old before I figured out there was another way of asking the very same thing:

How long before all the trouble started?

Because trouble is precisely what I was.

Never mind that my appearance was inevitable, all but foreseen and foreordained before the cosmic ink on my parents' marriage certificate was dry. Sooner or later, I was bound to put in my appearance, and that meant that, sooner or later, a husband would have to be found for me. This caused friction between my parents while I was still an infant, drooling in my cradle.

I can tell what you're thinking:

That must have been uncomfortable.

Not drooling, a thing all infants do, but growing up knowing you are the primary source of tension between your parents, both of whom you would like very much to love. Since you've already been intelligent enough to come to this conclusion, I see no reason to deny it. Why begin my story with the telling of a falsehood?

You're absolutely right. It was.

Imagine you have ants crawling over your body, so many you can never quite brush them all off. No sooner do you relax, thinking, *I've finally done it this time!* than you feel a prickle and an itch in some body part you could have sworn you'd taken care of only moments before.

The sensation isn't horrible. Not exactly. It certainly isn't painful. These are only tiny black kitchen ants, not ants red with anger, ready at a moment's notice to sting and bite. The trouble is, the sensation never ends. Those ants are with you every single moment of your life. You never have an instant's peace, awake or asleep. For, when you lie down to rest, with no distractions, it sometimes feels as if the ants will smother you completely, flowing over your body like a great black tide.

That's what it feels like to live in a house divided.

Let me take a moment to describe it for you. I think it will help you to understand what I'm talking about. The house where I grew up, where my parents lived together, yet apart, is set into the top of a mountain, the tallest in any direction as far as the eye can see.

Actually, I suppose it would be more accurate to say that the house *is* the top of the mountain. Two great buttresses of stone and glass facing opposite directions, set back to back. Like a statue with its arms stretched open wide, each reaching for a prize unobtainable by the other.

My father's side of the house faced due east, the better

for him to catch the very first rays of the morning sun. My mother's side faced west, the better to keep an eye on the moon and the stars. And the mountain itself comprised the whole wide world, so that there was no part of creation in which my parents did not play some part. No place where creatures lived and breathed that did not know both light and dark.

This, of course, is just as it should be. It may even sound familiar. But I will say again that the world was a very different place when it was young. In that time, sunlight and shadow did not live in the world together in the same way that they do now. When the sun shone, its light bathed all the world. When it went down, darkness covered all.

And, as the years went by, people came to worship the one even as they came to fear the other. So that, even though my parents shared the world, they did not have an equal share of power, for the love of the world was most definitely lopsided. This had pretty much the effect you might expect. My parents first grew to resent, and then to distrust, and, finally, to fear one another.

They say that opposites attract. I've heard this. Haven't you? I don't know what you believe, but I think that it's true. The trouble is, between attraction and understanding there can be a very great distance. Too great for any one individual, no matter how strong and powerful, to cross on her or his own. It is a distance which must be crossed by both, together. How long this takes is not important. What matters is that the journey commence in the first place, that the parties involved move steadily toward one another until, at long last, each is safe in the other's outstretched arms.

As far as I can tell, my parents never even packed their bags, let alone set out. With the possible exception of me, they weren't all that interested in the things they might have in common. They were more interested in the things that kept them apart.

And so my mother never saw that the rising of the sun could be a thing of beauty. Never saw the way the color returns, first peering over the edge of the world, then tumbling over and over and over itself, like brightly dressed children turning somersaults.

And my father never took the time to see the beauty of the moonlight. Never noticed the way it caresses everything it touches with a sweet, white kiss, turning even the branches of dead trees into decoration as fine and lovely as mother-of-pearl inlay on an ebony box.

What he would have seen had he looked at me, I never knew, for he never saw me. Or, if he did, I never knew it. Due to an agreement made at my birth, the result of a cryptic and dire prophecy, I would not officially see my father until the day I turned sixteen. On that day, I would be considered of marriageable age and would move from my mother's side of the house to my father's, the better for him to select the proper husband for me.

Asking for my opinion about whom I might like to spend the rest of my life with was not, apparently, considered an acceptable option.

And so, though he was only half a house away, for all intents and purposes, I grew up without a father. Though I did catch glimpses of him from time to time. Unlike my mother, unlike either of my parents, for that matter, I was not confined to the dark or to the light. I could move freely in either.

As I grew older, I began to make it my business to discover as much about my father as I could without him knowing about it. In this way, I learned that he never laughed, that his hair was dark chestnut flecked with gold, and that, when the weather turned chill, he wore a cloak of this exact same color. But it is difficult to learn much about someone when you can't let them see you.

I did learn one other thing, however. And that was that there lived in my father's household a girl who was almost exactly my age. One he was raising as if she, not I, were his daughter. She was tall and graceful, where I was merely tall and often awkward, and dark, where I was fair. And her eyes were as green as holly boughs.

She was the daughter of his forester, my mother finally told me, though only after I had pestered her so often and for so many years I must have driven her almost out of her mind.

As a general rule, my mother refused to speak about my father. Her business was her business, and his was his. She could no more explain his actions than he hers. It did no good for me to ask *Who? What? Why?* and certainly not very often.

But, as my sixteenth birthday began to grow close, then closer still, my mother seemed to change her mind. The only conclusion I can draw is that it finally dawned on her that it would be in my best interest to have some understanding of my father's side of things, of which the dark-haired girl was clearly an important part. And so, she finally gave me the long-awaited, much-asked-for explanation.

She waited until almost the very last minute. She told me the night before my sixteenth birthday.

"Her name is Gayna," my mother said.

We were sitting in her observatory, my favorite room in our part of the house. The ceiling was all of glass and almost completely round, poking out from the side of the mountain like a great soap bubble. Sometimes, when I was younger and would awaken in the night, I would find my mother in this room, standing absolutely still with her eyes upon the stars, as if they held some message she had yet to decipher.

"Whose name?" I asked, a little sulkily.

We had both been on edge all day, knowing it might be our last together for who knew how long. My mother had arranged for dinner to be served in the observatory, a thing which was usually one of my favorite treats. Tonight, neither of us had eaten much.

"The girl you've pestered me about for time out of mind,"

my mother replied. "The one who's always with your father."

At this, I sat bolt upright, my food altogether forgotten.

"Why?"

"Why what?" my mother asked with just the hint of a smile. "Why is she called Gayna? Why is she always with your father? Or why am I telling you this now?"

"I don't care what she's called," I said boldly, though we both knew I did care, very much. "And I can figure out why you're telling me now. It's because I turn sixteen tomorrow."

"That leaves the middle one, then," said my mother. "She resides with your father because she is an orphan. Her mother died giving birth. Her father was gored by a wild boar when she was five. There being no one else to raise her, Sarastro took her in."

"So," I said after a moment. "He will raise a stranger's child but not his own."

"Gayna's father was not a stranger," my mother said. "He was your father's forester. This I have already told you."

"But *why?*" I burst out once more. "Why should he care for her and not for me? It isn't fair."

"No," said my mother. "Perhaps not. But it would be a mistake to think your father cares nothing for you, Mina. If anything, I fear he cares too much. Your marriage is the most important thing in the world to him. He sets great store by it."

At this, I could feel my understanding, to say nothing of my patience, stretch almost to the breaking point. This may seem somewhat precipitous to you. I'd ask you to remember I'd had fifteen long years filled with precious little information in which to try to figure all this out.

"My *marriage*," I echoed, and even I could hear the bitterness in my voice. "But not me, myself. How can he choose a husband for me when he doesn't even know who I am?"

"A just question," my mother agreed, her own voice calm. "And one I once posed myself. Now finish your dinner," she went on briskly as she rose from the table, and in this way, I knew the brief period of answering questions was over. "The hour grows late and I have work to do."

At her words, I felt a spurt of panic. *This may be the last night I hear her say this,* I thought. Tomorrow night, for all I knew, I would be having dinner with my father and the daughter of his forester in some great hall filled with smoking torches. Some place where I could be pretty certain they did not welcome the night.

"May I not come with you?" I blurted out.

A smile touched my mother's marble features. "Of course you may," she replied. "Eat something while I fetch you a cloak with a nice big hood. If you're coming with me, that unfortunate hair simply must be covered up."

With that, she turned and left the room. I ate my dinner as fast as I could, in a manner that wasn't at all ladylike.

I'll eat all my dinners this way from now on, I thought, suddenly inspired. *Then perhaps my father will be so appalled by my manners he'll give up on me entirely and send me back where I belong.*

This thought cheered me so much I took the biggest bite yet and dribbled gravy down my chin. Quickly I wiped it off. Who knew when I might spend time with my mother again? I didn't want to begin our last night together with a scolding.

"Hold still, now," my mother said as she returned with a cloak and a rosewood box full of hairpins. Black ones, of course. Swiftly she tucked and pinned every strand of my unfortunate bright hair up out of sight and tied a black scarf around it beneath the hood for good measure. Then, together, we went out into the night.

How shall I describe it to you? How shall I tell what it is like to move through the darkness with my mother at my side? She cannot be separated from the night, for she is its living embodiment. Her face, as pale as the moon when it is full. Her eyes, as silver as the stars. She has no need to bind up her hair, for it is as dark and lustrous as the sky at midnight. She is beautiful, my mother, and the great sadness of my childhood has always been that I look so little like her.

At least we have the same name, Pamina, though Mina is what I prefer, most often, to be called.

I don't mean that my mother rules the darkness. She doesn't, not precisely. She doesn't make it come and go, for instance. The universe does that all on its own. It's more that she is the guardian of the night, of the things that belong to it. She keeps them safe and in their proper place, just as my father does for the things that belong to the daylight hours.

We walked in silence for quite some time before I realized

where we were going: through the thickest part of the forest to where my father's favorite room looked out over his side of the top of the mountain. It was but a short journey, even on foot, a thing I always found surprising, showing, as I thought it did, that my parents were much closer than they cared to acknowledge. There, my mother stopped, her face turned up to where, almost at the mountain's top, a shaft of golden light stabbed out into the darkness.

"Do you see, Mina?" she said softly. "Do you see the way your father tries to impose his will? The way he will not accept, but seeks to defeat, the darkness?"

I did see, of course. But my mind, which even moments ago had spontaneously plotted ways to displease my father and so encourage him to return me to my mother, now leaped to his defense.

But what if he just wants to read a good book? What if he's come to the very best part and doesn't want to stop just because the daylight has gone? Must the lighting of a lamp always be considered a crime? Do we not pull the shades to keep out strong sunlight?

Of course I did not say these things aloud. Instead I said, "Why did you ever marry in the first place?" A question to which I'd wanted the answer for as long as I could remember.

"Because it was necessary. It is still necessary," my mother replied after a moment. "There are some things which must be in order for the world to exist, Mina. The marriage between your father and me is one."

I bit down, hard, upon my tongue to keep from asking just one thing more, the thing which I had always wished to know the very most. It didn't do any good. I asked the question anyway. I'm just made that way, I suppose.

"But did you never love each other?"

My mother was silent, gazing up at the light streaming out from my father's room. Silent for so long I became all but certain she wouldn't answer at all. Then, just as I was beginning to feel altogether wretched, she said:

"Yes, we loved each other. Once. It might even be the case that we still do. It's been so long since I've thought of such things that I no longer know. But I do know your father and I have never understood one another. And without understanding—"

My mother broke off, her eyes still fixed on the light.

"Love is like water, Mina," she continued after a moment. "Water, in all its forms. It can squeeze between your fingers like your own tears. Burn and freeze your heart at the selfsame time. It can evaporate before your very eyes in no more than an instant. Making a reservoir to hold your love is the most difficult task in all the world. You will never do it if you do not understand first yourself, and then your beloved.

"Have you heard the saying, *Still waters run deep*?"

"Of course I have," I said.

"But do you understand its meaning?" asked my mother. "It's the best way I know to describe abiding love. Remember that phrase when your father marches his parade of potential husbands before you. Look for the place within, the reservoir where love may reside until it fills to overflowing. Do not be dazzled by outside appearance, for that is merely what the sun does best: It shines."

"I will remember," I promised.

"Good," said my mother. Then she turned and laid her hand against my cheek. "Go inside now. Sleep, and have sweet dreams, my daughter. For tomorrow is a big day. You will be sixteen and I must take you to meet your father."

"Yes, but will you?" I asked, intending to tease, for my mother had never gone back on her word as far as I knew. Not to me, nor to any other. I knew that she would keep her part of the bargain made at my birth, no matter what it cost her.

She laughed, but the sound was without mirth.

"Now you sound just like your father. His greatest fear all these years has been that I'll change my mind at the very last minute, find some way to keep you all to myself."

"He doesn't know you very well, then," I remarked.

"On the contrary," a new voice said. "I know your mother very well."

With a cry, my mother spun around, thrusting me behind her. Not that it did any good. For, in the same instant, torches flared to life all around us. As if the very ground had opened up and spewed forth fire. And so, in the space of no more than a few heartbeats, we were surrounded by my father's soldiers.

I think my mother understood what he intended at once,

though I wasn't far behind her. There could be but one cause for this. My father intended to take me away before the appointed time.

"No," my mother said, a statement, not a plea. "Do not do a thing you may come to regret. This is not the way, Sarastro."

"It is the only way I can be sure," the voice said, a voice I now recognized as my father's. "And I've had almost sixteen years to think about it."

A figure stepped forward. In one hand, it carried the largest, brightest torch of all. So bright it made my eyes water and caused my mother to muffle her face inside her cloak. My first true sight of my father was thus obscured by tears, and I learned a lesson which I never forgot:

Darkness may cover light, but that is not the same as putting it out. Whereas, to overcome darkness, all light need do is to exist.

Yet, even beaten back, my mother was not cowed.

"This is not the way, Sarastro," she said again. "There is no need to do this, and the day may come when you will be sorry you have made this choice."

But my father simply laughed, the sound triumphant and harsh.

"Don't think you can threaten me with words, Pamina," he said. "It is simple. I have won, and you have lost. It was never much of a contest in the first place, really."

"It should never have been a contest at all."

"Enough!" my father cried. "I will not stand around in the dark and argue with you. Instead, I will simply take my daughter and go."

At this, I saw him give a signal, and I braced myself. I expected several soldiers to try and drag me from my mother's side. Instead a single man stepped forward. Even through the water in my eyes, I could tell he was the most handsome man that I had ever seen. Eyes the color of lapis lazuli. Hair that shimmered in the torchlight, almost as bright a gold as mine. He extended one hand toward me, as if inviting me to dance.

"Give me your hand and come with me," he said, "and I swear to you that your mother will not be harmed. Resist, and there is no telling what will happen."

And, in this way, I learned a second lesson I never forgot: Beauty may still hide a treacherous heart.

"What do you take me for?" I asked, and I did not hold back the scorn in my voice. "I will not give you my hand. For to do so is to give a pledge. This, I think both you and the Lord Sarastro know full well.

"I will not be tricked into pledging myself to a stranger. But I will come with you for my mother's sake, for I love her well and would not have her harmed."

"Strong words," my father said.

"And a strong mind to back them up," my mother replied. "I say again, you will regret this act, Sarastro. Thrice I have said it, and the third time pays for all."

"Step away from your mother, young Pamina," the Lord Sarastro said. "I will not ask again. Instead, I will compel."

And so, I stepped away, pulling my hood down over my face, for I had begun to weep in earnest and did not want to give my father and those who did his bidding the satisfaction of seeing me cry. The second I stepped away from my mother, I could feel the wind begin to rise. Tugging on my cloak with desperate, grasping fingers. Howling like a soul in hell.

Over the scream of the wind, I heard my father shouting orders in a furious voice. Then I was gripped by strong arms, lifted from my feet, and thrown like a sack of potatoes over someone's shoulder.

The last thing I saw was the flame of my father's torch, tossing like some wild thing caught in a trap.

The last thing I heard, dancing across the surface of the wind like the moon on water, was a high, sweet call of bells.

BIRD SONG

THE LADY MINA HAS GIVEN ME MY CUE, AND SO, JUST when you are wondering what happens next to her, I must doom you to disappointment, at least for a little while. For now it is time for me to enter and take up the story.

What cue, you are no doubt wondering?

She has called you intelligent. I know she has. Not only that, I know it pleased you. Don't bother to deny it. I know much more than I appear to, particularly if it has to do with Mina's story, for parts of it are also mine. Our tales are wrapped together, twisted around one another like point and counterpoint. Melody and harmony. But as for me, I'm not so sure how smart you are. How clever can you be if you failed to see my entrance coming?

She used the oldest trick in the book. The very last thing she said. How much easier did you want her to make it for you?

That's right. It's the bells that announce my entry into this story. I'm the one playing them, for they are mine. And who am I, you are no doubt wondering? I am Lapin, a name that means rabbit, though, fortunately, in a language not my own. There's a bit of irony for you. I couldn't care less about rabbits, unless they're in a stew.

It's the birds I care about.

See, this is where that great intelligence of yours is going to get you into trouble. You're trying to make sense of this, when it would really be so much better not to. Some things cannot be reasoned out, though they may be explained, a thing I will do shortly. In the meantime, you must do what I have learned to do: accept things as they come along without making too much of a fuss about them.

So just believe me when I say that I am called Lapin the bird catcher. Though, I prefer bird caller, if the truth were to be told. It's not precisely accurate to say that I *catch* birds. I don't set snares or traps. I don't lure them or capture them by force.

What I do is play my bells and the birds come to me. To wherever I am, from wherever they are. And once they have come, they never depart. This is how I came to know the Lady Mina.

But I'm getting ahead of myself.

I need to explain about the bells, and to do that, I must back up. The first member of my family to possess them was my grandmother. Though, as they never would have come to her had it not been for the actions of her own father, I suppose I must back up one step further to my great-grandfather. His name was Pierre-Auguste, and he was unlucky in love.

This is hardly an unusual circumstance. And, when it does occur, the disappointed party is generally considered to have two options. He can pull in his breath and expel it in a laugh, thereby ensuring that his heart will mend and his life will go on. Or he can pull in a breath and expel it in a sigh, a signal that his heart will remain broken for as long as it continues to function. It was this second path that my great-grandfather chose.

But Pierre-Auguste did not stop there. He cherished his heartbreak, nourishing it like a sick child, until, with time, both it and he became something else altogether. A thing like the rind of a grapefruit left out in the sun. Hard and bitter. Sour enough to cut your mouth on.

In spite of this, he married, hoping for sons to carry on his name. He got a daughter, and at that, only one. A thing which, as the years passed, caused my great-grandfather's bitterness to increase to such an extent that it completely slipped its bounds. One day, he struck a servant, over nothing more important than the breaking of a teacup. She fell, and in so doing, pierced her temple upon the sharp edge of a table. She was dead before she hit the floor. And now, at long last, the powers who watch over the universe decided enough was enough. It was time for them to get involved.

Yes, there are powers who do this. Watch over the workings of the universe, I mean. I've never met any of them in person, so I don't know what their names are. I'm not even certain that they *have* names. Not like you and I do, anyhow. The only thing I know for sure is that they don't interfere in the lives of mortals very often.

To see the entire universe at a single glance requires excellent vision. And so it was that the powers that watch over the universe saw something no one else would have noticed when they looked upon my great-grandfather. And this is what it was: that the break in the heart of Pierre-Auguste might provide an opening to mend a rift between two others. This is the real reason they decided to get involved.

And so they appeared before my great-grandfather, who was understandably startled, not to mention frightened. They coshed him on the head, thereby giving him pretty much the punishment he expected. But instead of striking him dead, they sent him a dream. A dream of what might have happened if, at the very moment he'd sucked in a breath at the pain of his own heartbreak, he had released it in a laugh instead of in a sigh.

All the things my great-grandfather had never known were in that dream, the life he had denied himself. He awoke with tears upon his cheeks, the first he had shed since he was a boy. And so it was that my great-grandfather came to experience the one kind of bitterness he had never known: the bitterness of remorse. And thus was he justly punished.

But this was not all. For my great-grandfather had done more than blight his own life. He had taken the life of another. And so the powers that watch over the universe now turned to his descendant, to my grandmother. And, through her, to those whose lives had not yet been dreamed of, let alone begun.

This means me, of course.

The powers that watch over the universe gave my grandmother, then a young woman, a set of bells. In number, twelve. Mounted on a board of mountain ash. To be struck with a hammer whose head was polished stone cut from the mountain at the heart of the world. And this is what they told her about them: If she could hear the melody of her own heart and sound it out upon the bells, she would call to her side her heart's true match. Its one true love.

Kind of sappy. Yes, I know. Also somewhat predictable. Great, nameless powers often make pronouncements of this sort, or so I'm told. Deceptively simple too. Hearing the melody of your own heart, then rendering it up, is not such an easy matter. You can trust me on this one. I know.

Not only that, but in the meantime, while you're practicing, there are many other creatures who may be listening, and the melody you play may be the one that calls to their heart, even though it doesn't match your own. A thing my grandmother discovered the day the grizzly bear showed up in the garden.

The first she knew about it was a great screech issuing from the house next door. My grandmother didn't pay much attention at first. The neighbors on that side were always making noise about something or other. It was the ominous silence that followed the screech that finally got her notice. That and the great, dark shadow that had suddenly come between her and the morning sun.

My grandmother looked up from the bench upon which she was sitting. There was a grizzly bear standing at the edge of her vegetable garden. As grizzly bears are primarily carnivorous, it seemed reasonably safe to assume it hadn't come to pick greens for a salad. In fact, being eaten right there and then was pretty much the only thing that came to my grandmother's mind.

In her astonishment and fear, my grandmother let drop the hammer with which she had been playing upon the bells. It struck the largest one on its way to the ground. At the sound it made, the bear made not a roar, but a soft, crooning sound. Its dark eyes gazed straight into my grandmother's, as if beseeching her for something.

Slowly, hardly daring to breathe, my grandmother bent and retrieved the hammer. Then, her hand shaking so much she feared the hammer would slip back out again, she began to play the bells once more.

As she did, the grizzly gave a great sigh of perfect contentment, turned around three times just like the family dog, curled up and went to sleep in the sun. Right on the bed of zucchini, which turned out to be a fine thing as my grandmother had, as always, planted too many of them anyhow.

And in this way did she come to understand that playing your heart's true melody upon even so beautiful an instrument was a thing much easier said than done.

She didn't give up trying, of course. Would you? I thought not. Soon the grizzly was joined by a brown bear, a sun bear, and a beaver suffering from an identity crisis of magnificent proportion. It was right about then that the neighbors began to murmur the word *witch,* and my grandmother and great-grandfather, who was now much nicer, began to contemplate leaving town.

Fortunately for them, the next living, breathing thing my grandmother's attempt to get her song right summoned was a carpenter. A young man as finely made as any house he hoped to build, who looked at my grandmother with dreams of castles in his eyes. She looked him up and down and thought it over. The melody she had played upon the bells that day was as close as she had ever come to getting her heart's true song right. All things considered, she decided it was close enough.

She and the carpenter were married. Together with my great-grandfather, they moved to a nearby hillside with a pond for the beaver and lots of land for the bears to roam. My grandmother raised grapes, my grandfather built a house, many, many arbors, and, eventually, my great-grandfather's coffin. My grandmother put the bells away until her children should be born.

And if, sometimes, in the dead of night, she heard her heart beating in ever so slightly a different rhythm than that of her sleeping husband, my grandmother simply pulled the pillow over her head. She had made her bed, or, actually, my grandfather had. But my grandmother was content to lie in it beside him.

Eventually, my grandmother bore a set of twins, a girl and a boy. The boy marched away to war at an early age, leaving his sister, the girl who would become my mother, behind. She was in no hurry to try the magic of the bells. Not until she was a young woman, until the music of her heart became too much for her body to contain, did she sit in one of her father's many arbors and attempted to sound it out.

She, too, ended up summoning animals, though not such alarming ones as her own mother. Her first attempt to play the bells summoned field mice from miles in every direction. They gathered around the bench on which she was sitting, noses twitching, and regarded her with round, dark eyes. There were so many of them, the family cat ran away that very afternoon.

Her second attempt brought squirrels with tails like bushy feather pens. The third, possums so homely they made her glad the animals themselves didn't see all that well. By this time, I'm sure you've gotten the general idea, and so had my mother, to her great dismay.

It seemed her specialty was to be rodents of all shapes, sizes, and kinds.

This fact upset her so deeply she married the first man who came along. He happened to be a baker, which was a good thing because, in her distress over what her playing called to her, my mother forgot to eat half the time.

My grandfather built them a house, not far from his own. The baker built a brick oven in the backyard and set about doing what he did best. Soon the townspeople were deciding to overlook their concerns that witchcraft might run in our family. Instead, they concentrated their attentions on my father's bread and my grandfather's wine. My mother put the bells away on the highest shelf that she could find, which happened to be in the bedroom closet. And there they stayed, all but forgotten, until the day I was born.

On that day, a momentous event occurred, and I don't mean just my own arrival. My mother was in one of those lulls which occur during labor, brief spells between one round of pain and the next. She lay still in her bed, panting just a little as the late afternoon sun was warm upon the bed, exhausted from working so hard.

She had just begun to feel the grip of the next contraction, when she forgot about the pain entirely. More rabbits than she had ever seen in one place together abruptly leaped in through the open window, and ran across the room and out the bedroom door.

Before my mother could so much as draw a breath to shout my father's name, they were followed by a group of foxes, and then a swarm of bees. That was the moment my mother realized the bed had begun to tremble and then to shake. Within instants, the whole bedroom had begun to sway from side to side.

My mother found her voice and shouted for my father in earnest. He arrived just as the closet door went crashing back and the set of bells hurtled to the floor. They struck the ground in such a way that all twelve bells sounded at the selfsame time. At which the trembling of the earth ceased, and my parents stared at one another in open-mouthed astonishment.

Oh, yes, and I was born.

When she had recovered sufficiently to tell my father of the events immediately preceding my birth, Papa, who was somewhat superstitious, decided that we had received a series of omens impossible to ignore.

And so I was given the name Lapin, after the rabbits who had been the first to understand that something momentous was about to occur, and the right to play the bells, not when I turned sixteen, but from the very day that I was born.

Three

LAPIN COMES TO THE POINT, FINALLY

YES, I KNOW. YOU SHOULD HOPE SO. FOR HEAVEN'S SAKE, just calm down. I do have a tendency to take the long way around, I admit it. But melodies and stories both can be like that. Besides, it's not as if I don't have my reasons for telling things the way I do. If you don't know where you've already been, how can you know which way to go?

I didn't start playing the bells right away. Not in any truly musical sense, anyhow. I did bang on them at a very young age, a circumstance which ended up with me and my playing being relegated to the great outdoors. Children were allowed a bit more freedom when I was young than they are nowadays. I didn't even have a nursemaid, but no one seemed to worry that I'd come to any harm.

I wasn't likely to be attacked or carried off, after all. I was making far too much noise.

I was five when I called my first bird down from the sky. It was a chickadee, a bird whose song is its own name. One moment I was sitting on one of the comfortable wooden benches my grandfather had made, trying to sound out an actual tune for the very first time. The next, there was a flurry of wings, and a small bird appeared by my side.

It had a sharp black beak, gray wings, and a white breast. It regarded me first with one expectant, inky eye and then the other, cocking its black-capped head from side to side.

I knew the legend of the bells by then, of course. My father had assured this by making them the subject of many a bedtime story. I played the melody again, at which point the chickadee threw back its head, opened its throat, and harmonized. And as it did, though I was only five, I understood that my future would be filled with the songs of birds. From that day to this, that moment is still the happiest of my life.

The week after that, I played a song that summoned a red-bellied woodpecker. After that came a bird with a white body and a dark hood pulled over its head, looking for all the world as if it was in disguise. This was a dark-eyed junco, or so my grandfather informed me. These were followed in succession by a green jay, and, close upon its tail feathers, a blue one. Small birds all, as befitted my overall size at the time.

Then came wrens, sparrows, and warblers of all shapes, colors, and varieties. An indigo bunting as blue as a cold autumn sky. An oriole as yellow as newly churned butter. A cardinal with feathers as red as the bright drops of my own blood that I saw the day I accidentally cut my finger on the sharpest of my father's bread knives.

Sometimes, I would play a song and nothing seemed to happen. Days would go by. Then, without warning, and generally when I was engaged in something altogether different, there would come the flutter of bird wings. The sound of the bells, or so it seemed, could travel as far as any bird could fly.

Before too long, my grandfather, getting on in years but still hale and hearty, set to work building bird feeders and bird houses. I began to play the bells at all hours of the day or night. For I had heard an old woman who'd come to buy bread say that not all birds like to sing in the bright light of day. There are some who prefer the soft shadows of the night.

And here, at last, my story is about to intersect with Mina's. For it was in calling down a night bird from the sky that I first came to the attention of the Queen of the Night.

I have already told you how the house my grandfather built for my grandmother came to be located on a hillside near the town where they'd both grown up, with my parents' house close beside it. But, as is often the case with hills, the one on which our houses resided did not stand alone. It was one of a series of many hills, all rolling together until, from their very center, a tall mountain shot straight up.

Among the many tales whispered about this mountain was that it was the first in all the world. The one, in fact, from which the world itself had sprung. And this was the reason, it was further whispered, that the mountain was the chosen dwelling place of Sarastro, Mage of the Day, and his consort, Pamina, the Queen of the Night.

Not that anyone had ever seen them, of course.

But it was spoken that, in the time when the world began, they had wed and chosen this mountain in which to dwell. Like all the local children, I was curious about these tales. But I never thought I'd discover the truth of them for myself.

I did so when I was eight years old.

On the night of my eighth birthday, in fact. In honor of the occasion, I had been allowed to stay up a little later than usual. As always, I had with me the set of bells. My parents had thrown me a wonderful celebration. My heart was full of joy. And so, after all the guests save my grandparents had departed, I did the thing I always did when my heart was full. I sat in the orchard with my family around me and attempted to play the music of my heart upon the bells.

I'm not sure I can describe the melody I played. It was born in my heart and, if it lingers, it is there alone, and not in my mind. But I do recall that, for a long time after I ceased playing, nothing happened, save that the sounds of the world around me grew silent and still, as if they, too, had listened to my song.

The silence stretched for so long that I had pretty much decided there was no bird song to answer it, or, if there was, it lived in a breast that was very far away from mine. I had just risen to my feet, the bells tucked beneath one arm, when I heard the sudden rush and sweep of wings. And then a voice so sweet and clear answered my music that I swear I felt my own heart skip a beat.

"Mercy upon us," I heard my mother whisper. "You've called down a nightingale. They do say that's the favorite bird of the Queen of the Night."

No sooner had my mother finished speaking than the nightingale swooped from the branch on which it had landed and alighted on my shoulder. From there, it refused to budge. Together with my family, I returned to the house and went to bed, the nightingale perched upon my headboard with its head tucked against its breast. It became a fixture in our household from that night on.

I never saw it during the day. But, for the next week, each day at precisely the moment the sun slipped over the horizon, the nightingale would appear with that same rush and sweep of wings, finding me no matter where I was. Though I cherished all the birds my playing summoned, I freely admit I harbored a special spot in my heart for this one.

One week to the day after my birthday, there came a night when the moon was no bigger than a crescent of cut fingernail floating in the sky. All day long, my mother was edgy, murmuring under her breath that it was on nights such as this that the powers of the Queen of the Night, whom she sometimes called *die Königin der Nacht*, were strongest.

More than that, on such dark nights it had long been whispered that die Königin der Nacht walked abroad. Many had felt her passing, though few had seen her. For only those to whom she wished to reveal herself had the power to see her in the dark.

And, sure enough, as soon as the sun slipped over the horizon in a riot of color, the Queen of the Night arrived.

Her coming made the hillside around my parents' house tremble as it had the day I was born, a thing that convinced my father that the events attending my birth had now come full circle. He only hoped we would all survive them.

How shall I describe her to you, die Königin der Nacht?

Even though I was only eight, my eyes were old enough to recognize her beauty, my heart steady enough to feel the beat of hers and know that it was filled with anger and sorrow in almost equal parts. Her dark hair streamed out from her head, so long and fine it seemed to mingle with the darkened sky. Beaten silver was the color of her eyes. They were filled with tears, and when she wept the tears slipped down her cheeks like a shower of stars.

In her arms, she held an infant. It, too, was crying.

"Selfish, foolish boy!" scolded the Queen of the Night.

"Where is the bird that you have stolen from me? Speak quickly, or I will put an end to your miserable life!"

It was at this moment that the first of several very astonishing things happened, as if what was happening already wasn't astonishing enough. My mother, the same mother who'd panicked at the sight of a group of field mice, stepped in front of me, standing toe-to-toe with die Königin der Nacht.

"How dare you!" she shouted. "Stop threatening my son right this instant! He didn't mean to take anything from you. He's a good boy. Besides . . ."

Here, my mother reached behind her back, hands flapping as if searching for something. Understanding immediately, my father rushed forward, snatched the set of bells from my hands, and thrust them into my mother's. Triumphantly my mother whipped them around, holding them out before the Queen of the Night.

"It was *these* that summoned your bird down from the sky. They have been in this family for three generations, given to us by the powers that watch over the universe. I'm thinking that means we're under their protection. You'd better watch out."

What the Queen of the Night might have replied to this very remarkable speech none of us, not even she, were ever to know. For, at that moment, as it did each evening, the nightingale shot down from the sky. It settled into its usual position on my left shoulder.

"You picked a fine night to be a little late," I whispered as softly as I could, and felt the soft prick of its beak against my cheek. The wailing of the infant picked up a notch.

"You see? You see?" cried die Königin der Nacht. She held up the child. At this, the next very astonishing thing happened.

"Oh, for goodness' sake," my mother snapped in her most exasperated voice. She turned to me, thrusting the bells back into my arms. "Hold these," she commanded. "They're yours, after all."

Then she turned, took two steps forward, and snatched the crying infant from the Queen of the Night's arms.

For the span of eight heartbeats, the same number of years that I had lived, nobody else did anything at all.

"There now, there now," my mother crooned to the infant as she rocked it gently, a thing that only seemed to make it wail all the louder. I saw die Königin der Nacht pull in a breath.

We are all about to die, I thought.

That was the moment the nightingale fluttered from my shoulder to my mother's, threw back its head, and began to sing a song so beautiful I swear it made the stars come out. The infant abruptly stopped wailing, hiccuped exactly once, and began to suck its thumb.

"There now," my mother said again as she gazed down at the infant in perfect satisfaction. As for me, I kept my eye on the Queen of the Night. I wasn't so certain she was finished with us yet.

"This is my daughter, Pamina," die Königin der Nacht said

after a moment, in a voice just like anyone else's. "The nightingale was singing, just as it is now, at the moment she was born. Ever since, it has had the power to soothe her, a power even stronger than a mother's love. But, a week ago, the bird flew from my side and did not return. Since then, my daughter and I have had no rest, by day or by night."

"She's beautiful," my mother answered. "But I think that she's too warm." She pushed the cloak in which the baby Pamina was swaddled back from her head. "Oh my."

Beneath the cloak, the baby's hair wasn't dark like her mother's, a thing I think we had all expected, but bright and shining as the morning sun, curling up from her head like steam rising from water set to boil. And in this way, I saw the beauty of the Lady Pamina for the very first time.

"So it is true what the old tales say," my father murmured, speaking up at last. "Night and day are joined together, and they have made a child."

"As you see," the Queen of the Night replied. "But until she turns sixteen, she is mine alone, to raise as I see fit. To prepare her for what is to come. But I'm hardly going to get anywhere if I can't even get her to go to sleep at the proper time."

She turned her beaten-silver eyes on me.

"Please," she said, and I heard my mother catch her breath. "Release the nightingale. Let her come home."

I tried to open my mouth, to explain the way I thought things worked, and discovered I couldn't move my jaw. The

Queen of the Night, die Königin der Nacht, had just said please. How on earth could I say no?

It was the nightingale who finally helped me out. With a great cascading waterfall of notes, she ended her evening song. The Lady Pamina was, by this time, fast asleep in my mother's arms. The nightingale now left my mother's shoulder and returned to mine. She bumped her round, soft head against my jaw, as if to knock some sense into it.

"If you please, Your Majesty," I managed to get out.

"Pamina," said die Königin der Nacht. I think she was trying to put me at ease by letting me know her name was the same as her daughter's. I wasn't so sure it helped any, though. The most powerful being I had ever encountered, was ever likely to encounter, had just given me permission to call her by her first name.

It was all a bit much for an eight-year-old.

"If you please, Your Majesty Pamina," I said, and was rewarded by the glimmer of a smile. "I would if I could, but I don't think I can."

Not particularly eloquent, I admit, but it did get the point across. Not only that, I'd managed to mean *no* without actually having to say it right out loud.

The Queen of the Night's dark eyebrows drew together. "Explain," she said. "Why not?"

"No bird who has ever come to me has left me again, not for good," I said. "I don't know why. I'm sorry."

"It's the bells," my father said. "The sound of them just plain gets inside your heart. If their sound calls to you, then you must answer. More than that, it is your wish to answer, just as it becomes your wish to dwell forever with the player of the bells.

"The bird stays not because my son keeps her captive, but because there is no other place that she would rather go. Wherever he is, that is now the place where she belongs. She cannot return to you, not in the way you wish. The bells have called and she has answered. The nightingale has given, and been given, her heart."

"That is it exactly," my grandfather put in.

The Queen of the Night was silent for a very long time.

"I perceive that you speak the truth," she said at last. She opened her arms, and my mother placed the sleeping Pamina into them. "What, then, shall become of my daughter?"

"Ow! All right!" I cried.

Five pairs of eyes turned in my direction, four mortal and one a great deal more. But they all did exactly the same thing: They stared straight at me and at the nightingale perched upon my shoulder. I'm sure she was doing her best to look innocent, assuming that's a thing a bird can actually accomplish. She'd just given me a sharp jab with her beak. It was this that had prompted me to cry out.

"I have an idea," I went on now. "I'm older than the Lady Pamina, so I must go to bed much later than she does. What if I come every night, just at bedtime? The nightingale will follow me and sing the baby to sleep. Then all will be well."

"Ah!" exclaimed die Königin der Nacht, and her gaze shifted away from me to my mother and father. "I begin to see why your son has called to him the most beautiful song on earth. He has a generous heart. What is your name, boy?"

"I am called Lapin, Madam," I answered.

The Queen of the Night's dark eyebrows flew straight up. "Your name means rabbit, yet you call down birds from the sky?"

"It's a long story," I replied. "But, if you please, I really do prefer Lapin. Not everybody knows that it means rabbit. Not everyone around here, anyhow."

The Queen of the Night nodded, and I could have sworn I saw a twinkle in her eye.

"Very well. I understand. I thank you for your generous offer, Lapin, but I'm afraid it is impossible. You can't travel back and forth from your home to mine. The distance is simply too great, even on a swift horse. If your parents and grandparents were willing to consider such a thing, however, there might be another option. You all could come and live with me."

"No," my mother said at once. "Not that we aren't grateful for the honor you bestow upon us, Lady, but we belong here." She reached for my father's hand, and he moved to clasp hers. "This is the life that we have chosen."

"You have chosen it, and chosen well," replied die Königin der Nacht. "But surely your son has a life of his own. Will you deny him? In my house he will have greater scope to discover what his heart holds. And what, in time, it may call to him."

"No," my mother said again. "He is just a boy."

"Please, *Mutter*," I said, surprising everyone present, myself most of all. "Let me at least try. I want to go."

And, as I said this, I realized how much it was so.

"Oh, Lapin," my mother said.

"Do not grieve," said the Queen of the Night. "For I will send him back to visit you when the days are shortest, and his coming will brighten your lives when the dark is long. And this I promise, now and forever: Neither I nor any who belong to me will ever hold your son against his will. Are you content?"

"No," my mother answered honestly. "But it is fair, and I will learn to live with it."

And that is how I came to be a servant of die Königin der Nacht and went to live in her great house which lies inside a mountain.

Though I missed my parents, I never regretted my choice. Die Königin let me do as I pleased, as long as the nightingale and I were there to sing the Lady Mina to sleep each night. I played the bells in every corner of her great house until the mountain itself rang with birdsong. I watched the Lady Mina grow to be a beautiful young woman. And, from a distance, I did what I could to keep my eye on my mistress's husband, the Lord Sarastro.

What he made of me, I never knew, for we never actually

spoke. But it was impossible to live in my mistress's house and not be aware of his presence. Most people think it is the dark that lurks, sly and treacherous. But I tell you that I think it is the light. For it is always hovering, just over the edge of the horizon, waiting to leap out and strike you blind.

And so, the years passed, moving inexorably toward the moment when the Lady Mina would turn sixteen and leave behind the only life that she had known.

"What is it like, Lapin?" she said to me one night in the year in which she was fifteen years old. We were doing a thing we often did, gazing out the window of her mother's observatory. A full moon gazed back down. As always in the evening, the nightingale was with us, though the bird now preferred the Lady Mina's shoulder to my own.

"Is it hard to leave behind all that you have known?"

"What's hard is never having an evening free from questions," I said. For the Lady Mina always had at least one up her sleeve. At my reply, she smiled. "I left what I knew of my own free will," I said, "though I was just a boy at the time."

"And I may not. Because my departure is a bargain already made, one in which I had no part. That's what you mean, is it not?" the Lady Mina both pronounced and asked at once.

I hope her father loves her, I found myself wishing fervently. *But more than that, I hope he appreciates her, especially her quicksilver mind.*

"That is what I mean," I acknowledged.

She fiddled with the hem of one long sleeve, worrying it between her fingers.

"He'll probably marry me off to some sunburned oaf."

"Definitely a possibility," I said. "Allow me to suggest you take along a hat when you go."

She chuckled, and left the sleeve alone. "It's a great pity I can't stay here and marry you instead."

At this, I took up my stone hammer and played a soft tune upon the bells. Nothing in particular, just whatever came to mind. To mind, but not to heart.

"Do you think that we belong together, then?" I asked. "That my heart calls to yours?"

The Lady Mina sighed. "No, Lapin. I think as I believe you do. That our hearts do not call to one another, though we love each other well. But it doesn't stop me from wishing that I need not marry a stranger."

"Then don't," I said, and I struck a brave sound upon the bells. "Don't be docile about all this. Be stubborn. Insist that you be allowed to marry the choice of your heart and no other."

"Easy for you to say," the Lady Mina said.

I ran the hammer along the bells, from high note to low, from top to bottom. The sound it made was jumbled and not at all harmonious.

"You think so?" I asked. For, though I was eight years older than Mina was, no song I had ever been able to play had brought me anything other than another set of wings.

"Of course not," the Lady Mina said at once. "I'm sorry. I'm out of sorts and taking it out on you. Pay no attention to me."

"I won't," I said. "I almost never do, you know."

This won a chuckle from her, as I had hoped. "Oh, Lapin," she said impulsively. "What would I do without you?"

"That is a thing you will never need to know."

She turned her head and looked with both her eyes into both of mine. I'm one of the few people who will meet her eyes, for a reason I will let her tell you herself at the proper time.

"Is that a promise?" she asked softly.

"It is a promise," I replied.

"I will hold you to it. You know that, don't you?"

"Of course I know that," I said. "Why else do you think I said it? Unless you doubt me."

"No, Lapin," the Lady Mina said. "I would never doubt you. Now let's both stop talking, shall we? Let me hear some music instead."

And so I sat and played the bells until the moon went down.

A week later, the Lord Sarastro took her away. A thief in the night, he stole her from her mother before the proper time. I saw it all, but could do nothing to prevent it. Even with my aid, die Königin, her daughter, and I would have been but three against many. Easily overcome.

Never will I forget the look upon my mistress's face as the

louts with their blazing torches departed, bearing away the daughter whom she loved. Always its image will stay with me, even if I live until the end of time.

"Do you see, Lapin?" she cried when the lights had gone, when she could shake back her cloak and I could leave my hiding place, for all was dark once more. Tears as hard and clear as diamonds streamed down her pale cheeks. She was weeping a fortune, and why shouldn't she? Had she not just been deprived of the first treasure of her heart?

"Do you see what he has done?"

"I see," I said. "Now what shall *we* do?"

At this, she laughed, and the sound was wild, matching the sound of the wind as it rose. The second the Lady Mina had stepped away from her mother it had started, answering the call of the storm in my mistress's heart.

"Lapin," die Königin der Nacht said. "The name which means rabbit."

"It does," I said. "But that does not mean I have the brains of one. I've understood for many years now the real reason you brought me here. It was because you feared this day would come."

"Then you know what I would have you do," she said.

"I do," I answered. "But I warn you, I don't think this has ever been done. I cannot truly control what I may call. Furthermore, once I have begun, you cannot intervene on your daughter's behalf. It must be that which I summon, or nothing."

"I know these things," die Königin der Nacht said impatiently. "Why do you waste time telling me what I already know?"

"I just want us to be sure," I said. "There's always the chance that what I call will end up being even worse than what her father has in mind."

"Impossible," die Königin der Nacht proclaimed. "For I think you see my daughter truly, and I know you love her well. Both those things, I fear, are more than I can say for the Lord Sarastro. Bring my daughter the one who will set her free, as you brought the one who lulled her to sleep so long ago.

"Do it, Lapin. Play the bells."

WHAT LAPIN'S BELLS SUMMONED

WHAT WOULD HAVE HAPPENED IF THERE'D NEVER BEEN A storm?

If there'd never been a storm, I might never have heard the bells. And if I'd never heard the bells, I would never have entered Mina's life, an event that changed the lives of all.

I wonder about these things sometimes.

Foolishness, of course. If something is meant to happen, then it will. That's just the way the world works. There's no use trying to stop it or get around it. You probably know this for yourself. Fortunately, not everything that happens carries the same weight as everything else. Was I meant to hear the bells and enter Mina's story when I did? Absolutely.

Was I meant to eat the last piece of royal chocolate birthday cake before my younger brother, Arthur, could get to it, when I was ten and he was seven-and-a-half? Probably not. All that was required for that to happen was a willingness to get out of bed and creep down cold stone stairs in the middle of the night.

I can hear Mina's voice laughing in my ear. Chiding me. *How can they follow your portion of this tale when you haven't even told them who you are?* And so I suppose I'd better get that out of the way. Things are no doubt confusing enough with so many different people telling you what happened.

I am a prince, and my name is Tern.

A tern is a seabird, something like a gull. Not even my parents have a good explanation for why this is the name I was given the day I was born. Neither of them had ever seen the sea before. The land my father governs lies many miles from any coast. Rivers we have in plenty. Also lakes, streams, swamps, and ponds. But you could ride for days on end on the swiftest horse in my father's stables and still not catch a glimpse of the sea. Yet a seabird is what I was named for.

If you decide to seriously press my mother, tell her you refuse to eat your broccoli until you get an explanation, she'll tell you that she named me Tern because she liked the sound. There's a problem with this. You can probably recognize it right off. All sorts of words may make lovely sounds when you speak them aloud: aubergine, tamarind, minaret, crevasse.

But the fact that they produce nice sounds doesn't mean

they make good names. Who wants to be named after some great gaping hole in the ground? A name needs to fit, to have some meaning. At the very least it ought not to get in the way of the person on whom it's been bestowed. A name ought to help a person fulfill his destiny, help make it clear, not make it more complicated than it already is. Destiny is tricky enough, after all.

In the end this is precisely what my strange name did. It made my destiny clear. It simply took its own sweet time about it.

As I think I said earlier, my part in this story begins with the storm. A storm like no other any person in our kingdom had ever seen. A storm that made it seem as if the very night itself was in a rage, a fury of lust for revenge which would be spent only with the rising of the sun.

Stars shot across the heavens like stones from a thousand catapults. The wind screamed in fury and howled with pain all at the same time. Its strength caused slate to fly from the roofs of houses in the village which had stood, untouched, for centuries. Trees let go of their hold on the earth and flew into the air and out of sight.

The land trembled, and a great roaring came from everywhere at once, so that it seemed as if my homeland itself had been yanked from the earth as easily as the trees, and was even now being carried miles away to be deposited beside the sea.

Just when it seemed as if there could be no other outcome than that the world would tear itself apart, a single bolt of lightning, sharp and jagged as a javelin, shot straight down from the sky. It landed in the very center of the forest near my father's castle. The King's Wood, our people called it.

Then, with a final shriek of anguish, the wind went still. There was a moment of absolute silence. For no reason I could name, my heart began to beat in hard, quick strokes, as if I were more frightened now than I had been at the height of the storm. *Something has happened,* I thought. *Something important.* But I did not know yet what it was.

Then, from the castle courtyard below, I heard my father's voice calling for the lighting of torches. Quickly, for I knew I would be needed, I threw on a cloak and went down. The people of the village were just beginning to creep from their homes. Like one cat under the hostile eyes of another, they moved carefully and cautiously, as if they expected to be pounced upon.

"Ah, Tern," my father said when he saw me. "Good, there you are. Stay by me a moment, will you?"

He paused to watch my mother and her ladies-in-waiting set off to see if there were any wounded or ill who needed tending. My younger brother, Arthur, who is very good at such things, went to see if there was any rescuing to be done. Finally my father turned back to me.

"Tern," he said, his dark eyes sober in the torchlight. "Take these two"—he gestured to his two most faithful retainers— "and find out what has happened in the wood. Send them back to me when you know."

"Father, I will," I promised.

For, suddenly, I knew what the important thing that had happened was, or at least what my father feared it might be. I knew exactly what my father wanted me to look for. Exactly where to go. And so it was that half an hour later, my father's most faithful retainers and I discovered where the lightning had struck. We saw what it had done, and undone.

In the center of the King's Wood there stands—there stood—a great oak tree, the only one of its kind. It was so old no one could remember when it had been any smaller, let alone when it had been young. It was called the King's Oak. According to the legends of my land, it had been planted on the day our very first queen had borne her lord his very first son.

Over the years, the tales about the tree had grown even as the tree had, until it was almost as important a symbol to our people as the king himself. A change in the oak would mean a change in the kingdom, or so the people said, and they believed it. If it should be struck down, so should we all.

The bolt of lightning had split the King's Oak in two, straight down the middle, one side falling to the left, and one side to the right. In the light of our torches, my father's men and I could see that, on both halves, the heart of the tree had been exposed. It was still strong and hearty. Save for the lightning, the King's Oak could have stood another number of untold years.

This was the good news, I suppose. But the bad news was that my father's fear had turned out to be well-founded. The lightning had struck the King's Oak. Clearly some great change was in store for our land. The only question was, what kind?

I pulled in a breath, turned my back on the tree and my face to my father's retainers.

"Return to my father the king and tell him this," I instructed. "The King's Oak lies in two pieces, yet even parted, it is strong. Say that I would have him return with you to see this for himself, so that he may decide what it means, and further, what should be done."

The retainers bowed and left me without a word, though I knew what they were thinking. They were afraid. Even by the light of their flickering torches, I could see it in their eyes.

It didn't take long for my father to return. Most of the village came with him, or so it seemed at the time. Soon the clearing around the King's Oak was as bright as day, filled with the light of many torches. Their flames were the only thing in the clearing that moved, save for my father himself and the eyes of his subjects as they watched him walk around the cloven tree once, twice, three times.

It was so quiet you could have heard a single leaf drop to the ground, had there been any left to fall. There were not. All had been swept down by the storm.

Finally my father halted and turned to face his subjects. At this, the eyes of the people halted, too, and so did their breath. I think even their hearts stopped beating as they waited for my father to speak, to say what he thought the future held in store.

"My son, Prince Tern, has spoken truly," said my father. "The King's Oak lies split in two, yet, in both halves, the heart is strong. So does the strength of our kingdom hold true, for do I not have two sons, and are not their hearts strong?"

At this, a great sigh went through the clearing as all the people expelled their breath at once. My father had not pronounced the cleaving of the oak to be a disaster. This was the good news. Yet even a small child could see that we still had a problem.

"I believe we have been given a sign this night," my father continued, "and that it concerns my two sons. Both are strong and fit to rule when I am dead, yet the crown can pass to only one. Tradition would dictate that it must pass to my firstborn. But all of you know well what is spoken of the King's Oak: that, if it changes, our kingdom shall change, also.

"Therefore, hear what I have decided shall be done. Let Prince Tern choose one half of the tree. Let Prince Arthur choose the other. Then, let them fashion from the heart of the King's Oak what their own hearts summon. In the morning, I shall judge what each has made, and in this way will your future king be chosen."

"You choose first, Tern," Arthur said, before I could so much as open my mouth to suggest that he do likewise.

Now, the King's Oak had been split straight down the middle. You might not think it would make much difference which side of it I chose. But, as my father stood to make his

263

decree, with his back to the tree and his face to his people, one half of the downed tree lay to his left side, and the other to his right.

Yes, of course, you are no doubt thinking, and no doubt with impatience. *How else would they fall?*

The point I'm trying to make is this: If I chose the left half, I chose the half closest to my father's heart. And in so choosing, I would make a statement, stake a claim: that I was the son whose heart was the most like my father's, and therefore most fit to rule when my father's heart beat no more.

This sort of thing is considered important where I come from. For my father believes, and I must admit that I agree, that the heart of a king is his most important attribute, not his proud bearing, his big voice, or even his fine mind. Any idiot in a decent suit of clothes may sit upon a throne, a thing usurpers have proved from time to time.

The best kings are the *true* kings. The ones born to rule. The ones who have known this was their destiny before they understood what it was they knew, for it commenced with the very first beat of their heart. And that's why regicide is such a terrible crime. A true king is a king in his heart, a heart which must be allowed to beat to the very end. To live its full and proper life. Only when the heart of a true king ceases to beat can the heart of his successor take its place.

As a general rule, that heart is expected to beat in the breast of his firstborn son. But every now and again, even nature can skip a beat, and the heart of a king will beat in a younger son. I had often wondered whether this was the case with Arthur and me, because of our names, if nothing else. I get named for the sea-gulls, most of whom are scavengers. My brother, for one of the most legendary kings of all time.

And so, after a hesitation that seemed like an hour but was, in fact, no longer than the time it took to take a breath, I bowed to my father and stepped to the tree's right side.

"I will choose the right," I said, "for the right hand of a king must be strong."

I heard a murmur of appreciation rise up from the people, and two other sounds. So soft I think only the three of us most closely concerned heard them. I heard my brother, Arthur, suck in his breath, and my father expel his in a sigh.

"And I will take the left," Arthur said, stepping forward in his turn. "The better to protect the king's heart."

"So be it," my father said. "I will judge what you have made at dawn."

Five

TERN MAKES A CHOICE
AND HEARS A SOUND

SWIFTLY MY BROTHER AND I SET TO WORK. HE ON THE left side of the King's Oak, and I on the right. My father and his subjects returned to the village, leaving Arthur and me alone within a ring of torches. What beat in my brother's heart during the rest of that strange night, I cannot tell. But in my own there pounded a desire more fierce than any I had ever known.

And it was simply this: to learn what my own heart might hold.

I could hear our father returning before I was finished. It was only then that I realized Arthur had been silent for some time. I turned, for we had been working back to back, and saw him sitting upon the ground. His head was bowed, as if in weariness. Across his lap lay a great spear, as long as the King's Oak was tall. And all carved from the heart of the left side of the tree.

Oh, well done, Arthur, I thought.

"You always have to try to be first, don't you?" I said. "It wasn't a race, you know."

At this, Arthur looked up with a smile, for this was an old joke between us.

"Still trying to compensate for the order of my birth," he replied. Then his face grew serious. "Tern," he began. "About the half of the tree you chose—"

"Arthur," I interrupted him. "Please, don't say anymore. I chose the right half." At the unintended pun, I made a face. "The *correct* half," I went on. "You know it, and I know it. I think even Papa knows it. Why else would he have come up with this particular test for us?"

"He could just want to see what kind of woodcarvers we are," Arthur remarked, his tone mild.

"Good gracious!" I exclaimed in perfect imitation of our mother. "I hadn't considered that."

"Old idiot," Arthur said.

"Young moron."

I cuffed him on the ear. He poked me in the stomach with one end of that impossibly long spear. We were standing with our arms around each other's shoulders, grinning like buffoons, when our parents arrived.

"Oh ho," my father said when he saw us. "So now you've

267

decided the fate of our kingdom is just one big joke?"

"He started it," Arthur said.

"Did not."

"Did too."

"My sons," my father said sternly, though his face twitched strangely, a surefire sign that he was fighting back a smile. "Enough. The people will be here soon and we must not confuse them with mischievous behavior. They're already worried enough."

"Yes, Father," Arthur and I said in unison, a thing which made my father's face twitch once more.

Arthur and I stepped apart. I could see my mother, who had, naturally, accompanied my father, looking first at Arthur and then at me. When she looked at my brother, her eyes were dry. When she looked at me, she had tears in her eyes. And so it seemed that the only people who did not know that the matter of who would succeed my father was already settled were his subjects.

They crowded into the clearing now, their faces wary, yet expectant. Together, my parents stepped back to stand among them, facing me and Arthur.

"My sons, have you completed the task I set?" my father asked, his tone formal.

"Father, we have," I responded.

"As Prince Tern chose his portion of the tree first, let Prince Arthur be the first to show what he has made."

"As the king commands," my brother said, and he stepped forward.

"I have made a spear," he said as he knelt and offered it to my father. "As long as the King's Oak is tall."

"And why have you done this?" my father asked as he took it from him. He hefted it, as if testing the weight, judging how far it would fly when thrown.

"So that there should be no portion of our land that my arm cannot protect in time of peace or defend in time of war," my brother responded.

"This is well done," my father said. And he gestured for Arthur to rise. He handed him back the spear. Arthur accepted it, then returned to my side.

"What have you made, Prince Tern?" my father asked.

And it was only as he asked the question that I realized something. An important something. A something you would have thought I'd realized before now: I didn't know. My heart had been so full of the desire to know itself that I hadn't even noticed what my hands had carved.

I looked down at them now.

"A flute," I said. *A flute? Oh, for crying out loud.* This was a bit eccentric, even for me, particularly after Arthur's very manly spear.

"And why have you done this?" my father asked, just as he had asked my brother.

I did the only thing I could. I pulled in the deepest breath

269

my lungs would hold, looked my father straight in the eye, and told the truth.

"My lord," I said, "I truly do not know. I listened to my heart when carving from the tree, and the flute is what my heart called forth."

I think even my father was somewhat at a loss for words at this. It's difficult for someone who has always recognized their destiny to hear the words, "I do not know." Fortunately for all concerned, my mother chose this particular moment to speak up.

"Let us hear you sound it," she said. "Perhaps, then, we all shall know."

"As the queen commands," I replied.

"Say as she *requests*, rather," my mother said, and she smiled.

And so I pulled in a second breath, as deep as the one I had just taken, lifted the flute to my lips, and began to play.

It's hard to describe what happened next. I think the simplest thing to say is that, for me at least, the world around me was no longer the world I knew. Or rather, it was the world I knew, but so much more.

My mind knew that I was standing in the King's Wood, facing my parents and my father's assembled subjects, with my brother at my side. My mind knew that there was grass beneath my feet and trees in a great circle all around. It even knew that I felt both foolish and afraid, for I was far from understanding what was going on.

But my heart . . . My heart registered none of these things, for it was filled with sound.

I cannot tell you what melody I played. I'm not so sure it was one you would recognize. Instead, it was as if the voice of the flute was the voice of the wide world itself and the beating of my own heart, all at once. Playing was like running as hard and fast as I could, simply for the joy of it. Like standing absolutely still with my bare feet in the waters of a clear, calm lake, with my face tipped up to face the sun.

Like starlight. Like moonlight. Like nothing I had ever experienced or could ever hope to describe. As if all the possibilities I could ever dream of, as well as countless others which had never even occurred to me, had suddenly become crystal clear and transformed into sound.

That was the music the flute made. And at the moment I ceased to play, I understood the truth: I had been playing the music of my heart. And no sooner did I understand this than I heard a new sound seizing the fading notes of the flute, as if it had been chasing after them. Holding on to linger when the sound of the flute was done.

Faint, yet clear, I heard the chime of bells.

Slowly I brought the flute down from my lips. The look upon my father's face was one that I had never seen before.

"I believe that Death himself would stop to listen to such music," my father said.

And, suddenly, for the first time ever, I saw into my father's heart, and saw that it was filled with doubt. Strong and true as Arthur was, it might be no bad thing for me to succeed my father after all. For the flute that I had made might inspire the people I ruled to greatness. Might halt an enemy without the spilling of a single drop of blood.

That was when I heard it again, louder this time: the high, sweet call of bells. The sound they made seemed to set my whole heart jangling, so near, so very near it was to my heart's own song. And at that moment, I knew what I must do. If I was ever to search out my own destiny, find the one whose heart beat with mine, I had to set out. Right now.

"My lord," I said, and I went to kneel before my father as my brother had done. "I honor you, and I honor this land. But as you commanded me to carve what I would from the heart of the King's Oak, now let me say what is in my own heart."

"I pray you, do so," my father said. And he stooped and put his hands on my shoulders, urging me to rise.

"Father," I said when I had gotten to my feet. "Let my brother, Arthur, be king when you are gone. For his heart bids him to stay, while mine urges me to go. I cannot be a good king, a true king, if my heart lies elsewhere, no matter how much I love our land or the people I would govern."

"Is this truly what your heart speaks?" my father asked.

"It is," I answered steadily. "I swear this on my honor, as your son."

"Then so be it," my father said. He embraced me, stepped

forward to embrace my brother, then, with one arm around my shoulder and the other around Arthur's, he turned all three of us to face the assembled crowd.

"Hear now, all of you!" he cried. "Prince Tern will travel through the wide world, listening to the music of his heart until he discovers what it may hold. Then, with all my heart, I hope he may return to us once more.

"Prince Arthur will succeed me. He will rule in this land after I am gone. Now let the kingdom be filled with rejoicing, for the riddle of the King's Oak is solved!"

"Long live Prince Arthur!" the people shouted. Caps flew into the air. Children clapped their hands as they were hoisted up onto shoulders. "Long live Prince Tern!"

"I'll thank you to notice they said my name first," Arthur murmured as my father went back to stand beside my mother, leaving the two of us to stand waving at the crowd.

"They're just brownnosing," I murmured back. "You're going to be king, after all."

At this, Arthur gave a shout of laughter, and the people hoisted us up onto their shoulders and carried the two of us home through the dawn.

Shortly after a good breakfast, in which it seemed to me the entire kingdom took part, I tucked the flute into a pocket of my tunic right above my heart and pulled a well-provisioned knapsack upon my back, for I am not entirely without good sense. Then I set out to answer the call of the bells.

THE LADY MINA
SPEAKS HER MIND

FEAR.

I could feel it in the arms that held me. Taste it on the tip of my tongue. Hear it in the sound of the wind as it tore through the trees. Fear and pain and rage combined.

My fear. My pain at the duplicity of my father. The breaking of my mother's heart. The fear of my father's soldiers. Where the rage came from, I could not tell. But, every now and then, like a flash of sheet lightning against a pitch-black sky, came an emotion that stood alone, and this one was easy to identify: It was the Lord Sarastro's triumph.

Just when I was sure my ribs would break from being bounced against the hard shoulder bone of the one who held me, I heard a barked command, and the company halted. Almost at once there came a great clang, like the raising of a portcullis. There was a second command, and, again, we moved forward. As we did so, I heard the hard-soled boots of the soldiers ring out upon stone. Since I was facedown, I could easily see the way that sparks flew up, so smartly did they march inside the Lord Sarastro's dwelling place. With a second clang, the great doors of iron closed behind us.

Trapped, I thought.

"Set her down," said the Lord Sarastro. "But bring her along."

At once, I was set on my feet. One strong hand remained on my arm. It propelled me through a series of narrow corridors so swiftly, it was all I could do not to stumble. Then, with a suddenness that reminded me of the way the earth will sometimes abruptly fall away on both sides of a twisting mountain path, the walls of the corridors winged back and a great hall yawned before us.

I could tell this mostly by the feeling of immense open space, by the way the room *felt*, not because I could see it for myself. My hood was still pulled over my face, so low I could see nothing save when I gazed straight down.

"Release her," the Lord Sarastro said. And, at his command, the hand fell away. I heard the scrape of a boot as my captor stepped back. I was left standing alone.

Of course my first impulse was to push my hood back, the

better to study my new surroundings. Or, if not that, then at least to stare with open defiance at the man who, within the last few moments, I had decided I would never call father.

I did nothing.

Instead, I kept my head bowed, my hands folded inside the sleeves of my cloak. For it came to me without warning, as inspiration often does, that my silence might be a weapon I could use in whatever battle I was about to fight with the Lord Sarastro. That there must be a battle seemed obvious.

He had broken the agreement made at my birth, broken his own oath. Set his will against my mother's and broken hers into pieces. But he had yet to learn how strong my own will was.

"Welcome, my daughter, Pamina," the Lord Sarastro said. "Welcome to your new home."

And, at his words, I felt my legs begin to tremble as a terrible emotion seized my whole body.

You are wrong, my lord, I thought. *I cannot have a new home, for I never had an old one. A home is a place one's heart creates and so recognizes as its own. A place it enters of its own free will. All others are merely dwelling places.*

I bit my lip to keep from crying out my pain, for it seemed to me, in that moment, that I saw my future spreading out before me. My father would marry me to some stranger of his own selection, a man who matched the criteria of the Lord Sarastro's heart but not mine. I would spend my life in the dwellings of others. I would never know my own true home.

The pain of this realization stopped up my voice, so I made no answer to the Lord Sarastro's welcome.

"Let me take you to your room," he finally said when it became clear that I would not reply. "Perhaps, when you have had a chance to rest, you will see that all will be well."

How can it be, when it has begun like this? I thought. Though the truth was that the pain of this moment had been started long ago, in the moment my parents first turned away from one another.

He must have made some signal, for, again, I felt that strong hand upon my arm. It piloted me across the great hall and toward a flight of stairs. As I lifted my foot to place it upon the first step, I suddenly cried out, for, as the torchlight fell upon the stair, light leaped into being, a light so bright it all but dazzled my eyes. Some vivid mineral flecked the stone, sleeping deep within until awakened by the light of the torch.

"This is porphyry," the Lord Sarastro said as he paused to let me catch up. "Do you know it? It is beautiful when the light shines upon it, don't you think?"

It is, I thought. *And it is not.* It seemed even the steps beneath my father's feet had been created to prove a point, the same point he had driven home to my mother by snatching me away. No matter how strong, no matter how beautiful, dark would always be overcome by light.

And so, for the third time, my father, the Lord Sarastro, spoke to me and I said nothing. But beside me, I heard the one who held me make a sound. In one ear and out the other before I could determine what it meant.

"Statos," my father said as if he'd understood precisely. "That will do. You must give her time."

Statos. The golden one, I thought. The one who had tried to trick me into giving him my hand. And I knew then what my father had in mind. There would be no parade of potential husbands. There would be no need. He already had the one he wanted.

Without another word, my father turned and continued to the top of the stairs, a servant lighting the way before, Statos and I following behind.

At the top of the stairs was a wide, curved corridor of white marble, gleaming like a river of milk in the light of the torches. Open to the air and bordered by a low balustrade on the left and by the stone wall of the mountain itself on the right. The Lord Sarastro moved down it at a brisk pace, so swiftly I almost had to run to keep up, an action which caused my hood to slip back. For the first time, I began to get a better look at my surroundings.

A row of illuminated sconces lined the wall on the right. Between them were hung tapestries depicting the course of the sun across the sky. Like the stairs which I had climbed to reach this place, the background of each tapestry was dark. But the sun was embroidered in gold thread so that it flashed in the light.

At the far end of the corridor, my father stopped. In front

of him was a single door. At his nod, the servant knocked once, then threw it open and stepped inside. My father waited until I had reached him.

"This will be your room, Pamina," he said. "If not tonight, then one day soon, I hope that you will find it to your liking."

Then, with a gesture that I should go first, he ushered me inside. It was like walking into a jar of honey, warm and golden. The floor was burnished amber. Great swathes of gleaming silk just a shade lighter adorned the walls. A bright fire burned in a black iron grate, with a great overstuffed chair and matching footstool pulled invitingly in front. An enormous bed covered in ivory damask stood on a raised dais in one corner.

But it was the windows that drew me most of all. One entire wall of lead-paned glass. *How it will sparkle in the sun!* I thought. Even now, the stars shone through, beautiful and hard as diamonds.

"How many times must I tell you to draw the curtains at night, Gayna?" I heard my father's voice say. And it was only then I realized that the room was already occupied.

She was tall, dark-haired, and beautiful. But then I knew these things already, for I had seen her often enough. At the sight of her, my heart gave a strange twist. This was the girl my father had raised instead of me, the forester's child.

He has given me her room, I thought.

"I beg your pardon, my lord," she said, and she moved toward the windows.

"Why not leave things as they are?" a new voice proposed. Deep and smooth as the velvet drapes for which Gayna's long fingers were even now reaching. *Statos,* I thought. His voice was like the color of the room, warm and golden as honey.

"Your daughter is accustomed to the night, my lord. Perhaps seeing one thing which is familiar will make this transition easier for her."

He was right, of course. Not that I liked him for it. I saw the girl, Gayna, hesitate, as if uncertain which man she wished more to please.

So that is the way things are, I thought.

"Very well," the Lord Sarastro said, though I could tell by the sound of his voice he wasn't pleased. "But for this one night only. Pamina is my daughter, as much as she is her mother's. Not only that, she lives with me now. That is a fact to which she must grow accustomed. The sooner the better."

He talks about me as if I wasn't even here, I thought.

Gayna's hand dropped to her side. The room filled with silence.

"I will leave you now, daughter," the Lord Sarastro went on. "Gayna will stay with you this one night, so that you will not be lonely. In the morning, I will send for you."

I laughed before I could help it. I didn't mean to, but the sound rose up and out, quick and bitter, before I even knew that it was forming.

"You're worried that I'll be lonely?" I asked, and I made no attempt to hide the derision in my voice. The disbelief. "Don't you think it's a little late to be concerned about that?"

In the shocked silence that followed, I heard a piece of wood snap inside the grate.

"So you can talk," the Lord Sarastro said, his voice curiously mild. "I was beginning to wonder."

"You should not speak so to the Lord Sarastro," Gayna burst out, as if she couldn't hold back her outrage for one second longer. "You owe him your respect, your allegiance, and your love. He is the Mage of the Day. He is your father."

"He is an oath-breaker," I replied.

And then, as if her rebuke had broken a dam inside me, all the hot words I had been storing up came streaming forth.

"An oath-breaker," I said again. And now, at last, I pushed my hood all the way back, so that all could see my face clearly, though my hair was still bound up in its dark scarf. I heard Statos hiss out a breath through his perfect white teeth. Save for the fire, it was the room's only sound.

This is how my father, the Lord Sarastro, seemed to me now that I looked upon him without tears, and with my eyes wide open: He looked for all the world like a lion in his prime. A full beard covered the lower half of his face, exactly the same color as the chestnut hair which curled back from his forehead, then tumbled down to brush his shoulders. He wore a doublet of bronze velvet. Upon his brow was set a circlet of beaten gold the same color as his eyes.

I felt a pain so sharp I feared my very bones would splinter and pierce my flesh. This was my father. All my life I had wanted him to know and to love me. The father whom, for all my life, I had wished to know and to love. If he had waited just a few more hours, who is to say what might have been possible between us? But he had not, and so I knew there could be nothing.

"By his own act, the Lord Sarastro has forfeited my respect," I said now, "and my allegiance, for one cannot pledge to serve where one does not trust. As for love ..." I turned to face Gayna where she still stood by the window. I saw her eyes go wide as she looked into mine.

"Let us hope you love him enough for both of us," I said. "For that must suffice him, as I find I do not love him at all. I will never be governed by his will. Never marry a man of his choosing. I will never call him father.

"And, for the record, my name is Mina."

"So it is true what the tales say," Gayna whispered. "The daughter of the Queen of the Night bears the evil eye."

"Gayna!" the Lord Sarastro said sharply. "Enough!"

But I simply laughed once more. "And which one would that be?" I inquired sweetly. "The gold or the silver? You'll want to be careful how you answer, for you may reveal more about yourself than you know."

For this is what they all had seen, a thing I have not told you until now: My eyes are two different colors. One as silver as the stars, the other as golden as the sun. A daily reminder that I was a child of two worlds. Worlds who could not live without one another, yet could not get along.

"In your grief, you speak things you should not," the Lord Sarastro said, and, though I turned back to face him, I could not read the expression on his face, in his voice, or in his eyes.

"For tonight, I will be understanding. But my patience will end with the rising of the sun. At dawn, you will be presented to my subjects as my daughter, whether you desire this or not, for not even you can deny who you are.

"The life that you have known is over, Mina. The sooner you accept this fact, the better for you things will be." He turned away then, motioning with one hand. "Come, Statos."

For a moment, I thought that Statos would protest. That he would speak to me directly, make some plea. But he did not. Instead, he made me a formal bow. Then he followed my father out of the chamber, leaving Gayna and me alone.

Seven

THE THOUGHTS OF THE FORESTER'S DARK-HAIRED CHILD

I DIDN'T WANT TO LIKE HER. THAT MUCH SHOULD BE obvious. I didn't even want to feel sorry for her, for sympathy is nothing more than the top of a steep and slippery slope.

So what did I want, you are no doubt wondering? The truth is that my desire was twofold. Preferably, that the daughter of the Lord Sarastro had never existed in the first place. But, if she had to, what I wanted more than anything under the sun was really quite simple.

I wanted to hate her guts.

I even managed it, for most of the first hour after we had been left alone. My anger, my outrage over the way she had spoken to her father was enough to carry me straight through that. It was as my anger began to fade that I began to perceive that I had a problem.

After her father and Statos's departure, the daughter of the Queen of the Night—I had already decided I would not call her *Mina*, not even in the privacy of my own mind—the daughter of the Queen of the Night moved to sit by the window, to stare out at I couldn't quite imagine what.

For what is there to see in a night sky, after all? It's nothing more than a dark blanket, stitched some nights with the moon and always with the stars. But, unlike the sun, which can pretty much be counted upon to do the same thing day after day, the night sky is as changeable as the one who governs it. Die Königin der Nacht.

The moon alters its shape, day by day, month by month. The stars change positions, dancing to the passage of the seasons. Never mind that such things can be predicted, even plotted out. You cannot trust the night sky. It's really as simple as that, in my mind. And in my heart, I know this truth: What cannot be trusted is difficult to love.

And so I sat on the bed, and the daughter of the Queen of the Night sat in a chair by the window. I looked at her. She looked at the night. I'm not sure when I realized that she had changed position, ever so slightly. She must have done it the one time I moved to stir up the fire. For the room was cold with the drapes pulled back from all those windows. A chill had taken possession of the air even though it was high summer. *Just another of night's perversities,* I thought.

But when I resumed my seat again, I saw that the Queen of the Night's daughter was resting her head against the cold windowpane, as if it had become too much effort to hold her head up. It was her only concession to the strain of what had happened to her this night.

But she did not speak. Not one word since her outburst to her father. I might have not existed at all for all the attention she paid me.

Perhaps that is her *wish,* I thought.

And with that thought, I made my very first mistake. For if she could make a wish, even if it was the opposite of anything I wished for, then she was not so very different from me, after all. I may be selfish. I admit it. But I am not stupid. And I've never been deliberately unfair, or at least I hadn't been at that point.

"What is that you see?" I asked, at long last breaking the silence. And this was my second mistake, a thing I probably don't need to tell you.

For, with this question, I had acknowledged many things. That I was curious. That I had let my curiosity get the better of me. But, most important of all, I think, I had acknowledged the fact that she might look upon the night sky and see things that I could not.

"Come and look for yourself," she said. She didn't even bother to lift her head from the windowpane. I stayed right where I was. But after a moment, she sat up straight and looked around. The light from the fire fell upon one half of her face, lighting up her golden eye like a new-struck coin. The eye of silver, the one that belonged to the night, was closest to the window, indistinguishable from the light of the stars.

"Unless you are afraid, of course."

There's a reason that this is pretty much the oldest trick in the book, and that would be because it works almost every time. I could almost feel the spurt of anger that pushed me to my feet and across the room toward her, even as my mind urged me to stay right where I was.

"I'm certainly not afraid of you," I said.

She turned back to the window as I approached, but not before I thought I saw the flicker of a smile. Not a smile that triumphed over me, just a lightening of her expression. I suppose it could have been a trick of the firelight, but I really don't think so.

"Then look," she said, "and I'll tell you what I see with my eyes, if you tell me what you see with yours."

"Fair enough," I said. I nudged her feet from the footstool upon which they had been resting and sat down upon it so that, for all intents and purposes, we were sitting side by side.

"Oh, my," I said after a moment.

"Exactly what I was thinking," said the daughter of the Queen of the Night.

"It doesn't do this often, does it?"

I heard, rather than saw her shake her head, for, now that I had dared to look, I couldn't tear my eyes away from the night sky. Never, not even on the clearest night I could remember, had I seen so many stars. Nor had I ever seen any behave in quite this way.

They were falling from the sky. Each and every one.

Some shot from one side of the window clear across to the other, as if chasing one another, racing around in circles, desperate to tire themselves out. Others arced up, like divers leaping off high cliffs, then shot straight down.

Earlier, during the time in which I now knew the Lord Sarastro had first laid hands upon his daughter, there had been a terrible storm. Trees had writhed as if in agony. The wind had made so terrible a sound I'd wanted to crawl straight underneath my bed and stay there until morning.

Frightening as that was, this was even worse, for it all happened without a sound. Below, the world was absolutely still, while in the heavens above, the stars committed suicide.

It was the most beautiful, the most bitter thing that I had ever seen. For it seemed to me I understood its cause.

The Queen of the Night was weeping for her stolen child.

"It's your mother, isn't it?" I asked.

"I think so, yes," replied the daughter of die Königin der Nacht.

"Do you think there will be any stars tomorrow?"

Without hesitation, she nodded.

"There will always be stars. There must be, just as there must be a sunrise. It is for this reason that the Queen of the Night and the Mage of the Day were joined. They cannot be parted, not unless the world itself is."

"But she weeps for you."

"Yes. I believe that she does."

I turned my head to look at her, then, and, for the first time, I saw that she wept also. Not from the eye of gold, the eye she had inherited from her father. That eye was as dry as ashes, and cold ones at that. But from the eye of silver there flowed one tear after another, exactly the same color as the stars in the sky. In so endless a stream I only barely stopped myself from glancing at the hem of my skirt, certain I would find it drenched with the tears that must, by now, have formed a great puddle around us on the floor.

Though they had been separated, they wept together for what had befallen them, the Queen of the Night and her strange-eyed daughter.

"Would she have brought you, do you think?" I asked. "Would she have kept the appointed time?"

The daughter of the Queen of the Night looked down at me, and now I could see that, though the gold eye did not weep, it too was filled with unbearable sorrow.

"I believe she would have," she answered. "For I have never known her to go back on her word, not to anyone. But we'll never know now. The Lord Sarastro has taken care of that."

"He is more than simply the Lord Sarastro," I said. I knew it was foolish, but I couldn't help myself. I had loved him too well, and too long. He had been everything to me. Father and mother both. Yet it seemed to me as if she threw him away, discarded what he was without a thought.

"He is your father."

Even in the dim light, I could see the way hot color flushed her face.

Nicely done, Gayna, I thought. *Who knows what she can do? What power she, herself, controls. If she turns you into a toad, it's no more than you deserve for your stupidity.*

She pulled in a breath as if to speak, then flattened her lips into a thin and unattractive line. At this, I have to say my spirits picked back up a little. I'm only human, and it pleased me to discover that, even for a moment, she could be ugly.

"More your father than mine, I should think," she said. "Is that why you dislike me so much? Not that I would blame you, of course."

Of all the dirty tricks, I thought. She hadn't turned me into a toad after all. Instead, she'd shown me how well I'd done that myself, all on my own.

"Who says that I dislike you?" I asked. "Maybe I do, maybe I don't. Not that I'd need a reason if I do."

This time, I was certain that she smiled, for I could see her face full on.

"Ah, so there is something more," she said. "Let me think."

She scrunched her face up in concentration, and it was then I realized that she had stopped crying. I wondered if the sky outside had done the same, but I didn't want to turn my head to look. I didn't want to break our strange tableau.

"There's really only one thing that it can be, of course. The golden boy. Statos."

"He's not a boy," I said hotly as I sat up a little straighter on the stool. "He's a grown man, and the Lord Sarastro's apprentice."

"Is he indeed?" the daughter of the Queen of the Night asked softly. "The Lord Sarastro's *chosen* apprentice?"

"And what if he is?"

"If he is, then he would make a fitting consort for the Lord Sarastro's daughter."

If she'd shot a burning arrow straight into my chest, she couldn't have hit the mark more accurately, nor wounded me more.

"That seems to be the general consensus of opinion," I said, and even I could hear my voice was bitter.

She cocked her head to one side, just like a bird considering which way to pluck a worm from the ground.

"How long have you loved him?"

I opened my mouth to deny it altogether, then shut it with a snap. *Why deny the obvious?* I thought. There were days it seemed to me the whole world must know how I felt about Statos, even Statos himself.

"Do you believe in love at first sight?"

She considered for a moment. "In theory, I do, I suppose. Though not from personal experience. That doesn't quite answer my question, though."

I sighed. "Since I was five. He entered the Lord Sarastro's household the same year my father was killed."

"The same year the Lord Sarastro took you in to raise as his own," the Lady Mina said, her tone thoughtful. And I realized with a start of horror that I had done the thing I'd sworn I'd never do. I had given her her name in my own mind.

"He raised you," she said again, "as his own daughter. But now he wishes to give the man you love to a total stranger. One who is a daughter by nothing more than a trick of birth. It must be very difficult for you, Gayna. I'm sorry."

"Oh, for pity's sake!" I cried. "Stop it, can't you? Just stop it!"

I shot to my feet, unable to stay still a moment longer. I took several agitated paces away, then whirled back.

"Why can't you just be mean and nasty and ugly? Why must you be understanding and long-suffering? I liked you a lot better when you ranted and raved. It was much easier to dislike you. And nobody said that you could call me by my name."

I stopped, panting just a little, and we stared at each other. I half expected her to get to her feet as well. It's what I would have done. Even the playing field so that we could really go at it. Look each other in the face, stare each other down, eye to eye.

But she did not. Instead, she continued to sit in her chair, her hands folded in her lap.

"You liked me better when it was easier to dislike me?"

"Don't you dare make fun of me," I said, abruptly all too aware of how ridiculous I'd just sounded. I could feel the laughter swarming up the back of my throat. The trouble with being angry is that it not only makes you feel stupid, it encourages you to say stupid things as well. Stupid things that are hard to take back and impossible to erase. And suddenly, there you are.

"I wouldn't," she said. "I mean, I'm not. I always sort of envied you, if it makes you feel any better."

"Envied me," I echoed. "What for?"

"Because you had two fathers," the Lady Mina said simply. "Yours, and mine, even though you didn't get to know yours very well. Whereas I, for all the attention he paid to me, had none."

"You had your mother," I said.

She nodded. "True enough. That was another reason I sometimes envied you. You look much more like her than I."

I stared at her, appalled. All my life I had heard tales of die Königin der Nacht, and none of them good.

"What do you mean?" I asked. "I don't."

"But you do," the Lady Mina said simply. "You have dark hair, as she does. Skin so pale you can almost see right through it. You could be her daughter, except for the eyes."

"Well, but your hair is dark," I said. I was sounding ridiculous again and I knew it, but it was genuinely the first thing that came to mind.

"You think so?"

At this, she reached up and, with two quick motions, untied and pulled the dark scarf from around her head. Her hair came spilling down around her shoulders.

I think I must have made some sound. To this day, I still don't quite know why I didn't raise a hand to protect my eyes. The only reason I can come up with is that I didn't want to look away. As if, even as my mind went completely blank, it knew this was as close as I would ever come to gazing straight into the rising sun, for that's exactly what color her hair was. Streaming over her shoulders in just the same way the sun spills over the horizon.

"You are beautiful," I said simply. "Why doesn't that make me hate you even more? It certainly ought to, don't you think?"

"Only if what you felt was truly hate to begin with," the Lady Mina replied.

"You're doing it again," I said. "Sounding all sensible and like you know everything. Statos isn't going to like that, you know."

She did rise to her feet at this, the dark scarf falling from her lap, and all that mass of golden hair tumbling down, down, down, until it almost reached the floor.

"I don't care what Statos likes or doesn't like," she said, her tone forceful. "I don't want him, Gayna. I don't want anything the

Lord Sarastro has to give. I don't want to take anything from you."

I pulled in a breath. "Do you not even want a father?"

Absolute silence filled the room, more complete than when the Lord and Statos had departed.

"Yes," the Lady Mina said at last. "Yes, of course I want a father. One who sees me for what I am, or wishes to, at the very least. For only then may he see what I may become. I don't want a father who steals me away in the middle of the night. Who breaks his word. Who sees me only as a pawn in some gigantic cosmic game of one-upmanship against my mother.

"Do you think the Lord Sarastro can be that kind of father?"

He has been a good one to me, I thought. But all my life I had known that I was not the Lady Mina, not the Lord Sarastro's true blood daughter, and so I remained silent.

"I'm not so sure I think so either," the Lady Mina said, taking my silence for assent to her view that the Lord Sarastro could not be the father that she wanted. "As he's the only one I've got, it seems simplest not to want him at all."

"You will be very lonely here, then," I said, then bit my tongue. "I'm sorry. Perhaps I should have offered words of comfort."

"No," the Lady Mina said with a quick shake of her head that had her golden hair rippling like the flames of the fire. "Not if they were false. I'd rather know the truth, however unpleasant."

"Even in that case, I really hate to tell you this," I said. "But

I think it's nearly dawn. The sky is that funny color that isn't a color. Do you know what I mean?"

"Yes," Mina answered as she turned to look over her shoulder. "I have seen the dawn. There is a moment when the sky goes blank, as if the world is trying to remember what it looks like in the light."

"That's it exactly," I said as I moved to stand at her side. She turned, and together we stood for a moment, gazing out the window. "You should get dressed," I went on finally. "The Lord Sarastro will send for you soon."

"I should be well dressed when I go to be sacrificed? Why should I do anything to please him? Answer me that."

"Then don't do it to please him," I said at once. "Do it to please yourself, and do it for your mother. You speak brave words. Now match it with brave deeds. Show them what the daughter of die Königin der Nacht is made of."

At this, to my complete astonishment, she threw back her head and laughed. "Now you're appealing to my vanity," she said. "That is well done. All right, show me this finery."

"This doesn't mean we're friends, you know," I said as I moved to a wardrobe tucked into an alcove on the far side of the fireplace and flung it open.

"Of course it doesn't," the Lady Mina said, her tone calm. "I think I'm sorry for that. It would be nice to have a friend. I never really had one other than Lapin."

"Lapin?"

She shook her head, as if sorry that she'd spoken. "Not now," she said. "Perhaps another time. What do you think of this one?" she asked. And she pulled from the wardrobe exactly the dress I would have chosen had I been in her place, one made of cloth of beaten gold. "If the Lord Sarastro wishes me to make an impression on his subjects, this ought to do the trick."

Without thinking, I said, "You'll be absolutely blinding."

She laughed again, but it seemed to me there was sadness in the sound. "My thought precisely," she said, and she carried the dress over to the bed and laid it out. "Who knows? Perhaps, while they're hiding their eyes at the mere sight of me, I can make good my escape."

I felt the breath back up inside my lungs. "You would do that? You would try to run?"

She turned her head, then, and those strange eyes looked straight into mine. I'm pretty sure that's when it happened. A single thought, the same thought, appearing simultaneously in two different minds.

"I would," the Lady Mina said as she straightened slowly. "But I could not do it on my own. The dwelling of the Lord Sarastro is large, and I do not know my way through it. Help would most definitely be required."

"And if you had it?" I asked.

"Then I would go and not look back," the Lady Mina said. "Particularly not at any man with golden hair and bright blue eyes."

"I will help you," I said.

By way of answer, the Lady Mina smiled.

At the sight of it, I felt my heart skip a beat inside my chest even as my determination strengthened. *Statos must never see that smile,* I thought. If he did, he would never look at me again, not that he looked at me all that often now.

"But we must hurry," I said, and I moved toward her. "The sun is nearly up. The lord will send for you at any moment."

To my astonishment, she laughed, as if the danger only added pleasure to the challenge.

"I have an idea to buy us a little more time," the Lady Mina said. "Give me your cloak, and I will give you mine." Then she leaned down and swept up the golden dress, holding it against me. "Let us see how well you look in this finery, shall we?"

THE OUTSIDER

I'LL NEVER FORGET MY FIRST SIGHT OF THE LORD Sarastro's daughter, standing fearful yet uncowed at her mother's side. Nor my second one, for that matter, standing motionless and alone in her father's great entry hall. Did not die Königin der Nacht say three times that the Lord Sarastro would regret his actions in stealing their daughter away? And did she not say that the third time pays for all?

Well, I say this. That lady knows what she is talking about.

I cannot say for certain whether the Lord Sarastro came to regret the actions he performed. It is a thing of which we never spoke. But I do know my third sight of the Lady Mina was the one that sealed my fate, assuming it hadn't been sealed already, long before. Standing in the room her father had prepared for her, the hood of her cloak at long last pushed back, I could see her face clearly for the very first time.

This is the picture of her that has never left me, the one that beats with my heart, runs with my blood, holds up my body right along with my bones. It will stay in my mind until my brain itself becomes as blank as a sheet of new-made parchment, a thing that will mean my heart has stopped.

The simplest way of saying it is this: Even in her pain and defiance, the Lady Mina was beautiful. So beautiful she outshone the moon and the stars alike. Had it been in the sky at the time, I have no doubt she would have outshone the very sun.

The fourth time I saw her, she wasn't the Lady Mina at all.

It was shortly before dawn when the Lord Sarastro summoned me to his study. I was ready, had been for hours. The truth is, I hadn't gone to bed at all. How could I sleep when I knew that everything I'd worked so long and hard for could, should, *would* be mine with the rising of this single sun?

"Ah, Statos, good. Come in," the Lord Sarastro said when I had been ushered in. The servant who had summoned me bowed and departed, leaving me alone with my lord. My lord and master, I probably should say. For, as his apprentice, my master is precisely what the Lord Sarastro was.

I know several of the others have told you their life histories, or something of them. Have no fear that I will follow their example, for I have no intention of boring you to tears with the many details of my life until this moment. For one thing, my life isn't all that unusual or uncommon.

Like many a younger son of parents rich and poor alike, I was sent to join the Lord Sarastro's household as a boy, in the hope that I might prove worthy enough to join his order. This I did, and in time achieved an unlooked-for honor. I became his chosen apprentice, the one above all others to whom he revealed his thoughts.

None of which may make much difference to you, of course. For I have not forgotten that your first glimpse of me was through the Lady Mina's eyes. Don't think I don't know what that makes me: the villain of this story. I will say this much, though, and suggest that you remember it as you read along.

My desires were, are, no different from the others'. All I wanted was precisely what they did: a place to call my own, a home, and a heart to share it with, to beat in time to mine. And if I did not always do quite what you would have done to accomplish these ends, let me ask you this: How far would *you* go to achieve your heart's desire? If it was almost within your grasp and about to be snatched away, how much farther would you go?

"You conducted yourself very well last night," the Lord Sarastro said, and he gestured me to take a seat while he stayed beside the window. "You made me very proud. I am sure that, with the coming of the sun, my daughter will see reason."

I bowed my head, acknowledging his compliment which

pleased me greatly, and showing that I agreed with him when, in fact, I did not. I was far from believing that the Lady Mina would change her opinion of what had happened to her simply because the sun was about to come up. That was nothing new, after all.

And I think that this was the moment I first began to feel afraid. For, if the Lord Sarastro did not see the situation clearly, truly, then the fact that I was the one he had chosen for his daughter would make no difference. All might still be lost. But I did not speak my fears aloud. If there's one thing an apprentice should never do, particularly one attached to a magician so powerful he is literally the living embodiment of the sun, it's to let his master know that he has doubts about his judgment.

"This morning, Mina will be presented to my subjects," the Lord Sarastro continued, by which he mostly meant the members of his court, other magicians of our order, and the people of the nearest town. The lord looks after too many people for them all to be assembled in one place at once, even on so momentous an occasion as this.

"After she has been made known to them, I will present you as her future husband. Then, in the grove most sacred to our order, the ceremony will take place at once.

"Do you not think—," I blurted out, before I could prevent it. I stopped and bit my tongue. Hadn't I just finished promising myself I wouldn't speak my fears?

"What?" the Lord Sarastro asked as he came to sit beside

me. "Don't be afraid. Speak what is in your mind."

"Might it not be better to wait?" I asked. "To present me as your daughter's intended husband?"

Give her more time, I wanted to cry. *Time for her to get to know me. Time for me to win her heart. You have control over her body. You've certainly proved that much. But do you think that's all I want?*

"If she makes a public denial, her pride may make it difficult for her to take it back," I went on.

This was a thing I knew the Lord Sarastro understood: the power of pride. It had ruled his dealings with his own wife for many a long year.

At my words, the Lord Sarastro's eyebrows winged up, and I felt my stomach clench. Though I had not spoken all I might have wished, still, I had never contradicted him even this much before.

"That is well thought of," he said after a moment's pause. "For she will certainly have pride, if she is anything like her mother."

He rose and returned to his former position, gazing out the window. Had he stood at his window all night, I wondered, as I had at mine? Had he watched as the night tore itself apart in grief, and all in perfect silence? How had he felt to know he was the cause?

"I will not be governed by the pride of a sixteen-year-old girl," the Lord Sarastro said at last. "Particularly not my own daughter. She is subject to my will, as are all who dwell within my lands. The sooner she is made to acknowledge this, the better. Therefore, all shall proceed as I have already spoken."

At this, I rose also and made a bow.

"It shall be as you wish, my lord."

"Indeed," the Lord Sarastro said. "Indeed it shall. Now go. Take those who are without and bring my daughter to the audience hall, Statos. The sun is about to rise."

And so I made my way to the Lady Mina's chamber, the Lord Sarastro's servants following the proper distance behind. Was I proud of myself as I walked along? As every step I took brought me closer to my desire, did I celebrate the fact that, in spite of what her own wishes might be, in a few moments more, the Lady Mina would be made to bow to her father's will, and therefore, to mine?

Surely, the answer must be yes if I am truly the villain you'd like to think I am.

And so it pains me to tell you the truth. Mostly, I concentrated on trying to control my heart, which was suddenly beating high and fast, prancing inside my chest like a racehorse. I tried to figure out if it were possible to wipe my palms upon my pocket handkerchief without the Lord Sarastro's servants noticing, for my hands were clammy and had begun to sweat.

I wondered if I might simply throw up.

I'm sorry if this destroys the image you have of me as a villain, but it is you who have cast me in that role. It is not one I took on for myself. And so, step by painful step, I made my way to the Lady Mina's door.

Upon reaching it, I stopped, pulled in a breath, then nodded for one of the lord's retainers to knock and announce me. The Lord Sarastro is strict on matters of protocol. I was here as his emissary, his representative, and should therefore be accorded the same respect that he would be due.

There was a moment's silence following the servant's brisk knock. Then, "Enter," called a high, clear voice. The servant opened the door and threw it back. I advanced into the room, making a sign that the retainers should close the door behind me, then wait in the corridor.

I had no idea what to expect from the Lady Mina this morning. Was it possible, as her father maintained, that she would come to accept her new situation in just a single night? She was standing with her back to the room, gazing out the great bank of windows, swathed in her great, dark cloak. Even the hood was pulled up over her head. Of Gayna, I could see no sign.

At the click of the door closing fast, the Lady Mina made a small movement, and I could see a flash of gold fabric beneath the cloak's hem.

That is a good sign, I thought. She would not defy her father completely, for she had dressed to attend the audience.

"Sarastro, Mage of the Day, sends you greetings, Lady Mina," I said. "He welcomes you to your first dawn, and requests that you accompany me to the audience scheduled in your honor."

"My first dawn as his subject, you mean," the Lady Mina said, her voice subdued, muffled by the hood of her cloak. Still, she did not turn around.

"He seeks only to honor you," I said, wishing I didn't feel, and sound, quite so stupid. Wishing I could throw protocol aside and say what I truly wanted.

"And to honor you, as well," the Lady Mina said. "For does he not intend that I shall be your bride? Come now, tell me the truth, Statos."

"That is the lord's desire," I said, choosing my words carefully. "And mine, above all else."

"Truly?" the Lady Mina asked. Again she moved. And again I caught a sudden flash of gold. "More than anything else in the world, you wish to be my husband?"

"I do, Lady," I said.

At this, at long last, the Lady Mina turned around, pushing her cloak back from her face as she did so. At her gesture, I felt the very blood inside my veins congeal.

"And now, Statos?"

"Gayna," I said, my voice no more than a whisper. "For the love of heaven, what have you done?"

WHAT SOMETIMES HAPPENS TO THE BEST-LAID PLANS

(A THING YOU MAY NOT NEED TO BE TOLD)

"WHAT I HAD TO DO," I ANSWERED, MY TONE IMPASSIONED. "What any subject who truly holds the Lord Sarastro in her heart would have done."

"You helped her get away."

"Yes," I said simply. What was the sense in denying what I had done?

I watched as Statos moved to the chair in front of the now cold fireplace, his movements slow yet jerky, and sat down upon one arm. I have seen men, competitors in the tournaments the Lord Sarastro sometimes hosts, move like this sometimes, when they have taken a blow which does no lasting injury but confuses all the body, the mind most of all.

Then he looked up, his blue eyes dazed, and spoke a single word:

"Why?"

"To show the Lord Sarastro the truth about his daughter's heart," I said. "To prove that she will never bend her will to his, for she does not love him. She does not love you. She is the lord's daughter by blood, but this does not make her worthy of either of you. Forget her, Statos."

To my astonishment, he laughed, and the sound was so bitter it made my throat close up.

"Forget her," he echoed. "Why do you not simply suggest I forget my whole life? Merciful sun in the sky!" he exclaimed as he shot to his feet and began to pace around the room. "How shall I tell the Lord Sarastro of this? You have no idea of the trouble this brings down upon us."

"Then perhaps you'd better tell me," I said. "It would be nice if someone explained something."

He swung around to face me, pivoting swiftly on one heel. His eyes moved over my face for what seemed a lifetime. Long enough for me to feel myself color, then grow pale beneath his scrutiny. For me to feel first hope, then fear take hold of my heart.

"You really don't know, do you?" he finally said quietly. There was in his voice a thing that I had never heard there before, though this is not the same as saying I did not recognize it for what it was.

No, oh no, I thought.

For the thing in his voice sounded remarkably like pity. And, much more than hate, it is pity which is the opposite, the doom, of love. For to love or hate truly, you need to be equals, or at least close in strength. But pity is a thing which flows from the strong to the weak. From the *haves* to the *have-nots.*

"Know what?" I asked, though the truth was, I was far from certain that I wanted to know.

"There is a reason the Lord Sarastro did not take his daughter into his household before now. A prophecy was made in the hour of her birth."

"A prophecy," I said. "I suppose I should have known. Wait a minute. Don't tell me." I raised a hand as I saw him take a breath to go on. "It doesn't just concern the Lord Sarastro's daughter. It also concerns her husband."

"That is so," Statos replied. He began to move about the room again, though not with the agitation he had showed before. This was the way he moved when he was thinking something through, trying to come up with an explanation for a difficult problem. A thing he did without being aware he was doing it, and one of the things I loved most about him.

"According to the prophecy, when the Lady Mina weds, the very world itself will change," he said softly now. "And the powers of her parents, of the Night and the Day, will also change. They will at once grow weaker and more strong."

In spite of myself, I gave a snort. "Just once, I'd like to hear a simple, straightforward prophecy."

Statos gave a bark of surprised laughter. For a moment, I saw genuine amusement and appreciation light in his cobalt eyes. I felt a clutch inside my chest.

How much easier my life would be if I did not love you! I thought. *How much less painful, but how much plainer. How much less color there would be in the world.*

"Who comes up with such things, anyhow?"

"I don't have the faintest idea," Statos replied. "The powers that watch over the universe, I assume."

"And they're interested in the Lady Mina and whom she might marry."

He nodded, and the smile faded from his eyes.

"It seems that they are. The Lord Sarastro's interest is only natural, of course. He has devoted the Lady Mina's lifetime to finding the true meaning of the prophecy. Since it tells that the world will be altered not by the birth of a daughter but by her marriage, the lord has reasoned that the key lies in finding the right husband for her.

"But he hardly saw her until yesterday," I protested. "How can he find her the right husband when he doesn't even know her?"

"He does not need to know her," Statos said, both his tone and his expression betraying his surprise at my agitation over what he considered to be obvious. "In fact, he does not wish to."

I think my mouth actually dropped open. I loved the Lord Sarastro, and I had trusted him since I was a small child. But there are some things that simply don't make sense.

"Don't be ridiculous," I said. "Of course he needs to know her. How else can he find the proper husband?"

"By reason," Statos said simply. "Reason and nothing more. This is why, much as he sometimes mistrusts her, he gave the raising of Mina over to her mother, the Queen of the Night. The Lord Sarastro feared that, if he raised his daughter himself, if he watched her grow as other fathers do . . ."

"It might be difficult for him to deny her if her choice was different from his own," I filled in softly.

"That is it, precisely," answered Statos. "He could not afford to run the risk that he would be swayed by his, or the Lady Mina's emotions. More than her happiness is at stake in this. There is the fate of the world itself."

"To say nothing of the fate of his own power," I said suddenly, and I think it's fair to say that I surprised us both. This was as close as I had ever come to criticizing the Lord Sarastro. "The prophecy says only that the Lady Mina's parents will each grow weaker and stronger upon her marriage. It doesn't say in what proportion."

Statos nodded, his expression thoughtful. "That is true also. Therefore, the lord reasoned that the best choice for his daughter would be a member of his own order. Someone he knew he could trust absolutely, for he had helped to guide his steps himself."

"You," I said. "His favorite, his chosen apprentice. How well everything works out."

"The Lord Sarastro has a reason for everything he does," Statos said simply. "It is his way, the way of our order."

"Why did he choose to raise me, I wonder?"

Then, even as I posed the question, a reason occurred to me. One my mind informed me just might break what was left of my already-battered heart.

"But surely you know the answer to that," Statos said.

"So that he could know what a young girl was like," I said, and I thought my own words might suffocate me. "To raise a girl without actually having to raise his own daughter. I am a stand-in. An experiment. A cipher."

"Of course not," Statos said at once. He moved to where I stood, turned me to face him, and grasped me by the upper arms. "He honored your parents, especially your father, Gayna. Raising you simply shows his respect."

I felt a dreadful impulse to laugh and fought it down.

"Respect," I said, and I looked up into those blue, blue eyes. "Honor. Those are fine words, Statos. But for all they speak of noble things, they come from the mind and not the heart. So tell me, what of love? Does the Lord Sarastro love me? Do you? *Can* you even love?"

I felt his hands flex, involuntarily, upon my arms.

"Gayna," he said. "I-it does no good to ask such questions. They can change nothing."

"My lord!" A brisk knock sounded on the chamber door. At the sound, Statos started, his grip tightening yet again. "The hour grows late."

"Merciful heavens!" Statos whispered. "The Lord Sarastro's audience. How can I tell him that his daughter has run away rather than bend her will to his?"

"Let me tell him," I said, though the very words brought despair to my heart. "It is I who should bear the brunt of his displeasure, not you, for I showed her the way out."

"No," Statos said at once. And now, at last, he let me go. "I will tell him. I will do my duty."

He turned toward the door.

"Just tell me one thing," I said, and, at the sound of my voice, he stopped, though he did not turn around. "I have no idea what's going to happen next, but I don't imagine it's going to be very pleasant for me. Tell me the truth about this one thing before you go to the Lord Sarastro."

"What do you want to know?"

More than anything in the world, I wished to close my eyes, so that I might not have to see his reaction. I kept them open.

"*Could* you have loved me? If there had been no prophecy, if it made no difference whose blood flows in my veins and whose in the Lady Mina's, would she still have been your choice? Or might you have made another?"

"Why do you ask me such things?" Statos said, and his voice was weary. "Have I not already told you they can change nothing?"

"I'm not asking that anything change," I said. "All I'm asking for is knowledge. You ought to understand that. Knowledge is a thing of the mind. If you had been free to choose, would you still have chosen the Lord Sarastro's daughter?"

"I have always been free to choose, Gayna," Statos said.

Then he went out, and closed the door quietly behind him.

IN WHICH A NEW FRIENDSHIP IS FORMED

ALL THAT NIGHT, I PLAYED THE BELLS.

I played until my hands went numb to the wrists, and then the elbows, and, finally, the shoulders. Until calluses formed upon my palms, hardened, and then split open. Until the bright blood trickled slowly down my fingers in a never-ending stream, and the bells themselves were colored red and gold. I played until I was beyond hunger, beyond thirst, beyond pain, but still within the bounds of hope.

Just as dawn was breaking, the birds arrived.

Every single bird I'd ever called to me in the course of my life swooped down in a great wheeling mass just as the sun burst over the horizon. Some settled on the ground at my feet in the clearing where I sat. Others lined the branches of the nearby trees. Still others turned in spirals above my head, making a great exclamation point in the lightening sky.

Yet, in spite of these different actions, all had one thing in common. Save for the beating of their wings, not one bird made a sound, as if knowing in their hearts, as I did in mine, that no other voice should be raised. Nothing must come between the ears of the wide world and the call of the bells.

Last to come was the nightingale, who settled into her usual position upon my shoulder, though this was hardly her usual time of day to do so. I knew that she was there only by the quick flash of wings I caught out of the corner of my eye. I think my entire body had gone numb by then. The only parts still functioning were my arms, my hands, and my heart.

My mind felt as thin and blank as a sheet of pounded metal. Not that my mind was really all that important at the moment. The mind is a wonder and can accomplish many things. But it cannot accomplish the impossible. That is a thing only the heart can do, though a strong will helps also.

The impossible began to happen shortly before noon. That's when the young man finally showed up, stumbling into the clearing like a drunkard, then pulling up short. Blinking, as if he couldn't quite trust the sight in his own eyes.

At his arrival, every single bird turned to stare. Those on the ground looked up. Those in the trees looked down. Those still in the air ceased to beat their wings, opened them to glide, and craned their necks. As for me, I continued to play the bells. It had taken a long time for anything to show up, it was true. But there was no guarantee the first thing to show up was going to be the right one.

"I'm here," the young man gasped, and he sounded so out of breath I wondered if he had run the whole way from wherever it was that he had started out. "I'm sorry it took so long. I'm not too late, am I?"

At his words, the stone hammer slipped from my numb fingers and fell upon the ground, and the bright noonday was filled with silence.

"You are not too late," I said. "Who are you?"

"I am called Tern," the young man said. "And I'm a prince, if that's important."

"Tern," I echoed, not quite certain I had heard him right.

He made a face. "It's an unusual name, I know. It's a kind of sea-bird, to tell you the truth. But my younger brother's name is Arthur."

"How nice for him. I am called Lapin," I said. It was the first time I'd volunteered my name in as long as I could remember. "You don't have to tell me what it means. I already know."

"Your name means something too?" the young man asked, his voice surprised. And at this, three separate things happened, all at once.

I threw back my head and laughed.

The birds opened their throats and began to sing.

And, muffled in a cloak to guard against the light of day, die Königin der Nacht arrived.

And New Plans Are Formed

"Do you know who I am?" she asked.

I felt a wild impulse to laugh and fought it down. It could, quite truthfully, be said I wasn't all that sure I knew anything anymore, though I had managed to find the one who played the bells and produce my own name upon request, both of which I took to be good signs.

Pull yourself together, Tern, I thought. *You are a prince, after all.*

"Madam," I answered, wishing I could say something other than what I was about to. "I regret that I do not. Though please don't take it personally. I seem to be saying, 'I don't know,' an awful lot all of a sudden. Though it might help things if I could see your face."

I watched her turn her head in Lapin's direction, the movement as eloquent as if she'd spoken aloud.

Is this the best that you could do? it asked.

"He said his name was Tern," Lapin offered mildly.

"Did he, indeed?" the woman said, and her head turned back toward me. "Perhaps this will help," she said. And she pushed back the hood of her cloak.

For the span of my swiftly indrawn breath, the world grew still. A great darkness reached out to cover the sun, though there was not a cloud in the sky. And, in that moment, I released my breath, for I thought I knew. She pulled the hood back over her face and the sun shone out once more.

"Well?"

"There are tales in my land," I said, "told mostly to lull children to sleep. Tales of a great queen who watches over the night. She is complicated, the tales say. Like the night, she is many different things at once. Some say she has a voice of silk. Others, that she has a will of iron. But all agree on one thing: Her beauty has no equal."

"Just one," answered the Queen of the Night. "My daughter. Will you look upon her likeness?"

"If it pleases you," I said.

"Oh, for crying out loud," Lapin suddenly exclaimed. "I didn't play the bells until my fingers bled just so the two of you could sound like you're in the middle of a court audience. We haven't got a lot of time here, in case you've forgotten. Can't you just tell him what needs to be done and get on with it? Some of us haven't had much rest and are tired."

I half expected her to strike him dead for his impertinence right on the spot, always assuming she actually had the power to do so. Instead the Queen of the Night simply smiled.

"You'll have to forgive Lapin," she said calmly. "He can be annoying, especially when he's right and he knows it."

"There's something you need me to do?" I asked. Perhaps all of this was about to make sense.

"Why did you come here, young Tern?" she asked by way of a reply.

"Because I had to," I said simply. "The bells didn't give me any choice."

"Bells," said the Queen of the Night.

I nodded. "I heard bells," I said. "And it seemed to me that they called to me. More than that, their call was a summons."

"And so you answered it, just like that?"

"Not precisely," I acknowledged. "I don't know how things are where you live, Lady, but, where I come from, knowing your heart and what it holds is considered pretty important."

The Queen of the Night took another step toward me, so close that, if I had dared, I could have reached out and touched her.

"Did the call of the bells match what is in your heart, young Tern?"

"No," I answered truthfully. "Not precisely. But it was as close as anything has ever come. Too close a match to be ignored, even if I had wanted to. And so I came. It's as simple as that. What does it mean? Do you know?"

"I do," said the Queen of the Night. "But answer me just one more question first. What color are your eyes?"

It would have to be that, I thought.

"That is a question not even my mother can answer, not to her own satisfaction, anyway," I replied. "For I am told that my eyes change color according to the light.

"In the morning, they are golden. At midday, green. By late afternoon, they have mellowed to fawn brown. My brother, Arthur, insists that they turn gray as a pewter plate at twilight, then silver when the first stars appear in the sky. At full night, things are easier for all concerned, for, at a certain point, I simply close my eyes. My father calls them hazel, and says we should simply leave it at that.

"My hair is just plain brown," I added after a brief pause.

The Queen of the Night smiled. "There is nothing plain about you, young Tern," she said. She looked over her shoulder at Lapin. "Let your heart rejoice, for you have done well."

At this, Lapin got to his feet and swept her a tired bow, a thing that made the birds around him eddy like leaves in a gentle wind.

"My heart can never truly rejoice until the Lady Mina's does."

"Well spoken," the Queen of the Night said, and she turned back to me. "Come walk with me, Tern, and I will tell you what you need to know."

* * *

"I have a daughter," the Queen of the Night said. "Mina, my only child. Last night, she was stolen from me by a mighty sorcerer, the Lord Sarastro, who intends to choose a husband for her. Unfortunately, he's also her father."

That would be the night of the storm, I thought. *The night the world began to change.*

"I would have my daughter set free," the Queen of the Night continued. "But more than that, I wish her to have the freedom to know, and choose, from her own heart. While her father holds her, this can never happen, for he would have her bend her will to his."

"But—," I said.

The Queen held up a hand for silence.

"I know what you will say," she pronounced. "That many a father has chosen a daughter's husband. The fact that this is true has never made it right. But more than this, Mina's father broke an oath when he took her from me. I cannot trust him to do what is right for our daughter.

"Therefore, Mina must be set free, and so I set Lapin to play the bells."

"Wishing your daughter to be freed from captivity I understand," I said. "But I don't understand about the bells."

"The bells have been in Lapin's family since his grandmother's time," the Queen said. "They were a gift from the powers that watch over the universe. If struck correctly, they

322

enable the player to summon their true love to their side."

"I don't think Lapin is my true love," I said.

"I'm pleased to hear it," the Queen of the Night answered with a smile. "But I set Lapin a special task, to play the bells in a way they had never been played before. He has known my daughter since she was an infant. It was his hopes for her that he held in his heart when he played the bells, not his hopes for himself. And this was the hope that I held in mine:

"That Lapin's playing would call to the one who could both rescue my daughter and win her heart, for the call of the bells would come so close to the music of his own heart that he could not refuse to answer its summons."

"Oh," I said. It was a pretty accurate description of what I'd experienced, I had to admit.

At this, the Queen of the Night gave a laugh as silver as her eyes. "Come," she said, and she reached inside her cloak and drew out a locket made of silver. "Let me show you my daughter's likeness."

"It doesn't matter what she looks like," I said swiftly. "Not if she is the true match of my heart. And even if it turns out that she isn't, she's been wronged and needs to be rescued. I can certainly do that much."

She paused then, with the hand that held the locket half-extended toward me. "I do believe you are afraid, young Tern."

"Well, of course I'm afraid," I said.

"Of what?"

"Of every part of this," I answered, seeing no reason not to be completely honest. "It's changed my whole life. I'd be foolish not to be afraid, I think. But that doesn't mean I won't do what needs to be done."

"Perhaps your whole life has been spent in waiting for this moment and you just didn't know it," the Queen suggested. "In which case, all you are doing is fulfilling your destiny and not changing anything at all."

"Perhaps," I acknowledged.

"All right. Let's say you end up rescuing my daughter, but nothing more," she said. "Not that that wouldn't be quite a lot. It would still be helpful to know what she looks like, don't you think?"

"You'll have to excuse me for being an idiot," I said. "I think I've been up as long as Lapin has, for, as long as he played, I listened."

The Queen of the Night threw back her head and laughed once more. Then she sobered, and those eyes like stars looked straight into mine.

"When Mina was taken, I was sure I'd never laugh again. Sure that my own heart was broken. I think you will do very well, young Tern. Now take this, and look upon my daughter."

I've never really believed in love at first sight, though that could be nothing more than rejecting the notion because it hadn't happened to me, I suppose. And it isn't altogether accurate to say that love at first sight is what happened to me at that particular moment. Because the truth is, this wasn't my first glimpse of the Lady Mina's face. I had seen it before.

This was the face that my mind had been conjuring, slowly yet surely, ever since I first played the flute that I had carved from the heart of the King's Oak, and heard it answered by a call of bells. Hazy, at first, its features indistinct, growing more and more clear the closer I came to the sound of the bells. Right up until the moment that I had burst into the clearing, at which point the sight of Lapin and all that had happened since had driven the image to the back of my mind.

But not, as it happens, from any portion of my heart. For, at the sight of the face in the locket, my heart gave a great leap, and, after that, all my mind needed was but a small step to understand the cause. It was the Lady Mina's face I had been moving toward, her call I had heard in the voice of the bells. And, as her mother hoped, so, now, did I. That the reason I had been summoned would be because the Lady Mina's heart was the one true match for mine.

"Well?" the Queen of the Night inquired softly. "Will you know my daughter when you see her again?"

"I would know her anywhere," I said. "For her face is written in my heart."

At this, she laid her hand upon my arm. "You give my heart hope, young Tern," she said. "Lapin!"

A moment later, slightly disheveled, as if he had fallen asleep, Lapin appeared in a flurry of birds.

"Did I hear my mistress's voice?"

"There's no need to be cheeky just because you know I'm pleased with you," said the Queen of the Night. "Besides, there's no time to rest on your laurels. I want you to go with Tern."

"He's a prince!" Lapin protested. "They're supposed to be good at this sort of thing. He doesn't need my help."

"He does. Mina knows you, while he is still a stranger. Though not, I hope, for very long."

Lapin gave a great, exaggerated sigh. "Oh, very well. If I must do everything, then I guess I must."

He is making it all up, putting on an act, I thought. *He wishes to go as much as she wishes to send him.*

"I will be glad of your company," I said, and found that I meant it.

"Oh, well, that settles it then," Lapin said, but I thought I detected a twinkle in his tired eyes. "It's not every day I get to be a sidekick to a prince."

"Enough!" said the Queen of the Night. "Let my women tend to your hands, Lapin. Then you and Tern should set out at once."

"Which way shall we go?" I asked. For, now that I didn't have the call of the bells to guide me, I realized I wasn't quite sure precisely where I was, let alone where the path by which I had arrived had gone.

"Lapin knows the way," replied the Queen of the Night. "I have done all that I dare. Now it is up to you."

In Which Many Things Begin to Converge

THOUGH THIS MAY TAKE MORE THAN
A SINGLE CHAPTER TO ACCOMPLISH

IT SEEMED LIKE SUCH A SPLENDID IDEA, AT THE TIME.

To run away, and thereby escape from the Lord Sarastro and show my defiance of him, both at once. And not only that, to run away just at dawn. At the moment when the sun begins to reclaim its ownership of the world, just as the lord wished to claim ownership over me.

Could there have been a more complete rejection of his plans for me, of all he stood for? I thought not. Oh, yes, it was a brave and splendid idea, one worthy of a heroine in an adventure novel. One who was going to have a happy ending beyond her wildest dreams.

Eventually.

In the meantime, she—I—was being forced to admit a painful truth.

Running away really isn't all that much fun.

In the first place, the tunnels through which I was making my escape were dark. Not a problem for me, or so you and I would both have thought. But the darkness of the hidden passageway through which I moved was not the kind to which I was accustomed. It was close and cold. The further I moved along it, the more it seemed to me that I was walking through my own tomb.

Gayna had discovered the series of passages as a child, she had told me as we raced to put our spontaneously made plans into effect. Though the Lord Sarastro had taken her in, there were few women in his household. As a result, Gayna was often left unattended for long periods of time. Like any child, she'd been eager to explore, and, consequently, she had discovered a series of narrow passages that seemed to her to run between the very walls of the Lord Sarastro's dwelling.

What this meant, what their purpose was, Gayna had never learned, for she had never confided her discovery to anyone. As she had grown older and her household duties had increased, she'd visited the tunnels less and less frequently, but she had never forgotten them. There was an entrance to one behind the wardrobe in the room in which I'd spent the night. And it was through this passage that Gayna proposed I make my escape, while she, dressed in the finery intended for me, would stay behind.

"Stick to the main passageway," Gayna had said as she bundled me into her own cloak. "This should be easy, for it is wider than the others. Turn neither to the left nor to the right. Keep walking until you come to a great stone door. If you put your two hands together in the center and push with all your might, the door will open. You must then hurry through it quickly, for, as soon as you have let it go, it will swing back all on its own. I don't know how it does this, but I do know it's heavy enough to crush you."

"I will take care," I said.

We stood back and regarded one another. She was beautiful in the fancy dress we'd found, its gold a perfect complement to her dark hair and her fine, pale skin.

"He's a fool not to want you," I said, then cursed *myself* for a fool when I saw her cheeks flush and the tears rise, unwanted, in her eyes. "But perhaps he does, and cannot show it," I hurried on. "The Lord Sarastro is his master, after all. And if he has other plans for Statos—"

"Perhaps," Gayna interrupted. "And perhaps I'll ask him and see what he does. But as for you, you'd better go. There isn't much time. It's nearly dawn."

Moving past me, she fiddled with the back of the wardrobe. I heard a click, then watched as Gayna put her hands in the center of the back of the wardrobe and pushed. It swung back, and a draft of cold and musty air poured out. Gayna stayed where she was, her weight against the door. Beyond her, I couldn't see a single thing.

"Thank you for everything, Gayna," I said. "Good luck."

"And to you," the girl my father had raised instead of me said.

Then I stepped forward into the passage. She stepped back. And the door swung closed behind me.

"Do you actually know where we're going?" I asked. "Not that I'm complaining or anything. But we have been walking for several hours."

Lapin yawned hugely, a thing he had been doing off and on ever since we'd started out. I couldn't precisely blame him, but it was starting to get on my nerves. It's not exactly as if I'd had any more sleep than he had, after all.

"Of course I know where we're going," he said now. "I'm just being careful, taking the long way around. We can hardly march right up to Sarastro's front gates, pound on the door, and demand that he let the Lady Mina go."

"Oh, I don't know," I said after a moment. "He and all his retainers might die laughing. Then we could walk right in."

There was a moment of silence. Then Lapin gave a chuckle, a pleasing sound. All the more pleasant because it seemed to have put an end to the yawning.

"You will be a worthy adversary for the Lord Sarastro," he

said. "I don't think he'll be expecting a sense of humor, some-how."

"What will he be expecting?" I asked. A question that had been much on my mind.

"I'm not sure, to tell you the truth," Lapin acknowledged. He gave a grunt of exertion as, together, we scrambled up a series of boulders.

We had been climbing steadily since we started out, as if the course Lapin had set would take us to the very top of the mountain. The slope had been gentle, at first, the forest dense all around us. As we climbed higher, the land began to change. The trees thinned and the ground grew rocky.

"He may not be expecting anyone at all," Lapin continued, pausing for a moment to catch his breath. "I don't think any-one's ever truly challenged the Lord Sarastro's authority before."

"Not even your mistress?" I asked, then bit my tongue. I have a tendency to speak before I think, a trait which I know often worried my father, for it's the kind of thing that can get a person into serious trouble.

"Actually," Lapin said, "they stay out of one another's way as much as possible. Not that this has prevented either from feel-ing threatened, if you know what I mean."

I thought I did. "Oh," I said after a moment.

"Precisely," Lapin commented. "And now, young prince, if you are rested, we'd better keep going. I'm thinking standing on the top of these rocks leaves us too exposed to prying eyes."

With that, he began to clamber down.

"Wait just a minute," I said as I followed. "We stopped so *you* could rest, not I."

"You just go right on believing that," Lapin suggested.

In the air above us, I heard a single bird call, sounding as if it were laughing at us both.

"Gone," the Lord Sarastro said. "What do you mean my daughter is gone?"

"She isn't in her room, my lord. It would appear that she has run away."

There, I thought. *I've done it.*

I'd told my lord and master that his daughter had fled rather than be subject to his will. Rather than be my wife. Now all I had to do was to wait for the explosion. The only bright spot about the situation that I could see was that I'd been able to reach the Lord Sarastro before he'd entered his great audience hall. He'd still been in his antechamber, and this meeting between us was, therefore, private. I'd stationed the retainers who had accompanied me to the Lady Mina's chamber outside the door to help make sure of that fact.

"Run away! Impossible!" the Lord Sarastro exclaimed now. "She would not dare. She is still my daughter."

"She *is* your daughter, my lord," I replied. "It would seem that this means many things, including that she will dare much."

At this, the Lord Sarastro stopped, and his face grew hard.

"She is her mother's daughter also," he said. "Surely the Queen of the Night has had some hand in this. I should never have left my daughter alone, Statos. I should have married her to you at once."

I'm not so sure that would have made a difference, I thought. Not to the Lady Mina's desire to escape, at any rate. Though it might have deprived her of the means.

I must tell him how it happened, I thought. *I must do my duty.* But I discovered I was filled with a strange reluctance. Try as I might, I couldn't shake the image of Gayna from my mind. Gayna, who had grown up here as an outsider, just as I had. Who longed for many things, just as I did. But longed, most of all, to be loved.

Just do it and get it over with, I told myself. *You can't afford to think of Gayna now.*

I drew a breath to speak, but the Lord Sarastro suddenly spoke before I could.

"But I didn't leave her alone, did I?" he asked, his tone quiet, almost as if he was speaking to himself and not to me at all. "I feared she might be lonely, and so I did not leave her on her own. I left Gayna with her, did I not, Statos?"

Now I did find my voice. "You did, my lord."

"My daughter is unfamiliar with my dwelling," the Lord Sarastro continued, "for she never set foot in it before last night. She could not have run away all on her own. I did not aid her, and I'm certain you did not. To do so would destroy both our hopes. In fact, I can think of only one member of my household who might have wished my daughter elsewhere."

He moved to the door and yanked it open.

"Bring Gayna to me at once."

There are many fine sayings in the world. This one, for instance: *The darkest hour is just before the dawn.*

Not true. I can tell you this from personal experience. For on the morning that I helped the Lady Mina run away, it was the hours before the dawn that had been filled with the brilliance of hope. Despair didn't set in until the sun came up, for, with the sun, came Statos.

He did not love me. Not because he couldn't, but because he wouldn't. He was not looking for love alone, as I was. He was looking for his marriage to make him a place in the world, a place no one could take from him. A desire I could understand all too well. A fact which made the situation even worse, somehow. Why could he not see how well matched we were?

All of a sudden, I couldn't stand it anymore. What good did it do me to love? Had I not loved Statos from the first moment I saw him? Loved the Lord Sarastro better than his own flesh and blood? Yet in neither case would my love do me any good, for mine was not the love that was desired. It was as valuable as a counterfeit coin. It would buy me nothing.

There is no reason for me to stay here, I thought. I could see the future, and it was bitter and bleak.

Moving quickly, my body in motion before my mind could contradict, I walked across the room, untying the Lady Mina's cloak and folding it over one arm as I did so. To appear in a cloak might arouse notice. There was no real reason for me to go out, as all were being summoned to the Lord Sarastro's audience that morning. But appearing in the finery I wore beneath would be quite appropriate.

Now all I could do was hope that Statos hadn't posted any men in the hall outside. I pulled in a breath, grasped the knob, twisted it, and pulled open the door.

"What do you mean you cannot find her?" the Lord Sarastro roared.

The retainer swallowed audibly, and I knew a moment of pity. By rights, I should have been the one facing the lord's anger.

"I went to the chamber as you commanded, my lord. But when I knocked, announcing your summons, there was no reply. Three times I called, and still there was no answer. So I opened the door and went inside. The Lady Gayna is not in her room. She is nowhere in your dwelling that I can discover."

The Lord Sarastro gave a bark of unamused laughter. "It seems we have an epidemic of disappearances on our hands, Statos. But those who run would do well to remember they invite others to pursue."

He turned his golden eyes upon me, then, and though the

anger was plain to see, it seemed to me there was something else in the Lord Sarastro's eyes. A thing that I had never seen before. And that thing was doubt. Perhaps even fear. For no one had truly set their will against his until this moment.

"Find my daughter, Statos," he said. "Do this yourself. You may dispatch others to search for Gayna."

"My lord, I will," I promised. Though my heart knew a sudden and unexpected pang. Perhaps Gayna had been right to be bitter after all. She would always come second to the Lord Sarastro's blood daughter.

"When you have found her, send word, then take her to the grove most sacred to our order," the lord went on. "There, I shall decide what must be done."

"My lord, I will," I said again. Then I departed in haste, leaving him alone.

Meetings

I walked for what felt like hours, though, as I had no real sense of where I was going, I also had no real way to gauge the time. The passage twisted and turned, sometimes narrowing so abruptly that I had to slide sideways, my back against one wall and my skirts brushing against the one opposite. Eventually, though, it always widened out again, a thing which made me glad. For I discovered that I did not like to be so closely confined.

When it wasn't widening, narrowing, or twisting, the passage climbed until my breath labored and my heart pounded in my head, then plunged so steeply my legs ached walking down the incline. Sweat first gathered, then cooled on my skin, causing me to pull my cloak close around me. But no matter what direction the tunnel took, two things remained constant:

The dust and the dark.

The first was simply an annoyance. I found I was unable to rid myself of the fear that I might sneeze and give myself away, in spite of the thickness of the stone walls with which I was surrounded. Had Gayna not warned it was better not to risk a light? But, as the moments slipped by and still my journey continued, I discovered a strange thing. One I had never thought to learn.

I discovered how it is that people come to be afraid of the dark.

Until now, the dark had never been an enemy, for it had never been, nor had it contained, anything unknown. Everything about the dark had been comforting and familiar, and so it was little more than a change in my ability to distinguish my surroundings.

But all of that was different now.

Now, for the first time, the darkness brought no comfort, for I did not know what it might hold. And the longer I moved through it, the more uncertain I became. The longer I walked, the more the dark seemed to be a living, breathing entity. A thing with a will that might set it against mine.

Or perhaps it was nothing more sinister than this: In the dark, I began to doubt the course that I had chosen.

What if Gayna has played me false? I wondered. Wouldn't

this be the perfect way to get rid of an enemy? To guarantee an escape that led instead to a dead end, no way out, and an endless journey in the dark? Almost at once, I was rewarded for this ungenerous thought by stubbing my toe against the wall.

I leaned for a moment against the passage wall, wiggling my stubbed toe in the air, waiting for the pain to subside.

It does no good to think that way, I chastised myself. *Either she's false or she isn't. And either way, it's too late to worry about it now. You made your choice. All you can do is keep on going. Unless you'd like to go back and give yourself up.*

I tried to imagine what might happen then. Just for an instant, it seemed the Lord Sarastro stood in the passageway beside me, so clearly could I picture his anger in my mind. I could see his golden eyes cloud with it, furious that I had escaped from him in the first place, completely disregarding the fact that I hadn't gotten very far.

"You will be married to Statos right this instant!" the lord would no doubt thunder.

So all my running away would have accomplished would have been to land me right back in the place from which I'd run. Except this time, I'd be married to Statos, and the chains which bound me would be even tighter.

No! I'm not going to let that happen, I thought. I put my foot back down and kept on walking.

Moments later, I found the door. I did this by quite literally walking straight into it, a thing which made me take two staggering steps back and sit down, hard, on the dusty stone floor. It then took me several more moments to determine that it really *was* the door and not simply another wall. But Gayna had told me to continue straight. To turn to neither the left nor to the right. And, as turning was the only way I could continue, I could reach but one conclusion: At long last, I had come to the way out. Now all I had to do was open the door.

Push in the very center with both hands, Gayna had said. And I remembered that this was the same way she had opened the door in the back of the wardrobe. But it is one thing to find the center of a door when you can see it clearly. It's quite another to do so when you can't see anything at all. So I did the only thing I could. I began to explore the stone with my fingers, hoping to discover the seams that marked the outline of the door.

My fingertips were raw and bleeding before I was through. And, in the end, much to my surprise, I found that I was smiling. For the door was small, shorter than I was. In all likelihood, not much taller than Gayna herself must have been when she'd first come here as a child. In order to push in the very center, I would have to kneel, then crawl out as quickly as I could before the door swung closed. It would probably also help to roll to one side as I did so, the better to prevent my skirts getting caught in the door.

I could just imagine the looks on the faces of the Lord Sarastro's soldiers when they found me, sitting on the ground with my skirts trapped in solid rock.

Stop being foolish, Mina, I scolded myself. *You've come this far. You'll do what needs to be done. Now stop procrastinating and get this over with.*

And so I knelt, put my hands side by side in the center of the door, and pushed with all my might.

I think that, in spite of Gayna's assurances, I expected some resistance. This couldn't be an exit used very often, after all. But the door gave way so suddenly I tumbled straight out. Then, as it happened, rolling to one side to avoid catching my skirts proved to be a totally unnecessary precaution. The door opened onto a steep slope. My own momentum propelled me forward and out.

For one terrifying moment, I stared straight into open space. Then, after giving one great cry of dismay, I somersaulted down the mountainside.

It was the scream that got our attention. A scream in the forest is pretty hard to ignore. One moment, we'd been climbing silently, yet steadily, our breath moving in and out the only sound. In the next, a great cry split the air, and then there came a great rustling and scraping, as if the top of the mountain lost its hold and was sliding toward the bottom.

"This way," Lapin said, his tone urgent. Together, we began to run. We hadn't covered much ground at all before Lapin stopped so abruptly I ran right into him. The two of us tumbled unceremoniously to the ground.

"Thanks a lot," he whispered as soon as he'd cleared the leaves from his mouth.

"Thanks yourself," I whispered back, hoping I hadn't broken anything useful in the fall. "You might give a fellow a little more warning next time. Why are we whispering, by the way?"

Lapin nodded his head in the direction in which we'd been moving before we'd come to our sudden stop.

"See for yourself."

I looked. "I see what you mean," I said.

"I thought you might."

In front of us, across a rocky space of ground, stood the largest bear I had ever seen, reared up on its hind legs, its muzzle peeled back in a snarl, though it made no sound. A short distance in front of it crouched a cub. And, in between, lying flat and unmoving on its stomach, was a figure with hair as golden as the sun.

"That's the Lady Mina," Lapin whispered.

"I know."

"Well, don't just lie there. Go and rescue her."

"Lapin," I sighed. "I can't go charging in front of that bear any more than we could go knock on Sarastro's front door. We have to be clever. We have to have a plan."

"I'd think of something quickly, if I were you," Lapin said. "I don't think that mother bear is going to give us much time."

"Maybe we can distract it, lure it away," I said. Slowly, I began to ease myself to my feet. But, even as I spoke, I knew such a plan was hopeless. No mother bear alive would leave her cub if she could help it.

No mother bear alive, I thought.

At that moment, as if sensing my intentions, the she-bear swiveled her muzzle toward me, glowering at me with dark brown eyes. And now, at last, she made a sound. A growl in her throat that caused the very marrow in my bones to quiver. I reached for my sword. Yet, even as I drew it, I paused. She was only doing what any mother would. Seeking to protect her child.

"It's a pity my grandmother isn't here," Lapin murmured as he eased to his feet. "She summoned bears when she played the bells, and not one of them growled. But then music soothes the savage beast, or so they say."

"Idiot! Lamebrain! Peahead!" I suddenly exclaimed in a loud voice, a thing that caused the she-bear to give another growl and turn more fully toward us.

"There's no reason to get personal about it," Lapin said.

"I'm talking about myself, not you," I answered. "Here. Hold this."

I thrust the sword in his direction.

"Now wait just a minute!" Lapin protested. "I'm just the sidekick around here, remember? Besides, I'm no good with anything sharp. I always end up cutting something I'm not supposed to, usually some portion of myself."

"I don't want you to use it," I snapped. "I want you to hold

343

it. I have something with me that may work better than a sword. You were the one who said we didn't have much time. Suppose you just shut up and do as I ask?"

"You're as grouchy as the bear," Lapin complained, but at least he took the sword. Moving quickly now, I reached inside my tunic and brought out the flute that I had carved from the heart of the King's Oak.

"A flute," Lapin said. "You're going to tame a bear with that?"

I pulled in a breath. "I'm going to try."

At that exact moment, the Lady Mina lifted her head. The she-bear swung around. From her throat, there came much more than a growl. She took two menacing steps in the Lady Mina's direction.

"Any time would be just fine, I'm thinking," Lapin said.

I put my lips to the flute and began to play.

I was dreaming. That had to be it. What other explanation could there be for what was going on?

I remembered walking through the dark for an endless amount of time, then light so bright it was blinding. A vicious tumble downhill. And after that, nothing for I had no idea how long. But, at last, my slowly returning senses began to tell me many things.

First and foremost, that every part of my body was bruised and aching. Secondly, that I was lying, facedown, upon the ground. The cold, damp ground. Lastly, that I wasn't alone. I could hear whispers, couldn't I? And wasn't that something that sounded distinctly like a growl?

You'll think me cowardly, though I'll remind you that I never actually claimed to be all that brave. And even if I had, considering all I'd been through in the last several hours, it might be that my bravery was all used up. Perhaps that is why, for a moment or two, I was tempted to simply lie where I was and not even bother to open my eyes. If I was going to be captured or eaten, what could I do?

You ought to be ashamed of yourself, Mina, I thought. *You didn't get away from the Lord Sarastro only to give up now.*

That was when I heard the voices again, louder this time. I distinctly heard the word *flute.*

That is Lapin's voice! I thought.

I lifted up my head. There was a bear standing right in front of me. The largest I had ever seen, though any bear looks large, I imagine, when you, yourself, are lying flat upon your stomach on the cold, damp ground. It was certainly the angriest bear I had ever seen. Of this there could be no question. Angry with me. There wasn't much doubt about that either.

That was the moment two separate things happened: I discovered just how much I didn't want to be eaten, after all, and the song of the flute began to weave through the air, tantalizing as a whiff of smoke.

How I wish that you could see into my mind! Or better

still, into my heart. For it seemed to me that this was the flute song's intended destination. The bear was just a convenient excuse for the flute to play. My ear, my mind, just convenient conduits for its song to reach my heart. I suppose I could tell you that, with the sound of the flute, the world changed. But the truth, I think, is that it did not.

I was the one who did the changing. For, as the song of the flute wove through me, I realized that I wanted it there, forever. I wanted to make it mine, to not ever let it go.

And this is a very remarkable thing, if you stop to think about it. In fact, as I realized some time later, it's precisely the same as falling in love. For, to do this, your whole being must accept something new, a thing that starts out as foreign, but ends up so much a part of you that your imagination, which is pretty good, fails utterly when trying to imagine life without it.

Still waters run deep, my mother had said, speaking not of my heart, but the heart of some other. But the flute spoke both *to* my heart and *of* it, its song pouring into me straight and true, finding its way to where it belonged as surely as any waterfall finds the pool into which it flows. And no sooner had the flute song reached my heart, than I was changed. For it seemed to me that I was now complete, whereas something had been missing before.

"Mina!" I heard a frantic voice whisper. "Stop daydreaming! Get up!"

And it was only then that I remembered my danger. Remembered Lapin and the great, angry she-bear. I pushed myself upright and saw an astonishing sight. The bear was dancing among the trees, crooning to herself. The song of the flute, or so it seemed, had won her heart also. I couldn't see the one who played it clearly. He—I thought it was a he—moved in and out of the trees, as if trying to draw the bear off.

"Move, Mina," Lapin said again. "You have to get away from the cub."

"What cub?" I asked as I got to my feet and began to move toward him. Lapin was about as far away from the bear as he could get and still be close enough for me to hear him, I couldn't help but notice. At my question, he pointed, and I turned around. Just behind where I had fallen, a bear cub lay curled up, fast asleep. For it, the song of the flute had been as sweet as any lullaby.

"Things should be all right now," Lapin said as he took me by one arm. "You're no longer between the mother and her cub. What are you doing out here, anyhow?"

"I ran away," I said.

"Did you, now?" Lapin asked, and all of a sudden his grin spread wide. "Bet that shook up the Lord Sarastro. Your mother will be proud."

"Oh, Lapin," I said. And I threw my arms around him. I don't think I'd ever been so glad to see someone in my entire life. "How is she? Is she all right?"

"She's just fine," Lapin answered. "It's you we need to be

worried about. Come quickly now, Mina. I promised Tern we'd meet him over by those rocks."

"Tern is the one who plays the flute?" I asked as I let Lapin hurry me along.

"That's right."

"Who is he?" I asked.

Lapin shook his head. "That is a question he can best answer for himself. Though he is a prince. I can tell you that much."

"A prince who plays the flute," I said, "rather than use his sword. This fellow may be worth a look."

"You're about to get your chance," Lapin said. "Here he comes."

I turned and saw a young man approaching. His clothing was travel-stained. His hair, the color of warm summer earth. And his eyes . . .

"I think we should be safe now," he said. "Mother and child have been reunited."

I watched as Lapin handed him back his sword.

"Lapin says you are a prince and that your name is Tern," I said.

"Lapin is correct on both counts."

"Tern," I said. "That's a bird's name, isn't it? What did he do, call you with the bells?"

"He did," Tern answered simply. "But he tells me his heart was full of you when he played them."

And at that, the waters of my heart became as clear as

moonlight on a calm lake, and I discovered what it was that the flute had added. What my heart held now that it hadn't before.

"You think you love me," I said, and watched his eyebrows shoot straight up.

"I don't just think it. I know I do," answered Prince Tern, as fearlessly as any dragonslayer ever faced down his adversary. And now he looked me full in the face, his strange eyes meeting the strangeness of mine.

"Will you love me, do you think?" he inquired.

"I might," I replied honestly. "In the meantime, I can tell you this much, though."

"What's that?" he asked.

"I love the color of your eyes."

At this, he smiled. "What color do you see?" he asked.

"One that has no one name," I replied. "For it is comprised of too many things to be called by only one. Your eyes hold all the colors in the world, I think."

"And yours, of the heavens."

"Oh, for pity's sake!" Lapin exclaimed. "Why don't you just give each other a kiss and be done with it? I'm not sure how much longer I can stand this soulful carrying-on. I'll just leave you alone for a while, shall I?"

And so he did.

A thing which, in the end, turned out to be just as well.

PARTINGS

THAT'S RIGHT. I DID IT. I LEFT THEM ALONE.

A thing you may wonder at, though, in all honesty, I think the wonder is that I didn't even think twice about it, at the time.

If you could have seen them together. Seen the way they looked into each other's eyes. I imagine that great explorers have this same look, upon finally sighting the new land for which they've spent their whole lives searching. A look of discovery and recognition, all at once. It seemed to me that I could almost hear their hearts change rhythm, striving to find the way to beat as one.

You've heard the saying, *Two's company, three's a crowd?* Of course you have. But I'll bet you didn't know I was the one who coined it. Well, I did. And this was the moment of its inception. The moment Mina and Tern first beheld one another.

It's not as if I went very far, though it may have been farther than I intended. The truth is, I wasn't paying all that much attention to where I was going. I was too busy feeling sorry for myself. A thing I am naturally somewhat embarrassed to admit, but which I must, for, without this confession, what happened next makes no sense at all.

When will I find love? I thought. Surely, *my* time had come. I was older than the Lady Mina by almost eight years. Not only that, I had been playing the bells, trying to get the music of my heart right, almost literally from the day I was born. Fond as I was of them, one would think, by the law of averages alone, that I would have called to me something other than just another bird by now.

And so I have, I thought. *I called to Tern.*

A thing completely unique in the history of the bells. But, nevertheless, a thing that had ended up being much more important to the Lady Mina's heart than it was to mine.

It was at this point that I stopped my aimless walking and sat down with my back against the nearest tree. Above me loomed a rocky overhang. I took the bells and the hammer from the pack upon my back, settled the bells upon my knee, and cleared my mind. Then, I simply began to play, with no other desire than to hear the sound the bells made, to bring some consolation to my sore and lonesome heart.

I'd like to be able to tell you that the tune I played was sprightly and hopeful. But it was not. Instead, it was the most melancholy set of notes that I had ever brought forth. Filled not with hope, but with fear, and the fear was this: that the future would simply be a continuation of the present. That it would hold no more than the past had held.

You should be ashamed of yourself, Lapin! one part of my mind said. But the other part had a ready answer: *No. Let your melancholy have its voice, for despair is just as true a thing as that which is its opposite.*

And, through the conflict in my own mind, I came to realize a thing I never had before. Always before when I had played the bells, my mind had played an active part. Thinking of the future. Commanding my hands to sound out every hope my mind might conjure. Wondering what the next moment would bring. Would it be another bird, or might this be the song which would, at long last, summon my true love?

But now, abruptly, the battle of my wits had ended in a draw. And so my mind fell silent and withdrew from the fray, leaving behind the thing I should have been listening to all along, of course. To say nothing of playing it.

The music of my heart.

And if, in this moment, both my heart and the music I played were full of despair, what of it? It was the truth, just as true as the love for Mina which had filled my heart when I had played the bells and called to Tern. And so I played of my weariness of summoning birds no matter how beautiful they were, and the pain and pleasure it brought me to be able to call another's true love forth but not my own.

I cannot tell you how long I played. I don't think the heart keeps time the same way the mind does. But, at last, my hands slowed and then grew still, for my heart was still a heart and not a bottomless well. I lifted the hammer above the bells and let it hover there, as if deciding whether or not to play just one more note. And, in that moment, I heard a rustle from the overhanging rock above my head.

I wonder what kind of bird it is this time, I thought.

I looked up. The face of a young woman stared back down.

Dark hair swung over her shoulder in a single plait, so long it seemed to me I might have reached up to tug on the end, though she was high above me. She had eyes as green as the boughs of the tree beneath which I still sat. I felt my heart begin to pound like a fist against a stout oak door.

I don't believe it, I thought.

My playing had called to another human being at last. Surely, she could be no other than my own true love.

Slowly, I got to my feet.

Speak to me, I thought.

And, as if she'd heard me, the young woman's lips parted and she spoke thus:

"Have you lost your mind?"

* * *

He stared up at me like the imbecile I was pretty sure he had to be.

"What?"

"It was a simple enough question," I said, trying to keep my voice low. A difficult thing to do when you're calling across even the short distance which separated us.

"Have you lost your mind?" I asked once more. "Don't you know the woods are filled with the Lord Sarastro's soldiers? Do you want them to know where you are?"

"Of course not," he answered automatically. Then I watched as his face paled. "Mercy upon us," he exclaimed, and he spun around. "Mina and Tern."

"You know where Mina is?" I asked. "Where?"

"Not far," he answered as he quickly put away his set of bells. It was the sound of them that had brought me to him in the first place, though I'd been going in the opposite direction at the time. I wasn't quite sure what this meant, but I was quite sure I didn't have the time to think about it now.

"You have to get her out of here," I said.

"I intend to," he said. "Just as soon as you stop talking."

"There's no need to get nasty about it," I said. "Wait a minute and I'll come with you."

I eyed the distance from the edge of the rock to the tree under which he stood, gathered up my skirts, then jumped. I heard his startled exclamation from below as I embraced an armful of pine needles and rough tree bark. Heedless of what it might be doing to the fine garments I still had on, I clambered down.

"What?" I said when I reached the bottom. He was staring at me as if I'd grown a second head. "You never saw a girl climb a tree before?"

"Of course I have," he answered back. "I've just never seen one fly through the air to do it until now. Are you finished playing twenty questions? If so, I suggest we get a move on."

"I'm not the one who was making enough racket to bring the soldiers in the first place, you know," I couldn't help but remark.

"For your information—," he began. But he never finished, for, at that moment, several things happened all at once, and all of them enough to chill the blood.

I heard a man's voice cry out, followed by a quick and vicious clash of arms. A woman's voice, raised sharply in fear. And then, a voice I knew too well.

"Do not harm her, by the Lord Sarastro's command."

Statos, I thought.

"Harm him, and you harm me, too," I heard the Lady Mina say. But I had no time to wonder at the words, for the bell player beside me was starting forward.

"No!" I hissed as I caught him by the arm. I pulled back with all my might and still he dragged me halfway across the tiny clearing where we stood.

"No," I said again, desperate to convince him now. "Think!

Don't just run off. If you go to her aid, they'll catch you, too. Then there will be no one to help her."

At this, he stopped, though I felt the way his body trembled, like a horse longing to lunge out and race.

"How can I help her?" he asked. "Do you know?"

"I do," I said. "At least, I think so. Not far from here, there is a grove that is sacred to the magicians of the Lord Sarastro's order. The lord intended his daughter to be married there this morning. Even if that no longer occurs, it is certainly where he will pass his judgment on her."

"Them," the one beside me corrected automatically. "Don't forget about Tern."

"I can't forget about someone I didn't even know was there," I said.

All of a sudden, his gaze met mine, and I felt that he saw me truly for the very first time.

"You are Gayna," he said. "The daughter of the Lord Sarastro's forester."

"And what if I am?" I asked. "Now suppose you tell me who you are."

"I am Lapin," he answered simply. "I serve die Königin der Nacht, the Lady Mina's mother. Do you truly wish to aid her?"

"I do," I said. "And we've stood around talking about it long enough. Come on. Let's go."

THE BRIEF CALM
BEFORE THE STORM

THEY TOOK TERN'S SWORD, THEN BOUND HIS HANDS before him, a rope passed between them so that he could be led like an animal. Statos himself tied a thick cloth around Tern's eyes. His hands looked strange, quivering ever so slightly, the veins on the back of them raised, as if there flowed through them some powerful yet suppressed emotion. I realized then how tight was the leash Statos kept upon his self-control. But what he longed to do instead, what it was inside him he was afraid to let burst forth, that thing I could not tell.

When he had finished, he turned back to me. I held out my hands.

"Bind me also. For what you do to Tern, you do to me."

"I will not," he said. "This man is a stranger, but you are the Lord Sarastro's daughter."

"He isn't a stranger," I said. "Not to me."

I saw something that looked like pain come and go in the blue of Statos's eyes.

"Is that why you ran away?" he asked, as if he couldn't help himself. "To meet your sweetheart?"

I gave a sudden laugh. For though that had hardly been my intention when I fled, it was nevertheless a reasonable enough explanation of what had actually occurred.

Color flooded Statos's face. In the next moment, it went bone white.

"You think this is a matter for laughter?" he demanded.

"No," I said. "Of course I don't. But I say again, if you bind him, you must bind me. If not, I'll refuse to budge from this spot and you'll have to carry me like a sack of potatoes. But then you've done that before."

"Mina," Tern said in a low voice.

Statos spun toward him, then. And, in that moment, I saw what it was he held so tight and fast inside. Pain, first. But hard upon its heels was the desire to rid himself of it by inflicting it upon some other. And who better than Tern, who had materialized as if from nowhere and claimed all that Statos had so longed for?

"Let word be sent to the Lord Sarastro that his daughter is found," Statos said after a moment. "Tell him we are on our way to the grove."

The leader of the soldiers saluted smartly. With a flick of his fingers, he gave a signal which sent one of his men scurrying off. Then he turned to Statos.

"Her eyes, at least, must be bound, even if she is the Lord Sarastro's daughter. For the location of the sacred grove is forbidden to all but the members of the lord's order and those who most closely serve them."

"I do not need to be reminded of that," Statos said sharply. Then he pulled in a breath. "Give me a cloth and I will bind her eyes. But, by my command, let her hands remain free."

The soldier gave a second salute. "It shall be as you wish."

And so, for the second time that day, I made a trip in the dark. My eyes wound about with thick, rough cloth. My senses dulled save for the feel of Statos's hands upon mine. How long I walked thus, I cannot tell. But just when I was beginning to feel so weary I couldn't take another step, Statos halted.

"Let the Lady Mina be seated, for she is tired," he said. "But let her eyes remain bound until her father arrives. The other, leave standing. Guard him well."

Other hands moved me gently across what felt like a carpet of soft grass beneath my feet.

"Here is a smooth rock, my lady," a voice said, and I thought I recognized the leader of the soldiers.

"I thank you," I replied. But when his hands fell away, I made no move to sit.

"Will you not take some rest, lady?" he inquired after a moment.

"I will rest when Tern is permitted to," I said, and heard Statos give an exclamation of impatience.

"Leave her to her stubbornness," he called. "We shall see how long it lasts once the Lord Sarastro arrives."

And with that, the clearing filled with silence.

"So, what's the plan?" I asked, though I was careful to keep my voice low. "Actually, before we get to that, how do you know where we are going? Surely the location of this grove is supposed to be a secret."

"It is a secret," Gayna said simply. She paused to hold a branch filled with sharply pointed leaves aside so that I might pass by, unscratched, then fell into step beside me. We had been traveling for several minutes, she leading, me following behind, swiftly and in silence. But, at last, my curiosity had gotten the better of me, a thing it has often done.

"None may know where it exists save the members of the lord's order and those who serve them most closely. That is the Lord Sarastro's law," she went on.

"Oh, that's just great," I said. "Now I'm *officially* breaking the lord's law. But you still haven't answered my question. How do you even know where the grove is?"

She turned her head to regard me for a moment, as if trying to weigh how I might take the information she was about to impart.

"I followed the lord and his party one day," she said, her tone matter-of-fact. "Dressed as a boy. No one even noticed I was there, let alone that I wasn't what I seemed to be. Men are often quite unobservant, you know. They see only what they wish to see."

"Particularly those devoted to the sun," I said, matching my tone to hers as closely as I could. "Their minds lack subtlety, for they look only for what is brightest."

She was silent for a moment. "I hadn't thought of it that way," she finally admitted. "But you could be right. While you, of course, are much less likely to be fooled, as you are accustomed to subtlety, being a servant of the Queen of the Night."

"You catch on fast," I said, and she smiled. "You still haven't answered my first question," I reminded her. "What will we do once we reach the grove?"

"How on earth should I know?"

At this, I stopped and put a hand on her arm to halt her.

"Wait just a minute," I said. "You're saying we're going to rescue Tern and the Lady Mina but we don't know how?"

"I didn't know I was going to help her escape in the first place until I was actually doing it," Gayna said. "So I'm hoping it will be enough just to get to the grove and wait for what comes along."

"That's very brave of you," I said. "Not to mention fool-hardy and terrifying."

"All right, let's hear your plan," she said.

361

"What makes you think I've got one?"

She put her hands on her hips, and a long-forgotten image of my grandmother flashed across my mind.

"In that case, I think you should just shut up about mine," she said.

"What do you mean yours?" I asked. "You haven't got one either!"

"For heaven's sake," she hissed. "Keep your voice down. What, precisely, would you like to do? Something, or nothing?"

"Something, of course," I said. "I'd just like to know what it is ahead of time."

"We do know what it is," she said. "We're going to help the Lady Mina and what's-his-name."

"Tern."

"Tern. The fact that we don't have all the details worked out yet doesn't mean we won't be successful. Now can we please stop talking and keep on going? Preferably in silence, which I understand is golden. I never in my entire life met anyone so devoted to making noise as you."

"And I never met anyone so argumentative," I said. But by then I was talking to her back. So I did the only thing I could.

I followed.

I saw the Lord Sarastro for the very first time standing with the sun behind him. A thing I'm absolutely certain he did on purpose, for he was absolutely blinding. And, for a moment, I must admit, my heart quailed. For it seemed to me there was no difference between the lord and the sun itself.

How can I set my will against such a one and survive, I wondered, *let alone, triumph?* Then, in the next moment, I answered my own fear with hope. *Because I will do more than stake my will. I will stake my heart, also.*

But it would not be alone. Mina's would be with it. My eyes did not have far to look for her. Her father had placed her at his side, her eyes now unbound, and in them an expression that reminded me to hope.

And when I saw this, the brilliance of the Lord Sarastro seemed to dim, and I noticed that, though the light was bright, it was also low in the sky. The hours of the day were growing short. Soon, the night would come.

But if the Lord Sarastro were in a hurry because of this, he did not show it.

"I am told you are called Tern," he said. "And that you are a prince in your own country. Are these things true?"

I bowed my head. "They are, my lord."

At this, the lord motioned to the soldier who stood beside me. "Let his hands be unbound," he commanded. "For if I take his word about these things, then I must trust that he is a man of honor."

And so, at last, I stood unbound before Mina's father and all whom he had gathered to him in this place that was most sacred to the magicians of his order.

CAMERON DOKEY

"Why have you come here?" he inquired.

"Surely the Lord Sarastro must know that already," I answered. "For I was brought here by his followers."

At this, the lord's lips twitched, whether in irritation or amusement, I could not tell.

"A clever answer," he commented. "Let us hope, for your sake, you are clever with more than just your tongue. Why have you come into my country, Prince Tern? That is the thing that I would know. Speak true, for I will know if you are lying."

"I followed where my heart led, my lord."

"And it led you to my daughter, is that what you're trying to tell me?"

"It did," I replied.

"And what would your heart ask of me?"

"That you give your blessing to Mina becoming my wife. For, this, we both desire."

"Do you, indeed?" said the Lord Sarastro. "What do you have to say to this, Mina?" he asked, turning to her abruptly. "You have kept silent long enough."

"The Lord Sarastro has not addressed me until this moment," Mina said. "But since he has now, I will say this: Prince Tern speaks the truth, as you commanded. Therefore, I have nothing to add."

"You desire to be his wife."

"I do, my lord."

"And what of the prophecy spoken at the hour of your

364

birth? What of the pains I have taken to choose a husband for you? Do these things mean nothing?"

"What should they mean to me?" Mina inquired. "You have dedicated yourself to the prophecy, not to me. You do not know me, Father. Why should your mind choose for me, while my own heart goes ignored?"

"Father," the Lord Sarastro said, and, to my surprise, I heard bitterness in his tone. "You call me that now, only when you want something from me."

"Which only goes to prove I am your true daughter," Mina responded. "For you have not claimed me until now, to help you fulfill your own desire."

"And you think you know what that is," the Lord Sarastro said. A statement, a challenge.

"But surely it is obvious," Mina replied. "To marry me to the one of your choice, and so control the outcome of the prophecy. On the day I wed, the world will change. That cannot be altered. But you would try to have the world change according to your will. That is why you broke your own oath, and stole me away before the proper time.

"You do not think of me, but only of protecting your own power. If your efforts to this end mean nothing to me, we are even, I think. For my happiness means nothing to you."

"Of course it does," the Lord Sarastro protested, shocked.

"Then prove it. Let me marry Tern."

"My lord!" the one called Statos suddenly burst out, as if he could hold himself in check no longer. "You cannot give your consent to such a thing. He is a stranger, unproven and unknown."

"Then let me make a trial and prove myself," I said at once, and I stepped forward, a thing which made the Lord Sarastro's soldiers lay hands upon their swords. "For then I will be a stranger no longer. My worth shall be known."

"You would undergo any trial I set?" the Lord Sarastro asked, and I could not read the expression in his eyes.

"I would, my lord," I answered steadily. And I held those eyes I could not understand with my own.

"Without fear?" the lord asked softly.

"Of course not," I replied. "But fear is no fit means to measure anyone, for fools have no fear, or so I've heard it said."

"And so have I," the Lord Sarastro said, and he released my eyes. "That is well spoken. Very well. Let you and Statos face the same trials together. By the outcome Mina's husband will be chosen."

I heard Mina draw in a quick breath, but before she could object, Statos spoke once more.

"How can you propose to test me like some stranger?" he demanded, and all there assembled must have heard the pain in his voice. "I have been your apprentice, and your choice to wed the Lady Mina, for many years. I have no need to prove myself."

"Perhaps not," the Lord Sarastro said. "But my mind speaks that this is the only way to be fair to all. Therefore, it is my will that you undergo these trials."

"I tell you, I will not!" Statos shouted. "For you do not use your mind in this, but your heart. And not even yours, I think, but your daughter's. You do the very thing you have sworn you would not. Already you have broken one oath. Now it seems you will break another."

The Lord Sarastro's face flushed bright red.

"Enough!" he roared. "Either face the trials that I will set or give up all claim to Mina's hand."

"My lord," Statos said, his voice strangled as if holding himself in check only by the force of his will. "I will not, nor is that all. For I call upon those members of our order here assembled to witness the fact that you do me a great wrong.

"But I will stay while this prince faces his trials, and see the outcome. For he may fail, and, in his failure I may see my triumph."

"As you will," the Lord Sarastro said, and now I heard nothing but weariness in his voice. He turned to me. "Prince Tern," he said. "Hear now the nature of your trials. Carrying what you have with you in this moment but no more, you must pass through the fires of hell unscathed and return from the embrace of Death alive.

"If you can do these things, my daughter will be yours."

There was one moment of absolute silence. Then Statos laughed, and the sound was like the clash of sword on shield, metallic and harsh.

"But surely these are impossible tasks," he said.

"How fortunate for you, then, that you refused them," I heard the Lady Mina answer softly.

Statos flushed and took a step toward her. But, at a signal from the Lord Sarastro, the members of their order held Statos back.

"Do you accept these trials, Prince Tern?" the lord asked.

"I do accept them," Tern answered in a steady voice.

And then, to the astonishment of all present, with the possible exception of me, for I knew her well, the Lady Mina stepped forward. In fact, so great was their astonishment that it seized all their limbs and held them fast. They made no move to stop her. And so, she walked across the circle and took Tern by the hand, gazing for a moment into his eyes.

"You are certain?" he asked.

"Absolutely," she said. Only then did she turn to face her father. "I accept them also."

"It is well that you do," the Lord Sarastro said. "For you may not balk at the outcome. Now let him go, that the trials may commence."

He still doesn't understand, I thought. *But, then, how can he? For he doesn't really know her.*

"I don't think you understand, Father," Mina said. "I will not stay behind like a small child to await an outcome decided by others. Tern is the one my heart has chosen. Where he goes, even into danger, I will go, also, for that is where I belong."

"Do not be so foolish, Mina!" the lord exclaimed, and I

realized then that this possibility had simply never entered his mind. "The trials are for Tern, to determine his worthiness."

"And what of my own worthiness?" Mina inquired. "Or is that already decided for no other reason than that I am your daughter? You treat me like a prize at the village carnival, my Lord Sarastro. But I am not some thing for you to give away. I am myself. I have a mind and heart of my own. And both say this: I will go with Tern. I will not stay behind."

Slowly the Lord Sarastro moved to where his daughter stood, took her face gently between his hands, and tipped it up.

"It seems you have been telling the truth," he said at last. "For I think I do not know you at all. But this much I can see for myself: that your mind is set. Very well. You may go with Prince Tern."

"No! Wait!" I cried.

For, in that moment, I saw that it was not only Mina who had spoken true. Gayna had spoken the truth, also. A time to aid Mina and Tern had, indeed, presented itself. Not in the way we might have hoped, for escape was plainly impossible. But, if there's one thing life has taught me, it's to be prepared for anything.

And so, I dropped down from the tree in which I had been hiding, much to the delight of Mina and Tern and the consternation of the Lord Sarastro and his soldiers.

"Lapin!" Mina cried.

"Spy!" the Lord Sarastro said, and he signaled his soldiers

forward. "How did you come to know about this place? How long have you been here?"

"Which question would you have me answer first?" I managed to get out before the soldiers surrounded me and pinned me fast by both arms.

"I'd show a little more respect, if I were you," the Lord Sarastro said.

I did my best to make a bow. Difficult, given my present circumstances. "You misunderstand my intentions, my lord. I wish only to give your daughter a gift."

"What gift?"

"If I might have the use of my arms?"

At a nod from the lord, the soldiers released me, though they stood close and tense as I reached inside my cloak.

"The bells!" Mina exclaimed when she saw what I intended to give. "Oh, Lapin."

"Bells," the Lord Sarastro said. "You wish to give my daughter a set of bells?"

"It is all I have to give," I said simply. "For she has had my heart from a week after she was born. She may not carry a weapon, is this not so? But surely she may take a gift from an old friend. It is only a simple set of bells."

"There is nothing simple about these bells, I think," the Lord Sarastro said, and he came close to study them, though he made no move to take them from me. "For I have heard tales of them before now."

"Do not permit this, lord," Statos burst out suddenly. "You cannot trust him. He serves the Queen of the Night."

"That is so," I answered. "But I am also myself. I have my own will. I know my mind, my heart. That is more than you can say, I think."

"Enough!" commanded the Lord Sarastro. "I will permit this gift if you answer me this question: How did you come to know the location of this grove?"

"I told him," Gayna said. And she dropped down beside me, her skirts flaring like a great golden bell.

"Gayna," Lord Sarastro said. "I suppose I should have known."

"The hour grows late, my lord." Statos spoke up once more. "The sun is going down. You should make a decision, and let the trials commence."

"Give my daughter your gift, Lapin," the Lord Sarastro said. "Then let Tern and Mina be taken to the place of trial."

Sixteen

Trial the First, and Trial the Second

ANY PERSON OF SENSE WOULD HAVE BEEN ABSOLUTELY terrified.

But, as I think my story's already proved, the one with sense in my family is my younger brother, Arthur. He's the one who took the traditional route, inheriting a kingdom from our father. Me, I set out to roam the wide world to see if I could find my heart. And I had done so.

Naturally, having been successful, I wanted to live as long and happy a life as I possibly could. I'm not a complete idiot, after all. As Mina and I followed the Lord Sarastro to the place where we would undergo our trials, my heart did beat quickly, it is true, but more with anticipation than with fear. My heart had accomplished its mission. It had found its match. No trial Mina's father or anyone else might set could take that away from me.

Not far from the location of the sacred grove, the trees of the forest gave way altogether, and the sheer rock of the mountain itself rose straight up in a great wall. Upon its face were carved a series of symbols, all depicting the sun on its path across the sky. The Lord Sarastro moved to the one in the very center, where the sun was at its fullest and brightest, and struck the image three times with the staff of his order.

At that, with a motion that was all the more astonishing for the fact that it was accomplished in perfect silence, a door in the rock wall swung open. A series of white stone steps plunged straight down. As I stared at them, I felt a sudden burst of fierce heat.

The fires of hell, I thought.

"This is your last chance to turn back," the Lord Sarastro said. "Once you have set your feet upon this path, there is no other course but down. If you walk the path to the very end, you will be successful and emerge upon the other side. If not, you will be lost forever in the bowels of the very earth itself. No power in the universe will be able to call you back.

"Do you still accept these trials?"

"I do, my lord," I answered steadily, and felt the way Mina's hand tightened upon mine.

"And I do, also," she vowed.

"Then let these trials commence," the Lord Sarastro said. "And may the strength of that which you hold in your hearts be your shield and your reward."

"I can't believe I'm thinking this," Mina said as we made our way down. We had been moving steadily downward for the space of no more than a few minutes. Already, the heat was near to overwhelming. And now we could hear the fire's roar. It had a voice like a living thing, a hungry predator whose only thought is to devour.

"What?" I asked.

"We're facing trials which could end our lives," Mina went on. "But all I can think is, who knew that hell was so close? Just a short flight of stairs away."

"Perhaps it is some magic of your father's," I suggested.

"Perhaps," Mina agreed. "And perhaps hell is this close to us every single day. Perhaps it is only our commitment to joy which holds it down, for do not those who give up joy claim to suffer hell on earth?"

"I have heard it said so," I acknowledged, and gripped her hand all the tighter. I could feel the way the sweat pooled in the very center of her palm, but whether from the heat or from fear I could not tell.

"It's getting hotter, Tern," Mina gasped. "Do you hear the way the fire roars? The path and walls have a strange glow. Do you see it?"

I nodded, for I did see it. The white stone on which we walked was stained red as blood.

"I think we are very close now. Are you sorry you came with me?"

"Of course not," Mina said. "Now is hardly the time to start asking silly questions. You should save your strength."

"Just one thing first," I said.

And I took her in my arms and kissed her. The first kiss that we had shared. It wasn't much like other first kisses, I think. Her lips weren't smooth as rose petals, but dry and chapped from the heat of the fires of hell. But the touch of them so filled my heart with music that, for the instants the kiss lasted, I no longer heard the fire nor felt its heat. All I heard was the music of my own heart. All I felt was joy.

When it was over, Mina lifted a hand to my cheek.

"Your eyes are as white as ice," she said.

I smiled. "Let us hope it is ice enough to put this fire out." Then, still hand in hand, we turned to face the fire's glow. As it turned out, Mina was right.

Hell was close.

The turn of the very next corner brought an end to the passage. Here, in spite of all my joy, all my desire to be brave, I stopped short. Before us, a great lake of rippling flame spread out. So vast, it completely filled my vision, even when I turned my head from side to side. It had no end, this lake of flame.

This is the worst thing about hell, I thought. Not the heat, and not the pain, though these were horrible enough. But most horrible of all was that it had no end. Once hell takes you, you are there forever. There is no way out.

"How do we cross? Can you see?" I asked.

For, as I stood there, it seemed to me that my eyes began to dim, and the only sense I truly possessed was that of my ears, and they were filled with the fire's roar. Then I felt Mina's touch upon my arm.

"There, Tern. I see a way!" she said.

I shook my head to clear my vision, and looked to where she pointed.

Across the lake of fire, like an arm reaching out to ask for help, stretched a single span of stone. From where I stood, I judged it wide enough for two people to walk side by side, but not a single step wider. Hungry tongues of fire lapped up at its deck. With every step we took, Mina and I would feel their touch. Yet the Lord Sarastro had said we must pass through the fires of hell unscathed, unharmed. If we could not, we would lose the trial. Then Death himself would come to claim us.

You are a fool, Tern, I thought. *What makes you think you are strong enough or clever enough to brush back the fires of hell? You couldn't even succeed your own father, claim your own birthright. You will fail, for you are nothing.*

And no sooner had I thought these things than it seemed to me that I understood the fire's roar. It was not one single voice, as I had previously perceived, but a multitude of voices, all raised at one and the self-same time. Each crying out its own doom. But more than that, mine.

"This one thinks the Lord Sarastro will abandon his daughter in this place!" I heard one call out. And it seemed to me every single voice the fire held laughed in response.

"If so, he is an idiot and deserves his fate," a second observed. "For surely the lord will rescue his daughter at the last moment."

"Rescue her, leave this one here, then marry his daughter to the man of his own choice," put in a third voice. "That's what a smart father would do, and the Lord Sarastro is no fool."

I am lost, I thought.

It seemed to me that the voices of the fires of hell made perfect sense. Why should the Lord Sarastro abandon the daughter he so loved to a horrible fate when he might save her? His claim that no power on earth could save us was surely a lie. A lie to trick me into putting myself in harm's way so that he could be rid of me and bestow Mina where he pleased: on Statos.

Darkness filled all my vision, my knees gave way, and I sank down. At once, the call of the fire increased. So many voices that I could not distinguish between them anymore. But I knew what they said. In my heart, I knew it, for did they not speak what my heart feared most?

There was no point in trying, for I would fail. No point in hoping, for I was already lost.

How long I stayed so, I cannot tell you, for it is a thing I do not know. I'm not even sure time is measured in the regular way in that terrible place. But, slowly, gradually, I began to hear a new sound. A sound that was not a voice of the fire, but a voice from the world above. Mina's voice.

"Tern! Tern!" I heard her cry, and her voice was dry and hoarse. As if she had been calling my name over and over, for a very long time. And in her voice I heard fear. I heard sorrow and pain.

You might think that hearing such things in Mina's voice would have increased the fear and pain in my own heart. But they did not. Instead, at the sound of her voice, my heart opened, just a crack. Fear receded. Love and hope returned. And in that moment, I perceived that I had misjudged hell. It was stronger and more terrible than even I had imagined, for I had thought it was a place that was simply external. I knew now that it was not, for the seeds of hell are sown in each and every heart.

Hell is pain. An agony which goes on forever. And you choose it for yourself.

I will not! I thought.

"Mina," I gasped out. With one hand, I scrabbled at the front of my tunic. "Mina, help me. . . ."

"See how pitiful he is," the voices of hell jeered at me. "He refuses to admit what must come, even now."

With a cry of frustration, I tore the fabric of my tunic, exposing the place where the flute lay in its sheath, just above my heart.

"Mina," I said again, and felt her hands upon mine, willing them to be still.

"It's all right, Tern. I understand what you would have me do," she said. "But, in spite of your pain, I think the solution to this trial is for my heart to solve, not yours. For I have watched your suffering, and longed to end it, and is that not what love does? But only if you trust me."

"I will. I do," I said. And I watched her smile. Her face was red and splotched with tears. Her hair was in wild disarray, as if she had pulled it in frustration. Never had I seen a more beautiful sight.

"Then let us see if I am right," she said. "And whether I am or not, remember this: I love you, Tern."

"And I you," I said.

At this, with some effort, Mina helped me to my feet. And, as she did so, the fires of hell fell silent, as if they could do no more. Whether this was a good sign or a bad one, I could not yet tell. Not that it mattered, anymore.

I had made my choice. I would trust in Mina. If we failed, we would do so together, not because I had chosen my own despair, chosen hell over the woman I loved.

Mina pushed back her cloak and pulled out Lapin's bells, glowing red and gold. She cradled them in the crook of one arm, as one does an infant.

"Walk by my side, for that is your place," my true love said.

Then she turned her face to the fire and set her foot upon the stone bridge, and, at the exact same moment, she began to play the bells.

This is the song that the Lady Mina played: the story of our love. She played its unexpectedness, the long odds of its ever existing in the first place. She played its sweetness and its joy. She played its determination and its strength. But she played of its uncertainties, also. For not even the strongest love is proof against all fears. Had I not just proved that, myself?

And no sooner had she played of love's uncertainties than her song passed beyond any description that I can give you, for what she played was no longer just a song of love. It had become the thing itself.

Below us, alongside us, in perfect silence now, the flames of hell writhed. They reached for us with every step we took, fingers of flame curling greedily upward, held back only by the sound of Mina's bells. Then, high above us, a new sound began to fill my ears. The beat of wings. I lifted my face up, and saw that all the air above us was filled with fluttering white.

Doves, I thought.

And, suddenly, I understood what it was that Mina had done. In playing love itself, she had played much more than the love for me which filled her heart. She played all the love that she had ever known, or hoped to know. Her love for her mother. Her love for Lapin. And the birds which so loved him had answered the call of the bells.

In a great flurry of white wings, they swooped down around us. And, at the beating of their wings, the very fires of hell fell back and were put out. A fine layer of ash rose into the air, so that my nose and mouth were clogged, and my eyes watered. But it clung most tenaciously to the doves.

Now, at last, they opened their throats as well as their wings, and, at the sound of their calls, Mina stilled the voice of the bells. Together, we listened to the doves' lament for their fine, white wings. And for this reason, forever after, have they borne the name *mourning doves*.

Still making their soft, sad calls, they rose into the air in a great, gray spiral. Up, up, up they flew, one after the other, and then were gone. I don't know where they went to any more than I know where they had come from. But I think now as I did then, that they were summoned by the power of love.

And with their going, the first trial was over. Mina and I had crossed the bridge, unscathed by the fires of hell.

"One down, one to go," Mina said. And through the ashes that stained her face, she smiled.

At the far side of the bridge over the flames of hell was a great cavern. In spite of its size, it had been hidden from us until now. For the fires of hell burned so hot, so bright and high, that they had obscured anything that might have lain beyond them.

"Do you suppose this is what the underworld truly is?" Tern asked quietly as we stood side by side. "A series of never-ending rooms, one after the other? A great labyrinth of trials?"

"I do not know," I said. "I know only that we must go inside. We cannot come to the end if we do not move forward."

But even as I spoke, I felt dismay seize my heart. For the cavern before us was as bright as day, hewn from the same white stone as the path which, all along, Tern and I had followed. And it was cold as ice. Across its great distance, I could discern a small, black opening at the far end. Along its walls stretched two great wings of darkness, one to the right and one to the left. And it was these which made my heart, so lately brave, go still with fear.

"Look, Tern," I cried. "Surely those must be the wings of Death, himself. Perhaps he is a great, black bird. A carrion crow. I cannot play the bells in this place. For if I do, I will not beat back Death. Instead, I will summon him."

And at this, I began to weep, for it seemed to me that I had offered only false hope. I had brought us this far only to fail, and our lives and love would be utterly extinguished by Death's embrace. I could not win this trial.

"I think you must be right," Tern said after a moment. "For crows are clever, and surely this is the most clever trap of all. See how the reach of the wings is almost upon us? All we need do is take a step and Death's arms will be around us. The trial will be over as soon as it begins."

"I don't know what to do," I said.

"Mina," Tern said. "Let me see your eyes. But dry them first. I cannot see truly if you weep."

And so I did as he asked. I ceased to weep and looked into his eyes.

"Tell me what you see," he said.

"Myself," I answered. "And that is all. Your eyes have no color in this place."

"And when I look into your eyes," Tern answered, "I see myself, and that is all. Perhaps that is the answer to this riddle. In this place, we have only one another. You aided me in my fear; now I will aid you in yours."

"But how?"

"I will deal honorably with Death," Tern said. "I will not try to cheat him or outsmart him, for he is ready for such things. He has laid his trap too well."

So saying, he reached inside his torn tunic and pulled out the flute that he had carved.

"The first time I played this," Tern continued, "my father said he thought the beauty of its music would make even Death pause in his course. I will give Death an offering no one else has thought to give. I will give him beauty. Let us see if he may be charmed. But only if you trust me in this. If it is your wish, as well as mine."

"It is," I said, and found that hope had returned to my heart once more.

"Then stay by my side," Tern said, his words once again echoing my own. "For that is where you belong."

"I will," I said. "And let us not be parted, whatever comes."

"That is my wish also," Tern said.

And now, at last, he raised the flute to his lips and pulled a deep breath into his lungs. The fires of hell no longer burned. The ashes their passing had left behind had all been carried away by the mourning doves. And so, in that moment, my true love pulled in a pure, true breath. And, in the next, he breathed out, and I heard the flute's song.

High and sweet was the sound it made, as high and sweet as the hopes for the future which Tern and I both held in our hearts. A future that acknowledged Death would come at the end.

Oh, Tern, I thought.

For it seemed to me, as I listened, that I understood the meaning of his song. I had played of love, of life. But Tern played of the end of these things, or at least the end as living beings may know them. His was a song that did not deny Death, but gave him his due, as all things which live and breathe must.

Accept this gift, I thought, *as we will accept your embrace, one day. But for now, let us pass. For our day is not yet come.*

The great wings of darkness began to quiver, and, for a moment, I could have sworn I felt my heart stop. Then, the great wings of Death fell back. The bands of darkness vanished from the cavern walls. In the opening at the far end of the cavern, a small figure stood alone.

I touched Tern's arm. Still playing, he nodded his head to show he understood. To move forward was no longer to enter Death's embrace. And so, the flute still at his lips, Tern and I walked across the cavern which separated life from death, in the same way we had crossed the fires of hell, side by side. Until, at last, we stood before Death himself.

He wasn't a bird after all, but a small, wizened man, his body wrapped in a threadbare cloak. Still, Tern played his music. And so, I seized my courage with both hands, pulled in my own deep breath, and looked into Death's fathomless eyes.

I am not presumptuous enough to say that I understood or even recognized everything I saw there. But, where it seemed to me that Tern's eyes held all the possibilities in the world, at least for me, the eyes of Death held all the possibilities for everyone. For, sooner or later, all possibilities come down to just one thing: the moment Death finally takes us in his arms.

With my own eyes, I asked a question. And it was then that the last thing I expected happened. Death smiled. Showing a set of perfectly straight and even white teeth in that crooked old face. Then, like a rusty door hinge, he pivoted slowly on one heel and stepped aside. Together, Tern still playing the flute, the two of us moved past him and through the far door of that great cavern.

And so the second of our trials was done.

IN WHICH MANY STORIES
DRAW DOWN TO A SINGLE CLOSE

THEY STEPPED BACK INTO THE OPEN AIR JUST AS THE SUN went down. Tern, with the flute still at his lips. Mina, with the bells that I had given her cradled in the crook of one arm.

At the sight of them, a great shout went up among the Lord Sarastro's followers. Statos fell to his knees, his head bowed down. The lord himself rushed forward. As I saw the look upon his face, I realized that his heart had not truly believed he would see his daughter again until that moment.

As for me, I'd had no doubts. But then I'd known Mina much longer than the Lord Sarastro had, even if he was her father.

"Mina," he said, and his voice was filled with many things,

but chief among them joy and wonder. "My child. My daughter."

"Sarastro, Mage of the Day," she answered. "Father."

Now, finally, Tern lowered the flute, and its song fell silent.

"Prince Tern," the Lord Sarastro said. "If you will let me, I will embrace you as my son."

"With all my heart," Tern said. And so it was done.

"At the first light of day tomorrow, you will wed," the Lord Sarastro went on.

Still trying to control everything, I thought.

"Say by the light of the full moon instead," Tern suggested quietly. "For I will not marry Mina without the presence of her mother."

"Well spoken, Prince Tern!" a voice I recognized all too well said.

There followed several moments of confusion while the servants of the Mage of the Day and those of the Queen of the Night got used to the presence of one another, a thing that had not happened in years beyond count. In the midst of this, Statos suddenly rose to his feet and rushed forward. He threw himself at my mistress's feet.

"Hear me, great queen!" he cried.

At this, complete silence fell over all assembled.

"I will hear any who makes a just petition," my mistress answered quietly. "Stand, that I may see your face, and identify yourself."

"I am called Statos," he said as he got to his feet. "Chosen apprentice of the Lord Sarastro until this moment. But, as he broke his oath to you and stole your daughter before the appointed time, so did he break his word to me when he said that she might be my bride. But, if you will give me what I ask, I will render up all my lord's secrets to you, and you will have great power over him.

"So will the world be changed indeed when the Lady Mina weds, and all in your favor, if you will consent that she shall be my wife."

"Let me see if I understand you," my mistress said. "You would wed my daughter though you know she has given her heart to another."

"Lady, I would," answered Statos.

The Queen of the Night was silent for many moments. "But why?" she asked at last. "What joy could there be in such a life for you?"

"Perhaps I do not look for joy," Statos said, "but only for the honoring of a promise. I have been taught that such things have much value."

"And so they do," replied die Königin der Nacht. "Yet, for all that, you plead with the wrong person. No one may honor the promise of another, just as no one may give another's heart.

"If you ask me, I will share your grief at the promise broken. But I will not replace it with one that I must break, myself. My daughter is not for you. Let her go, Statos."

"I cannot," he said softly.

"May I speak?" Tern suddenly asked.

"To me, most certainly," my mistress answered. She regarded Statos thoughtfully for a moment. "I suggest you listen to what Prince Tern has to say. He has just proved his worthiness in a rather spectacular fashion, after all."

So Statos turned, and the two men faced one another.

"Will you gloat, then?" Statos asked.

"Of course not," Tern said, his voice showing clearly that such a thought had never occurred to him, and, at the sound of it, Statos blushed.

"I would offer you a gift, if you will take it."

Statos's eyelids flickered, as if sheer force of will alone kept him from looking in Mina's direction.

"There is only one thing you possess which I want."

"By which you mean Mina, I suppose." Tern sighed. "Remarks like that only show how much you're the wrong man for her, Statos. I don't possess her at all. But I'm not trying to argue. I'm trying to offer you this."

He held out the flute.

"I carved this on the night that Mina was abducted," he explained. "Though I did not know that at the time. It is carved from the heart of the most ancient and powerful oak tree in all my father's country. The King's Oak, it is called. And as my hands shaped it, this was my desire: to create that which would let me know my own heart."

He turned then, and smiled at Mina.

"This, I have done. But when I look at you, Statos, I see one who has not yet discovered what his heart holds. So I would give the flute to you, in the hope that you might use it to find your own happiness. My need for it is over."

"You think I want your charity?" Statos asked, his voice strangled. "Your used possessions?"

"I'm trying to give you a gift," Tern said. "The greatest I have to bestow. Will you not take it? Will you not be my friend, and Mina's, rather than our enemy?"

Statos took a breath. But before he could speak, Gayna broke in.

"Take it," she said. "Take it, Statos." And it was she, rather than Mina, who stepped to Tern's side. "All your life you have lived by the rules of another. Worked so that his dreams, his desires, might be given life, even the desire to make the Lady Mina your wife.

"You told me once that you had always been free to choose. Now you stand in the place to which all your choices have brought you. You are betrayed and alone. Why should you reject such a rich gift? Take it, and learn what your own heart holds."

"You would have me take this gift, then," Statos said.

"I would," Gayna answered.

"And if it tells me that I should leave?"

"Then go. Look forward, not back."

"Would you wait for me?" asked Statos.

This was the moment I discovered I was holding my breath,

had been holding it, in fact, from the time that Gayna first stepped forward.

"No, I would not," Gayna answered softly. "For I, too, am done with living my life according to the desires of one who does not love me. Instead, I will stay, and see if my heart holds what I think it might."

And with that, she looked straight at me, and I felt my heart roll over once.

"You would have me be alone, then?" Statos asked.

"Well, of course I would," Gayna answered, as if she thought he was downright silly. "But only for the time it takes to know yourself. How long a time that ends up being is up to you, I think."

At this, Statos looked Tern full in the face, and, for the first time, it was with no anger coloring his own.

"I will accept your gift with thanks," he said, "and wish you and the Lady Mina much joy together."

And so, Tern handed him the flute and Statos accepted it. Then he bowed, and turned as if to go. At that moment, I heard a rush and sweep of wings. *That is the nightingale,* I thought. But, instead of settling upon my shoulder, she settled upon Statos's. She ruffled her feathers once, twice, as if accustoming herself to this new perch, then opened her beak, and poured forth her song.

Never had I heard her sing a song so beautiful. But the most astonishing thing was yet to come. For, no sooner had she finished, than Statos put the flute to his lips and let the notes fly forth. And the song he played was so lovely, yet so sad, that all eyes were filled with tears when he had done.

Then the nightingale flew from his shoulder, singing as she went, and, as if spellbound, Statos followed, wrapping his own song around the nightingale's notes. They may be traveling together still, for all I know. For with his departure, he leaves this story forever, and where he is now or what became of him, I do not know.

Though I hope he's happy, don't you?

FINALE

COME CLOSE, AND I WILL FINISH A STORY, FOR THE END IS very near, now. Tern and I were married that very night, by the light of the full moon, while my father's retainers and my mother's danced together on the ground, and the stars turned reels in the overhanging sky.

The revels ended just at dawn. For then, as they had for untold years, my parents prepared to part company. But, before this could happen, I had my own gift to give. One I had discussed beforehand with Lapin, for it required his blessing.

"You are sure?" I asked.

"I am," he replied, and he had Gayna at his side. "We may

not be quite as sudden in our love as you and Tern are, but then we are small folk, not great ones."

"Speak for yourself," Gayna said.

At which Lapin laughed. "Have I ever mentioned that my middle name is Robert?"

"Why should you wish to be called anything other than what you are?" Gayna inquired.

"That's it," Lapin said. "Now I'm sure it's love."

And so, as the musicians at last fell silent, and the tired dancers sat upon the ground, I went to stand in the center of my father's sacred grove and called my parents to stand by my side.

"Mother, Queen of the Night," I said, "and Mage of the Day, my father, I have a gift for you, if you will accept it. But only if you both agree, for it must belong to both of you, or to neither."

"She sounds just like you," my mother observed.

"She does not," my father protested. "I'm nowhere near that pompous and stuffy."

"You think not?" my mother asked, and I could see the way her eyes danced with laughter in the thinning dark.

"Do you suppose I might speak for just a moment?" I inquired. "I'd like to get this done before the sun comes up. The timing of this is sort of important."

"I apologize, Mina," my mother said. "Please, go on. And of course I accept your gift, even if it means I must share it with your father."

"Anything your mother can do, I can do," declared the Lord Sarastro.

I sincerely hope this works, I thought. And I held out Lapin's bells.

"You know the history of these bells," I said. "But I think they have a future, also. In order for it to be fulfilled, you each must answer the same question: Do you love each other?"

Not a soul stirred in the clearing as we waited for my parents to answer. "Speak from your hearts," I charged. "Anything less doesn't count, and not only that, it will bring about disaster."

"Then from my heart, I answer this," said the Lord Sarastro. "That though I do not always understand her, I do truly love your mother."

"And I say this," my mother replied. "That I love your father, though he has wronged me. And because I love truly, I forgive those wrongs."

"Then these belong to you," I said. "To both of you, equally, to share and share alike. To the Lord Sarastro in the day, and to Pamina, die Königin der Nacht, in the dark.

"Each day as the sun sets, Father, you must give them to my mother. And each day as the sun rises, Mother, you must give them to my father. Let the rising and setting of the sun be a time of coming together, not of dividing. Play the bells, and let all creation hear the music of your hearts, for you have hidden it away for far too long."

"Actually, I think you're right. She does sound like me," my father said.

My mother laughed and took the bells from my arms. She had time to sound just one note, but it was a note of such incredible beauty and joy that it caused the sun to leap straight up over the horizon. Then my mother turned and gave the bells to my father.

"I will be interested to hear the song you play," she said.

And now my father laughed in his turn. "And so will I."

Then he began to play, and at this, the full glory of the world burst forth. For, in that moment, the hopes of the powers that watch over the universe were fulfilled, and the world was discovered to be much more than a mountain, albeit a very tall one, but an entire globe, spinning in the sky.

And with this discovery, day and night no longer warred with one another. For, in its new shape, the world could never be all one thing or all the other. The night that I was married is the time night and day began to live side by side in the world, a circumstance with which you are familiar, for it has existed ever since that time.

In time, the music my parents play came to be known as the music of the spheres. It may still be called this, for all I know. For they are still playing. They will play until the last gasp of the universe itself. You can hear them for yourself, if your heart knows how to listen.

And as for me and Tern, we did not settle in just one place, but decided to spend our days wandering through the new world which had just been born. Naturally we stop to see both his family and mine upon our travels, at holiday and birthday time, as often as can be managed.

But I think the truth is that neither Tern nor I needs a fixed place, as other people do, for the true place of each is in the heart of the other. That will be true for as long as our hearts beat and maybe even longer. I don't yet know.

So here, I think, is where the story ends. Or at least the portion of it I am able to tell you.

Author's Notes

THIS STORY WAS INSPIRED BY MY FAVORITE OPERA: Mozart's *Die Zauberflöte. The Magic Flute.* That's right. I said opera. Not only that, I said I liked it. Why do you think they put author notes at the end of the book and not the beginning, if not to avoid scaring readers off entirely?

Seriously, though. You ought to try it. Opera is so fantastical, so much bigger than life. It's not all overweight sopranos marching around in weird costumes that always seem to involve helmets with great curved horns sticking out of the top. And *Die Zauberflöte* is a great place to start.

There's even a film version by the great Swedish filmmaker Ingmar Bergman, which is one of my favorite movies on the entire planet. In fact, it was Bergman, not Mozart, who first created a husband and wife relationship for Sarastro and the Queen of the Night. It seems just right, though. What has always appealed to me about this story is its combination of whimsy and distress. Of sunlight and shadow. Yes, this would explain my title. I'm also drawn to the notion that, to truly win what your heart desires, you must conquer your own fears. In our own ways, we all face trials.

I've definitely reshaped some elements to fit my world view, rather than Mozart's. The truth is, men didn't think much of women, or at least not of their brains, in Mozart's time. In the original trials, Tern (named Tamino in the opera) is steadfast and brave, and Pamina mostly tags along. And the character of Statos (Monostatos, in the opera) is strictly a bad guy for no other reason than that he's a Moor. So there's definitely some misogyny and racism going on. All the more reason to have a fresh look at the material, I say.

Thanks for reading. I hope you had as good a time as I did writing.

WINTER'S CHILD

To Annette Pollert, editor extraordinaire,

with many thanks

A FEW WORDS CONCERNING STORIES

THE WORLD IS FULL OF COUNTLESS STORIES, ALL BEING told at the same time.

Some are so quiet you have to strain your ears to hear them. Stories like the one the grocer tells to the first autumn apples as they jostle for position on his shelves. He murmurs as he polishes them with his flannel sleeve, promising to make them shine so brightly that every single apple will take a journey in a market basket to be made into a pie before the sun goes down.

Only a little louder is the tale that the sea captain's young daughter tells her rag doll in the dark of night. She huddles in her bed, listening to the wind moan. "Soon," she whispers into one rag-doll ear. "Soon Papa will return, safe and whole." That is what the wind is saying, she promises the doll. Papa will come home again. He will not leave us. Outside, the wind continues its endless sob and moan. But as long as her lips have the power to tell the tale, the sea captain's daughter's eyes stay dry.

Then there are the tales that shout; stories that can shake the rooftops with their wonder: the tales that sweethearts tell. Most wonderful of these are the ones when both the tales and the love prove true.

And then there are the everyday tales, the tales that make the world go around. Stories children tell themselves so they believe they're growing up faster than is possible; tales parents tell each other as they cling together, watching their youngsters strike out on their own; tales the old folks tell to help them remember what it felt like to be young; stories the voices of the living chant over the graves of the dead, mourning those whose storytelling days are done.

Pick any time of the day or night and somewhere, everywhere, stories are being told. They overlap and flow across one another, then pull away again just as waves do upon a shore. It is this knack that stories have of rubbing up against one another that makes the world an interesting place, a place of greater possibility than it would be if we told our tales alone.

This is impossible, of course. Make no mistake, everyone's story touches someone else's. And every brush of one life tale upon another, be it ever so gentle, creates something new: a pathway that wasn't there before. The possibility to create a new tale.

In this story—which, as I'm sure you've already figured out, is not one but several all flowing together, parting ways only to bump into one another again—in this story, something very remarkable takes place:

All paths begin and end at the door of the Winter Child.

STORY THE FIRST

IN WHICH THE WINTER CHILD RECEIVES HER NAME,
AND ALL THE TALES THAT MAKE UP THIS STORY
ARE THEREBY SET IN MOTION

MANY YEARS AGO, WHEN THE WORLD WAS MUCH YOUNGER than it is today, a king and queen dwelt together in a castle made of ice and snow. No doubt this may seem uncomfortable to you, but as this royal couple ruled over a kingdom where there was so much ice and snow that not a single day went by without some sight of both, the king and queen had become accustomed to their situation. It suited them just fine. They found nothing unusual about their circumstance, in fact.

But I am straying from my path already, and I've no more than packed my bag and started out the door.

The king and queen had been married for several years

when the stories you are about to read were preparing to begin. The royal couple had loved each other truly when first they had wed, but, as the years went by, the queen began to fear the march of time. She began to ask herself a series of impossible questions, questions with no answers:

If her looks should start to fade, as inevitably they must, would the king still care for her? Or did he love her for her appearance alone?

In all fairness, it must be acknowledged that the queen was very lovely. Her face was a perfect oval. Her lips were the color of the bright red berries that flourished even in the depths of winter, and her skin was as white as snow. Her eyes gleamed like two jet buttons, and her hair was a waterfall of black as dark as a night without stars.

In equal fairness, it must be acknowledged that, by giving in to her fear, the queen performed a great disservice, both to herself and to her husband. The king had not fallen in love with her simply because of the loveliness of her face, but also for the strength and beauty of her heart.

But giving in to her fear was precisely what the queen did. Her heart didn't even put up a fight. The moment that happened, all was lost, though the queen didn't realize this at the time. As soon as fear's occupation of the queen's heart was complete, she retreated to the castle's highest tower. All she took for company were her baby daughter, just six months old, and a mirror made of polished ice.

First days, and then weeks, went by. The queen sat in a hard-backed chair, gazing at her face for hour after hour, searching for the first sign that her beauty—and the king's love—were poised to take flight. The king visited the tower morning, noon, and night. The nursemaids came and went, caring for the princess. The housemaids came and went, dusting the room and lighting the fires. The king sent first the royal physician, and then every other healer in the land to see if any could cure the queen's strange malady.

None of it made any difference. Nothing the king did or said could penetrate the fear that had captured the queen's heart. And so, as the weeks threatened to slide on into months and still the queen's heart refused to listen, something terrible began to transpire. The king's love began to falter, for not even the strongest love can survive all on its own. Love cannot thrive simply by being offered. Sooner or later it must be accepted and reciprocated. It must be seen for what it is and nourished according to its needs, or it will die.

The queen's face remained as beautiful as ever. But the king's love could not stay the course charted by his wife's fearful heart. His love began to diminish with every minute of every day that the queen stayed in the tower, until at last the morning dawned when the king awoke and discovered that his love for the queen was altogether gone. And in this way, the queen's own actions brought about the result she had so feared: The king no longer loved her.

411

Love must go somewhere, however, and the king still had one family member left, his baby daughter. Determined that she should not suffer because her mother had eyes only for herself, the king decided to love the princess twice as much as he had before.

The baby had her mother's coloring. She, too, had hair and eyes as black as night. Her skin was as pale as fine white linen, and her mouth, a perfect little red rosebud. This caused the king both pain and joy. Every time he gazed into his daughter's face, as he did each morning, noon, and night, it seemed to him that he felt the clutch of fear wrap itself around his love.

Search though he might, the king could find nothing of himself in his daughter's face. In every particular, she seemed to be her mother's child. The queen's fate was hardly turning out as might have been predicted, let alone desired. The princess's resemblance to her mother could not help but make the king wonder about his daughter's own fate. What might it hold in store?

Now, it was the custom in the land of ice and snow for mothers to bestow names upon their newborns. Every family followed this tradition, from the royal couple to the woodcutter and his wife. Most people named their children right away, for it was dangerous to let a child go without a name for too long. Without a name, it is hard to develop a sense of direction. Without a name, it is difficult to set out on your life's journey and so discover who you are.

This is not to say that any name will do, of course. In fact, it's just the opposite. Every child must be given her or his true and proper name, and this is a task that cannot be rushed. It takes time.

So when at first days, and then weeks, went by and still the baby princess had no name, though it made the king uneasy, he kept it to himself. But as the weeks slid into months that added up to half a year, the king's uneasiness turned into genuine alarm. Day after day, the infant princess lay in a basket by the tower window, kicking off her blankets no matter how tightly her nursemaids wrapped her up. This, the nursemaids took to be a sign.

"She is trying to escape her destiny," whispered the first, as the nursemaids sat together near the kitchen fire one night. They were having a bedtime snack of tea and scones.

"Oh, don't be daft," the second replied. She took a gulp of tea, then winced as it burned her tongue. "There's not a soul alive can do a thing like that."

But it was the third nursemaid who came closest to the mark. She sipped her tea, for she was more cautious.

"She's only six months old," the third nursemaid remarked. "The princess doesn't have the faintest idea what her destiny is yet. And she won't, poor mite. Not until she has a name to call her own."

Not long after this conversation took place, there came an afternoon when, just like always, the queen sat in her hard-backed chair gazing at her reflection. Her baby daughter lay, kicking her legs, in a basket on a nearby window seat. The window was open for, though cold, the sun was shining and the day was fine. High above the castle, so high as to render the legs of the baby princess so small they were almost invisible, the North Wind was passing by.

Now, the North Wind is a cross wind, a contrary and unpredictable blusterer. The plain and simple truth of the matter is that the North Wind hates to be cold. But as bringing cold is the North Wind's reason for existence, it really has no choice. This is why, in the dead of winter, the North Wind howls so. It's lamenting its own fate and wailing a warning. It will do some mischief if it can, and never mind the consequences.

And that's precisely what happened that day at the palace. The North Wind passed by with mischief on its mind.

It did not care that the sun was shining and the day was fine. It could not bring about such things itself, and so they provoked only jealousy in the North Wind's soul. So when it spied an infant lying unwatched and unprotected by an open window, the North Wind swooped down to take a closer look. Perhaps it might be able to use the baby to conjure up enough mischief to summon clouds that would blot out the sun.

But no sooner did the North Wind come in through the window than it caught sight of the queen gazing at her reflection in the mirror made of ice. The North Wind was so struck by the queen's beauty that it forgot completely why it had come. If it had been possible for something to deprive the North Wind of breath, the queen's beauty would have done so.

But no matter how the North Wind tried to get the queen's attention, frisking around the hem of her skirts, teasing the ends of her midnight-dark hair, nothing compelled the queen to look up. She never even shivered, as if she didn't feel the North Wind's presence at all. Instead, the queen's eyes stayed fixed upon her mirror and her reflection. Thoroughly vexed, for it was not accustomed to being ignored, the North Wind swirled around the tower room. There, on the window seat, was the infant who had drawn it down to the castle in the first place.

Aha! the North Wind thought. It dashed to the window and caught the child up in its arms, sending the basket and cushions beneath her out the open window in a great *whoosh* of air. Surely whisking away the beautiful woman's infant would get her attention.

Sadly for all concerned, it did not.

The North Wind carried the princess straight out the window, and still the queen did not so much as stir or turn around. When it realized this, the North Wind behaved true to form. Having stirred up some mischief, the North Wind lost interest and released the child, letting her fall.

Down, down, down the baby princess plummeted, kicking her legs the entire time. She fell past the window where her mother's ladies in waiting sat busy with the castle mending. Past the window where her father's pages were dusting the leather spines of all the books on the library shelves. And finally, past the royal study where her father sat at an open window of his own, jotting down notes for a State of the Kingdom address he would be making in about a week's time.

At the sight of his daughter hurtling inexorably downward, the king gave a great cry. He abandoned his papers, leaped to his feet, and dashed down the stairs from his study to the castle's front door. He hadn't a chance of reaching his daughter before the ground did. The situation was simple as that and, even as the king ran for all he was worth, he knew this in his heart. But just as the king was sure his heart would burst with fear and love combined, the unseen forces that shape the world around us interfered for a second time.

Just before the princess hit the ground, a different wind caught the baby in its arms. It was a small and playful wind, a delicate wind, a harbinger of the spring that comes after the North Wind passes by. A wind like this was not about to watch a baby be dashed to pieces, particularly not on such a beautiful day.

With a touch as gentle as a shower of flower petals, the wind set the princess on a nearby snowbank. And this was where the king found her moments later, no longer kicking her legs, for the Spring Wind had carried away the princess's blanket, but had left her otherwise completely unharmed.

"Unharmed." It's a nice word, isn't it? A comforting word, though not quite all-encompassing. "Unharmed" is not the same as "unchanged," after all. And "changed" is precisely what the princess was.

The baby's hair, once as dark as the feathers of a raven, was now as white as the snowbank on which she rested. Her eyes, no longer dark, had become the fine and delicate blue of a winter sky. Her skin always had been white, but now it seemed so thin that the king could see the blue veins weaving their intricate patterns, like lace, beneath the surface. The princess's lips, previously as red as a rosebud, had faded to the pale pink of that same rose now kissed by a winter's frost.

The embrace of the North Wind had changed the princess forever. She had become a Winter Child.

The king loved her no less for this, however. In fact, as he cradled his daughter against his thundering heart, the king might even have loved her more. For now, at least a portion of her destiny seemed clear:

She must walk the ways of a Winter Child.

A Winter Child does not tread the same paths as the rest of us. The touch of the North Wind lingers on a Winter Child long after the wind itself is gone. There is only one way to remove this touch, and so return a Winter Child to her true and original form. She must help to right some great and terrible wrong. She must atone for a sadness that was not of her making.

This is what it means to be a Winter Child.

No sooner did the king come to realize all this than he realized he was angry. Angry with the queen, his wife, a mother so intent upon herself that she had failed to see the danger to her daughter, let alone to save her from it.

And so, still cradling the baby in his arms, the king returned to the castle and climbed all the way to the topmost tower, taking the steps two at a time. He burst into the chamber where the queen still sat, gazing at herself. She had not even noticed that the baby was gone.

"Look what our daughter has become! Look what you have helped to make her!" the king cried.

The king held out the baby toward the queen, and finally, the queen looked up from the mirror made of ice. The coldness of the North Wind had utterly failed to catch her attention, but the heat in her husband's voice turned the queen's head as if pulled by a cord. Even accustomed as she was to gazing at nothing but her own features, the queen could see at once that something was terribly wrong.

"But I never—," the queen began.

"Yes, I know you never," the king cried passionately, cutting her off. "You never even noticed our daughter was missing, because you never see anyone but yourself!"

He advanced into the room, still holding the infant out in front of him, and now the queen could clearly see the changes in her daughter for herself. She felt a fine trembling begin in the pit of her stomach and spread to her limbs. For the first time since coming to the land of ice and snow, the queen felt cold. Cold with the apprehension that something dreadful was about to happen, something that now could not be turned aside.

"How I curse the mirror that you clasp so tightly!" the king

418

went on. "More tightly than you have ever clasped our child. How I wish your mirror could show you the coldness of your heart. I wish that it could show what lies beneath your beauty. I wish it could expose your flaws."

Here, I will give you some important information, so important you may even wish to write it down and keep it somewhere safe. Put it in a place where you can take it out and look at it from time to time. And that important information is this: It is very dangerous to utter a wish and a curse at the same time.

That's ridiculous, you may answer. *Surely the two would cancel each other out.*

Don't you believe it. Not for a moment. Instead of canceling each other out, each magnifies the other, giving it more power, until both the wish and the curse have enough power to come true.

That is precisely what happened in the tower room that day. No sooner had the king finished speaking than the queen uttered a piercing cry. She flung the mirror away with all her strength. It struck the wall, shattering into pieces too numerous to count. Most flew out the window and were borne away by the wind. Only one did not. This icy fragment struck the baby princess and embedded itself deep in her heart.

The power of a wish and a curse together now had done its work. Each had fed upon the other's energy, growing in strength, until both were granted at the same time. In that instant, the queen's mirror had revealed not just her outer beauty, but also her innermost flaw. What she had seen so pained and horrified her that the queen's heart shattered into pieces too numerous to count, just as the mirror had. She perished on the spot. All that remained of her beauty was her daughter's pale and serious face.

Her daughter, the Winter Child, who now had a shard of cursed and icy mirror embedded in her heart.

The king sank to his knees, still cradling his baby girl in his arms. What his own heart felt in that moment, no living soul will ever know. But now, with cold tears streaming down his cheeks, the king spoke one thing more. He spoke his daughter's name aloud.

Deirdre. That was what he called her. *Sorrow* was the name the king gave to his only child. Then he bowed his head and, at last, his tears grew warm.

For now the king wept not just for what would be, but for all the things that could be no more. He wept for the fate of his wife, whom he had once loved so deeply, and for that of his young daughter, now forever altered by the North Wind's touch. As the king rocked her in his arms, dampening her pale face with his tears, he vowed that he would spend the rest of his life trying to prepare his daughter for whatever lay in store for her as a Winter Child.

But as to what, precisely, that might be . . . for that we must move on to another story.

Two

Story the Second

IN WHICH GRACE TAKES UP THE TALE

AND INTRODUCES US TO KAI

I CANNOT IMAGINE A WORLD WITHOUT KAI.

Part of this is simple mathematics. I've never known a world without him in it, for he was born three days before me. Part of it is simply love. Except that love is rarely simple, even when you think it is. Or maybe I should say that love is rarely simple in the *way* you think it is. I'm living proof of that.

Kai and I grew up together, side by side. We lived at the very tops of two old neighboring buildings that leaned toward each other ever so slightly, like sweethearts who couldn't bear the thought of being kept apart. The rooftops were so close together we could place a single plank across the gap between them and walk from one rooftop to the other. We did this every summer after Kai was strong enough to put the board in place and our courage was strong enough to carry us across.

Kai never looked down.

I always did. This was a difference between us, right from the start, a difference that became more pronounced as time went on. Kai's eyes sought out nearby things, while my eyes much preferred to search for far-off ones.

"Grace, don't," Kai used to plead when I would stop partway between my rooftop and his to wave at Herre Johannes, the flower merchant, as he pulled his horse and cart up in front of our buildings' front doors, far below. "Don't look down. It's dangerous. You'll fall."

"Of course I won't fall, silly," I answered back. I lifted one foot to take a step, then held it poised in midair. This worried Kai most of all.

"You can't fall if your feet know where they're supposed to be." And with this, I always put my foot back down on the board and continued on my way.

"Yes, but what if the board has a change of heart about letting you walk on it in the first place?" Kai would query every time he grasped my hand and pulled me to the safety of his rooftop.

This was our standard discussion, not quite serious enough to be called a true argument. I always insisted that I would be all right in the end if only I knew where to place my feet. Usually, it was as simple and straightforward as putting one in front of the other. Kai was equally insistent that even the most straight-forward of paths could turn out to be more complicated than it seemed at first. Which meant, in turn, of course, that even the most carefully placed footsteps could be sent awry entirely without warning.

Perhaps it will come as a surprise, then, when I tell you that most of the time it was Kai who made the trip from his rooftop to mine. This, despite the fact that he disliked heights. In addition to saving me from potential foolishness and danger, the plain and simple truth was that our rooftop was much more pleasant.

My grandmother, my oma, had one of the best green thumbs in town. Our rooftop caught the rain just like every-body else's did, but my oma knew just what to do with the rain that fell on ours. Almost every square inch of our roof was filled with a pot or planter of some kind. Some held fruit and vegetables that we would eat fresh in summer, then preserve to eat during the long winter months. But most of the pots were filled with flowers.

There were geraniums red as firebrands and marigolds as bright as spun gold. In early spring, sweet peas fluttered like flocks of tiny purple finches. In the autumn, mums clustered together like schoolchildren in their new winter coats, prepar-ing for the cold.

The flowers did more than bring us pleasure. They also brought in much-needed income. This money was important, for it was just my oma and me at home. My father, Oma's son, had been a soldier stationed in a faraway land. He died in a skirmish when I was very young. My mother had loved my father so much that, rather than stay at home in safety after I was born, she had left me behind in Oma's care and followed her husband and the drum.

When word of my father's death was brought to my mother, she left the camp and walked to the edge of the river along whose banks the battle had been fought. There, she filled the pockets of her apron with stones. Then she waded out until the swift current swept her feet from under her and the stones in her pockets pulled her down to the river's floor. In this way, I lost both my parents on the very same day.

No doubt you're waiting for me to say that I missed them, but it would be more truthful to say that I missed the *idea* of them most of all. They had departed, first our city and then this world, when I was so small as to have had no true memory of either of them. I had only Oma's memories and her stories of my father as a little boy. Much as I treasured these tales, they were not quite the same as memories I might have created had I known my parents myself.

I took careful note of the other children's parents as I grew up, however. Children are always interested in what other children have that they do not. It seemed to me that some of the parents I saw were happy together, but many were not. Happiness can be difficult to hold onto, I think, when your body is weary, your stomach is never quite full, and your hands are cold even in the summertime.

Take Kai's parents, for instance. His father worked in the coal mines just outside of town. In the summer, whistles blasted, summoning the miners to work just as the sun came up, but in winter, they did so long before the sun even had its eye on the horizon. Kai's father walked to work in the dark, and he labored in the dark. In the dark, he walked home. Then he had many flights of stairs to climb before he could take off his boots outside his own front door. To keep the choking dust of his labors out of the house as much as possible, Kai's mother cleaned out her husband's boots in the hall.

On many nights, or so Kai once told me, his father never said a word. He was so weary, it was as if the coal dust had closed up his throat. But sometimes, raised voices lifted themselves into the air and flew from Kai's building to mine. On those nights, I could hear them, even when it was winter and the windows were tightly closed.

After those nights, I would awaken to find Kai asleep at the foot of my bed. He would be curled up in the nest of blankets Oma kept for him in the trunk that had once held her trousseau. Kai's mother would come for him in the morning, her face pale, her mouth pinched so tightly it was a wonder she could drink Oma's sweet, dark tea. Circles would be inked beneath her eyes.

Kai and I never spoke about those mornings, just as we

never spoke about the nights that preceded them. But when his father died, killed by the very earth itself when a section of the mine collapsed, Kai wept. His mother sobbed so long and hard that she had to be carried home from the burial ground. That was the first time I realized love was not as simple as you might suppose. To me, Kai's father had seemed a cold, hard man, a man designed to frighten. But why would you weep over the loss of someone you feared?

This was also the first time I wondered whether or not Kai's eyes, so good at seeing what was near, could see things invisible to mine.

Both before and after Kai's father's death, his mother took in sewing. Oma and I had done this as well, starting when I was old enough to use a needle without poking myself. During the winter months the three of us often worked together. We took turns: one week in front of the stove at our house and the next week in front of the one at Kai's. That way, we weren't heating two houses at once.

I hate to sew.

I think it's one of the reasons my feet itch to take to the road and my eyes want nothing better than to be fixed on the horizon line. Sewing requires you to sit still, to look only at what is close to you. Even if you're setting a sleeve into an armhole, so that you are stitching around in a circle, sewing is all about that which is straight. Straight stitches, straight seams, straight lines. Kai sewed with us until he became old enough to be apprenticed to Herre Lindstrom, the watchmaker. He was always much better at it than I was.

The one good thing about sewing, however, was that my grandmother and Kai's mother would tell stories to help pass the time. Kai's mother had been born in the south. Her stories were often full of sunshine and warmth. But Oma had been raised in the far, far north. Her tales were comprised of ice and snow. It was she who first told us the tale of a girl forever altered by the North Wind, the tale of the Winter Child.

"Her name is Deirdre," my oma would say. "A word for sorrow, for sorrow and the fate of a Winter Child are intertwined."

"But why, Oma?" I would always ask, even after I had heard the story of Deirdre the Winter Child many, many times.

The fact that anybody, even a girl in a story, had a name like Sorrow always struck a strange chord in my heart. I liked my own name, Grace, just fine. But I don't think my affection for it made me swell-headed. I wasn't making any particular claim to being *graceful* because of it, and I certainly wasn't claiming to be better than anyone else. I can be impatient, and I have a nasty temper. I know these things well enough.

But my name did make me feel safe, somehow, as if it carved out a particular place for me in the world—even if I didn't quite know yet what that place would be. Being named Sorrow seemed a terrible fate.

"A Winter Child is unlike any other child on earth," my

oma went on. "She has been touched by the North Wind, enfolded in its arms."

"All of us have felt the touch of the wind," Kai said. But he shivered, as if the memory of how the North Wind felt on a winter day was enough to make him cold.

"True," my oma replied. "But a Winter Child has felt more of the North Wind than either you or I have, Kai. We feel only the brush of its passing. It does not truly see us as it hurries by.

"But a Winter Child is chosen, swept up in the North Wind's arms. People are not made to be so close to the forces of nature. They have the power to alter us. Before a Winter Child can be as she was before, she must remove all traces of the North Wind's touch by righting some great wrong."

"That hardly seems fair," I remarked.

"Righting a great wrong is not a bad thing," Kai countered before my grandmother could reply. His eyes were fixed on his sewing, but his voice was stubborn. "I think it's brave and noble, not a cause for sorrow at all."

"Children," Kai's mother said chidingly, "let Frue Andersen tell the story."

"No, no," my oma said with a smile. "I don't mind the interruptions. It is true that righting a great wrong is not a bad thing in and of itself," my grandmother continued, and I battled back a spurt of irritation that she'd addressed Kai's objection rather than mine.

"Though doing so is often very hard. The path is easiest to

walk when you choose it for yourself. But such a choice is not granted to a Winter Child."

I heard Kai pull in a breath, as if to speak again. I put my foot on top of his and pressed down, hard.

"What wrong must Deirdre set to right, Oma?" I inquired.

"The wrong committed by her parents," my grandmother replied. "You remember I told you how, when the queen's mirror shattered, all the pieces flew out the window and were carried away on the wind, all but the one that pierced her daughter's heart?"

I paused to carefully finish a seam before I answered. More than once I had been forced to take out stitches and do work over again after being caught up in one of Oma's stories.

"I remember," I said when the thread was knotted, the end snipped, and the seam done. I gave the sleeve a gentle tug, testing to see how my stitches held.

"Careful," Kai teased, as if he were seeking revenge for my stepping on his foot. "You'll pull it right back out again."

I stuck out my tongue.

"Those pieces flew throughout the world," my oma went on, "still filled with the magic of a wish and a curse combined. Each and every one found its way into a human heart. The persons so wounded have been changed forever in a terrible way: They are incapable of seeing with the eyes of true love."

There was a momentary silence while both Kai and I considered this.

"But . . . ," he said.

"How?" I asked at precisely the same time.

My oma smiled. "A heart that carries a sliver of that icy mirror is not what it was before," she explained. "It now contains both less and more. But the *more* that it contains is what creates the *less*, and so such a heart is at war with itself."

My oma paused, looking from me to Kai, and then back to me, as if waiting to see which one of us would figure out this riddle first.

"Fear," Kai suddenly burst out. "That's what the piece of mirror adds."

"Fear, indeed," my oma said. "You are right, Kai."

"But wait," I objected, doing my best not to show how irritated I was that Kai had figured it out first. "I thought the curse of the mirror was that it showed the queen her innermost flaw."

"You are right as well, Grace," my grandmother said. "Think about it for a moment. Why did the queen spend so much time at her mirror in the first place?"

"Because she was afraid," I answered slowly. "Afraid her beauty would fade and the king would stop loving her." I fell silent for a moment, considering what I could now see was the logical conclusion. "So fear was the queen's innermost flaw."

"I think it must have been, don't you?" my grandmother responded. "I've always thought that, when the queen looked in the mirror for that last time, she saw that she was just as beautiful as she had always been. Her face had not changed at all. Her beauty had not diminished, but still the king's love had fled.

"In that instant, the queen realized what she had done. She had brought the very woe she dreaded upon herself by giving in to her fear and closing off her heart. And her heart, grown smaller by staying so tightly wrapped, could not expand again. It could not contain this bitter knowledge and her fear all at once. Her heart shattered, just as she had shattered the mirror."

"And she perished in that same instant," I murmured, as I remembered what came next.

"She did." My grandmother nodded. "But she left behind her child and countless others, all with a sliver of ice in their hearts. So the wrong the Winter Child must right also was decided in the instant of her mother's death.

"To travel the world in search of all those wounded hearts and to mend them, one by one."

"But that could take forever," Kai protested.

"It will take as long as it must," my grandmother replied. "When the Winter Child turned sixteen," she went on, in a tone of voice that signaled she was returning to her storytelling and would tolerate no more interruptions, "the age when many young heroes begin their quests, the very day she turned sixteen, Deirdre, the Winter Child, set out on her journey.

"She put on a dress of linen, fine as gossamer. Over it she tied a woolen cloak as white as snow. She laced her feet into a pair of crystal boots as sturdy as the stars. She took a staff of pale ash wood into her hand, and she kissed her father the king good-bye. Then she turned and walked away from the palace made of ice, and she left the land of ice and snow behind.

"She did not look back, not even once. Though she must have wanted to, I think, don't you?"

I sat for a moment, my hands resting on the sewing in my lap, trying to imagine what it must be like to leave your home. Not because you wanted to, but because you must. Because you must right a wrong not your own.

Oh yes, I thought. *She must have wanted to look back very, very much.*

"She has been traveling the world ever since, seeking out and mending those damaged hearts, one by one. As long as Deirdre is on her journey, the magic of her quest embraces her, just as the arms of the North Wind did, so very long ago. She will never grow a day older, for she cannot continue her own life until her task is done. For most of us, the Winter Child is invisible, for she is not made to be seen by ordinary eyes.

"Even so," my oma continued in a hushed and reverent tone, "in the silence after a winter storm has ceased to howl, in the soft whisper of a morning snowfall, in the way the moonlight sparkles over new-fallen snow, you can feel when she has been nearby, ever searching. You can sense the presence of the Winter Child."

"But . . . ," Kai said yet again, and with that single word, he broke the storytelling spell.

"Oh, for goodness' sake," I cried. "Why must you always take everything apart to see how it works? Can't you just close your eyes and enjoy the story?"

"Grace," my grandmother said softly.

I immediately fell silent, for I knew that tone. All of us have heard some version of it at one time or another from those who love us most: the sound that says, *I am disappointed in you. That was badly done.*

"I'm sorry, Oma," I mumbled.

My grandmother fixed her dark eyes on me, but she said nothing. I gave an inward sigh. I love my oma with all my heart, but there's no denying her will of iron. She says I am like her in this, but I'm not so sure. For when my will comes up against hers, mine is always the one that bends.

"I'm sorry, Kai," I said, for my grandmother's point, of course, was that she was not the one who truly deserved my apology. "Please, go on."

"I just want to know one more thing," Kai said, and I could hear him struggling to keep the surliness out of his voice.

"And what is that?" my grandmother asked.

"What about the heart of the Winter Child? Who will mend that?"

At this, Kai's mother, Frue Holmgren, who had been silent for so long I'd almost forgotten that she was there, made a small sound. She performed a strange gesture, as if trying to snatch Kai's words right out of the air.

"Ah," my grandmother said with a sigh. "Now you have come to the heart of the Winter Child's tale, Kai.

"Even if Deirdre finds all the other wounded hearts and mends them, one by one, dissolving all the slivers of ice, driving out fear so that the hearts may know true love, there is still the matter of who will mend the Winter Child's own heart.

"Does the task fall to her or to someone else? No telling of the story I have ever heard has answered this question."

"Then perhaps," I said, determined not to let Kai outdo me when it came to observation, "the solution lies not in her tale at all, but in someone else's."

"Perhaps," agreed my oma.

There was a moment's silence. Kai stared down at his sewing. Out of the corner of my eye, I saw my oma reach out and take Frue Holmgren by the hand. And suddenly, I realized how late it was. The room was close and warm, and I was tired.

"I still think the king gave his daughter the wrong name," Kai said. "He should not have named her Sorrow."

Oma squeezed Frue Holmgren's fingers, and then let them go. "What name would you have chosen?" she inquired.

Kai looked up, his eyes fierce as they stared at my grandmother's face. "Hope," he said. "That's really what she brings, isn't it? So that's what her father should have named her."

My grandmother's expression softened. But as she leaned to place the palm of one hand against Kai's cheek, I was astonished to see that tears had risen in her eyes.

"Your true love will be fortunate in your heart, I think," she said. "For it is strong and whole. So will your love be, when you choose to give it."

With that, Oma leaned back and took up her sewing, and none of us said anything more.

Three

My grandmother told us many stories, but somehow, it was always the tale of the Winter Child that Kai and I loved best of all. Awakening in the morning, we imagined we saw the flare of her gossamer skirts in the patterns the ice formed outside our windows overnight. We heard the sound of her crystal boots in the noise the ice made as it scoured the walls and roof through the long, dark winter nights. Somehow, these flights of fancy helped to make our own winters more bearable.

Winter is not just a passing fancy in the land of my birth. It comes early and stays late. It can be beautiful, but it is also fierce and cunning, not to be ignored. Looking for traces of the Winter Child, wondering how many hearts she would mend that year, kept Kai and me busy until spring returned and we could be outdoors.

Even then, however, Kai always seemed to take the story more seriously than I did. It was as if, in his own heart, he didn't think of it as a made-up tale at all. Even as he used his sharp eyes to look closely at the world and so discover how it worked, Kai kept this one flight of fancy: He believed in the Winter Child.

As time went on, of course, we had less and less time for stories. We were both growing up. All too soon, our next birthdays would bring us to sixteen, the same age as the Winter Child herself. Kai had long since grown too old for staying at home. At twelve, he'd been apprenticed to Herre Lindstrom, who made and repaired clocks and watches.

Spending hour after hour hunched over all of those intricate pieces—springs so small and fine that if you dropped one it would disappear into the carpet and never be seen again, cogs with teeth and gaps between them designed to fit together in just one way and no other, even holding the tiny tools for such delicate work in my hands would have made me want to run screaming from the room. But Kai loved his hours in the watchmaker's shop.

"Everything makes sense, Grace," he said one afternoon, as we were walking together. Most days, when my sewing was done, I would leave home a little early to meet Kai, and we would walk home from Herre Lindstrom's shop. It was one of the few times when we were alone. There were not as many opportunities for Kai and me to spend time together, now that we were growing up.

"A clock, a watch, can only work one way. If you can see what that way is, you can fix anything if it breaks."

"I'm glad you like it so much," I said in perfect honesty. "It would make my head hurt and my eyes water."

Kai smiled. He turned his head to look at me, and then his eyes narrowed ever so slightly, as if I was blurry and he was trying to bring me into focus. Lately, I had caught him doing this more and more. There was always an expression in his eyes I couldn't quite decipher.

"I thought you said the sewing already did that," he said at last.

I gave a snort. "You're right. It does."

Over the years, my oma's eyesight had begun to fade. As a result, the fine handiwork that used to fall to her eyes and fingers now fell to mine. The curious thing was that the more I disliked the work, the tinier and more even my stitches had become, until at last I became somewhat famous as a seamstress. Even the ladies in the finest part of town desired my sewing.

Slowly, I had begun to earn enough money so that Oma and I could have moved into a nicer flat, or at least to one on a lower floor. But, by mutual consent, neither Oma nor I ever spoke of such a thing. She did not want to leave her rooftop garden, and I did not want to leave Kai.

"I'm sorry, Grace," Kai said quietly.

Because we knew each other so well, he understood how,

as my hands grew more proficient, my spirit struggled. As if the stitches I placed in other people's garments somehow all conspired together to bind me to a life that wasn't what I wanted. Not that I knew what I *did* want, mind you. It's often easier to see what you don't want than what you do. This is a fact of life that I'm hardly the first to have noticed.

"You don't have to be sorry," I answered as we rounded a corner, leaving the shop district behind. We were entering the poorer quarter now, the place where we lived.

"It's not as if it's your fault," I went on. "I'm happy that you like your work, Kai. Honestly, I am."

"I know you are," Kai said. "It's just—"

"I know," I said, cutting him off.

The fact that Kai spent his days doing something that matched his temperament so well, while I did something that matched mine so little, genuinely distressed him. I told myself that this was why he watched me in that close and quiet way of his.

"You could try something else," he suggested now.

"Oh yes?" I answered, my tone short in spite of my best effort. We crossed the street, careful to avoid the horses.

"And just what did you have in mind, taking in laundry or scrubbing floors? Girls don't get apprenticed like boys do, Kai, in case you hadn't noticed. It's not as if I have a lot of options."

I could read and write, which was unusual for a girl from a poor family, but I did not possess any of the other skills that might have made me eligible to work as a governess or a teacher, even if that had been what I'd wanted.

Perhaps if I had seen a clearer vision for my handiwork, I might have dreamed of opening up a shop, of paying others to stitch clothes that I had designed. But I did not. I didn't know quite *what* I wanted. I just knew I was tired of sitting still. There were days when it felt as if my whole body itched to be in motion.

So I headed to the rooftop as often as possible. Even in the dead of winter when I had to bundle up in so many layers that I looked like one of the snowmen the children dressed in cast-off clothes, I went. First thing in the morning, last thing before I went to bed at night, I climbed the stairs from the rooms I shared with my grandmother and clambered out onto the roof.

On the rooftop I could breathe. I could stand in one place and turn in a circle, catching a glimpse of at least some portion of the horizon in whichever direction I sent my eyes. At night, when I could no longer see the shapes of the world around me, I could tilt my gaze upward toward the stars.

On the days when my world felt so small I feared that I would suffocate as Kai's father had so long ago, crushed by the weight of the world itself falling on top of him, standing on the rooftop was the only thing that revived me. On the rooftop I felt free, if only for a few moments.

And then something happened that changed both my life and Kai's forever. My grandmother and his mother died and Kai and I were left alone.

*   *   *

It was the diphtheria that took them. Regular as clockwork, it came with the thaw each year, as if to make a mockery of the hope that spring should bring. Wrapping bony fingers around unsuspecting throats, and then slowly squeezing the life out of them. Kai's mother fell ill first, and Oma went to nurse her, though both Kai and I urged her to stay at home.

"Your mother has no one else on earth but the three of us, Kai," my grandmother said sternly as we huddled outside the Holmgrens' door. Oma's scarf was tied in a determined bow at her chin. She'd set her hands on her hips and had planted her feet, sure signs that she meant to have her way.

"Neither of you can be spared from your work. That leaves me. There's no sense arguing about it, so you might as well save your breath. Now go out and buy me a chicken so I can make Hannah a nourishing broth."

Kai and I exchanged a glance, and then Kai stepped aside and my grandmother marched through the Holmgrens' front door. Oma did her best to nurse Kai's mother back to health. In addition to the broth, she made a poultice for Frue Holmgren's chest. She kept the fire going day and night to keep her warm. Nothing made any difference. Kai's mother was dead before the month was out. The day Frue Holmgren was buried, my oma took to her bed.

"Grace," she murmured late one night. By now, we both knew that Oma, too, was dying. "I want you to promise me something."

"I will promise anything you like," I said. "Only don't tire yourself."

My oma smiled. She held out a hand, and I slipped mine into it.

Cold, I thought. *She is so very, very cold.* Yet the room around us was so warm that I didn't need the shawl I wore indoors in all but the warmest weather. *It will not be long now,* I thought.

"Promise me that you will use your eyes," my oma said. "Promise me that you will let your heart follow them."

"I will, Oma," I said.

My grandmother squeezed my fingers. "Do one thing more for me, will you?" she asked.

"Anything," I said.

"Tell me a story."

If she'd asked me to stand on my head I could not have been more surprised. Oma always had been the storyteller. I leaned forward, resting my elbows on the bed, one hand still clasping my grandmother's.

"Once upon a time," I began, "there was a brave girl named Grace. . . ."

Oma smiled. All through the night I sat beside her, spinning a tale about a girl who bore my name. And that was how Kai found us the next morning. Sitting together, hands still clasped, but by then my voice had fallen silent and Oma breathed no more.

* * *

We buried her in the old graveyard on the hill outside of town, not far from Kai's parents. Beside Oma's headstone were the markers that stood in memory of my father and mother who had been buried far from home. Many in the neighborhood came to pay their respects, but it was the flower vendor, Herre Johannes, who stayed the longest.

"If you need anything, Grace," he said as we stood beside the grave. Herre Johannes turned the soft cap he always wore over and over in his hands. "Your oma and I were always good friends to each other. Don't forget that."

"I won't, Herre Johannes," I said. "Thank you."

Herre Johannes settled the cap back onto his head. He nodded to Kai and to me, then made his way back down the hill. Kai and I stood together, not quite touching.

In the days since Oma's death, a strange awkwardness had fallen between Kai and me. We were on our own now, our lives forever altered by the loss of those we loved. And we were both sixteen, old enough to be considered adults. We had been together, living side by side, for as long as we could remember.

"Let's go home now, Grace," Kai said quietly. "If you want to, you can come back tomorrow."

Without a word, I nodded, turning away from my grandmother's grave. *Which home?* I wondered. *Yours or mine?* Who were Kai and I, how did we fit together, now that those whom we loved were gone?

I had seen Kai watching me, in that quiet way of his, in the days since Oma had died. Several times, I thought he was about to speak, but each time, he held his tongue. But I had a feeling today was the day I would learn what was on his mind.

"Do you think about the future, Grace?" he asked as we walked along.

Spring had come in earnest during Oma's illness. Crocuses bloomed on the hillside. Above our heads, the sky was a perfect arc of deep, rich blue.

"Of course I think about it," I answered, my tone shorter than I intended. I thought about the future all the time. Worried about it was more like it, not that worrying did me any good. Kai stayed silent.

I pulled in a breath and held it, my eyes on the green grass of the hill, the bright, new green that only appears with the first flush of spring as the earth renews itself. I let my breath out slowly and tried again.

"I'm sorry," I said. "I didn't mean to snap. It just seems like kind of a silly question, that's all. Of course I think about the future. What else is there to think about? It scares me."

To my horror, I heard that my voice had dropped to a whisper. I felt the sudden sting of tears at the back of my eyes. All through the days of Oma's illness, through every moment that had followed, I had done my best to overcome this fact. Without success.

"The future terrifies me," I confessed now, my voice rising. "I don't know what to do. I can't see my way, Kai."

"Marry me," said Kai.

Four

I ABRUPTLY STOPPED WALKING.

"What?" I cried.

"Marry me," Kai said again. My sudden halt had caught him by surprise. His momentum had carried him several steps along the path, so that now he had to turn around. We faced each other. I saw Kai's own eyes widen in surprise as he caught sight of the astonished expression on my face.

"For heaven's sake, Grace," he said. "You must have thought of this too. It can't be a total surprise. It's the logical next step, and surely it's what my mother and your grandmother always wanted."

"What about what we want?"

Kai's head jerked back, as if I'd struck him. And all of a sudden, I felt more wretched than I ever had in my entire life.

Too fast. It's all happening too fast, I thought.

Quickly, I closed the distance between us, reached out and gripped Kai tightly by the shoulders.

"I spoke without thinking," I said, gazing straight into his eyes. "I did not mean to hurt you. I'm sorry, Kai. Of course I see the sense in what you're saying. It's just . . ."

Kai gazed back, his eyes intent on mine. "It's just that you don't love me enough to marry me," he said.

I tightened my grip further and gave him a shake. "I didn't say that. Did you hear me say that? Stop putting words in my mouth."

I released him and hurried down the hill, my stride just short of a run. *Away. I have to get away,* I thought. Perhaps, if Kai and I hadn't been standing quite so close together, I wouldn't now feel so responsible for the hurt and confusion I'd seen in his face. We'd scrapped, as all children do, quarreling over nonsense. But neither of us had ever really refused the other anything before, not anything important.

"Grace, wait," Kai called. He caught up, matching his pace with mine.

Only someone who understood me as well as Kai did would have done this. Another man might have put a hand on my arm to stop me, at the very least to try and slow me down, but not Kai. He knew it would give me just the opportunity I needed to take the ultimate step: to turn and fight, or to turn and run.

Instead, Kai simply chugged along beside me, the sound of our feet shushing through the new grass. Gradually, my burst of emotion wore itself out and my pace slowed. My exertions had carried us to the bottom of the hill. With just a few more minutes of walking, we would reach the outskirts of town. We would return to our empty rooms.

If I married him, I thought, *I wouldn't have to be alone.* But was that enough to do the thing that Kai was asking? Were holding back fear and trying to prevent loneliness good enough reasons for us to marry, even if they helped us both?

Maybe Kai is right, I thought. *Maybe I don't love him enough.*

"Don't expect me to apologize again," I said without looking at him.

"All right," Kai replied, his tone agreeable. I thought I felt his glance slide in my direction. "Though you know what they say."

"Do I?"

"The third time's the charm."

I felt laughter bubble up inside my chest and decided to let it go. "They do say that, don't they?" I said with a sigh. Kai stayed silent. I turned my head to look at him. "I'm being awful, aren't I?"

"You are," Kai said.

I couldn't quite read his tone. "Thanks for nothing," I said. "I'm trying to apologize."

"Yes," Kai said. "I know you are. You're also trying to get yourself off the hook. Don't think you can fool me, Grace. We know each other too well."

We walked along in silence for a moment. Then, ever so softly, I felt his fingers slide along the inside of my arm until they were laced with mine. It was the first time we'd held hands in a long time.

"I didn't mean to add to your fear, Grace," Kai said quietly.

"You didn't," I protested. "Hey—ow!" At my answer, Kai had squeezed my fingers so hard I thought the bones might crack. "All right, you did scare me, just a little," I admitted.

Kai gave my arm a little shake. "The thing is, Grace," he said, "I don't see why."

"Well, for starters, you might have picked a better place and time."

Kai gave a snort. "All right, I'll give you that," he said. "Though it does make sense, you know. We're both alone now, Grace. If we were to marry—"

"I see that. I honestly do," I interrupted. "It's just . . ."

Both my words and my feet faltered and came to a stop. I looked at Kai. As he always did, he gazed back at me with clear and steady eyes. And suddenly I felt a spurt of irritation, in spite of my best efforts. How could it all look so simple and right from his position, yet so complicated and uncertain from mine?

Our eyes see different things, I thought. *They always have. Even when we're looking in the same direction, standing side by side.*

I let go of his hand. "Is this what you really, truly want, Kai?" I asked. "Is this all?"

A frown burrowed between his eyebrows. "That's a trick question," he said. "I can tell. I just can't see what the trap is yet."

"That's because there isn't one," I said. "I do love you, Kai. I honestly do. And I know our getting married was close to your mother's heart and to my oma's. I guess I always thought we *would* get married some day. I'm just not sure that day can be now."

"Well, I hardly meant today," Kai said, his tone testy.

I gave him a shove. "Stop it," I said. "You know what I mean. Stop pretending that you don't. It doesn't matter that it's the logical next step; it doesn't even matter if it's the step our families would have wanted. What matters is what you and I choose for ourselves."

"All right, I give up," Kai said, throwing up his hands. "What do you choose, Grace? *What is it that you want?*"

"I want to see the world," I burst out. "And I don't mean a glimpse from the rooftop. I want to see more than just the horizon, Kai. I want to see what's beyond it. And if we get married—"

"You think I'll hold you back," he said, his tone strange and flat. "You think I'd try to stop you."

"I don't know what I think," I all but shouted. "What's the matter with you? Can't you see that's just the problem?"

There was a moment's ringing silence. In it, I stared at Kai and he stared back.

If either of us had taken a step, we could have reached out and been in each other's arms. Either one of us could have drawn the other in and held on tight as if we'd never let go. Neither of us moved a muscle. I don't think we'd ever been farther apart than we were in that moment.

"So you don't love me enough to marry me," Kai said.

"I *do* love you enough," I countered. "Just not yet, not now. I want to see what's around the corner first. I want to *do* something. If *you* loved *me*, you'd understand. You'd let me go."

Kai's mouth twisted. "You're making an awfully big assumption, aren't you?"

"What's that?"

"You assume I'll be here when you get back. But I might not be. Who knows? Maybe by the time you finally remember me, I'll have found someone else. I can *do* things too, you know. So don't start thinking I'll be sitting around here *doing nothing* while you're off on your great adventure, because I won't be! Maybe I'll even have an adventure of my own!"

Kai spun away and began to walk toward town, his legs pumping with long and angry strides. I stood where I was, arms at my sides, my hands clenched into fists.

"Fine," I called after Kai's retreating form. "I hope you *do* do something. I hope you *don't* sit around staring at the insides of clocks all your life. And I hope you *do* find someone else! Someone whose heart is so different from yours you have to work the rest of your life to figure out how it works."

As I spoke, I felt the wind come up. A strange wind. It swirled around my head, lifting my hair as if to tangle it into knots. It traced my face like it wished to commit it to memory. Then, as abruptly as it had come to encircle me, it departed. A moment later, I saw Kai's shirt push flat against his back.

Kai stopped, as if he'd encountered an invisible brick wall. I watched the way his chin lifted, nose scenting the air, head swiveling from side to side. For just one moment, I thought Kai was going to turn back to me. In the next moment, the wind died down. With a shake of his head as if to dispel some errant notion that had caught him unawares, Kai resumed his brisk pace. He didn't look back, not even once.

Just like the Winter Child, I thought suddenly.

And it was only then that I realized what I had done. Like the king in Kai's favorite tale, I had uttered a wish and a curse combined.

That night, I dreamed of loss.

I was in a strange country, walking through an unfamiliar landscape. My heart pounded in my chest and a fine, cold sweat seemed to cover every inch of my skin. I was searching for something, searching for Kai.

There were times when I could see his outline in the distance, hear his voice drifting back to me on a wind I thought I recognized. The wind from the afternoon—the one that had come up, as if from nowhere, to scuttle between me and Kai.

Wind of change, I thought.

But no matter how I strained my ears to listen to the sound of Kai's voice, I could not understand what he was saying. Was he calling for me, asking me to follow him? Or was he trying to drive me away, demanding I turn back and leave him alone?

Did he love me as he always had? Or had my words driven a wedge between us, opening a gap wider than the one that separated our buildings, a space not even I would be brave enough to cross?

"Kai! Kai, wait for me," I called. I saw his head turn toward me, gazing over his shoulder. Just for an instant, his eyes met mine.

In the next second, he turned away, and I saw for the first time the dark expanse in front of him, reaching out from side to side like a pair of outstretched arms. The chasm was so wide that I could not see across it.

"Kai, wait for me!" I called once more. "Kai, no!"

But I was too late. I watched as Kai raised a leg and stepped out into the open space. Between one of my horrified heartbeats and the next, he was gone.

I sat up in bed, my heart a bright pain inside my chest. My gasping breaths showed white in the air. *Cold,* I thought. *How can it be so cold?* Just that afternoon, it had been spring. Now, as I looked toward the window, I could see a thin etching of frost on the outside of the glass.

I began to shiver. *It's a late storm,* I thought. *This is nothing more than Winter trying to have the last word, the same as it does every year.* Surely I had experienced such late storms before. But even as I tried to reassure myself, I knew it wasn't true. This was not some late-season frost. The cold I felt was something much, much more.

I threw back the covers and got out of bed, hissing between my teeth as my feet hit the icy floor. I dashed to the window, undid the fastening, and pushed it open. Frigid air flowed in to wrap me in its cold embrace. A bright moon floated in the sky overhead. By its light, I could see that Kai's window was wide open. The street below me sparkled with hoarfrost. In the rime, I could see a single set of footprints leaving Kai's building and heading down the street.

I don't remember putting on my stockings and shoes. Don't remember throwing my winter cloak around my shoulders. What I remember clearly is standing in the street, gazing down that straight line of footsteps. It led to the corner, then turned, vanishing from sight.

Gone. My heart thundered in my chest. *Gone. Gone. Gone.*

It did no good for my mind to assert that Kai was safe in bed, for it to reason with me that the footprints could belong to anyone. My heart knew the truth.

Kai was gone. He had followed the Winter Child.

Five

STORY THE THIRD

ENTER THE WINTER CHILD

I AM NEVER COLD.

Cold's absence is my first clear memory, as clear as the stars on a frosty winter's night. Clear as the way a voice can carry over an expanse of pristine snow in the still, predawn air. And with this memory comes understanding:

I am not like other girls.

Well, of course not.

You were never going to be like other girls anyway, you're tempted to say. I am a princess, after all. But there's not a princess on the planet with my attributes. Many may be called upon to keep the peace and to settle treaties by marrying some prince they've never seen. Others may labor under enchantment, twiddling their thumbs in boredom until some fellow on a white horse, or a horse of any color for that matter, rides up to break the spell.

But I defy you to find another princess who can do what I can, what I must: right a wrong she did not commit. Mend hearts too numerous to count with a single icy touch.

"Why me?" I used to ask my father over and over, and with such regularity that I'm sure he could have set his watch by the question. "Why did the North Wind choose me and not someone else? Why must *I* be a Winter Child?"

The answer, which my father never failed to give despite the way it must have pained him, was as plain as the nose on my face. A face that was much like the face of another—one whom Papa never spoke of if he could help it.

"Because of your mother," he always replied.

I knew the story, of course, though not from Papa. Not from any one person at all, in fact, but rather from everyone— and everything—around me.

There wasn't a person in my father's kingdom who didn't know the tale of what had happened, the details of how I had become a Winter Child. Nor did the knowledge end there. Every tree, every rock, every flower that bloomed and every frost that killed it knew the tale as well. The story was so much a part of the fabric of my father's kingdom that it was in the water we drank, the air we breathed, the first flush of green that came in spring, the last winter snowfall.

Speaking the details was simply unnecessary. Each time I

was laced into a dress for some fancy court occasion, I felt it in the way my ladies in waiting worked hard not to let their fingertips touch my skin.

So cold, and she can't feel a thing. It's unnatural, but what can you expect? She is a Winter Child.

I felt it in the way the castle servants turned their backs each time I snuck out of the castle dressed in a set of the head cook's youngest son's outgrown clothes.

Another princess would never be allowed to get away with such a thing, but then we must make allowances for her, mustn't we? Her time for fun and games will end soon enough—and then just think of what comes next.

Poor little Deirdre. Poor little Winter Child.

It isn't easy being different, let me tell you. But it's even more challenging to be different in a way that's so obvious nobody ever feels the need to acknowledge it. An obvious that is so well-established you can almost fool yourself into believing it's going overlooked.

Almost.

"Then why didn't the North Wind just take my mother instead?" I would ask my father.

One particular interrogation occurred when I was eight years old. Halfway to the milestone of sixteen, the year in which I would be called to fulfill the destiny *she* had mapped out for me.

She. Her. My mother. I'd never called her by her given name.

I couldn't. I didn't know what it was. Though I'd pestered my father with a million other questions, this was one I'd never dared to ask.

"If the North Wind wanted her attention so much, why didn't it just snatch *her* up in its arms?"

"You know I don't have an answer to that question, Deirdre," my father said. "It was the North Wind's choice, not mine."

"But I *want* you to have the answer, Papa!" I said, restraining the desire to stamp my foot with momentous effort. Such behavior might be acceptable at six, but never in an eight-year-old. "You're a king. You should have an answer for everything."

A strange expression came over my father's face, as if two factions were battling for possession of it. On the one hand, he looked sad and weary. On the other, it seemed that he wanted to smile. Before the matter could be settled, my father held out his arms. I crawled into them, settling into his lap with my head against his shoulder. He rested his chin on the top of my head. I couldn't see him do it, but I was pretty sure my father closed his eyes.

"I want you to listen to me, my daughter," he said. "What I am going to say may not make much sense to you now, but you will understand as you grow older."

I squirmed a little, in spite of the comfort of my father's embrace. Nobody likes to be told they're not old enough to grasp something important.

"I'm eight," I remarked. Halfway to the sixteen years I would need to possess in order to set out on what I was already sarcastically referring to as "my great quest."

"I know how old you are, Deirdre," my father replied, and I thought I caught a hint of laughter in his tone. This was enough to stop my squirming in an instant. My father didn't laugh very often. He hardly even smiled.

"I was there the moment you were born, when you had all the possibilities of the world before you. That person is still there, inside you. The North Wind's embrace has not changed that. It has not changed who you truly are."

"But you gave me a Winter Child's name," I said. "You called me 'Sorrow.'"

"Only to prepare you for what would lie ahead," replied my father. "You must learn patience, Little One."

"Maybe you should have named me that instead," I interrupted, and this time, I felt a tremor of what I was sure was laughter shimmy through my father's body.

"Perhaps you're right about that," he said, giving me a quick squeeze. "But listen to me now. When your task is complete, you may choose a name for yourself, the one you desire above all others. On that day, your life will begin anew. It will be as if you have been reborn."

I twisted in my father's lap so that I could look into his eyes.

If my first memory is of being cold, my second is of my

father's eyes. They were a deep and piercing green, like the needles of the evergreens that grow in the woods that mark the boundary between our kingdom and the lands beyond my father's realm.

Always, it seems to me that I feel my father's gaze, even now that death has closed his eyes. Watching over me with love and concern, promising that, in the end, I will find the way to solve the puzzle of my own existence, to right all the wrongs not of my own creation and, at the last, even find the means to mend my own wounded heart.

"I can choose my own name?"

"Absolutely," my father vowed. "You were not born to be called Sorrow."

His eyes kindled now with a bright green flame. "Just think, Deirdre," he went on. "You have a chance almost no one else is granted. The opportunity to choose your own name, one to match who you truly are inside."

"But how will I know what to choose?" I asked.

"Excellent question," my father replied. "All I can tell you is that you will know when the time comes. In the meantime . . ."

My father's eyes began to sparkle with laughter, which always made my heart sing with joy.

"We could start to compile a list of possibilities," he said. Making lists was something my father did a lot. It could be because he was a king or just because that's who he was. I've never quite been able to sort this out.

"Ermyntrude, for instance. Now *there's* a name to be reckoned with," my father went on. "Three syllables, a nice round name. And I'll bet you wouldn't have to share it with too many other girls."

My father paused and raised his eyebrows. If the game were to continue, it was now up to me.

"What about Hortensia?" I proposed. "That has four syllables."

My father nodded, as if I'd made a very astute point. "Esmerelda," he said. "Also four. Or what about Gudrun? Only two, but when I was a lad it was very popular. Gudrun is a name with staying power."

"Penelope is nice," I said.

"Zahalia," my father countered.

"Oh, Papa, I know," I suddenly exclaimed. "Brunhilde. I should have thought of it before. 'Brunhilde' is a name that always gets a reaction."

To my surprise and dismay, it got a reaction from my father I hadn't anticipated. He made a face, as if he'd tasted something sour. I watched as the laughter faded from his face, and the sadness moved to the front of his green eyes once more.

"Your mother had a cousin named Brunhilde," he said. "She was the maid of honor at our wedding."

And just like that, the game was done.

"I'm sorry, Papa," I said quietly. "I didn't know."

My father reached out to twist the end of one of my pale

locks around his finger, and then he gave it a tug.

"Of course you didn't, Little One," he said. "So you've nothing to be sorry for." He lifted me from his lap, set me on my feet, and then stood up.

For a moment, I thought he would say something more. That at last he would speak of her, my mother, his wife, the woman who had changed the course of both our lives. But he did not. Mine was the heart with ice inside it, but even as a child I knew my father's heart carried a wound far greater than mine. A wound that was beyond even my power to heal, a wound he would carry into the grave itself.

"I should get back to my study," my father announced. He bent to give me a kiss, then turned to go. "Speaking of names, I need to review the list of all the foreign ambassadors I'm going to meet tomorrow, and then I'll have to remember to ask Dominic to . . ."

Dominic was my father's steward, his right-hand man. I could tell from the sound of Papa's voice that his thoughts had already traveled far ahead of his body. I could only hope he would forgive me for calling them back.

"Papa," I burst out, after he'd gone no more than a dozen steps. "Come back. I have to ask you something."

"Gracious, Deirdre," my father said, snapping back to the present and turning around quickly at the fierceness of my tone. "What on earth is the matter, Little One?"

"It's her name, my mother's name," I said, and with that, I

suddenly discovered I was crying. "I have to know it, don't you see? So I don't add it to the list by accident. I don't want her name. I don't want to be like she was."

"Deirdre," my father said.

I think that was the moment when I grew up, for in the two syllables of my own name I suddenly heard and understood something I previously had not. My father hadn't just bestowed the name of Sorrow on me. He'd also bestowed it on himself.

"Joy," my father said. "Your mother's name was Joy."

Then he turned and walked away. This was the last time we spoke about her.

Six

THOUGH MY FATHER AND I NEVER DISCUSSED NAMES again, that afternoon marked the beginning of my fascination with them. I began to make a study of names, collecting them much like other children collected coins or stamps or dolls.

It wasn't simply the sound of a name that appealed to me, though I did enjoy this: the way a name felt inside your mouth as you formed its syllables, the space it occupied in the air when you pronounced it. But there was also the way a name and the person who bore it got along together. For this, or so it always seemed to me, was the heart of what a name is all about.

Was the fit between a name and its bearer seamless and comfortable? The castle baker was called Amelia, for instance, a name that seemed to suit her quite well. It sounded soft coming and going, like a flourish of icing on a fancy cake, but in the center there was a core of strength, the press of bread being kneaded against its board. Amelia.

Or did the name sit uncomfortably upon its wearer, did it chafe and rub? My father's steward could enter a room so soundlessly you'd never know he was there until he cleared his throat. Yet he was called Dominic, a name that always sounded to me like the sharp clatter of heels along a hall of flagstones.

Had Dominic known his name did not suit him and deliberately set out to cultivate a set of traits to counterbalance this? Did his name cause him discomfort? Did moving silently help to ease this pain? Did we grow into our names, and if so, could we grow out of them? Did we shape them, or did they shape us?

The names that interested me the most were the ones that belonged to people who paid them no attention at all. The people who carried their names around like sacks on their backs, never really recognizing the power of the name they bore. Such an interest was hardly surprising, I suppose. Did I not carry the name Sorrow all because my mother had overlooked the power of her own name and forgotten that she was named Joy?

And so I quietly continued my pursuit of names as the years pursued me, until at last, the day of my sixteenth birthday arrived.

You know what happened already, of course. How I dressed

myself in a gown of finest linen, sheer as gossamer. Upon my feet I wore a pair of crystal boots. But what the stories never remember is that it was my father who put the staff of ash wood into my hand. It was he who threw the snow-white cloak around my shoulders.

The stories also fail to share that Amelia baked me the largest cake anyone had ever seen, the inside as dark and rich as fertile earth with an outside covered in snow-white icing. It was so large there was enough for every single person in the kingdom to have a piece, so sweet it brought a tear to each and every eye.

The stories fail to tell how, after eating their pieces of cake in celebration of my birth, the people of my father's kingdom faded away, like snow upon warm ground, until only my father and I were left—the king and his daughter, the princess, the Winter Child, standing outside the gates of our ice palace. My father fussed a little with the lacings of my cloak, tying the strings so that they lay tight against the base of my throat.

"Papa," I said, astonished I could speak with the lump that filled my throat, a lump made up of all the things I feared I had forgotten to say but would never have the chance to now.

"I don't even need a cloak. I'm never cold. Please, stop fussing."

"I'd like you to wear one anyway," my father answered. He tweaked the cloak, adjusting it so that it hung perfectly straight from my shoulders. "Neither of us knows how long a road you must travel, Little One. A cloak may be useful along the way."

After all these years, he still called me Little One, the nickname he'd given me as a child so that neither of us would have to spend our days listening to him call me Sorrow.

"There may be days when your heart feels cold, though your body does not. On those days, it will be good to have something to draw in close around you."

"And this?" I asked, gesturing to the staff of ash wood he'd placed into my hand.

"So that you can imagine I am with you on your journey," my father said at once. "And when you need to, you can lean upon me."

Suddenly, I found it almost impossible to breathe.

"I don't want to," I choked out. "I don't want any of this. I don't want to leave you, Papa."

"Ah, Deirdre," my father said, drawing me into his arms.

For sixteen years I had been so careful never to speak those words. I might have asked a thousand questions about it, but not once had I truly railed against the fate my father and I both knew could not be avoided. But standing with my father before the gates of the palace on my sixteenth birthday, I could hold in my true feelings no longer.

I did not want to leave. I did not want to be a Winter Child.

The thought of mending all those hearts was daunting enough, but there was something more, a sorrow that would come to my father and me alone. I would not change. From the moment I set out to fulfill my Winter Child's destiny, I would not grow one day older until my task was done.

But my father was as mortal as the rest of the world was. He would continue to age, to feel the passage of time. Once I left him to set out on my journey, I would never see him again, not in any way that felt familiar to me now. His mortal life would be over before my task was complete.

"If I could have spared us the pain of this parting, I would have," my father said. "But there's no way to do it. There hasn't been since the day the North Wind first snatched you up in its arms. A parting of this nature would have come upon us even if you had not been called to be a Winter Child, Deirdre. It comes to all parents and children, to all who truly love."

"If you're trying to make me feel better, it isn't working," I managed to say.

And suddenly, my father laughed, a bright, clear sound. It seemed to carry on the cold air, as if setting out ahead of me. And I knew that, somewhere along my journey, I would remember that even in our moment of greatest sadness, I had made my father laugh.

"I want you to listen to me now," my father went on. "This is going to be a lecture, so pay close attention."

I couldn't quite manage a laugh, but I attempted a smile.

"I'm listening," I promised.

"The world is full of change, Deirdre," he told me. "That is its nature, for the very globe itself spins around. It is never still—always moving, therefore always changing. Today is the day that the curve of the earth will catch us in its spin and whirl us apart. But I will never truly leave you, just as you will never leave me."

My father placed a hand on the center of his chest. Suddenly understanding, I reached to cover his hand with one of mine. And so we stood together with our hands pressed against his heart.

"You will be inside my heart," my father said, "just as I will be in yours. Even when my heart ceases to beat, I will be with you. You will never be alone and neither will I."

How I wanted to be brave!

"But it won't be the same," I whispered.

"No," my father answered simply. "It will not. Nothing stays the same, Deirdre. That, too, is part of life. Sometimes, pushing against change only makes it push back twice as hard. But even the most bitter fruit may contain something sweet at its core. A taste you would never have encountered if you had not been willing to endure the bitter first."

He looked at me, his green eyes steady. I held my breath, waiting for him to say more. But it had never been my father's way to offer more words than were needed, just as it was not his way to offer false comfort. And so I knew that the next words spoken would not be his; they would be mine.

"I can do it, Papa," I promised.

And then, finally, I saw the bright sheen of tears in my father's eyes.

"I know you can," he said. "I have never doubted that."

"That doesn't mean I'm going to like it," I went on.

"I'll tell you a secret," my father said. "I've never cared for it very much myself."

The sound of my heart beating was loud in my ears. I could feel the winter sun on my back, even as the cold air stung my nostrils. A bird called in the sky overhead, and another answered from far off. A small wind, a curious wind, suddenly arrived to investigate the hem of my cloak. My father and I did not move. But I felt the world begin to shift and turn around me. The path that I must follow was unfurling at my back.

"So," I said.

"So," my father echoed.

And with that, I took a single step back. I felt a quick, hard pain spear my heart. I saw a spasm shoot across my father's face, and I knew he felt the same pain.

"I love you, Papa," I said.

"And I love you," my father replied. "I have loved you every day of your life. I will love you for every day of mine and more. My love will never diminish, no matter how many steps you take throughout the world, no matter how many years you wander until your task is done."

"I will love you as long as I draw breath," I replied. "And the moment I stop breathing, I will find you. Wherever you are."

"I will be waiting for you with open arms," my father said.

I took a second step back, and then a third and a fourth. With each and every step I took, I felt my heart give a painful tug. It seemed to me that I could almost see what caused it: the invisible line that connected my father's heart to mine. Thin as spider's silk, incredibly strong. It would stretch between us always, winding around the earth like a map of my wanderings. Never breaking, never releasing its hold.

"Don't look back when you turn to go," my father said. "Set your face to the path and keep on going. Will you do this for me?"

"Only if you'll do the same," I said. "Please don't stand here and watch me walk away from you."

"On the count of three, then," my father said.

"No, five," I said quickly. "Make it five, Papa."

I saw my father smile for the very last time.

"Five, then," said my father. "Are you ready?"

"No," I answered with a shaky laugh. "But you can start counting anyhow."

"One," my father said, as his eyes stayed steadily on mine. I gripped the staff of ash wood tightly in my right hand, feeling every groove, every whorl. Trying to ignore the fact that my palm was slick with sweat in spite of the coldness of the day.

"Two," said my father. "Three." I heard the soft *shush* as a nearby tree branch let go of its burden of snow and it fell wetly to the ground.

"Four." My stomach muscles tightened. Just one count more. One syllable, and I would turn away from my father forever.

"Five," my father said softly.

At that moment, the wind snuck beneath my cloak and tugged it out behind me. The lacings pulled against my throat.

No! my heart cried. *Not now. Not yet. Not ever.*

But even as my heart protested, my mind accepted the truth. I did not have a choice. Again the wind tugged, and this time, I let it turn me. The pain in my heart was so sharp I thought it would surely split in two.

Through my pain, I heard the scrape of my father's boot heel. I knew that he had kept his promise. This was what finally gave me the courage to take a step. My first upon my quest as a Winter Child.

Away from the palace made of snow and ice I walked, away from all I knew and loved. The wind was like a guiding hand at the small of my back, as if to make sure I would keep going.

Seven

STORY THE FOURTH
IN WHICH SOME PATHS CROSS AND
OTHERS MERELY WALK SIDE BY SIDE

HOW LONG DID I WANDER? HOW MANY HEARTS DID I meet, how many hearts did I mend before I encountered Grace and Kai? Good questions, all. The trouble is, I can't answer them.

It will help if you remember that I have a somewhat unusual relationship with time.

I was on my journey, fulfilling my quest, performing my duties as a Winter Child. As long as I did this, I would not age. I would stay precisely as I was.

Therefore, keeping track of time served no purpose. Some years felt long, other years felt short. They weren't what mattered anyway. What mattered were the hearts I found and mended, one by one.

I can tell you that by the time the wind, who was my only companion, brought me the sound of the name "Grace," I had crossed the world and recrossed it many times in my journey as a Winter Child. Along with my age, my interest in names remained constant. The longer I journeyed, the more hearts I encountered, and the more I began to see a pattern forming:

Those whose names fit them least on the outside often were the ones who carried a wounded heart on the inside.

Occasionally, though only very rarely, I also came across someone else: a person whose inside and outside were such a perfect match they almost had the power to mend hearts themselves. So is it any wonder that, when the wind brought me the sound of a girl named "Grace," I hurried to see what she looked like?

Grace.

What a lovely possibility-filled name. Possibility for generosity, for forgiveness. If there was an opposite to Sorrow, it seemed Grace just might be it. So I hurried to see her, following the wind, and discovered that this Grace was not alone. She had a young man with her, and even eyes much less perceptive than mine could have seen that these two were in the midst of a quarrel.

Most people can't see me. The tales told about me say that this is because I'm not meant to be seen by ordinary eyes. The truth is slightly different, I think: I'm not intended to be seen by ordinary hearts.

Nevertheless, over the years I have learned to be careful, learned it's best to keep out of sight. Sudden revelations that bedtime stories might actually be real are unsettling, to say the least. I'm here to mend hearts, not to stop them with fright.

For obvious reasons, it's easiest for me to conceal myself when the world around me contains a lot of snow or ice, but even on a warm summer's day I can usually find a pocket of air in which to hide. The trouble with being concealed, of course, is that sometimes you witness events you wish you hadn't. This is precisely what happened with Grace and Kai.

That was his name, the young man with her. Kai—to rhyme with sigh. And Grace was giving him plenty to sigh about, I soon discovered.

With both hands, Grace was pushing away love.

I don't get angry very often. There's just no purpose in it. Getting mad about something usually makes whatever caused your anger in the first place even worse. But the sight, the sound, of what was happening between these two made me angry, angrier than I'd been in a good long while. Angrier than I could ever remember being, in fact.

Grace was doing two things no one ever should: She was denying the possibilities of her name, and she was denying the potential of love.

Gently putting love aside is one thing. None of us can accept all of what we may be offered in this life. Sometimes we must say no, even to love.

But this girl named Grace was pushing love away with both hands, arms straight out in front of her, elbows locked. With all the force of her being, she was pushing away a great gift, and the worst thing of all was that it seemed to me she was doing it without truly consulting her heart.

Oh, she thought she was. She thought she was doing just what her heart wanted. Her words made that clear enough. But with a name like Sorrow, I can always spot it in another. I have to. It's part of my job.

And so I knew that this girl, this Grace, had sorrow and pain and fear in her heart, and I also knew she was denying they were there just as fiercely as she was refusing love. In spite of all her words about freedom, her heart was bound.

You are just like my mother, Grace, I thought. A name and a heart so at odds that one could not find the other.

And with this realization, I felt my anger fade. I watched as the argument reached its conclusion and the young man spun on one heel and set off for home. The wind hurried after, barely taking the time to swirl around Grace before dashing against Kai, plastering the shirt he wore against his back.

He stopped, and my heart began to beat so hard and fast the sound of it rang in my ears. I watched as Kai's head turned quickly from side to side, as if hoping to catch a glimpse of something he was sure was there but could not quite see.

And suddenly, I was dizzy. Possible paths opened before me only to splinter and then re-form like the colorful pieces of a kaleidoscope. That was the moment I understood, even as Kai was hunching his shoulders against the wind and continuing to walk. As Grace was standing alone, her expression stricken and desolate as she watched him.

The three of us were not finished with one another. Not by a long shot. We all had a very long way to go.

Eight

I WAITED UNTIL THE MIDDLE OF THE NIGHT. WHEN THE world grows still and the hearts of dreamers lie wide open. This is when I do most of my work.

Most people never even know I've touched their hearts. They simply wake up the next morning feeling better than they had when they closed their eyes the previous night. Usually, it's only after many such mornings have come and gone that those whose hearts I've mended recognize there's anything different about themselves. Even then, they might not be able to tell you what it is.

It isn't happiness, not quite yet. Instead, it's a lessening of that for which I am named, a lessening of sorrow. It is the creation of a space so that something else can come and take sorrow's place, the thing for which my mother was named but which she could not find within herself. I create a space for joy.

Every once in a while, though, I encounter someone who can truly see me. Not just the traces that I leave behind, like the frost on the windowpane that children are taught denotes my presence. I mean my actual form. There's a reason for this, I think: These are the hearts that have been willing to believe I exist, against all logical odds.

I've only met a handful of them during my journey, but each and every one holds a special place in my heart. For it is these hearts that have schooled my own to hope. They remind me to hold fast to the belief that there is a heart that can help me mend my own.

Standing in the narrow street that divided Grace's tall building from Kai's, I gazed at her dark windows high above. The full moon that had been playing hide-and-seek among the buildings abruptly gave up the game and leaped over the rooftops to hang like a great white plate in the sky. The street around me was flooded with its pale light.

Nothing ventured, nothing gained, I thought.

I turned and directed my upward gaze toward Kai's windows. Like Grace's, his were dark. Sensible people were asleep, even if what they dreamed wasn't sensible at all.

What do you dream, Kai? I wondered. He'd come so close to seeing me that afternoon. Dared I hope his dreams were of the Winter Child?

I spread my arms. Instantly, the wind appeared, filling my cloak. Up, up, up into the air the wind carried me, until I could place my hands against Kai's windows. Beneath my palms, the panes of glass grew cold. I knew this because I could see a thin film of ice begin to form, spreading out, then cracking like sweet sugar glaze.

Wake up, Kai, I thought. *Wake up!* And then the window opened and I was looking straight into Kai's eyes. They were blue. I could see this by the light of the moon. Not a pale blue such as mine, but the deep blue of an alpine lake after the sun has gone down behind the mountains. They gazed out steadily, though the expression in them was startled. I could hardly blame him for that. It's not every day you literally come face-to-face with someone straight out of a fairy tale.

When I spoke, his eyes widened. "Hello," I said.

"Hello," he replied. His voice was quiet and steady, the kind of voice made for making promises. Then, just like that, Kai's eyes narrowed, as if the light of the moon had grown too strong for him.

"How do you do that?" he blurted out. And I discovered that even a girl named Sorrow can still smile. It was a reasonable question. He did live on the top floor. It just wasn't the question I'd been expecting.

"I can do anything," I boasted. "I'm a Winter Child."

He shook his head in a quick, determined motion of contradiction. "No," he said. "That isn't right."

I lifted my chin, as if in defiance, though, as it had that afternoon, I could feel my heart begin to pound. "What can't I do?" I asked.

"You know the answer to that as well as I do," Kai replied without hesitation. "You cannot heal your own heart."

I felt a sharp pain as my heart contracted, then expanded, opening wider than it had known how to until this moment.

"Can you do it?" I asked. "Are you the one who can heal my heart?"

Kai looked at me for several moments, his eyes still narrowed in a slightly unsettling way. It was as if he thought he could figure out the way I was put together, how I worked, if only he could stare at me long enough. Again, my heart felt a painful, hopeful pang. If someone can see the way something works, they can see how to fix it when it breaks, can't they? Wasn't this precisely what I did myself?

"I don't know," Kai finally said. His voice was troubled. "Is that why I can see you, because you want me to try?"

"You can see me because you believe in me," I answered.

He gave another quick shake of his head.

"No," he said. "There's something more. It's because *you* believe in *me* that I can see you, isn't it? And because *I* want to try. I always have, I think, from the time I first heard your story when I was just a boy.

"I always knew there was more to the tale than just being a bedtime story. I knew that you were just as real as I was."

"And so I am," I said.

He smiled then, and I felt my own lips curve up in answer. "Yes," he said. "I see that you are."

My heart had become a rushing river. *So this is what it feels like to hope,* I thought. *It makes you lightheaded, and sets all your limbs to trembling with strength and weakness combined.*

"And my heart?" I asked, amazed to hear my voice come out just as steady as his. "Do you want to try and heal it?"

"I think I must," Kai answered slowly, as if the admission were welling up from someplace deep inside him. His eyes slid from mine to fix on something just over my right shoulder. At first I thought it must be Grace's window, but when he spoke again, I realized I'd been wrong.

"I used to ask about your heart," he went on softly, "when Grace's oma would tell us your story. It always seemed so unfair to me, to give you the power to heal so many hearts but not enough to heal your own."

The past. He is looking at the past, I thought. *The past that has made him what he is now.* A past that would give me a chance for a future. We stood in silence for several minutes. I gazed at Kai. He gazed at his former self. With an effort I could almost feel inside my own body, Kai shifted his eyes back to me.

"Where must we go?"

I pulled in a breath before I spoke. "Just like that?"

He made a sound that reached toward laughter. "Well, hardly. I *have* been hearing your story my whole life."

481

"Don't you dare ask me how old I really am."

This time, Kai did laugh. "I wouldn't dream of it," he promised. "Besides, I already know. Grace's oma used to say that you would stay the same age until your quest was done. You're sixteen, just like Grace and I are."

"Very cleverly answered," I replied. "So what makes you think we have to go anywhere? Why can't we settle things right here and now? Perhaps all you need to do is kiss me and be done with it."

"I'm not a prince," Kai said. "I think that only works for them. Besides . . ."

He drew the second syllable out, as if he were formulating his answer even as he spoke. "Having an answer as simple as a kiss wouldn't make sense. It wouldn't fit with the rest of the tale. You're on a journey, a quest, in search of all those other wounded hearts. So I think a journey must be the way to heal your heart as well.

"In which case I'll repeat the question. Where must we go?"

That was the moment when I realized how very much I wished to be in love.

Certainly it was the moment that I felt the future begin to open up before me, as my heart had opened itself to hope just a few minutes before. Perhaps love and hope are one and the same. I don't know. I do know this was the moment when the future ceased to be a desolate place, a place where I would always walk alone. By the use of a single pronoun, one simple "we," Kai had created a path where two might walk side by side.

If I was very lucky, the two might even hold hands. I extended mine.

"Home," I said. "We're going home."

I hadn't known what the answer was until I spoke. But now that I had, I knew it was right. *Home*. Back to the place where my strange journey had begun.

"I'll come with you," Kai said. "But I'm not going out through the window, if you don't mind. I don't think I'm ready to fly through the air. I'm just a mortal who likes to keep his feet on the ground."

"Suit yourself," I said. "Though you don't know what you're missing. I warn you—someday I hope to change your mind."

He turned from the window.

"Kai."

He turned back. "What?"

"Will you tell her good-bye?"

If Kai was surprised by my question, he didn't show it. Nor did he ask whom I was talking about.

"No," he said after a moment. He gazed past my shoulder, as he had done earlier. I knew he was thinking of Grace this time.

"I don't think so. There isn't any point. I used to think we'd always understand each other, that we would always walk the same path. I don't think that anymore."

His eyes shifted. Now they looked straight into mine. "I'm going to walk a new path," he said, "and see where it takes me."

"I'm glad," I said.

"So am I."

And that is how it came to pass that Kai left his warm bed and all he had once held dear, and he embarked upon a journey with no milestones to guide him. A single line of footprints in an unseasonably late frost was all that remained to mark his departure.

Kai did not look back. So, just as he turned the corner at the end of the street, when he could not see me do it, I looked back for him. My gaze went straight to the rooftop of Grace's building, with her darkened windows just beneath.

What will you do when you discover Kai is gone? I wondered. *Will you find a way to follow? Or will you give in to pride and let him go?*

I found the courage to venture my heart, Grace. Now let's see if you have the courage to venture yours.

STORY THE FIFTH

IN WHICH GRACE MAKES A CHOICE

HE WAS GONE. KAI WAS GONE. HE HAD FOLLOWED THE
Winter Child.

I stood in the street, staring down the trail his footprints
had left in the frost until I could no longer feel my feet and the
hem of my nightgown was soaked. Until I could hear Oma's
voice in my mind, clear as a bell:

*For heaven's sake, Grace, get back inside this minute before you
catch your death of cold.*

Though I never catch cold.

It's the strangest thing. Not even Oma could account for
it, which meant the familiar scolding was also something of a
joke. But suddenly, catching cold was precisely what I feared.

I feared my luck might run out just when I needed it most.

Kai had asked me to marry him, and I had turned him away. I had turned him away and now he was gone.

Oh, Grace, I thought as I finally began to shiver. *What have you done?*

It took all day to sort out my affairs. Unlike Kai, I didn't simply walk out and leave everything behind me. There was the landlord to speak to, completed work to send to my patrons, and incomplete work for which I needed to make arrangements for others to finish.

"I'd feel better about all this if I knew when you were coming back, Grace," the flower vendor, Herre Johannes, said late that afternoon.

He and I were standing together on the rooftop, *my* rooftop, among Oma's pots and planters. It was still too cold to sow seeds, but I had turned the soil over on the first clear day in preparation for when it would grow warm enough.

I had given Herre Johannes all of the notes that Oma and I had made about what should be planted where, and I was sure the old flower vendor would have some thoughts of his own. He was moving into my old rooms and would care for the rooftop garden in my absence. This suited both Herre Johannes and my landlord well.

Oma's garden had made our building famous. My landlord never lacked for tenants, even when times were hard. Standing on the rooftop now, I felt my first pang of regret. The rooftop garden was the one thing I would be sorry to leave behind.

"I'd be happier if I knew where you were going," Herre Johannes continued.

"That makes two of us," I said. I caught the worried expression on Herre Johannes's kind and wrinkled face and bit down on the tip of my tongue.

I am going to miss him, too, I thought. Strangely, it made me feel better to know that I would miss not simply a place, which could not miss me back, but a living, beating heart of flesh and blood.

I placed what I hoped was a comforting hand on Herre Johannes's arm.

"I spoke without thinking, Herre Johannes," I said. "I'm sorry. I have thought about what I'm doing, honestly."

But I hadn't been truthful with Herre Johannes, not entirely. I'd let him believe the obvious, that Kai had gone off in a huff following a sweethearts' quarrel. I kept to myself the knowledge that he'd actually chosen to do something much more dangerous and difficult than that: He was walking the path of the Winter Child.

Herre Johannes reached to give my hand a pat, and I dropped my arm. He rubbed one set of knuckles against the stubble on his chin. It made a rough and scratchy sound.

"You've been dreaming of striking out into the world for a good long while, I think," he said.

It was all I could do to keep my mouth from dropping open. Something of my struggle must have shown in my face, for Herre Johannes gave a chuckle. I laughed too, as I shook my head.

"Was it so obvious?"

"To someone who sees only the outside of you, no," he answered promptly. "But for anyone able to catch a glimpse of the inside of you . . ."

He broke off for a moment, gazing over my shoulder. It came to me suddenly that Herre Johannes was doing what I always had done when I came to the rooftop: He was gazing into the distance, his eyes seeking out the horizon.

"I have known you for a long time, Grace," he said. "I have watched you grow up, and your grandmother and I were good friends. I think, sometimes, that you are like the plants in her garden, always turning your face toward the sun.

"But I want you to remember something," Herre Johannes said, his eyes on my face now. "A plant needs to do more than stretch its leaves toward the sun. It also needs to send down roots deep into the ground. They hold on tightly in the dark, out of sight where it is easy to forget about them. But it is the fact that a plant can do these two things at once, anchoring itself to the earth even as it reaches for the sky, that makes it strong.

"If the roots fail, the plant will die every time. Do you understand what I am trying to say?"

"I think so." I nodded. "You are trying to remind me not to

488

get so consumed in what lies ahead that I forget about where I came from. You want me to remember to look both forward and back."

"There now," Herre Johannes said, and he pressed a kiss to my forehead. "Your grandmother was right. She always said you were a smart one."

Not smart enough to keep Kai from leaving, I thought. *Not smart enough to truly see him even though he's spent his whole life standing at my side. Not so smart that I stopped myself from driving him away, straight into the arms of the Winter Child.*

But I did not say these things aloud. "I will never be as smart as you are," I said as I put my arms around Herre Johannes and held on tight.

Herre Johannes made a rumbling sound deep in his chest. "Yes, well," he said. "It helps if you remember that I am very old."

"And your roots are strong," I said as I let him go. I stepped back, the better to see his face in the fading light.

"As are yours," Herre Johannes replied. "Remember that, when your journey seems difficult. Remember that I will be thinking of you as I tend the garden."

"I will," I promised.

We left the rooftop just as the sun went down.

STORY THE SIXTH

IN WHICH KAI FINALLY FINDS HIS VOICE

I SUPPOSE YOU'RE WONDERING WHY I HAVEN'T SAID anything until now.

If Grace were here she'd tell you I don't talk all that much, not unless I really have something to say, anyhow. Which makes me sound like some strong and silent type. Totally untrue, of course. And Grace isn't here. That's part of the point. If the two of us hadn't quarreled, if we'd stayed together, neither of us would have much of a story to tell. Or at the very least, they would be different from the one—ones—you're now holding in your hands.

You may also feel as if I owe an explanation. Why did I do it? Why did I follow the Winter Child? This would be difficult to put into words even if I were a big talker. The closest I can come is to say that the moment I beheld Deirdre, I felt . . . affirmed. For as long as I can remember, my heart has harbored a belief in spite of my logical mind: the belief that the Winter Child truly exists, that she is much more than a character in a bedtime story.

So I ask you, what would you have done? If your most cherished fantasy suddenly had appeared and looked you in the eyes, offered you the chance to become a true part of her tale, would you have refused? Would you have stayed home?

No. I didn't think so.

"Is this some sort of test?" I asked, that first night, as we walked along.

Somewhat to my surprise, once I'd declined Deirdre's invitation to fly through the air, she'd let me set both the pace of our journey and its course. My feet chose the way of their own accord: through the graveyard on the hill outside of town, heading in the direction of the mountains where my father had died. It was almost as if I wanted to say good-bye.

"Is what some sort of test?" she asked in return. This turned out to be a habit of hers. She often answered a question by posing one of her own. Perhaps it simply had become part of her nature. She'd been alone for so long that she'd fallen out of the habit of regular conversation.

"Letting me choose which way to go," I explained.

Deirdre shook her head, and I watched the way the moonlight shimmered over her pale locks. I narrowed my eyes, trying to imagine what she would look like when she was restored to her natural coloring—midnight hair and dark eyes. I simply couldn't do it. Imagination has never been my strong suit, but it seemed to me that everything about Deirdre fit, just as she was then.

"Of course it's not a test," she answered now. "Why would I want to test you?"

I shrugged, feeling slightly foolish. "I don't know. Because that's the way these things always seem to work, at least in stories. The hero gets tested, needs to prove himself."

She turned her head to look at me then, and I thought I caught a hint of a twinkle in her eye.

"Wait," I said before she could speak. "I don't think I'm a hero. That isn't what I meant at all."

Deirdre bit her lip, as if to hold back a smile. "You might be. You never can tell."

I gave a snort. "I'm a watchmaker, not a swashbuckler, so don't even think about me wielding a sword. I'd probably drop it on my foot and slice off a toe."

"Fortunately for us both"—Deirdre spread her arms wide, the cloak fanning out around her and revealing the dress she wore beneath—"I seem to be fresh out of swords."

"I'm just saying," I plowed on. "I mean, just so you know."

We trudged along in silence for several minutes, both of us looking ahead. What Deirdre was thinking, I couldn't tell. As for me, I was giving serious consideration to the physics that allowed me to walk, even though I'd just managed to put both feet in my mouth.

"Does the path we take make a difference?" I asked after a while.

"Yes . . .," Deirdre said at once.

She tilted her head to look at me, and I caught my breath. *If I live to be a hundred,* I thought, *I'll never get used to those eyes.* They were a color that usually resides only in nature, at the heart of a glacier or in the fine, pale height of a wind-scoured sky. They were beautiful and strange, and they drew me in, right from the start.

What must it be like to possess such eyes? I wondered. *Eyes with the power to see into a human heart?* What did Deirdre's eyes see when they gazed into my heart? Did they see things about it that I could not?

". . . and no," Deirdre went on.

I sighed. "I suppose I should have seen that coming," I remarked.

Deirdre turned her gaze back to the path in front of us, but I thought I caught a glimpse of a smile.

"You know what they say, don't you?" she said.

"I think I do," I answered. "They say that all paths are open to the Winter Child."

"All paths that lead to the living," she amended. "The hearts of the dead are beyond my help."

"But you fly," I protested, then bit my tongue. *It's just like in the old days,* I thought, *when Grace's oma used to tell us stories.* I always had questions, always saw loopholes.

"That was unexpected," Deirdre acknowledged. "A benefit, if you will, of the brief time I spent in the North Wind's arms. When my time as a Winter Child is finished, my flying days also will be done."

Deirdre cast another sidelong look at me. "To tell you the truth, I don't do it all that often. Like you, I prefer to keep my feet on the ground. That's where the hearts I must heal are to be found. But flying is glorious," she added with a smile. "And I *will* get you to try it sometime, so be forewarned."

"And the path we walk now?" I inquired, bringing the discussion back to where we'd started. I was still curious as to why she'd let me choose our course.

"I thought it might make the transition easier if you chose your own path away from home," Deirdre said simply. "I am accustomed to being a stranger in the world. You are not, and besides . . ."

"Besides what?" I prompted.

"You think you know me," Deirdre answered slowly, as if trying to decide how best to explain. "For you have heard my story all of your life. But every time a story gets told, it changes a little. Things get left out. You don't know me. We've only just met."

"Not a test," I said suddenly, grasping her point at once. "More like an introduction."

Deirdre's face lit up. "An introduction," she echoed. "That's it precisely."

On impulse, I stopped walking and held out my hand. She stared at it, her expression puzzled. Then, without warning, she laughed and placed her hand in mine. It was like holding ice. Never in all my life had I felt anything so cold. It took every ounce of willpower I had not to shiver.

"Pleased to make your acquaintance," I said. "My name is Kai Holmgren. What's yours?"

"Do you know?" Deirdre said suddenly. "I don't think I have a last name, or if I did, I've long since forgotten it." Her mouth gave a funny twist, as if it were full of a taste she couldn't decide if she liked.

"I only have titles, really, don't I?" she went on. "Take your pick. Which shall it be? Princess, Winter Child, or Sorrow?"

"I would like to call you Deirdre, if you'll let me," I answered steadily. "At least it's a proper name."

"Deirdre it shall be, then," said the Winter Child. She took her fingers from mine, and not a moment too soon. My arm was numb up to the elbow. We resumed our walk, continuing in silence for several minutes.

"If that conversation *had* been a test," Deirdre said finally, "you'd have passed with flying colors. You gave both a true and sensible reply."

"Oh, I'm just filled with common sense," I said, surprised at the bitterness of my own tone. "Though if Grace were here, she'd tell you I have too much of it. It made *such* good sense to ask her to marry me. I had it all worked out."

We hadn't talked about Grace, not since we'd left town. But the truth was, even with Deirdre beside me, Grace was always on my mind. For here I was, embarking on precisely the type of journey Grace always had wanted, exploring what lay beyond the horizon. It didn't seem quite fair, somehow.

Still, the fact that I was thinking about Grace irritated me. I had offered her everything I had to give, offered her myself, and she had turned me down.

"And are you sorry?" Deirdre inquired.

"Now I know *that's* a test," I said with a short laugh. "Or at the very least a trick question. How can I know how to answer unless I know what I'm supposed to be sorry for?"

"Sorry for coming with me, of course," she answered. "Sorry for leaving Grace behind."

"No," I said, and as I spoke the word, I felt the certainty of it, right through to the marrow of my bones. "I am not sorry I came with you, and if I'm not sorry for that, then I must not be sorry for the other.

"But I *am* sorry that Grace and I quarreled," I went on, and I felt the truth of this as well. "We almost never do, and we've been friends our whole lives. And I'm sorry that we parted in anger. Our friendship deserved better than that, I think."

"Perhaps there will be the chance to make amends," Deirdre said.

"Perhaps," I said. "I hope so."

Though I noticed that neither of us specified who would be making amends. Was the responsibility Grace's, or was it mine?

We walked all night and on into the morning. Each time we came to a fork in the road, I chose which path to take. The course I set took us higher and higher into the mountains. Deirdre had declined testing me, but it seemed I had some desire to test myself.

I had been happy in my previous existence, working for the watchmaker, figuring out how all the delicate pieces went together and how to mend them if they broke. I'm good with mending broken things, though I never expected to mend a broken heart.

What if I couldn't do it? What if I wasn't strong enough?

"Kai," Deirdre said suddenly, her voice slicing through my troubled thoughts. I felt the cold touch of her hand upon my arm. "Stop."

I did as she instructed, just in time. Two more steps and I'd have walked right off the face of the mountain. In front of us, the path stopped abruptly. The mountains fell away and I could see the world spread out below us. I stood for several minutes, catching my breath.

"The world is a very big place," I observed.

"That is so." Deirdre nodded.

I let my eyes roam over the patchwork landscape. "Have

you traveled everywhere?" I asked, and then I winced, for I sounded like a child.

"Not quite everywhere, but close," Deirdre answered.

We stood together, looking out at the great expanse. "I feel very small," I said.

"As do I," Deirdre replied honestly. "But small and insignificant are not the same thing, Kai."

"I think my brain knows that," I said, though my tone expressed my doubt. "But my heart . . ."

Deirdre laid a hand on my arm. With the other, she pointed across my body to a dark smudge on the horizon.

"Do you see that?" she asked. "That speck of green?"

"Yes," I said. "I think so."

"That is the forest that borders my father's kingdom," she said. "The land of ice and snow, the land where I was born."

I heard the longing in her voice, and suddenly, I saw the way to go. The path we could take to ease the longing in her heart and prove the strength in mine.

Fear, I thought. Hadn't that been Deirdre's mother's innermost flaw? The wound that her shattered mirror had scattered throughout the world. I would not give in to it now.

I reached for Deirdre's hand. Without a word, she reached back.

"Deirdre," I said, "will you teach me how to fly?"

Eleven

STORY THE SEVENTH

IN WHICH GRACE SETS OUT IN SEARCH OF THE HORIZON
AND DISCOVERS MORE THAN SHE BARGAINED FOR

KAI'S FOOTPRINTS TRAVELED NORTH. THE DIRECTION WAS
not surprising.

The Winter Child is taking him home, I thought. *Back to the
place where her long journey began. Why?*

I pondered this, and a thousand other questions, late into
the night. Common sense suggested I should be getting a good
night's sleep so I'd be fresh when I set out the following morning. My brain insisted this was the best course of action. My
heart rebelled.

My heart whispered that common sense already had been
proved wrong, for common sense had not believed in the Winter Child. It reminded me that Kai and the Winter Child already

had a day's head start. Who was to say where they might be by now? Though Oma had told us Deirdre's story for as long as I could remember, I had never heard anyone speak of what might happen to a person who chose to journey beside the Winter Child.

Kai was in her world now. Even more, he had chosen this for himself. Would he cease to age so that he and Deirdre would stay perfectly matched until her task of mending hearts was done?

The trouble with common sense was that my heart had too many questions my mind could not answer. So, in the end, I listened to my heart. Instead of curling up beneath my blankets, I spread out a selection of my belongings on top of them, trying to decide what to pack for my journey. It was not as easy as it sounds. I might have known where I hoped to end up, but I had no idea how to get there. I had no idea how long it would take.

Let's see if common sense can work on this, I thought.

I was going north. That meant cold. But, in spite of the weather at the moment, I knew winter already had given way to spring. It might be cold where I was going to end up, but along the way it would be warm.

I walked to the wardrobe that stood in the far corner of my room. From it, I selected my second-warmest cloak: the green one I often wore for rambling in the woods. I laid it on the bed. Beside it on the floor, I added my sturdiest pair of walking boots, followed by several pairs of socks. The boots might have been heavy, but they would last. And they were well-worn. No blisters, no matter how far I walked. I knew the socks were sturdy and in good repair. Oma and I had knitted them ourselves.

I will need a second dress, I thought, wishing, not for the first time, that I could wear boys' clothes. I chose my third best, one made of sturdy, serviceable calico. It would be a good choice when the weather grew warmer, and it would not take up too much room in my pack in the meantime.

Food to last for several days. A water skin. These, too, were added to my growing pile. I considered for a moment, then added some examples of my needlework. These I might barter for food or sell. Perhaps I could even hire myself out as a seamstress, if necessary. Finally, I placed the shawl I had given Oma in honor of her last birthday on the bed. It was made of pale green silk, embroidered with images of the flowers from our garden. It was too fine to wear, but I could not bear to leave it behind.

I stood back, hands on hips, gazing at my selections.

What else, Grace? What else?

There is nothing else, I realized. Nothing that I could pack, anyhow. My memories of Oma lived inside me, just like my love for Kai. Those would go with me wherever I went.

Go! my heart cried suddenly. *Don't wait for morning. Don't wait another moment to go after who you love. Go now.*

And with that, I was desperate to be gone. Filled with a fierce determination, I bundled the items I had selected into my pack, put on my boots, tossed the cloak around my shoulders, and headed for the door. Here, finally, I paused to look for one last time at the rooms in which I had grown up. On the small table beside Oma's favorite chair was her seed-saving box. I had left it for Herre Johannes.

Oma saved garden seeds every year, each kind in its own slip of paper that was carefully folded so that no seeds could escape. On impulse, I crossed to the box and plucked out a paper containing the seeds of Oma's favorite sunflowers. I carefully tucked it into the bottom of my pack, then slung the pack onto my shoulders. I felt the weight of it settle against my back, felt the way the straps gripped my shoulders. Then I left the apartment, closing the door quietly behind me.

Outside, it was cold. A great round moon, just past full, drifted in the sky. By its light, Kai's footprints were easy to see.

Why? I thought again. *Why?*

I had no answer. But I was not about to let that stop me.

Wish me luck, Oma, I thought.

My breath making fat white clouds in the cold air, I began to walk alongside Kai's tracks.

A girl doesn't need luck, Grace. I suddenly heard Oma's voice inside my mind. *What a girl needs is a good head on her shoulders. She needs to learn to keep her wits about her and her eyes open.*

I will, Oma, I thought. *I promise.*

I reached the end of the street, following Kai's footprints as they went around the corner. I was so intent on following this strange path that it wasn't until I reached the outskirts of town that I realized the truth:

Kai's steps headed straight toward the horizon.

Twelve

BY MORNING, I WAS WELL INTO THE MOUNTAINS. THOUGH the sunlight made Kai's footsteps more difficult to see, I was glad for it. The mountains, with the entrances to the mines yawning like great dark mouths, were an eerie, unsettling place to be at night. Were it not for the steady pace of Kai's footsteps showing me the way, I'm sure I would have become lost.

Sometime during the night, my ears had caught the voice of a stream, and in the morning light, I could see that my path ran right beside it. It rushed ahead, flush with snowmelt. I continued to walk until I came to a place where the flow of water broadened, becoming wide and shallow.

Here, a clump of fat boulders clustered together, as if inviting weary travelers to sit down and take a rest. I obliged, resisting the temptation to take off my shoes and stockings and wade into the stream. The thought might have sounded inviting, but it was still early spring and I knew the water would be icy.

I sipped from my water skin, ate a piece of cheese and an apple, and contemplated my surroundings. The mountains were beautiful. They also made me claustrophobic. They pressed close together, leaning in as if wishing to peer over one another's shoulders. I could not see the horizon. I remembered Kai's father, buried to death deep within the earth, and I shivered.

Time to keep moving, Grace, I thought. It was far too early in the journey to be indulging in such morbid thoughts.

I got to my feet, then bent to refill my water skin. I hadn't consumed much, but I had no idea how long my journey might take and I knew I could not be without water. Food I might forage or beg for if it came to that.

The water was cold enough to make me gasp. I filled my skin as quickly as I could, and then returned it to my pack. I settled the straps of the pack over my shoulders and turned back toward the path. I could just see the faint outlines of Kai's footsteps.

I began to walk once more.

By midday the sun had grown warm enough that I could take off my cloak. I added it to the contents of the pack. Without the extra layer of the cloak, the straps of the pack dug into my shoulders. *I will have blisters if this keeps up,* I thought.

In the span of no more than half a dozen steps, I was cross. Cross with myself, but most of all, I was cross with Kai. What did he think he was doing, stealing away in the middle of the night? He hadn't even said good-bye. He had made the most momentous decision of his life without me. He'd gone off and left me behind.

"So much for *me* not loving *you* enough," I muttered aloud as I stomped along.

The path was more uneven now, filled with sharp chips of slippery stone. Somewhere, I felt certain, there had to be a broader way, an easier way; the path the traders with their carts and horses used to cross the mountains.

"But you couldn't go that way, could you? Oh, no," I said, continuing to speak aloud. "You had to go and pick the hard way. You had to follow the Winter Child.

"Ow!"

Busy stomping out my thoughts, I'd let my eyes stray just long enough for my foot to find a large and contrarily shaped stone. It had rolled over, turning my ankle right along with it.

"Oh, fine. You're happy now, aren't you?" I exclaimed aloud, still talking to Kai.

I always had insisted that all you needed to do to get where you were going was to put one foot in front of the other. Kai always had been equally insistent that this only worked if the path was on your side. Apparently, the current path hadn't quite made up its mind as to how it felt about me.

Several steps ahead, a particularly sharp stone sat in the middle of the path. I sent it skittering with a quick, defiant kick.

"All I did was ask for a little more time!" I shouted. "Was that so wrong? We were talking about the rest of our lives. Just because I wasn't ready to settle down right that second. . . . For the record, I never said I didn't love you, Kai. I *do* love you, and if you weren't such a pigheaded idiot, you'd know it!"

At that moment, as if the sound of my voice had startled it into flight, high above my head I heard a bird call, the sound keen and fierce. I paused and looked up, shading my eyes from the glare of the sun. I caught a flash of white as the bird plummeted downward. In the next moment, it spread its wings, the shape of them sharp as an etching against the sun.

It must be a hunting bird of some kind, I thought. *A hawk or a falcon.* City birds I knew well from my many hours on the roof, but I was not as familiar with the wild birds. The bird banked low, and now I could see its dark head. Its body was dappled black and white, like the flanks of a horse.

I watched, my heart in my throat, as the bird's wings beat in the air, soaring upward once more. *He's not hunting,* I thought. *He's simply reveling in flight. Reveling in motion.*

"Oh, how beautiful you are!" I exclaimed, the words rising straight from my heart. "How I wish that I could be like you. How I wish that I could fly!"

What a glorious thing it must be, I thought, *to be able to leave the earth behind. To see it spread out below you in all its infinite possibilities.*

What did the horizon look like from the sky?

As if it had heard both my words and my thoughts, the bird cried out once more. Then it folded its wings and shot toward the earth. I lost sight of it in a fold of the mountains. As quickly as my elation had come, it abandoned me. I was hot and I was tired.

What do you think you're doing, Grace? I thought. *Kai left without saying good-bye. He left you for the Winter Child. An enchanted princess straight out of a bedtime story. You think you can compete with that?*

You turned Kai away. What makes you think he'll welcome you with open arms? Assuming you actually find him in the first place.

"Stop it. Just stop it," I cried aloud. Thoroughly frustrated with myself, I yanked off my pack and threw it to the ground. "If you're going to think like that, you might as well go home right now. You didn't even last a day. That's pretty pathetic."

I have no idea how the argument I waged with myself would have ended if it had been allowed to run its course. It wasn't. Before I could berate myself any further, I heard the falcon's cry, right behind me. I whirled around. The bird swept toward me, claws outstretched. I cried out and lifted a hand to protect my face.

With a rush of wings, the falcon swept past me. It scooped my pack off the ground and carried it away.

"Come back here!" I shouted. I began to run, stumbling as my feet sought purchase on the slippery stone path. "You can't have that," I yelled. "I need it. It's mine!"

Up ahead, the path took an abrupt turn to the right. I propelled myself around the corner, then skidded to a stop, abruptly
confronted by an unexpected confusion of images, a cacophony
of sounds. Before I could begin to make sense of any of them,
something rough and scratchy was tossed over my head. Sharp
pain exploded through my skull. Stars danced before my eyes,
and I remembered nothing more.

STORY THE EIGHTH

IN WHICH GRACE MAKES A NEW FRIEND
BUT ENCOUNTERS SEVERAL OBSTACLES

WHEN I CAME TO, I WAS LYING FLAT ON MY BACK. A ROCK the size of a goose egg was digging into my spine. Above my head, the light was beginning to dim; the sun hung low in the sky.

Slowly, I sat up. The motion made my stomach lurch and my head pound. I made a low moan of protest even as I persevered.

"I'm sorry about how hard he hit you," a nearby voice said. I swung my head toward the sound, then wished I hadn't as the world began to spin.

"I wish he hadn't hit me at all," I croaked out. I put my head into my hands until the spinning stopped, then raised it again, more cautiously this time. The figure of a girl about my age swam into view. She was sitting on a boulder near a small, bright campfire, stirring the contents of a pan suspended on a tripod. There was a tent pitched just beyond her.

"Who's *he*?" I asked.

"Harkko, my brother," the girl answered without looking up. "He and Papa think you mean to harm us. They think you're not alone. They've gone scouting to locate the rest of your group."

"They're wasting their time," I said. "I *am* alone."

The girl gave the side of the saucepan a sharp rap with her spoon.

"That's craziness!" she exclaimed. She turned to look at me now, her dark brown eyes wide. Her head was covered by a deep green headscarf. Hair the same color as her eyes peeked out at her temples. She wore a simple dress of coarse homespun wool. Her boots were even sturdier than mine.

"No one goes through the mountains alone." Her eyes suddenly narrowed. "You're lying."

"I'm not lying," I protested at once. "Why would I?"

The girl shrugged. "How should I know? You're a stranger," she replied. As if the fact of my foreignness explained everything and nothing all at once.

"Do you hit every stranger you meet over the head?" I asked.

"It's not a bad plan," the girl answered calmly. "It's always better to strike first and ask questions later. That's the way to stay alive."

"It's also the way to hurt innocent people or make ene-mies," I observed.

The girl did not reply. She took the pan off the tripod and poured its contents into a mug. Then she brought the mug over to me.

"Drink this," she said. "It will help to ease the pain in your head."

"How do I know it's not poison to put me out of my mis-ery completely?" I asked waspishly.

She grinned. "You don't. But I suggest you drink it anyhow. It really will help you feel better." I accepted the mug, and she sat down beside me. "My name is Petra," she said after a moment, as if making a peace offering.

I took a cautious first sip, grimacing as the hot liquid burned my tongue. The taste was bitter, but not so unpleasant that I couldn't bear it. I took several more sips. Petra was right. After a few moments, my head did begin to feel better.

"I'm Grace," I said, offering my name in return. We sat in silence for several moments.

"Now tell me the truth," Petra said. "How many of you are there?"

"I already told you. I'm alone."

She made a disbelieving sound. "You're a city girl. It's writ-ten all over you," she said. "Why would you come on your own into the mountains?"

"I'm following a friend," I said.

"Oh, I see!" Petra exclaimed at once. "You mean a sweetheart."

"No! Well, not exactly," I said. I set the mug on the ground. "It's complicated."

"Sweethearts are always complicated," Petra said. "But if he's jilted you, then it is much more straightforward. He must be caught and punished. Do you have no father or brothers to do this for you?"

"No, I don't," I said. "And Kai didn't jilt me. He . . ."

All of a sudden, I jumped to my feet. Adrenaline surged through my body. "The footprints!" I cried.

Petra got to her feet. "What footprints?" she demanded. "What are you talking about?"

I ignored her. Instead, I dashed from one side of the campground to the other, searching the ground. Kai's footprints were nowhere to be seen.

I had lost the trail. I had no way to follow Kai and the Winter Child.

Fourteen

I GAVE A LOW MOAN AND SANK TO MY KNEES, MY FACE IN my hands. What was I going to do now? I hadn't even been gone a day, and I had already lost the trail.

"Stop that," Petra said. She gave my shoulders a rough shake. "Stop it right now. That's a disgraceful way to behave! As if you had no courage at all."

"You don't know what I'm up against," I said fiercely, as I raised my head. "You don't know anything about me."

She extended a hand. "Then tell me. Quickly, before Papa and Harkko return."

I took the hand she offered and let her pull me to my feet.

Together, we walked over to the fire. Petra gave the contents of a cast-iron pot a stir.

"Now then," she said.

I took a deep breath, and told her.

"I take back what I said about you not having any courage," Petra remarked when my tale was over. "You're either the bravest or the most foolish person I ever laid eyes on. No one can do what you're attempting. No one can follow the Winter Child."

"I was doing a pretty good job of it," I said, "until your brother hit me over the head."

"I'm sorry," Petra said, and I heard the honesty in her voice. "There was no way to know. What will you do now? Will you go back to the city?"

I considered this for a moment. "No," I answered slowly. "I'll continue north, I guess. Surely I'll come to the land of ice and snow, if only I can walk for long enough."

"I wonder," Petra said, her expression thoughtful. Without warning, she stood. She marched over to the tent and disappeared inside it. A moment later, she returned with something slung over one shoulder.

"My pack!" I cried.

"*My* pack, I think you mean," Petra replied calmly.

"You're nothing but a thief!" I cried.

"My people prefer the term 'bandit,'" Petra said in the same infuriatingly calm tone. "It's so much more romantic, don't you think?"

"It amounts to the same thing," I said. "You take what isn't yours."

"But as soon as I've taken it, it *is* mine," she replied. "Be quiet now. That isn't what I want to talk about. I want to talk about how you and I can help each other." She resumed her position beside me.

"I don't understand what you mean," I said sullenly.

"Of course you don't. I haven't explained it yet." Petra opened the pack and rummaged through its contents. After a moment she pulled out my grandmother's shawl.

"Did you steal this?" she asked.

"Of course not!" I replied. "I made it for my grandmother. I did the embroidery myself."

Petra leaned in close, thrusting her face right into mine. "You made these stitches?" she asked fiercely. "You're telling me the truth?"

"I'm telling you the truth," I said. "Now *you* tell *me* why you want to know."

Petra sat back, Oma's shawl in her lap. After a moment she leaned forward and draped it over my shoulder. With one foot, she scooted the pack over until it rested in front of me.

"I've lived in that tent all my life," she said, jerking her head in its direction. "Traveling with my family from place to place, taking what we need to survive. I'm tired of it, so tired I could

scream. I want a *real* home. A home with four walls and a bed.
I'll never get one as I am now. But if I could do fine work like
that ..."

"You could earn a good living in the city," I said, grasping
her point at once. "It's what I used to do. But it didn't happen
overnight. It takes time."

"I'm already good with my needle," Petra insisted. "I have
to be, don't I? Who else would do the sewing? I just don't know
how to do fancy work like that."

"If I teach you, what will you offer in return?" I asked.

"What you need to know to continue your journey," Petra
answered. "I will teach you how to find your way by the light
of the stars."

By the time Petra's father and brother had returned to camp, we
had settled things between us. I would teach her the embroidery stitches she would need to know to do fancy needlework.
She would teach me how to follow the North Star. The first,
we would explain to her father. The second, we would keep to
ourselves.

"Papa will want to keep you with us," Petra explained as
we worked together to prepare the evening meal. "Particularly
once I am gone."

"Wait a minute. What do you mean once you're gone?" I
exclaimed.

"Shhh," Petra said. "Keep your voice down!"

From across the campground, Petra's brother lifted his head to gaze in our direction. Then he lowered it again, returning his attention to the snare he was mending. The falcon sat on a wooden perch nearby. The falcon's return had been the signal that Petra's father and brother were approaching the camp.

I did not like the look of Petra's brother, Harkko. His face was sullen and brooding, like an overcast sky before a storm. Both Petra's father and brother were harsh-featured. They did not speak much. When they'd first returned to camp, Petra's father had come directly to me.

"You will tell me the truth, if you know what's good for you," he'd said. "You are traveling alone?"

"I am traveling alone," I had said.

He'd given a grunt. "Then you are foolish but not a liar. I could find no other tracks. Make yourself useful and we'll see what I decide."

After that he had gone about his business and had ignored me.

"Tell me what you're talking about," I whispered to Petra now.

She gave the stew a quick stir. "Papa wants to marry me off to old Janos's favorite son," she said in a low voice. "This would give our family the right to trade in the flatlands. We could come down out of the mountains."

You mean you could steal in the flatlands, I thought. "But you don't want to get married," I said aloud.

Petra gave a snort. "Not to old Janos's son. He's a brute.

Compared to him, Harkko is a sweetheart. Hand me that plate."

I complied. She began dishing out stew. "I don't suppose it occurred to you to mention this before now."

"It's something else I'm teaching you," Petra answered.

"Oh really, and what would that be?" I asked.

She handed me the stew-filled plate. "How to drive a hard bargain. We'll talk to Papa after dinner," she went on. "He's always in a better mood when his stomach is full. We will tell him this skill you offered to teach me will increase my value as a bride. Say this is how you will earn your keep until we reach the far side of the mountains."

"And what happens then?" I asked, intrigued by her plan in spite of myself.

"That's when you will go your way, and I will go mine. Though that is something we will not mention to Papa, of course."

"No," I said. "Of course not."

After dinner, Petra approached her father and explained what I had offered.

"What good will it do you to know such a thing?" he demanded. He turned his head and spat into the fire. "You will have no time for it. We are not town dwellers."

"But your daughter's marriage will mean you will be able to spend more time in the towns, will it not?" I somehow found the courage to speak up. Petra's father turned his dark eyes on me.

"What is on your mind?" he asked. "Speak up."

"In the course of my work," I said, "I was often called to my patrons' homes. Often they were in the finest parts of town. No one questioned my right to be there. Within reason, I could come and go as I pleased. With this new skill, your daughter would be able to do so, as well."

Petra's father narrowed his eyes and I held my breath. *Now he knows that I see them for who they really are,* I thought. But if I could get Petra's father to believe the skill I could teach her would be an asset . . .

"Perhaps you have more sense than I gave you credit for," Petra's father said at last. "Teach my daughter well."

"I will," I promised.

I had a feeling my life just might depend on it.

Fifteen

I TRAVELED WITH PETRA'S FAMILY FOR A WEEK, AS WE wound our way through the mountains. Though my situation was still precarious, more than once I wondered what I would have done without them. The mountains were much more rugged than I had ever dreamed. No longer having Kai's footsteps to guide me, I might never have found my way across them.

Early each morning and after dinner each night, I showed Petra how to master the elaborate stitches she desired. Once her father and brother had fallen asleep, she taught me about the stars. She showed me how to look for moss on the north side of a tree. Most of all, she provided the bolster my courage needed as I prepared to go on alone, without Kai's footsteps to guide me. In the space of a week, she had gone from being a captor to being a friend.

Nor was Petra the only friend I made during this time. Though he would go off during the day, when the falcon was in camp, he often stayed close by my side.

"I think he's taken a shine to you," Petra observed on what would be our last evening together. The following morning, our group would come down out of the mountains. Both Petra and I would need to make our escapes that night. Her father and brother had not yet returned to camp. These would be our last few moments alone.

"Perhaps he knows how much I envy him," I said. "I've always wished that I could fly."

"It would certainly make it easier to get where you're going," Petra observed. "Maybe he'll go with you."

I looked at the bird, sitting calmly on his perch. He gazed back at me with clear, gray eyes.

"I always have the sense that he knows what we're saying," I said.

Petra smiled. "Perhaps he does. Falcons are about as smart as birds come. Now," she went on briskly, "tell me again what you're going to do once Papa and Harkko fall asleep."

"I'm going to take my pack and climb that ridge," I replied, nodding at the slope behind us. Petra and I had reasoned that this was the last direction her family would expect me to take. They would assume I would head down, toward the nearest town.

Petra herself would backtrack along the way that we had come. After much discussion, we had decided to leave at the same time. If we staggered our departures and something went wrong, there was a chance whoever went second wouldn't be able to leave at all.

"Now you tell me what you'll do once you reach the city," I said.

"I will ask for the flower vendor, Herre Johannes," Petra recited. "I will tell him you sent me, that you said he might be willing to help. I still don't see why," she added after a moment. "I'll be a total stranger."

She had voiced this concern many times.

"Not everyone believes strangers are not to be trusted," I said. But I could tell that Petra remained unconvinced. On impulse, I went into the tent, opened my pack, and retrieved Oma's shawl. Then I returned to where Petra stood, a puzzled expression on her face.

"Take this," I said as I placed the shawl into her arms. "And give Herre Johannes this message: Tell him I said you wished to put down roots, and that I thought he would be able to help you."

"But you can't—I don't understand," Petra cried.

"You don't have to," I said. "Herre Johannes will know what you mean. And he will know I'm the only one who could have sent such a message. He will know you are a friend, not a stranger.

"Petra," I said. "You have to trust me."

"I know that," she said. "I do. It just doesn't come easily, that's all. And you can't give me the shawl. I know how much it means to you."

"I want you to have it," I said. "All I ask in return is that you tell Herre Johannes I am well."

"I will," Petra promised. She gave me a fierce hug. "Thank you, Grace. I will never forget your kindness. I hope you find what you are looking for."

"I'm sure I will," I said. "I have the knowledge of the stars to guide me. Now we'd better see about dinner. Everything must seem just like normal."

It seemed that Petra's father and brother would never go to sleep. But at last, all was quiet in the campground. The fire had burned down low, until only the embers glowed in the darkness.

The moon was now a week off of full: no longer a sphere, but a chunky block of white suspended in the sky. This was a mixed blessing. The greater the cover of darkness, the better our chances of escape, yet the less light by which to find our way.

Petra and I waited until we heard her father start to snore before we crept from the tent. In the pale moonlight, I could just make out the two men's sleeping forms. As always, Harkko slept on one side of the fire and Petra's father on the other. With a chill, I realized that Harkko was sleeping on the side closest to the direction in which I would go.

Without a word, Petra flung her arms around me. I hugged

her back, squeezing tight. I shouldered my pack. Then, as silently as we could, we each began to make our way out of the campground.

The hair on the back of my neck prickled with each step I took. At any moment I expected to hear the sounds of voices crying out, raising the alarm behind me. I rounded the corner, breathing a little more easily as I did so. Just a few more steps and I would reach the place Petra had showed me, the safest place to begin my climb.

I don't think I'll ever know how it happened—what it was that alerted Petra's father to the fact that we were gone. Perhaps it was simply his own instincts, developed throughout a life spent looking after himself on the open road. No sooner had I reached the place where I would start to climb than I heard an explosion of sounds behind me—voices crying out.

Go, Grace! I thought.

My fingers reached above my head, frantically searching for the handhold Petra had showed me. Sharp pieces of rock rained down onto my upturned face, so loud they sounded like boulders. I heard a second shout, closer this time. *That is Harkko,* I thought.

Finally, my fingers found what they'd been searching for. Digging in with all the strength of my hands, I began to scramble upward. More rocks rained down.

"This way!" I heard Harkko's voice shout. I could hear the heavy sound of his footsteps now.

"No," I sobbed.

Then, without warning, the falcon was there. I felt the rush of air as it shot past me, flying up the cliff face. It gave a screech like a war cry. I redoubled my efforts to climb. I felt a second *whoosh* of air as the falcon darted back toward the earth. Below me, I heard Harkko give a terrified cry.

The bird is helping me, I realized. Petra had been right. I had made a second friend after all.

With a final burst of energy, I scrambled up the remaining few feet, then collapsed onto the ledge at the top of the slope. I did not stop to rest, but got to my feet and made my way as quickly as I could along the narrow path at the ledge's far side. Again, I heard Harkko cry out. His voice was answered by the falcon's. Then there was silence.

Keep on going, Grace, I thought. *Don't look back.*

I had walked for perhaps ten minutes when I thought I felt a familiar rush of air. I stopped and extended one arm. The falcon circled around me once, then alighted on my outstretched arm. My shoulder sang at the extra weight, but I kept my arm steady. In the pale moonlight, the bird and I regarded each other.

"Thank you," I said.

The bird cocked its head. Again, I had the eerie sensation that he could understand every word I said.

"I might never have gotten away without you," I went on. "I will never forget what you have done. I swear to you that someday I will find a way to repay your kindness."

The falcon ruffled its feathers, as if in reply. Then, with

a force that made me stagger backward, he launched himself back into the sky. I saw his silhouette cut across the moon, then swoop down. Flying on ahead of me, as if to show me the way.

One foot in front of the other, Grace, I thought.

I followed the falcon till the light of the waning moon gave way to morning.

Sixteen

THE PATTERN OF OUR JOURNEY NOW WAS SET. THE FALCON flew before. I followed behind. The days, which at first held their individual shapes as they were strung together like beads upon a string, at last began to blur and run together like raindrops. I no longer worried about time. Instead, I gave myself up to the journey itself.

It sounds grim, doesn't it? It wasn't. In fact, slowly but surely, I began to realize I was happier than I'd ever been in my life.

Not every day, of course.

There were days when I was lonely. Days when my solitude felt like the weight of a second pack, much heavier than the first. Days when the path beneath my feet seemed full of ruts just waiting to trip me. Days when my feet had blisters, my legs ached, and it seemed as if I was making no progress at all.

It's hard to know if the end is in sight when you don't know how to get where you're going.

On these days, two things kept me on course: my love for Kai and the falcon.

There were the practical considerations of having the falcon as a companion, of course. He was a fierce, determined hunter whose efforts kept me from going hungry. But there was also the simple fact of his presence, the keen edge of his call in the still morning air, the beat of his wings, the sight of his shape silhouetted against the sky. I might not have had a human companion, but as long as the falcon was with me, I was not alone. I was content to put one foot in front of the other.

Finding Kai remained the purpose of my journey, but there were days when I all but forgot about him. These were the days when the journey ceased to be a burden, when I celebrated the fact that each and every step brought me closer to the horizon.

Until the day came when two unexpected things occurred and changed the course of everything: I fell into a river, and my right shoe developed a hole.

It was the second thing that occasioned the first. For many days, I had been walking on the outskirts of a great forest. At times the falcon soared so high above me that he was no more than a dark speck against the sky. At others he swooped down to ride upon my shoulder. For the first time since we had begun our strange journey together, the bird seemed uncertain, unsettled.

"I wish I knew what was troubling you," I finally said, late one afternoon. It was our fourth day skirting the edges of a forest. The line of green seemed to stretch on forever beside me. The trees at the forest's edge were enormous. How large the trees in the forest's center might be, I couldn't imagine.

"Does the forest make it difficult to see which way to go from here?" I asked. "Is that what's bothering you?"

The falcon gave his wings a shake, as if trying to throw off my questions. I felt the sharpness of his claws against the skin of my shoulder. He was always careful never to pierce my skin. My clothing was not so lucky.

"That hurts, you know," I remarked, as I did my best not to wince. "There's no need to take your bad temper out on me."

The falcon butted its head against my cheek. "You are too grumpy," I responded. "I'd help you get over it if I knew what to do. I wish that you could tell me."

Without warning, the falcon launched himself into the air. I stood for a moment, rubbing my sore shoulder with the heel of one hand, watching as the bird arrowed into the sky. Not for the first time, a strange mixture of elation and envy filled my heart as I watched him soar. I resumed walking, my eyes shifting between the ground in front of me and the falcon above as he climbed higher and higher in ever-widening circles.

Then, as abruptly as he'd flown, the falcon folded his wings and dove back toward the ground. *He has found a way*, I thought. I quickened my pace. I'd gone no more than a dozen steps before my ears were filled with the sound of water. In front of me, the ground rose steeply. I picked up my pace, almost sprinting to the top.

I was standing on a riverbank. The river itself was broad. Its current flowed swiftly into the forest. The falcon sat on a boulder on the opposite bank.

"That's all very well for you," I called out after a moment. "You can fly across. How do you propose I follow?"

I had limited experience with rivers, but even I could tell that this one was much too deep and fast-moving for me to cross. I would have to find another place to try. I put my hands on my hips and surveyed my surroundings.

"I'm going into the forest," I finally announced.

At once the bird sent up a squawk of protest, though he did not move from his place.

"I'm sorry if you don't like it," I replied. "But I really can't see that I have much choice. I don't want to walk along the bank in the opposite direction. That would be turning back. I want to go forward. That means into the forest. Surely you can see that, Mr. Sharp Eyes.

"Why don't you try flying along the course of the river and find a spot where I can cross? Then come back and find me. Please," I finally remembered to add.

At this, the falcon launched himself skyward. He flew across the river and then skimmed above my head, just low enough so that I could feel the brush of his wings against my hair. Flying low and straight, he vanished into the forest.

The sole of my right shoe gave out about half an hour later, which was about five minutes after I'd begun to wonder if I'd made the right choice. Though we'd passed through several woods during the course of our journey, none of them had the feel of this forest. The canopy was so dense that little light filtered down to the forest floor. The air was damp and strangely oppressive. Surrounded by the trees, I lost all sight of the horizon.

I walked along the riverbank. The voice of the river was a great bellow beside me. Beneath the trees even the color of the water seemed subdued, a deep and muddy brown.

All right, so maybe the falcon was right about staying out of the forest, I thought. *Where is he, anyhow?*

At precisely that moment, I put my right foot down on a sharp stone. It pushed its way up through the sole of my boot, which was worn thin by my travels. I gave a yelp of surprise and pain, lifted my foot to extract the stone, and then promptly lost my balance and tumbled down the riverbank to land with a splash in the river.

The water was deep and icy cold. It soaked my skirts in an instant, making it hard to move my legs. It filled my boots, trying to drag me down. I could feel the swift current, pulling me along with it. I thrashed, desperately trying to keep my head above water.

"Help!" I called out. "Help!"

Through the roaring that filled my ears, I thought I heard a voice return my call. The current swept me around a bend. The river was wider and a little slower here. A broad mudbank extended into the water on the right-hand shore. I swam toward it as best I could. My arms felt heavy with cold.

"Good girl. You can do it," I heard a voice call. I made a final, frantic effort and felt a strong hand reach out to catch hold of my arm. With my other hand, I reached for it with the last of my strength. In the next moment I was on the mudbank, my chest heaving with exertion.

"Gracious, child!" the voice exclaimed. "It's fortunate I happened to come along. Another few minutes in that water, and you'd have been done for.

"Get up now," the voice commanded. "You can't just lie there. You'll catch your death of cold. You come along home with me. I've got a nice fire going. We'll get you warmed up in no time."

Slowly, painfully, I got to my feet. I was so chilled my teeth chattered. My whole body felt bruised and sore. Beside me stood a stout old woman, her face as wrinkled as an apple doll's. She had red cheeks and eyes as bright and dark as a robin's. There was a blue shawl wrapped around her head, a yellow one around her shoulders, and one of purple tied around her waist. She looked like a rainbow come to life.

"There now. I knew you could do it," she said. She placed an arm around my back and guided me up the riverbank. "Come along now. Let's get you home."

Home, I thought. Twice now, the old woman had used that word, and suddenly, a great longing for home rose up inside me. A home with Oma sitting at her sewing, with our flowers blooming all around me. A home with a special place that was mine alone, a place where I might rest.

Tired, I thought. *I am so very tired.*

"There now," the old woman said again, precisely as if she could read my thoughts. We reached the top of the riverbank. "Not much farther now, and you can have everything your little heart desires."

I stopped for a moment to get my bearings and to catch my breath.

I must have been in the river longer than I realized, I thought.

The trees were less dense where I now stood. The forest was more open and welcoming. Bright patches of sunlight slanted down through the trees' branches. In the largest patch of sun sat a cottage. It was painted white and had a thick roof of thatch. A riot of flowers bloomed in front, winding exuberantly along both sides to disappear around the back.

"Oh," I breathed. "A garden. You have a garden."

"Indeed, I do," the old woman replied. "Come along with me. It will feel like yours in no time."

How good it will be to feel the sun on my back! I thought.

How wonderful to smell the scent of flowers! I wondered if this old woman loved the same kinds that Oma had. Did she have sunflowers?

"My pack!" I suddenly exclaimed. "Where's my pack? I've lost it!"

"Tut," the old woman said. She clapped her hands, and suddenly we were surrounded by a flock of crows.

"This young lady has lost her pack," the old woman said. "Please see if you can find it for her."

The flock of crows flew off at once, their raucous cries loud even over the voice of the river. They wheeled upward, then vanished behind the riverbank. They reappeared almost at once. Each bird held a side of my pack within its beak.

"Be careful, oh please, be careful," I called out.

But it was already too late. With a sound of ripping cloth, the pack disintegrated. My few belongings tumbled through the air. My cloak spread out upon the breeze like a threadbare ghost. The crows began to caw in a great cacophony of sound.

That was when I saw it. The only memento I still had of home. The packet of sunflower seeds from Oma's rooftop garden.

"Oma's seeds!" I cried.

Then, suddenly, the falcon was there, his keen voice cutting across the harsh caws of the crows. Darting among them, as swiftly and accurately as an arrow, the falcon plucked the packet of seeds from the air with his claws.

The crows beset the falcon, shrieking in outrage, pecking at him with their sharp beaks. The falcon did not let go of his prize. His powerful wings lifted him high into the air, outpacing the wings of the crows. Nevertheless, the black beaks had taken their toll.

The falcon flew straight along the top of the riverbank before turning sharply and disappearing into the forest. The white seed packet was visible in its claws. But so were the black dots spilling to the ground in a fine black rain.

"Oma," I sobbed as the falcon disappeared from view. "Oma."

"That's right, dear," the old woman said. She began to propel me toward the cottage.

"Have no fear. I'll be your Oma from now on. Come into the house and take a rest. Don't you worry about a thing. Granny here can make you forget all your troubles."

Somewhere inside me a voice protested, saying that this wasn't what I'd meant at all. I didn't need a grandmother. I already had one. I didn't want to forget my troubles, for they were a part of what spurred me on. But my head felt fuzzy, my body ached, and the scent of flowers around the cottage suddenly seemed to rise up around me in a great cloud.

"That's right," the old woman coaxed. We reached the front door; she twisted an old brass knob and threw the door open wide. Before me was a room with dried flowers and herbs hanging from its rafters. A cheerful fire burned in a stone fireplace. The scent of something savory cooking in a cast-iron pot wafted toward the door. It was the most peaceful-looking place that I had ever seen.

"You just come right in."

With the old woman's firm hand beneath my elbow for guidance, I stepped across the threshold.

Seventeen

STORY THE NINTH

IN WHICH DEIRDRE RECEIVES AN
UNEXPECTED WELCOME

HOME!

How shall I describe what it felt like to see it again? What a powerful combination of joy and sorrow!

The great palace of ice and snow in which I had been born rose from the snowfield, solid yet whimsical somehow. The front gate had been made of iron once upon a time, or so my father always told me. But it had long been completely encased in the ice of the surrounding landscape, rendering it as white as the palace behind it. The gates were stuck open, a fact that had always pleased my father. We were a peaceful people. We had no need to bar our doors.

Behind the gates, the palace rose up like a great wedding cake, tier upon tier of floors, of battlements, of towers. In the very center, at the top of the tallest tower of all, was the room my mother had preferred. As I gazed upward, the sunlight caught the windows, casting a sparkle of rainbows across the snow. It was from one of those very windows that I had fallen long ago.

"Look." I suddenly heard Kai's voice beside me. "I think someone is coming out to meet us."

I felt the grip of his hand tighten on mine. All through the hours of our flight, Kai's hand had remained steadily on mine. When at last our feet had touched the earth, he'd swayed a little, like a sailor adjusting to dry land.

We had set down a little ways from the palace. I had wanted to walk toward my home as I once had been required to walk away from it. I tried not to think about the fact that my father would not be waiting there for me. But now, as I watched, a lone figure slowly made its way out of the palace and walked toward the gates.

"I wonder who it is," I said.

"There's an easy way to find out," Kai said with a smile. He took a step forward. I stayed rooted to the spot.

To my dismay and astonishment, my feet, which had carried me through so many foreign lands, abruptly refused to take me any farther. Much as I told myself I wished to, I could not move a muscle. I could not bring myself to take the last few steps, the ones that would truly bring me home.

I'm afraid, I realized. More afraid than I could remember being before.

"I can't," I whispered. "I can't, Kai. It won't be the same. *I'm not the same.*"

"Well, of course not," Kai said simply.

I felt a rush of emotion, so foreign that for a moment I could not recognize it. *Gratitude,* I thought. Kai hadn't argued with me, hadn't tried to talk me out of what I felt. He'd simply acknowledged the truth of my words.

I was home. But home was now a place that was both familiar and foreign.

Foreign I can do, I thought. And suddenly my feet began to move forward of their own free will, for they knew how to walk toward the unknown.

Together, Kai and I walked until we stood directly in front of the open gates. When we got there, the individual who'd come out to greet us bowed low.

"My lady," he said. I gave a start. I'd been so wrapped up in coming home that I'd forgotten the obvious: I was the ruler of this land now. As if to confirm my thoughts, the man before us spoke again.

"Your Majesty, I should say."

"Thank you," I said. *Well, that's going to take some getting used to,* I thought. "I appreciate your welcome. It is most kind."

Oh, for pity's sake, Deirdre, I thought. *Could you sound a little more stuffy?*

Slowly, as if my thanks released him from the need to bow, the man straightened up. Only then did I realize how old he was. For several moments, I gazed into his ancient face. He stared back, his eyes intent on mine. They were dark, and they did not seem to have aged. They were still quick and sharp. I felt my own eyes widen in disbelief.

"You look the same, yet not the same, if you will permit me to say so, Highness," the old man said. "I believe your father would have been proud."

"Dominic?" I breathed. "Can it really be you?"

The weathered face broke into a smile.

"I am honored that you recognize me," my father's steward said. "I always told your father that you would, when the time came."

"But how is this possible?" I asked. "I mean surely . . . I've been gone so long . . ."

"Not as long as you might think," Dominic answered. "But no matter. I made your father a promise, many years ago. A promise while he was on his deathbed, though I am sorry to speak of this on your homecoming."

"What did you swear?" I asked, even as I felt my heart cry out. I had known my father would not be here to greet me, had known it before I set out. But hearing his death spoken of was still painful.

"I swore I would be here to greet you upon your return, so that there might be at least one face in your kingdom that was familiar," Dominic answered quietly. "I swore I would do this no matter how long your journey took."

He gestured toward himself. "You see before you the power of this vow."

"I am glad of its strength," I said, speaking from my heart. Then, in a move that surprised us both, I stepped forward and threw my arms around him. I felt Dominic enfold me in a surprisingly strong hug.

"You are like your father," he whispered in my ear. "You inspire love."

"You are the one who knows best about love," I replied as tears blurred my eyes. "For surely your presence demonstrates its power."

I released him and stepped back. "There is someone I would like you to meet," I said. "Dominic, this is Kai."

But as I turned toward him, I saw Kai sway on his feet. For the first time I realized that his teeth were chattering and that his lips were all but blue with cold. I, who am never cold, had forgotten the fact that Kai might be, that he must be, and that he no doubt had been cold for many hours. We had flown through the air on the back of the wind. We stood in the land of ice and snow.

"Quickly," Dominic said. "Let us get him indoors. We will find a way to warm him."

And so, with Dominic supporting Kai on one side and me on the other, we passed through the gates of the palace and I was finally home.

Eighteen

MY FIRST WEEKS IN THE CASTLE PASSED IN ONE GREAT blur. There were so many new things to learn, now that I was the ruler of my homeland. I spent many hours each day with Dominic. Kai explored the palace on his own. But when Dominic and I were finished working for the day, Kai often joined us. Much to my delight, the two men liked each other at once. Their talents seemed complementary. Kai was always curious, and Dominic was a natural teacher.

"He is a fine young man," Dominic observed one morning. "He has a good pair of eyes and a keen mind."

We were alone in the room I would always think of as my father's study. I had been going over a list of the mayors in the

principal cities of the realm. My interest in names was coming in handy in a way I'd never anticipated. It made it easier to
commit the mayors' names to memory.

Dominic and I had had several discussions about the best
way for me to meet my subjects, but it was actually Kai who
suggested the course of action I decided to adopt. Instead of
waiting for people to come to me, I would make a tour of the
kingdom. Such a journey would be a good way to show my
people that I was as interested in them as they were in me.

The fact that the Winter Child had returned at last to take
up her duties as queen of the land of ice and snow had caused
great excitement throughout the land. Naturally, my people
were curious to see what I looked like. Almost none of them
had been alive when I'd first set out on my quest.

I had worried that, having fulfilled the vow he'd made to
my father, Dominic's strength would now begin to fade. If anything, it was just the opposite. He seemed to flourish under the
responsibility of tutoring me in my new duties. And he genuinely enjoyed the time he spent with Kai.

Kai and I had been given little time alone together since our
arrival. This was to be expected, of course, and I was genuinely
pleased that Kai had found so much to interest him around the
palace and grounds.

As the days went on, however, I found myself lifting my
head from my books, as if hoping to hear the sound of his footsteps in the hall. I never did. Instead, I was the one who sought

him out. I frequently found him at a window, staring into the distance, lost in his own thoughts.

Though he always turned to me with a smile when I spoke, there was also always a moment that caused my heart to miss a beat: the moment before he turned, when it was clearest that, though Kai's body was present, his spirit had traveled far away.

"Are you unhappy here, Kai?" I asked one afternoon. Dominic and I were taking a break from our session.

"Unhappy?" Kai echoed. He turned around quickly. "No, of course not. Why do you ask that?"

"It's hard to explain," I said, half wishing I hadn't spoken. What would I do if he said he was miserable and that he wanted to go home?

You know the answer to that, Deirdre, I thought. I would have to let him go. I could not hold Kai here against his will.

"Sometimes you seem pleased to be here, other times you seem far away."

Kai was silent for several moments. "I am far away," he finally said. "Far away from all that is familiar, far from my home."

I pulled in a silent breath. "Do you want to go home?"

Kai shook his head swiftly, and I felt myself relax a little. "No," he said, his tone firm. "I don't. It's just . . ." He turned to look out the window once again. "You have a true place here, Deirdre. I do not."

"Not yet," I said, just as firmly.

"Not yet," Kai said with a slight smile. He continued to gaze out the window, and I wondered if he was thinking of Grace. I moved to stand beside him, our shoulders just touching.

"Give it time, Kai."

"I will." He nodded. He turned to look at me then. "I'm used to being, well, useful, I guess," he went on. "I love exploring the palace, learning how things work, but the truth is, all I'm doing is satisfying my own curiosity. I'm not *doing* anything. I'm not accomplishing anything. It makes me feel unsettled and . . ."

"Useless?" I suggested.

Kai made a face. "I sound like an idiot, don't I?"

"I think you make perfect sense," I said. "In fact, I have a proposition for you. Dominic is going to travel with me, as you know. I need someone to run the palace in our absence. I'd like you to have the job."

"I don't know anything about running a palace," Kai protested.

"But you could learn," I said. "You could figure it out. That's what you're best at, isn't it?" I put a hand on his shoulder. "I want you to be happy here, Kai. I want you to feel that you are needed and that you belong."

"I want that too," Kai said. He lifted a hand and placed it on top of mine. "Deirdre, I—"

"Oh, there you are, Your Highness," Dominic's voice suddenly said from behind us. Kai and I started, then took a step apart. "And good afternoon, Kai," Dominic went on. "I am sorry to interrupt, but I'm afraid it's time for Her Majesty and me to resume our work."

"Kai has just agreed to run the palace in our absence," I said as I turned toward Dominic.

"Excellent," my steward said at once. "That is a sound choice. I will be happy to answer any questions you have before Her Majesty and I depart."

"Thank you," Kai said, his tone wry. "I'm sure I'll have some."

"See you at dinner," I said.

Kai nodded and moved off down the corridor.

"I apologize," Dominic said quietly as we turned our own steps toward the study. "Perhaps I should not have interrupted."

"No. It's all right," I said.

"Kai is a fine young man," Dominic said, voicing the opinion he'd shared many times before. "But might I ask what plans Your Highness has in store for him?"

"What makes you think I have plans for him?" I asked, unnerved by the question. *Are my feelings so obvious?* I wondered. "He's a human being, not a piece of furniture to be moved from room to room. I'm sure Kai has plans for himself."

"Of course you're quite right," Dominic said at once. We had reached the study. He opened the door, then stepped aside to let me enter first. "I should not have inquired. I have overstepped my bounds."

I waited until we were both inside with the door closed before I replied.

"Of course you should have inquired," I said. "I know my

father relied on you to speak your mind. I do too."

"It is my pleasure to assist Your Highness to the best of my ability," Dominic said. He sketched a quick bow.

"Even when I behave like a bad-tempered schoolgirl?"

"Especially then," he said with a smile. We looked at each other for a moment, and I thought I saw both joy and sorrow in his eyes. *Somewhere between the two,* I thought, *is where I want to be, just like everyone else.* I just didn't know how to get there.

"I should help you most when you need it most, Highness," my steward continued. "Would you like me to aid you now?"

"I'm not sure I know what kind of help to ask for," I confessed. "It seems my ability to read hearts is deserting me, just when I need it most."

"I doubt that very much," Dominic replied. "But if I may . . ."

I nodded. "Please, go on."

"I'm not sure you can read a heart in the way I think you mean," Dominic continued. "A way that would let you figure out what that heart will decide ahead of time. No one possesses that gift."

"Then what must I do?"

"Be patient," Dominic answered. "Learn to trust."

"Which one of us?" I asked. Dominic smiled. I caught my breath. I recognized that smile. My father's face had worn it every time I'd solved a difficult puzzle faster than he'd thought I might.

"If you can ask that question, you may need less help than you think you do, Highness," he replied.

"Dominic," I said suddenly. "Will you do something for me?"

"Anything that lies within my power," my steward answered promptly.

"Will you stop calling me 'Majesty' or 'Highness,' at least when we're alone? I'd like you to call me by a proper name."

"What name?" Dominic asked, his tone surprised.

"One that you choose," I replied. "A name that has meaning for you."

"Why do you ask for this?" Dominic inquired.

"Sometimes I feel that all I have are titles," I explained. "Your Highness, Your Majesty, the Winter Child. I know I get to choose my own name when my task is done, but in the meantime . . . I've never really cared for Deirdre," I admitted. "It's just another word for sorrow, after all."

"How do you feel about Beatrice?" Dominic asked.

"Beatrice," I echoed. I held the name in my mouth, felt the way it rolled over and around my tongue. It started out grandly, then seemed to quiet at the end, like a trumpet call rising and then fading in the clear morning air.

"I like it," I said. "Why did you choose it?"

"It was my mother's name," Dominic explained. A shadow passed across his face. "I always hoped I might have a daughter and pass on the name."

"But you didn't," I said, suddenly struck by the fact that Dominic had lived a long, full life and I knew virtually nothing about it.

"No," my steward said with a shake of his head. "I did not. In fact, I never married at all." He gave a rueful smile as if he had not intended to say so much. "Perhaps I am not the best person to offer advice when it comes to the heart."

"Nonsense," I said at once.

"Thank you," Dominic said softly. He cocked his head, his dark eyes on mine. "The question still remains, though: What are you going to do about Kai?"

"I don't know," I answered, matching his honesty with my own. "I guess I'll just have to wait and see what happens next."

"In other words," Dominic said, "you'll be just like everyone else."

Abruptly, my heart began to pound like a hammer inside my chest.

"What?"

"You'll be like everyone else," Dominic said once more. "You may be able to tell whether or not Kai's heart needs mending, but you cannot tell when, or if, it will decide to love. That, you must wait for him to reveal, just like any other girl would.

"Does it please you, to think you might be like everyone else?"

"Do you know," I said, "I think it does. I've never felt like everyone else, not for as long as I can remember. But it might be wonderful to be ordinary."

"Even if it means that, like many others, you end up being unlucky in love?"

"Even if it means that," I said. "Which is not to say I won't work hard not to be," I added with a smile.

"I wish you luck."

"Thank you." I walked over to the desk and retrieved the paper I had spent the day studying. I handed it to Dominic.

"I will now recite for you the names of all the mayors I am about to meet."

Two days later I rode out from the castle, leaving Kai behind.

Nineteen

Story the Tenth

IN WHICH GRACE MAKES SEVERAL
STARTLING DISCOVERIES

How long did I stay in the old woman's cottage? I cannot tell. Time seemed to pass strangely there, as if the usual rules didn't quite apply.

I was sick for many days, so ill and weak that I could hardly get out of bed, let alone go out of doors. As if all the steps that I had taken had conspired to make me lie down. My dunking in the river simply had been the final straw.

Throughout my illness, here are the things that I recall: the touch of the old woman's hands, the sound of her voice, the never-ending yet always changing scent of flowers. All these things should have been soothing, but somehow they weren't.

No, that's not quite right.

They *were* soothing. That was just the problem: so soothing that I ran the risk of forgetting myself. The old woman cared for me as tenderly as if I had been her granddaughter, and she encouraged me to call her Oma.

Have you ever been a character in one of your own dreams? That's what my days in the cottage in the forest felt like, as if I were on the outside of a window looking in at myself. But all the while, I knew that something wasn't right.

"You're feeling much better, aren't you, Grace?" the woman remarked as she brushed my hair one morning. This was a ritual she performed both morning and night.

Not even my true oma had done this, or at least not since I was a very small child. My true oma hadn't held much store in doing things for me; she'd much preferred teaching me to do things for myself.

"It's no wonder you were all worn out," the old woman continued. "Walking and walking, day after day with no end in sight, not even knowing if you were going in the right direction. How could you, when you didn't know where you were going in the first place?

"Tut."

As she often did when she wished to express disapproval, the old woman made a clucking sound, her tongue hitting against the roof of her mouth. As I'd begun to recover, she'd told me I had rambled during my fever, that I actually had tried to get out of bed, insisting I must keep on walking.

"Falling into that river might be the best thing that ever happened to you." She finished brushing my hair and set the brush on the bed beside me.

"The river brought you to me, and now you can stay right where you are. No need to go tramping through the world. You have me to look after you now."

She stroked her hand along the length of my hair, and then she leaned forward to place her cheek against mine. I wondered what our two faces would look like together, if I could have seen them in a mirror. As far as I could tell, the cottage had none.

"I'll bet you can't even remember what it was you were looking for," the old woman said softly. Her breath felt cool against my cheek. "Or maybe it's *whom*. Whom were you looking for, Grace? Won't you tell me?"

Day after day, she repeated these same questions. Day after day, I kept my lips pressed tightly together, refusing to speak Kai's name aloud.

I won't, I vowed silently.

There was something about the way the old woman posed these questions that alarmed me. The only protection I could give myself was to hold my tongue. Why she should ask these questions, why Kai's name was important, I did not know. I only knew I did not want to answer.

"I can't, Oma," I said, as I did every morning. Doing something of which my own oma would never approve: telling a lie. "I can't remember. I'm sorry."

"Nothing to be sorry for, my dear," the old woman said. "I'm sure you'll tell me in good time." Something about the way she said this always sent a shiver down my spine.

She's right, I thought. Sooner or later, this old woman would learn what she wanted to know. What would happen then, I did not care to guess.

I've got to get out of here, I thought.

As if recognizing it was pointless to ask any more questions this morning, the old woman stood.

"Come along now, Grace. It's time for chores."

"May I work in the garden today, Oma?" I asked as I stood as well. This was also part of the daily routine, my request to go outdoors. But not once since I had crossed the threshold of the cottage had I been permitted to set so much as a toe outside the front door.

"Gracious!" my new oma exclaimed as she snatched the hairbrush up from the bed. "Heavens no. Whatever put an idea like that in your mind? You're nowhere near strong enough to work in the garden. Be a good girl now and make your bed, and then sweep the hearth. I'm going to take this out for the crows. You know how they love it for their nests."

From the hairbrush, she pulled several strands of my hair.

"When I come back, we'll have some hot porridge. That sounds lovely, doesn't it?"

"Yes, Oma."

For the record, I hate porridge and I always have, so that made two lies I told every morning.

The old woman turned and walked to the front door. She plucked a shawl from a row of pegs that hung to one side of the door and wrapped it around her head. Then she opened the door. I took an involuntary step forward. Over her shoulder, I caught a glimpse of blue sky.

This was the moment I hated most of all. The moment she went out and left me all alone, for this was when the walls of the cottage seemed to close in around me. But this morning something unexpected happened. Just as the old woman opened the door, a sudden gust of wind swept into the room, wrenching the door from her grasp and sending it crashing open against the cottage wall.

Cool, clean air, dashed around the room, memorizing its contours. Then it moved to the window at the side of the house, stretching itself out against the windowpane as if to camouflage the fact that it was still inside.

"Gracious!" the old woman exclaimed as she quickly moved to recapture the door. "What a wind there is outside this morning. There must be a storm brewing. All the more reason for you to stay indoors."

She looked at me, her expression severe, as if she expected me to rebel. I remained silent. I remained still. I did not let my eyes stray to the window where I was sure the wind still hovered.

"You remember your chores now, Grace," the old woman instructed. "I don't want to come back and find them incomplete.

You know how unhappy it makes me when you disappoint me, don't you?"

"I do, Oma," I replied.

With a final glance around the room, the old woman stepped through the door and closed it behind her. A moment later, I heard the rasp of a key turning in the lock signaling the end of the morning ritual.

She says she loves me, but she makes me a prisoner, I thought. I walked to the window and leaned my forehead against the glass. Sure enough, it seemed that some of the wind still lingered there, pressed against the windowpane. I gulped in one deep lungful of the air and then another.

Help me, I thought. *I've got to get out of here. She doesn't love me, not really.*

What the old woman called love was literally keeping me a prisoner. This love did not think of me, it thought only of itself.

And suddenly, without warning, Kai's face came into my mind. I saw again the way he had looked when he had asked me to marry him. I had feared his love would hold me back, would hold me prisoner. That's what Kai had accused me of when I had turned him down. But now I knew what it was to be held a prisoner by love.

Oh, Kai! I thought. *How I misjudged you, misjudged your love.*

For now that I was thinking clearly, I realized that, like this old woman, I had been selfish. Kai had offered me a gift from his heart. But I had not recognized it, because I had only seen what my heart feared the most.

"I'm sorry," I whispered to the windowpane. "Forgive me, Kai. I think I understand why you chose to follow the Winter Child."

She could do the thing that I could not: look into Kai's heart and recognize the true value of what she saw.

Never again, I vowed. *Never again will I be so blind. Never again will I let fear rule my heart.*

I caught my breath as, in the next moment, the cottage around me seemed to change before my very eyes. No longer did it look homey and snug. Now that my heart and eyes were no longer clouded by fear, I could see the cottage for the ruin it was. The walls leaned inward. The fireplace smoked. Several of the windowpanes were cracked. My heart in my throat, I spun around.

The door sagged on its hinges. It wasn't locked at all! I could not be held a prisoner here, not now that I could see this place for what it really was.

Hurry, hurry, Grace! I thought.

Swiftly, fearing I would hear the old woman return at any moment, I thrust my feet into my boots and laced them up. She had mended the hole in the right one, then had positioned the boots right by my bed, as if in promise of the day I would finally be allowed to go outdoors. But now I knew the truth. The old woman would have kept me a prisoner forever, warping and distorting the name of love. She would have done her best to teach me to believe as she did.

And the moment I finally spoke Kai's name aloud would have been the moment all was lost. There is a power in knowing a name and in speaking that name aloud. A power to summon and a power to banish. But I had protected Kai. I had kept his name to myself. I had held him in my heart, and my refusal to let him go would help to free me now.

I crossed to the door. It was not quite ajar enough for me to slip through the space. *It's now or never, Grace,* I thought. I put my hands on the ancient wood and eased the door open a little more. The hinges shrieked like souls in pain.

Well, that'll do it, I thought.

Quick as a fish sliding through the narrows, I slipped through the opening. I was almost out when my skirt caught on a stray nail. Almost sobbing now from terror and hope, I yanked it free. The fabric gave way with a high tearing sound. And then I was stumbling down the path, the cackling of crows erupting in the air above me.

"Stop her!" I heard the old woman cry, her voice a wail of fury and despair. "Don't let her leave me alone!"

Straight as arrows the crows dove at me, their sharp beaks aiming for my head. I cried out, raising my arms to shield my face.

Which way? I thought desperately. Which way offered the best chance of escape? For the truth was, I feared both the river and the forest.

And then, suddenly, the falcon appeared. His voice was loud even over the caws of the crows. The bird had not abandoned me. He hurtled downward with talons outstretched, scattering the great black birds, then swept off in the direction of the forest. I followed his flight with my eyes. Through the trees, I caught unexpected flashes of yellow.

I began to run, laughing in joyful understanding, even as the old woman continued to shriek and the crows to caw. The falcon had shown me the way to freedom. It had even sowed the path itself.

All I had to do was follow the row of sunflowers.

Twenty

STORY THE ELEVENTH

IN WHICH ALL THE TRAVELERS WHO HAVE WANDERED

THROUGH THIS TALE FINALLY MAKE THEIR WAY

TO THE DOOR OF THE WINTER CHILD

I WALKED SWIFTLY FOR THE REST OF THAT DAY, DETERMINED
to put as much distance between me and the cottage as I could.
The falcon flew high overhead, as if to spur me on. After expressing my thanks, I did not speak. I concentrated on making up
for lost time. I kept my pace brisk. As the day wore on, the trees
began to thin. The air grew colder. Patches of snow dotted the
ground.

Late in the afternoon, the forest gave way completely to a
broad expanse of white. Here, at last, I paused. For surely this
could be no other than the land of ice and snow. Traversing it
would be my journey's final phase.

How far is it to the palace? I wondered. I had no food now, no water. I didn't have my warm cloak. I had only my determination not to give up.

Come on, Grace. There's no time like the present, I thought.

Cautiously, I tested the snow with the toe of my boot. I wanted to be absolutely sure the ground would hold me before I put my full weight down. Snow and ice were nothing new to me, not with the winters where I had grown up. But, as I began to move through this cold, white landscape, it seemed to me that the snow and ice were different somehow. Shaped by the forces that had created the Winter Child. This didn't necessarily make them treacherous, but it did make them unique.

There were no tracks in the snow. Nothing to show that any living thing had ever passed this way before. As far as my eyes could see, there was nothing but a dazzling field of white. I lifted my eyes to where the falcon was circling above me in the sky.

"Which way?" I called out. "Do you know?"

The bird made one last high circle, then arrowed down. He swooped low over my head, and then continued into the path of the setting sun.

"If you say so," I said though, for once, the bird had not given its piercing call. The *whoosh* the falcon's wings made through the air, the crunch of my boots against the snow, the steady rhythm of my heart as it knocked against my ribs, these were the only sounds. It was as if the entire land was holding its breath, waiting for something.

* * *

By the time the sun went down and then the moon rose, not even my own exertions were enough to keep me warm. I was tired and hungry. Even the horrible porridge that the old woman had fed me would have been welcome. Worst of all, however, was the feeling that I should be nearing my destination now.

Along about midnight, or so I judged by the position of the moon in the sky, the ground began to incline. I stood for a moment at the bottom of the slope, leaning forward with my hands on my knees, sucking in air.

Come on now, Grace, I thought. *You can't stop now. You'd never forgive yourself. Assuming you don't freeze to death before you get there.*

I straightened, and as I did, I felt the wind come up, frisking around me like a puppy.

"Oh, for heaven's sake!" I exclaimed aloud. "I'm cold enough. If you're going to show up now, the least you can do is to help me."

No sooner did I finish speaking than the wind died away, as if it was thinking things over. Then, having made a decision, it pushed against my back, strong as a pair of hands propelling me upward. I barely had time to snatch up my skirts to keep from tripping over them before the wind pushed me to the top of the rise.

There before me, in a valley curved like a large bowl, stood a palace made of ice, its towers dazzling in the moonlight. A great pair of gates stood open wide, as if to welcome all who approached it. Without warning, I grew dizzy. After weeks on end, after more footsteps than I could number, my destination was now no more than a five-minute walk away.

Then, as I watched, a figure made its way out through the gates and toward me. Suddenly I was running, no longer caring if I took a misstep, no longer remembering the long miles it had taken to get here, no longer thinking of anything else at all. All I wanted was to reach this solitary figure. To meet him halfway, and more.

"Hello, Grace," Kai said. "It's about time you got here."

Sobbing in relief, I hurled myself into his waiting arms.

Twenty-One

Story the Twelfth
IN WHICH KAI FINDS THE KEY THAT
OPENS MANY HEARTS

"I STILL CAN'T BELIEVE YOU CRIED LIKE A GIRL," I SAID.

"Well, why not?" Grace demanded. "I am one, aren't I?"

It was the morning following her arrival, and we were sitting in the room I had known she would wish to see most: the palace's tallest tower. The tower from which Deirdre had tumbled as an infant so long ago, thereby setting all our tales in motion.

Grace had slept deeply, which was hardly surprising. She hadn't asked about Deirdre at all, which was. But I knew better than to push her. The last thing I wanted was another quarrel. Once Grace was awake and had eaten a hearty breakfast, I showed her around the palace, finally taking her to the tower.

Grace was silent as we climbed the curving stairs. She stood in the open doorway, gazing into the room.

"I wish Oma could have seen this," she said at last.

"I thought that the first time I came here," I answered. "Come and sit by the window. I think you'll like the view. You can see the horizon."

"This may come as something of a shock," Grace said, her tone wry as she followed me into the room. "But I may have seen enough of the horizon, at least for a little while."

"I think it would shock me more if you didn't feel that way," I said.

We settled onto the window seat. In spite of the fact that Grace claimed she'd had enough, I noticed that the first thing she did was look out to see where the ground met the sky. Through the window, I could see a falcon making great lazy circles in the morning air.

"So," I said finally, "here you are. I still can't believe it." In spite of my flippant words at our reunion, I could hardly believe what Grace had done. She had set out after me. She had traveled for countless miles.

"That's several things you can't believe about me," Grace said without taking her eyes from the falcon.

"Well," I answered slowly, "maybe that's because I suddenly feel as if I don't know you as well as I once did."

Grace looked at me then, and I couldn't quite read the expression in her eyes.

"I could say the same about you," she finally replied. "If anyone had told me we'd have such a big fight that you'd go off in the middle of the night without saying good-bye, that you'd leave me to follow the Winter Child, I'd have told them they were out of their mind. Yet here we are."

"Here we are," I echoed. *And so,* I thought. *What now?*

"I'm sorry," I said, then stared in astonishment. Grace had spoken precisely the same words at the exact same time.

"No, really," I said. "Grace, I—"

"You should let me go first," she interrupted, with just the hint of a smile. "I'm the one who walked for ages to get here, after all."

"I knew you were going to rub that in sooner or later," I said. We hadn't had much time for conversation last night, but we had discussed flying. "You always did want to be first," I went on. "Oma used to say so."

"She did, didn't she?" Grace's smile turned just a little sad around the corners of her mouth. "Perhaps neither of us has changed so very much after all."

A silence fell between us then. Not quite as companionable as those we'd shared in the past, but not so strained as to be uncomfortable, either. It was a waiting-to-see-what-would-happen-next kind of silence. Grace broke it.

"I truly *am* sorry, Kai." Grace spoke quietly. "I'm sorry that we quarreled. And I'm sorry I let you believe I thought that if I married you, your love would require me to change, that it would require me to let go of myself. I'm sorry I believed these things, if only for a moment."

She made a gesture, as if to push away the past. "It was stupid. *I* was stupid. I should have known you better. I *do* know you better. I think"—she sighed—"I think the person I didn't know well enough was myself."

"But now you think you do," I said.

She looked at me, her gaze clear-eyed and steady. "Yes."

"Then that makes two of us," I said. "And for the record, I'm sorry, too. I never should have left without saying goodbye. It seems so childish now, doesn't it? But it felt like the right thing to do at the time."

"So what happens now?" Grace asked. "Do you still want to marry me?"

"If I did, would you say yes?"

"I asked you first," Grace said.

"How about this?" I asked. "I'm going to count to three. When I'm done, we'll each say whether or not we want to get married. We'll answer at the same time, just a simple yes or no. And we'll promise to speak the truth, because, whether we get married or not, we love each other and we always have.

"Will you do this?"

"Yes, I will," Grace said.

She held out a hand. I placed mine into it.

"Ready?"

"Ready."

"One. Two. Three."

"No," we said on the same breath, then stared in astonishment. I'm not sure which of us began to laugh first. We laughed until our sides ached and the tears streamed from our eyes.

"I don't know what's so funny," I managed to say when I could take a breath. "I walked out on you, you walked half the world to find me, and we don't want to be together. Oma would never have approved of this. Didn't she say stories were always supposed to end in happily ever after?"

"Who's to say ours won't still do that?" Grace asked. "I don't know about you, but I'm laughing in relief. I was so afraid I'd walked all this way only for us to hurt each other again."

"Why did you come after me?" I asked.

Grace was silent for a moment, her fingers fiddling with a tassel on the window-seat cushion.

"Because I had to," she finally said. "I couldn't bear the thought that you'd gone away in anger, though when I discovered that you'd left, I got pretty mad myself. And also . . ." Her voice trailed off. "I was afraid."

"Afraid," I echoed.

"Afraid that I'd never see you again," Grace said, her tone implying I was being stupid. Her fingers continued to worry the tassel. "What's she like?"

"What's who like?"

Grace heaved the cushion at my head. "Don't be an idiot. The Winter Child, of course."

"She's difficult to describe," I said. "She's very beautiful, of course."

"Oh, of course," Grace said.

I picked up the cushion and threw it back at her. "But in all my life, I don't think I've ever seen anyone so sad. You and I— we've always had each other, even when we've made mistakes. The fact that you came after me proves that. But Deirdre's spent years and years with no one at all."

"Except that now she has you," Grace said.

I made a face. "Is it that obvious? Being that obvious is just pathetic."

Grace gave a quick laugh. "You've never been pathetic, Kai," she said. "And the only reason I know you love her is because I know you so well."

She sat up a little straighter then, as if I'd poked her with a pin. "Do you mean to say you haven't told her?"

"Of course I haven't told her," I said. "How can I? She's a queen and what am I? A watchmaker's apprentice. Besides, I had pretty much given her the impression I wanted to marry you."

"Well, no wonder you were so happy to see me show up," Grace said with a laugh.

"That's it. I take it all back. I never missed you for a minute."

"Oh, yes you did," Grace protested.

"Yes, I did," I said more seriously. "I worried about you, too."

"Did you know I would come after you?" Grace asked.

"I didn't exactly *know* it," I answered slowly. "It was more a feeling that I had, as if I could sense your determination to find me, no matter what. It's part of why I agreed to stay behind while Deirdre toured the country."

"When will she be back?"

"She's expected today," I said.

"And then you'll tell her that you love her," Grace said.

I stood up. "It's not that simple, Grace," I protested.

She got up in turn, moving to grasp me by the shoulders.

"Yes it is, Kai," she said. "In its heart, in *your* heart, love is very simple. That is part of its great strength. It's only the world's expectations that complicate things."

"That's precisely my point," I said.

"Which means," Grace continued, her voice rising to carry over mine, "that you should tell Deirdre how you feel about her without delay. The worst that can happen is that she doesn't feel the same as you do, right?"

"Well, yes," I said tartly.

"But that would be no worse than the situation you're in right now," Grace said. "Not knowing how she really feels. Being afraid to speak up."

"I'm not afraid," I protested.

"Then prove it, Kai," Grace said. "If you don't tell her, you'll always wonder what might have happened. Surely you don't want to live a life of regret."

Grace made good sense, I had to admit. "What makes you so smart all of a sudden?" I asked.

Grace gave me a fierce hug. "I've had a lot of time to think things over," she said. She released me and stepped back. Then, to my surprise, she raised a hand to my cheek, just as her grand-mother always had.

"You have such good eyes, Kai," Grace said softly. "Don't waste what they can see."

"I won't," I promised.

In the next moment, I heard the falcon's piercing cry. Grace moved back to the window, undid the latch, and opened the casement. With a great rush of wings, the bird swept inside. It made a circuit of the room, then darted out again. Grace leaned out, the better to see the bird in flight.

"There's a train of horses coming," she said. "I think the Winter Child is back."

Twenty-Two

STORY THE THIRTEENTH
IN WHICH MANY IMPORTANT WORDS ARE SPOKEN

ON MY SECOND HOMECOMING, KAI WAITED FOR ME AT THE palace gates with Grace at his side. They stood close together, hands clasped, and I felt my heart begin to sing with joy and weep with sorrow all at the same time.

I came so close, I thought. *So close to finding love.* But it seemed it was not to be.

"Welcome home," Kai said, and then he smiled. "I'd like to introduce you to my oldest friend, Grace Andersen. She has traveled many miles to find me."

"Welcome, Grace," I said. *How right they look together,* I thought. *How long will it be before Kai leaves, I wonder?*

"Thank you, Your Highness," Grace said formally. She let go of Kai's hand to execute a curtsy. Then she stood quietly, hands at her sides.

"How did Deirdre do with the list of names?" Kai inquired of Dominic as the household servants rushed forward to help the two of us dismount. As my feet hit the snow, I gave a quick shiver. Why had I never noticed the way the cold seeped up through the soles of my shoes?

"She knew every name by heart. Not that I expected anything less, of course," Dominic replied. "And now, Your Highness"—he bowed low—"with your permission, I will retire indoors. My tired old bones are cold and would be happy for a little rest."

"It is cold today, isn't it?" I replied.

Dominic straightened up with a snap.

"What did you say?" he barked.

"I said I thought that it was cold today," I answered. "In fact, I can't remember when . . ." As the enormity of what I was saying hit me, my voice trailed off.

"What? What is it?" I heard Kai ask.

"I'm cold," I whispered. "Oh, Kai, I'm cold."

"It's happened at last," Dominic said, and I could hear the awe and wonder in his voice. "The last heart, her own, has been made whole. She is herself again, a Winter Child no longer."

At this, a great cheer went up. The servants who had gathered to welcome us fell to their knees as if with one body.

"Please," I said through teeth that suddenly wanted very badly to chatter. "Please rise. If I'm cold, I'm sure you are too. Let us all go inside."

But as I went to walk, I swayed on my feet, as if my body was suddenly a foreigner to itself. At once, Kai was at my side. He took off his cloak and draped it around my shoulders. It was warm from his body. He placed one arm around my back. With one hand, he grasped my elbow, firmly.

"Let us go in," he said.

And so I entered the palace of ice with Kai's arm around me.

A short time later we were seated in the tower room, Kai, Grace, and I. Dominic had retired to his rooms. I had changed from my traveling clothes to a gown of pale blue silk, with a dark blue shawl around my shoulders. I was still having trouble adjusting to the cold.

Before I'd joined Kai and Grace, I'd stood in front of the mirror in my room, studying my reflection for several moments. My face looked much as it always had. But my hair and eyes were both growing darker. All save a streak of white hair beginning at my left temple, a permanent reminder of my years as a Winter Child. I lifted a hand to touch it.

I'm glad it's there, I thought. *I spent too much time as a Winter Child for that part of me to ever be forgotten.*

I made my way to the tower. Even from this secluded location, I could feel a buzz of excitement throughout the palace.

First the Winter Child had returned home, and now she was a Winter Child no longer.

I wish I could tell you that I shared their excitement. The truth is, for the first time in a long time, I was absolutely terrified.

As I entered the room, I looked across it to Kai. He was sitting in a great wooden chair. Since ushering me into the castle, he had kept his distance. His face was tight, an expression that said he was dreading either the speaking or the hearing of bad news.

Grace sat on the window seat. At my insistence, she'd selected several dresses from my wardrobe. The one she was wearing now was a rich and vibrant green. A peregrine falcon perched on the windowsill beside her.

Just as we'd entered the palace gates, the bird had swooped down to land upon her shoulder. Grace had accepted his presence as if they were old companions, and so the two had come indoors together. She reached up absently from time to time to stroke a finger along the bird's white throat.

The room was filled with silence. A silence that was mine to break. *Quit stalling, Deirdre,* I thought.

"I suppose you'd like an explanation," I said.

"Only if you want to give one," Kai spoke up quickly.

I heard Grace make an exasperated sound. "Of course she wants to give one," she said. "Just as we both want to hear it."

She looked at me then, our eyes meeting for the first time.

In hers I saw a strange mixture of amusement, irritation, and compassion.

"You'll have to forgive him," she said. "He's feeling a little confused at the moment."

"I know just how he feels," I replied.

Grace cocked her head then, in perfect imitation of the bird beside her. "I didn't think I'd like you," she said suddenly. "And I was *very* sure I didn't want to."

"I could say the same about you," I said, and with that, I discovered that we were grinning like fools. In the next moment, as much to her surprise as to mine, Grace rose to her feet and curtsied low before me.

"Then may I ask you to speak, Your Highness?" she asked. "Will you explain why you are no longer a Winter Child?"

"I will," I answered, a good deal more calmly and regally than I felt.

Grace resumed her position on the window seat.

"I do not need to tell you how I became a Winter Child," I said. "For that tale is well-known. Just as it is known that, of all the hearts I would be called upon to mend, the one that would always remain out of reach would be my own.

"Only one thing could mend my heart. Only one thing could make it whole: the heart that was my heart's true match."

I heard Kai catch his breath.

So quick, he is so quick, I thought. He looked at me then, and I met his gaze. It took everything I had to keep mine steady.

"It wasn't my heart you needed at all, was it?" he said quietly.

"I wouldn't say that," I answered. "I *do* need your heart, Kai."

"What? Wait a minute." Grace suddenly exploded. "What are you two talking about?"

Kai turned to look at her. "Can't you guess?" he asked. "We're talking about you, of course."

"It was your heart that I needed, Grace," I said. "A heart willing to set out upon a journey of its own free will, a journey with no signposts along the way and no foreseeable end in sight. A journey that could only be completed by always putting one foot in front of the other.

"It is the heart willing and able to do all this that is the true match to mine. For this is precisely what my own heart was called upon to do."

"But I thought," Grace said, and then she paused. She shook her head, as if hoping to rearrange her thoughts. "I thought you loved Kai. What about his heart?"

"I do love Kai," I said, though I was finding it hard to speak around the lump in my throat. "I love him even though we must part. I need his heart. But his heart was not designed to mend mine. Yours was."

"Are you going to send me away?" Kai asked. I turned and saw that he had risen to his feet. "Is that what you want?"

"Of course it isn't what I want," I said.

"Then *why*?" Kai cried.

"Because—" I broke off. "Wait a minute," I said. "What do you mean, why? Don't you know?"

"Oh, for heaven's sake, Kai!" Grace exclaimed. "Don't just stand there. Tell her!"

"I'm trying to," Kai snapped back. "But you keep interrupting."

"Tell me what?" I asked.

"I love you," Kai said quietly. But in his quiet tone, I heard absolute certainty.

A great wave of emotion rolled through me.

"I think I have to sit down."

Kai laughed then, and the whole room suddenly was flooded with bright sunlight. From the windowsill, the falcon gave a sweet, sharp cry.

"But I thought you loved Grace," I said.

"And so I do," Kai replied. "But not the way that I love you." He knelt before me and took my hands. "The truth is, I've loved you my whole life." He stood and gently drew me to my feet. "Close your eyes, Grace," he said over his shoulder.

I was laughing as my true love placed his lips on mine. Kai's lips were warm. By the time the kiss was over, I knew I would never be cold again. With Kai's arm still around me, I turned to Grace. She was standing by the window with the sun on her face and the falcon by her side. Her eyes were wide open. In them I thought I caught the glint of tears.

"Kai will tell you I almost never do what he says."

"Thank you," I said. "For your heart has helped to mend mine twice. I would like it very much if there was something I could do for yours."

"But you're no longer the Winter Child," Grace protested.

"True enough," I answered. "Nevertheless, it lies within my power to grant a wish to the heart that has restored my own. What would your heart choose, Grace, if it could?"

"The same as it has always chosen," Grace replied. "My heart has never wanted to be in just one place. It has always longed for the journey, to see what lies over the horizon.

"It isn't that I don't love familiar things. It's that I love the unknown more."

At her words, the falcon suddenly spread its wings. It threw back its head and made the tower room echo with its cry. Without warning, the sunlight became blinding. I heard both Grace and Kai cry out, even as I lifted a hand to shield my eyes.

When I lowered it, the falcon was gone. In its place stood a tall young man with fine, pale skin and wide gray eyes. Long dark hair brushed the tops of his shoulders.

"Oh dear," Grace said.

The young man threw back his head and laughed, a bright, pure sound. Then he knelt at Grace's feet. He extended a hand, palm up. After a moment's hesitation, Grace placed one of hers within it.

"Thank you," the young man said simply. "Your words

have rescued me from an enchantment I have carried for many years."

"Now I'm the one who wants to sit down," Grace said.

The young man chuckled. Still holding Grace's hand in his, he rose to his feet, then turned to me with a bow.

"Your Majesty," he said. "I hope you will forgive my somewhat unusual arrival."

"Gladly," I said, my tone warm with surprise. "On the condition that you explain yourself."

"Long ago," the young man said, "I made a great mistake: I mistook false love for true. The young woman I rejected was a powerful sorceress. She placed a curse and a burden upon me, dooming me to wear the form of a falcon until I could find a heart that would choose me of its own free will, yet not be aware that it had done so."

"A heart that would choose the unknown," Kai suddenly said.

The young man nodded. "Precisely. I have flown throughout the world for many years, so many that I began to despair of ever breaking the curse."

He turned back to Grace.

"Until one day, I saw a girl in the mountains. A girl who refused to give up, who kept her wits about her. My heart has been yours from that day to this one."

"I don't suppose your name is Peregrine, is it?" Grace asked.

"It's Constantin, as a matter of fact," the young man said.

"Constantin," Grace echoed. "And will you be as true as your name?"

"With all my heart."

"In that case," Grace said, her tone mischievous, "I will give you mine again, knowingly this time. I only wish I could have learned how to fly."

"I will grant that wish, if you'll let me," I said. "If you will, for three weeks out of every month, you will both be as you are now. But in the fourth week, Constantin may return to the form of a bird and, since Grace's heart has chosen his, hers may also. Let your body soar as your heart has always longed to, and let this be the final gift of the Winter Child."

"I thank you with all my heart," Grace said.

"As I thank you for the gift of mine."

A FEW THOUGHTS CONCERNING
HAPPY ENDINGS

AND SO IT CAME TO PASS THAT THE TWO COUPLES WERE married in a single ceremony in the great palace of ice. People came to celebrate from miles around.

Grace sent word to the city far away. Petra and Herre Johannes came to the wedding, traveling all the way in Herre Johannes's flower wagon. He presented Deirdre with a bunch of snow drops, which she carried as a wedding bouquet. Petra gave Grace back her oma's shawl.

The wedding feast lasted for a full week, after which Petra and Herre Johannes began their journey home, while Grace and Constantin took to the skies. But Grace and Constantin promised to return to the land of ice and snow each year, for the bonds of love and friendship between the two couples were strong.

Of course they all lived happily ever after, and not just because that is the way these things usually go, but because their hearts had been tested and had remained true. That is the happiest ending of all.

"Well?" Kai asked, just at sunset on the day the wedding festivities concluded. He and his bride stood together at the palace gates, watching Grace and Constantin disappear from view.

"Have you decided?"

"I have." His new wife nodded. She leaned back against him, and then tilted her face to look into his. "I wonder if you can guess what my new name will be."

"I can tell you what I always thought it should be," Kai said. "Will that do just as well?"

She turned in his arms then, so that they were face-to-face. "Tell me."

"Hope," said Kai.

At the sounding of this single syllable, she threw her arms around him.

"I love you, Kai."

"I take it I got it right, then," Kai said.

She thumped a fist against his chest. "There's no need to be insufferable."

And now, finally, Deirdre, the Winter Child, she who had

once been named for sorrow, chose a new name, and the name that she chose was Hope. For, now that she was restored to her true self at last, she understood that this was the name her heart had carried within it all along.

For even as the winter carries within it the seeds of spring, her heart had nourished, as all hearts must, the strong yet fragile seeds of hope.

Author's Note

THE STRUCTURE OF *WINTER'S CHILD* IS A LITTLE DIFFER-
ent from other stories I've created for the Once upon a Time
series. This is a direct inspiration from my source material, Hans
Christian Andersen's "The Snow Queen." As a matter of fact, the
official title is "The Snow Queen: A Tale in Seven Stories." As is
the case with *Winter's Child*, in Andersen's tale each individual
"story" has its own heading giving a hint of what's to come.

In the original, the queen herself is pretty much the bad
guy. As I am never that interested in stories where one character
is always good and another always bad, I decided to mix things
up. It also took me more than seven stories to get my characters
where I wanted them to go! I tell myself this is okay as my tale
is much longer. I hope you enjoy the *Winter's Child* journey.
May it inspire your heart on the journeys it will make.

*Turn the page for a sneak peek
at another magical tale. . . .*

BEAUTY SLEEP

Cameron Dokey

Preamble

(A FANCY WAY OF SAYING "INTRODUCTION")

I'VE HEARD IT SAID (THOUGH I CAN'T SAY WHETHER OR not it's true) that all good stories begin in the same way, with the exact same words.

Since I naturally want you to find my story a good one, one that keeps you reading as much for the comfort of familiar details as for the new ones that surprise you, I've decided to stick to tradition.

You know the words, don't you?

Of course you do.

Once upon a time . . .

There. Thank goodness that's over with.

Now that I've gotten the traditional opening off my chest,

I'm free to tell my story any way I want to. Because isn't that at least part of the reason for telling your own life story? To tell the truth at last. Your truth, your way. Not the truth other people think you should tell in the way they think you should tell it. Which is really just another way of saying the way that makes them look best and feel the least uncomfortable.

Stories are tricky things, aren't they?

Because the thing about them is that the same events can be told any number of ways. It all depends on what you think is important, and, when the important stuff is happening, whether you're looking directly at it or looking away.

Here we come to my first true confession, which, coincidentally, may also be my story's first surprise. (By which I mostly mean that it surprises me.) Now that I've actually used those words (*once upon a time*) I have to confess that they don't seem so stupid and traditional after all. Actually I kind of like them. They have a certain ring. They conjure, like a spell. And I suppose the fact that I'm not the first to use them doesn't automatically make me unoriginal. Isn't it the words that follow *once upon a time* that make a story truly come alive?

All right. That settles it. If I'm going to tell my story (which I am), I want to tell it right. So I think this means I need to start over, this time really believing in *once upon a time*. Believing that it will draw you in, take you with me to a place you've never been before. (You only think you have—a thing that may well be my story's first surprise for you.)

I know.

Close your eyes. Now conjure up your favorite door within your mind. Perhaps it leads to a room you visit everyday. Or maybe it's for special occasions, the place you go to be safe and warm and comfortably alone. Perhaps the door is actually a garden gate, an entryway to a place filled with the mysteries of living things. Perhaps it's simply the front door to your own home. Are you going out, or going in? Never mind.

I'll tell you about the door I conjure. It is made of old, dark oak with iron handles and hinges. Not fancy, but sturdy and serviceable. A trustworthy sort of door. You know what lies beyond it, don't you?

That's right. My truth. My way. My story.

Can you feel its unseen forces gathering around you? The handle of the door slips from your hand and the door, my door, begins to open wide. Before you realize what you've done, you've accepted the invitation, put one foot across the threshold. That's all it takes. You're in for it now.

Begin at the beginning, the place where all good stories start.

You know the way. Of course you do.

One

ONCE UPON A TIME

   . . . and so long ago that the time I speak of can be remembered only in a story, a virtuous king and queen (my parents) ruled over a land that was fair and prosperous (though it wasn't all that large).

   Their kingdom being at peace, and their people being well fed and content, you might think the king and queen would be so also. But alas, it seems they were not. (Content.) For they lacked the one thing which would make their happiness complete: a child.

   For years, the king and queen had dreamed and waited. Long years, and so many of them that, one by one, their hopes for a child began to pack their bags and depart. And this stealing away of hope eventually took its toll. It compelled the king to do a thing he did not wish to do, a thing he never would have done, had he not lost hope for a child of his own. He named his younger brother's son as his heir apparent, the brother being deceased and therefore not available himself.

The boy's name was Oswald.

Not that anybody ever called him that. His propensity for skulking in corridors the better to learn other people's business (particularly their secrets), combined with his habit of playing nasty practical jokes based on what he'd learned, had earned him a nickname.

Everybody called him Prince Charming. Because he wasn't.

After many years of wishing for a child to no avail, a terrible day arrived. This was the day the king and queen awoke to discover that all their hopes were well and truly gone. But this turned out to have an unlooked-for benefit, for the absence of hope left a vacuum, a void. And now I'll tell you another thing I've heard said, and this I know is true: Nature hates a void. As soon as one occurs, something has to rush in to fill the empty space, for that is the way nature wants things to go.

And so it was that the void created by the desertion of their hopes turned out to be the best possible thing that could have happened to my parents. For in hope's absence, a miracle arrived.

On the very same day that she realized all her hopes had

fled, the queen also realized she was with child. A thing that, when she informed her husband, caused both their hearts to fill with joy. So much so that all their hopes heard the ringing of it, halted in their flight, turned around, and raced right back home. Between their hopes, their miracle, and their joy and wonder at both, my parents' hearts were therefore filled to overflowing before I was even born.

Many great things were predicted for me. Naturally, I would grow up straight and true, for that is what's supposed to happen when you are born royal. I would be beautiful if a girl, handsome if a boy. Above all, I would do my duty. First, last, always. When I put in my appearance on the exact same day the royal soothsayer had appointed, this was taken to be a sign that I would fulfill all these predictions, plus many more.

Several years and many disappointments later, my mother would be overheard to remark that the day of my birth was the only occasion she could recall on which I had been dutiful according to her definition. When my father protested that she was being too hard on me, she settled for the unarguable statement that it was most certainly the only occasion for which I had ever been on time.

In spite of all that happened later, every account I have ever heard concerning my actual birth relates that Papa and Maman were so delighted that a child had arrived at last that they were willing to overlook the fact that I was a girl and not a boy, boys being the preferred rulers of kingdoms, as you must know. For reasons that my nurse once explained to me were largely reproductive, but that I don't think I'll go into here and now.

I was born on a bright but chilly day in late September. Nurse has told me that my very presence warmed the room, for, even then, my hair was bright as the dawn. It made such a perfect arc around my head that it resembled a halo, an aureole. A combination of circumstances that caused my mother to immediately proclaim that the only name which could do me credit was Aurore.

This though she and my father had discussed naming me after his mother, whose name had been Henriette-Hortense. But, as my father was not about to deny my mother anything in the moments immediately following my birth, that plan was abandoned and the deed was done. From that moment forward, I was called Aurore.

It was, and still is, the custom in the country of my birth to hold a christening when a babe has reached the age of one month old. How this period of time came to be decided upon isn't clearly remembered, but it's generally assumed that the reason is twofold. A month is long enough after the birth so that a baby no longer appears quite so wrinkly and red, thus sparing those who come to congratulate the new parents considerable worry in the way of coming up with compliments on the beauty of the child. A month is also thought a long enough period to determine whether or not the infant is a good match in temperament for the name bestowed upon it shortly after its arrival. Many are the girls who are born Charlotte but end up as Esmerelda. Or the boys who begin life as Wilfrid but end up as just plain Bill. Well, not many, perhaps. But some.

In my case, however, there was no possibility that I might, even yet, become Henriette-Hortense. My hair having apparently grown even more golden with each passing day, and my eyes even more blue and my skin more rose petal–like, according to the nurse, anyway, the matter was considered settled. I was to be Aurore. First, last, always.

You know about my christening, of course. Everybody does.

Or the bare bones of it, anyway. What went right. But mostly, what went wrong. Given the size and scope of the event, what seems most incredible to me is that my parents never saw the disaster coming ahead of time. It's been suggested they were dazzled by the gold of my hair. (Though, now that I think about it, I seem to remember that this suggestion came from Oswald.)

What I do know—what everybody knows—is this: When the invitations were sent out, for the one and only time in her life, my mother failed to manage a social engagement to perfection, and her list was one person short. Not just anybody. *Somebody.* By which, of course, I mean Somebody-Who-Proved-To-Be-Important, even if that wasn't how she started out.

Who she was has been greatly distorted. Most versions of my story say she was an evil fairy and give her some fantastic name, usually beginning with the letters *m-a-l*. *Mal*, meaning bad, which over time has come to mean the personification of evil, just as Aurore has come to be the personification of all that is beautiful, innocent, and bright. I am the candle flame snuffed out too soon; she, the years of impenetrable dark.

This is for the simple-minded, I suppose. An attempt to show that she and I were opposites right from the start. All pure nonsense, of course. Not only didn't people think she was evil, they didn't think of her at all. And that, I believe, was the true heart of all the trouble that followed.

Her name wasn't "mal" anything, by the way. It was Jane. Just that, and nothing more. (And, for the record, there are no fairies in the land of my birth. They prefer the land just on the other side of the Forest, *la Forêt*, a place you'll hear much more about before my tale is done.)

After the big event, by which I mean my christening, people discussed Jane's life in great detail. Though I suppose I should say at great length, because there weren't really all that many details. Or none that anyone could accurately recall.

It was generally agreed that she was related to my mother, a distant cousin of some sort. And that she had been part of the entourage accompanying Maman when, as a young princess, she had come from across the sea to marry my father. There were even those who claimed to remember that Jane had been a member of the actual wedding party, that she had followed behind my mother, carrying her train. But when I asked Maman about this once, *she* claimed to have no memory of whether or not this was so.

When I remarked, very curious and a great deal put out, that it seemed incredible to me that Maman should be unable to remember whether or not a member of her own family had taken part in her wedding—been assigned, in fact, the important responsibility of keeping the bride's elaborate train straight and true during its long march down the aisle—my mother replied that she had been looking forward, not back, on her wedding day. In other words, her eyes had not been fixed on Cousin Jane. They had been fixed right where they should have been: upon my father.

Not long after, she sent me to bed without any supper for speaking too saucily, which was her way of saying I was asking too many questions, and furthermore that they were uncomfortable ones. This was neither the first, nor the last, time this happened. Nurse often remarked that I owed my fine figure not so much to all the time I spent outdoors, but to all the times I had spoken saucily to Maman.

Regardless of whether or not Cousin Jane actually took part in the wedding, on one thing everyone concurred. After the wedding, Jane simply dropped from sight and was forgotten. Or, more accurately, perhaps, she found a way to blend so perfectly with her surroundings that she became someone others completely overlooked. Everyone, in fact, except (perhaps) for Oswald.

Now we come to some important questions, ones to which we're never likely to have answers as only Jane can provide them, always assuming even she knows. The things I've always wondered are these: Did Jane choose to become invisible, or did it happen on its own, because of who and where and what she was? It's pretty plain she must have been unhappy for a good long while. But was her invisibility a cause or a result? Was it her unhappiness's root or vine?

Here's my theory: It was both.

I don't know how the world works where you live, but the place where I grew up is steeped in magic. This actually explains why ours is a place fairies don't call home. They prefer a more everyday place, where their own magic can have greater impact. There's magic in the air we breathe, the water we drink. When we walk, magic rises upward from the ground and enters our bodies through the soles of our feet, even when we have our stoutest boots on.

In other words, it's everywhere. In the wind and the rain. The feather from a bird that you find in a field during a country ramble. The hard, uneven surfaces of city street cobblestones. If you've grown up here, you're used to it. It's just the way things are. Almost everyone who's a native can do some sort of magic, even if it's something simple like boiling water for tea in the morning while you're still in bed, instead of having to crawl out of your warm covers to stir up the coals.

If you haven't grown up here but come to live, one of two things can happen, of course: Either the magic leaves you alone, or it doesn't. And if it doesn't, it does the same thing to you as to the rest of us: It makes you more of what you are.

This is a thing about magic that is greatly misunderstood. Magic isn't all that interested in change, which explains why things like love spells almost always backfire. And why those of us who grow up with magic don't use it nearly as much as people who haven't might think. (The boiling of tea water aside.) Nothing about magic is simple or straightforward, to be used lightly. And it's definitely not a substitute for what you can do just as well with your hands and your mind.

The people who end up with the strongest magic are the ones who are quickest to recognize this. Who see that magic's true power lies not in attempting to bend it to your will but in leaving it alone. Because if you do that, you'll discover an amazing thing. The will of the magic becomes your will of its own accord. For magic is a part of nature. It, too, hates a void. And the voids magic most wants to fill are the spaces that exist inside a person. It longs to strengthen that which is only waiting to be made strong.

Have you ever heard it said that somebody has shown her or his true colors? That's exactly what I'm talking about. The thing that interests magic is your true colors. Who you really are. And it can make you more powerful only if you first accept this. Which means, of course, that you have to be willing to accept yourself completely. Your virtues and your flaws. Most people shy away from doing this, another reason why magic doesn't get used as much as you might suppose.

But not Jane. She must have looked at herself without flinching. Unlike my mother, who has no time for magic, thereby making sure it has no time for her, Jane soaked it up, like a stunted plant in freshly watered ground. And herein lies magic's greatest danger. Remember what I said about the way it strengthens that which is waiting to be made strong?

If your virtues make up your true colors, that is well and good, for you as well as for the rest of us. But what about those whose true colors are comprised mostly of their flaws? These are the ones most likely to use magic for evil, even if they're not evil to begin with. For the things within them that the magic strengthens are like hunting knives: double-edged, wicked-sharp, and strong. They stick deep, cut both ways, are honed by power and pain alike. Such things cannot be held inside forever. Sooner or later, they must be released or they will slice their own way out.

What better way to release pain than to take revenge on the people you believe have wronged you? An eye for an eye. A tooth for a tooth. My power casts down your power, if only for a moment. Your pain replaces mine.

If Jane had been invited to my christening, who can say how much longer she would have held her pain locked up inside? Who can say what might *not* have happened? But she wasn't invited, and so something did.

"Little Princess, lovely as the dawn. Well-named Aurore."

This is what she is supposed to have said when, the last in a long line of wish-bestowers, she stood at my cradleside. By then, a horrible hush had fallen over my christening, a clotting sense of dread. Nobody recognized her, you see. Or (perhaps) nobody but Oswald. But her malice, that was an easy thing to recognize. Nurse has told me that the very air turned hot and tingled, the way it does right before a thunderstorm. You just knew that something bad was about to happen, she said.

As it happened, she was right.

"Yet even the brightest of sunrises must come to an end. *Tant pis.* Too bad," Cousin Jane went on.

Then, before anyone could prevent her, she reached down and scooped me from my cradle, holding me above her head so that her face looked up and mine looked down. I reached for her, my small fingers working to take hold of something, anything, for I wasn't all that sure that I liked my present situation.

At this, Nurse says, Cousin Jane smiled. As if I, myself, had provided the final inspiration for the pain she was about to unleash upon us all.

"Your end will come with the prick of a finger," she said, as she slid one of her own into my fist and I held on tight. Though everyone but Nurse has told me this is impossible, I swear I can actually remember this moment, what her finger felt like.

Smooth and cool, but not the smoothness of skin. I know that now, though I didn't at the time.

Several years later, when I was judged old enough not to choke myself on it, I was given a chicken drumstick as a special treat at a picnic we were having on one of the many palace lawns. Any opportunity to get messy always delighted me, according to my mother, and all went well, until I'd gnawed my way down to the bone. At the first touch of it, I became hysterical, and it wasn't until several hours later that Nurse finally managed to calm me down enough to tell her what was wrong.

That's what Cousin Jane's finger had felt like. Not smooth skin, but the smooth caress of cool, hard bone.

"The prick of a finger," she said again, giving hers a little shake, as if everyone hadn't heard her the first time around. "One sharp wound. One bright drop of blood. That's all it will take to cut your life down. Sixteen years, I give you, ma petite Aurore, lovely as the dawn. The same number I was given before I had no choice but to follow your mother to this gilded prison, so far from my home."

There was a moment of stupefied silence.

Then, *"Jane?"* my mother gasped out. A question, an uncertainty, even now.

At which point Cousin Jane tossed me high into the air and swept my mother a bow. "Well met, Cousin," she said. "You will remember me from now on, will you not?"

With that, she vanished in a puff of smoke, through which

I plummeted straight down into my nurse's desperate arms. Behind her, she left just the faintest tang of sulphur, and the ghost of a laugh that never quite died. It lingered in the air, like an elusive smell. Vanishing for days, for weeks, on end, only to creep around a corner and assault you when you least expected.

Haunting us all for more than a hundred years to come.

About the Author

CAMERON DOKEY is the author of more than thirty young adult novels. Her most recent titles include *The World Above* and *Wild Orchid*. She is also the author of *How NOT to Spend Your Senior Year*. Cameron lives in Seattle, Washington.

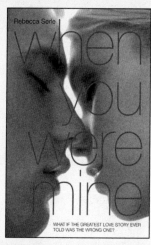

EBOOK EDITION ALSO AVAILABLE

WHAT IF THE GREATEST LOVE STORY EVER TOLD WAS THE WRONG ONE?

"Romeo didn't belong with Juliet; he belonged with me.
It was supposed to be us together forever, and it would have been
if she hadn't come along and stolen him away. Maybe then all of
this could have been avoided. Maybe then they'd still be alive."

From Simon Pulse | TEEN.SimonandSchuster.com | rebeccaserle.com

UNLOCK THE MYSTERY, SUSPENSE, AND ROMANCE.

Kissed by an Angel

Dark Secrets

New York Times bestselling author
Elizabeth Chandler

From Simon Pulse
TEEN.SimonandSchuster.com

alloy**entertainment**

THERE'S A FINE LINE
BETWEEN *bitter* AND *sweet.*

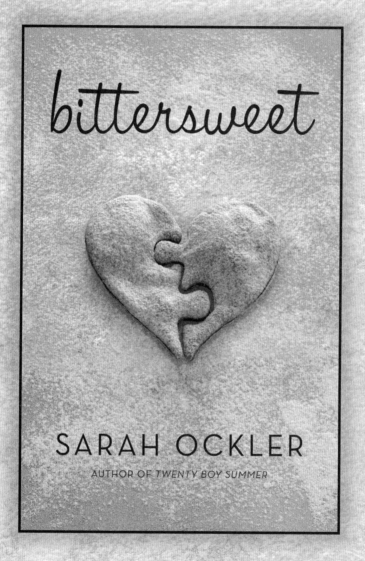

bittersweet

SARAH OCKLER

AUTHOR OF *TWENTY BOY SUMMER*

EBOOK EDITION ALSO AVAILABLE

From *Simon Pulse*
TEEN.SimonandSchuster.com
SarahOckler.com

Lose yourself in these devastatingly beautiful novels in verse.

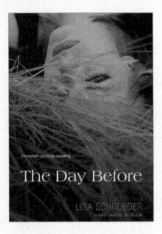

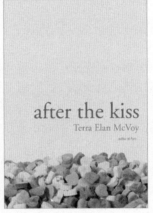

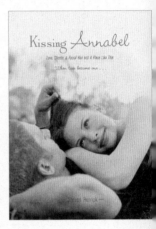

SiMONTEEN

Simon & Schuster's **Simon Teen**
e-newsletter delivers current updates on
the hottest titles, exciting sweepstakes, and
exclusive content from your favorite authors.

Visit **TEEN.SimonandSchuster.com** to
sign up, post your thoughts, and find out what
every avid reader is talking about!

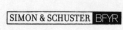